SHE WILL BUILD HIM A CITY

SHE WILL BUILD HIM A CITY

Raj Kamal Jha

BLOOMSBURY

NEW YORK · LONDON · NEW DELHI · SYDNEY

Bloomsbury USA
An imprint of Bloomsbury Publishing Plc

1385 Broadway	50 Bedford Square
New York	London
NY 10018	WC1B 3DP
USA	UK

www.bloomsbury.com

BLOOMSBURY and the Diana logo are trademarks of Bloomsbury Publishing Plc

First published in Great Britain 2015
First U.S. edition 2015

© Raj Kamal Jha, 2015

Every reasonable effort has been made to trace copyright holders of material reproduced in this book,
but if any have been inadvertently overlooked the publishers would be glad to hear from them.

Extract on page 7 from "On Killing a Tree" from Gieve Patel
Reproduced by kind permission of the author.

Extracts on pages 170–2 from *Magadhi and its Formation* by Dr. Munishwar Jha,
Calcutta Sanskrit Research Series, 1967. Reproduced by kind permission of the author.

Extracts on pages 248–8 from *The Aunt's Story* by Patrick White,
published by Vintage, copyright © Patrick White, 1994. Reprinted by permission of
The Random House Group Limited, and reproduced with permission of the author's estate.

Extracts on pages 320–3 from "The Story Teller," from the collection
Madwomen (The Locas Mujeres Poems of Gabriela Mistral), edited and translated
by Randall Couch, published by University of Chicago Press,
copyright © University of Chicago Press, 2008.
Reproduced with permission.

ISBN: HB: 978-1-62040-904-6
        PB: 978-1-62040-906-0
        ePub: 978-1-62040-905-3

LIBRARY OF CONGRESS CATALOGING-IN-PUBLICATION DATA HAS BEEN APPLIED FOR.

2 4 6 8 10 9 7 5 3 1

Typeset by Hewer Text UK Ltd., Edinburgh
Printed and bound in the U.S.A. by Thomson-Shore Inc., Dexter, Michigan

To find out more about our authors and books visit www.bloomsbury.com.
Here you will find extracts, author interviews, details of forthcoming events
and the option to sign up for our newsletters.

Bloomsbury books may be purchased for business or promotional use.
For information on bulk purchases please contact Macmillan Corporate and
Premium Sales Department at specialmarkets@macmillan.com.

~

To Rain,
his mother, his grandparents

&

Max Schneid (1898–1944)
Yasmin Malek (1996–2002)

~

~

Midnight had come upon the crowded city. The palace, the night-cellar, the jail, the Madhouse: the chambers of birth and death, of health and sickness, the rigid face of the corpse and the calm sleep of the child: midnight was upon them all.

Oliver Twist
CHARLES DICKENS, 1837

~

WOMAN

WINTER AFTERNOON

THIS, tonight, is a summer night, hot, gathering dark, and that is a winter afternoon, cold, falling light, when you are eight years nine years old, when you come running to me, jumping commas skipping breath, and you say, Ma, may I ask you something may I ask you something and I say, of course, baby, you may ask me anything and you say, Ma, when I am tired, when my legs hurt, when my eyes begin to close, I only need to call you, I only need to say, Ma, and you appear instantly, like magic, from wherever you are you set aside whatever you're doing you come running to me you lift me up you carry me you walk with me you.

Slow down, slow down, I tell you, but, of course, you don't, you say if it's sleep time, you place pillows on either side of me, you fluff them up, you switch off the light, you wait outside my room and only when you don't hear me move do you walk away, Ma, my question is.

And you pause.

You breathe in, deep.

You toe-tap the floor, the earth spins underneath, your eyes look into mine as if you are the mother and I am the child and you ask:

Ma, is there someone who can do the same with you?

What do you mean? I ask.

Ma, is there someone you can call when you are tired? Someone who can lift you up, carry you around until you fall asleep?

Is there someone like that, Ma? A man?

A woman?

Is there?

Is there? So many questions.

So many question marks, their dots and their hooks float in the air, block my view of your beautiful face.

And I say, yes, maybe there is.

~

Tonight is thirty years forty years later.

So quiet is this little house that I can hear, from upstairs, through the walls of the room in which you are lying, the drop of your tear, the rush of your breath.

One's like rain, the other wind, they both make me shiver.

~

And I say yes that summer afternoon, yes, maybe there is. Maybe there is a man or a woman who can lift me up although I will be much more comfortable if it is a woman because the only man I will let myself be carried by is your father and he is no longer with us and when I say this, a little cloud, cold and wet and dark, slips in through the window, hovers over our shadows on the floor before we both blow it back into the sky where it must have come from and when we do that, I feel your breath and I remember that it is warmer than mine.

The cloud gone, you ask, Ma, doesn't the woman who will carry you, just like you carry me, have to be tall? Very, very tall? More than twice your height? Like you are more than twice mine so that when she lifts you up, carries you around, your feet don't drag along the floor?

I guess so, I say.

How tall should she then be, Ma? you ask.

You tell me, baby.

You think for ten seconds, twenty thirty, your lips move, numbers small and big dance inside your head – multiplying? dividing? – and you say, at least 12 feet tall, a giant, like in *Gulliver's Travels*, Ma, in the land that comes after Lilliput, in which the little girl, nine years old, just like me, carries him like he were her doll. And to show what you mean, you raise both your arms, you stand on your toes, just over 3 feet in your socks, you try to stretch to 12, and you ask, Ma, how do we go looking for her?

Don't you worry, I say, we will meet her. Some day some night, I am sure, because how can you keep someone so tall hidden for so long?

Ma, if she is there, will she love you like you love me?

I don't know about that, baby, I say, maybe she will if you want her to.

Ma, will she have a mother and a father? Brothers and sisters? Friends? Will she live in a very tall house with many, many tall people?

Maybe, I say, but maybe she lives all by herself.

Let me know when you meet her, Ma, promise me that you will let me know, I want to see her carry you, I want to see you fall asleep on her shoulder.

Of course, I will, I say. Promise.

And, thus assured, you run away, leaving a hole in the air, shimmering, through which afternoon leaks away and evening drips in, mixes, dissolves the scents you leave behind.

Of winter cream and red wool.

Girl skin and baby shampoo, one night old.

~

Last night, I meet this woman.

This very, very tall woman. In this house, right here, where I stand, and, just as I promise you, I am now letting you know.

~

Have you fallen asleep?

May I lie down by your side, just for a while?

I won't wake you up, I will walk up the stairs on tiptoe, I will wipe all my sweat away so that not one drop falls, makes a noise.

If it helps, I will whisper each word I need to tell you, I will hold my breath – as if I am dead.

MAN

NIGHT METRO

HE is going to kill and he is going to die.

That's all we know for now, let's see what happens in between.

~

He waits to board the last train at Rajiv Chowk Station, the central hub of the Delhi Metro, crossover for Yellow and Blue Lines, through which move half-a-million passengers each day of whom he is one.

Nobody in this city notices one.

He is thirty years, thirty-five years old, 5' 10", 5' 11", his wrist so slim his watch slides halfway to his elbow when he raises his arm to brush back his hair. It's over 40 degrees but there's not a single bead of sweat on his face as if an invisible layer of ice-cold air sticks to him like cling film. Both hands free, he holds no bag, no phone as he waits at the platform, two levels below the street, next to Café Coffee Day under the Metro Clock whose hand shudders each time it moves a second.

Passengers ride escalators like toy men, toy women in a Shanghai factory he once saw on the Discovery channel: small and stiff, gliding up the belt, emerging face first. Followed by neck, chest, waist, legs, and, in the end, feet. That topple into a box to be hot-sealed closed, shipped across the ocean. To cities where there are more toys than children.

Next train 02 min.

The station is crowded, he closes his eyes, sees everyone naked and bruised.

Deep gashes scour bare stomachs and thighs like mouths of brown bags slit open.

Women squat on haunches blowing air into wrinkled penises.

Like children with balloons.

One is red, a womb floating in blood, inside which a foetus glows.

He feels an erection coming.

He opens his eyes, his heart aches, and a drowsy numbness pains, John Keats.

~

He likes poetry, he doesn't like wet, he doesn't like spray or spatter. No knife, no thick rope, no iron rods, the most popular weapons behind the headline murders in this city. Of Aarushi, the schoolgirl; mother Gurpreet and daughter Jasmeen; French tourist Lauren; Afghan woman Paimana and the elderly couple in Greater Kailash I, most of them stabbed, cut in many places. Or strangled, bludgeoned. Won't work for him because he knows his arms lack strength and even if he gathers enough force to hit, it's unlikely he will kill with the first blow which means he will have to keep hitting and, in the process, smear and stain larger areas. Perhaps, provoke a scream. There are 29,468 people per square kilometre in this city (Census 2011), twice that many is the number of ears.

Someone is bound to hear.

He could use a gun with a silencer, quiet and quick. As in movies he's watched, books he's read. Murder in Echo Park, Los Angeles, rain sliding down car windows, fogged in the cold. A park in Asker, near Oslo, a politician found in an empty swimming pool, a white tennis ball hammered deep into her throat. But this is fact, not fiction.

There are 20 million bodies in this city and then there is the heat.

Each body softened, warmed throughout the day in a marinade of its sweat and odours, hair oil, dust thrown up by diggers, cement mixers, earthmovers, dumptrucks. All tearing down, building up. New station, new flyover, new apartment block, new mall, new street, New City. Where everyone rubs against you, stands so close you hear their blood flow, skin crawl, hearts pump. Like the sound of trains running at night. You see remnants of meals lodged in teeth, trapped under nails stained yellow; cellphone screens smudged with wax from ears, flecked with flakes of dead skin.

Late at night, just before they close, eyes gleam with greed; during the day, they dim with despair.

~

He read a poem in school, *On Killing a Tree* by Gieve Patel, a doctor who lives in Mumbai. He has some lines by heart.

It takes much time to kill a tree,
Not a simple jab of the knife
Will do it . . .
. . . So hack and chop
But this alone won't do it . . .
. . . The bleeding bark will heal
And from close to the ground
Will rise curled green twigs . . .
No,
The root is to be pulled out –
. . . Out from the earth cave,
And the strength of the tree exposed,
The source, white and wet . . .
. . .Then the matter
Of scorching and choking
In sun and air,
Browning, hardening,
Twisting, withering.
And then it is done.

End of poem, he's never killed a human being. Only once, he has killed – a dog.

~

He hears the train.

He loves the Metro from the bottom of his heart, the place where he knows bad blood turns into good. He loves each train with its four, sometimes six, some have eight, Bombardier coaches. That's why, on nights like this one, he leaves his car at home to take the train back from wherever he is.

~

7

When he is nine years ten years old, he has a severe stomach ache, fierce spasms twist and crush his insides, make him cry into his pillow every night for a week. Father takes him to hospital where they make him swallow barium sulphate, then track its movement by taking X-ray pictures every half-hour until they have an entire album of black, translucent plates which, when held against the light, show the barium travelling through his body.

He holds that last image in his head: that of a thin, white trace moving straight down in the black, through the cloudy haze of organs, knotting into whorls and loops where the ulcers are, then travelling clear again, uninterrupted.

Like the Metro.

Each train a glowing pill swallowed, coursing through the dark insides of this sick city.

On the way home from hospital, Father buys him a cricket bat and a roll of Poppins hard-boiled candy to take the barium's taste away.

~

The train pulls in, pushing, in front, a wave of warm air from the tunnel to the platform. Doors open, people spill. A smell like rotting vegetables, bread and bananas gone bad.

Dead and damp.

Poet Gieve Patel is a painter, too. He did *Man in the Rain with Bread and Bananas.* (Oil on canvas, 2001.) That's his favourite because the man in the painting looks like his father. The same sad eyes, the same old glasses.

Next station is Patel Chowk, doors will open to the right, mind the gap.

Twelve stops before he reaches home in Apartment Complex, New City.

Standing, he closes his eyes.

CHILD

LITTLE HOUSE

THE night is so hot the moon shines like the sun, its light as bloodless white as bone, casting a cold shadow of a woman as she steps off an autorickshaw, carrying her newborn wrapped in a thin, blood-red towel, tells its driver to wait, walks up to Little House, a home for children, orphaned and destitute, leaves the baby on its doorstep, turns and walks away into a wind, slight but searing, that slaps her in the face and fills her eyes with water.

The only eyewitness to this abandonment is Bhow, a black-and-white dog, surprisingly clean given the garbage heap she's sitting on. She watches the woman leave the child, she watches her get back into the autorickshaw which drives away, the vehicle and its shadow both swallowed by the night heat rolling in from across the scorched bed of the Yamuna, the river with no water.

By night's end, this heat pushes the temperature to a few points above 40, the highest minimum in the city's recorded history.

It kills twelve people, seven over sixty, five under six.

The city's two night shelters, mandated to be kept open by the Delhi High Court during winter, turn into makeshift clinics to treat those with dehydration and heat stroke. These shelters, however, soon run out of beds, food and water, forcing hundreds to sleep on pavements, many on street dividers fanned by exhaust from passing vehicles. Some find spaces in the shells of broken-down buses, some at the entrance to Metro stations where, if they are lucky, they catch whatever they can of the air-conditioned draught that escapes from inside a coach when its doors open, when a train stops.

~

At nine the next morning, by which time the temperature has already touched 45, Mrs Usha Chopra, the conscientious receptionist and secretary to the director of Little House – she takes the Metro from her home in Dwarka and, underground, the air conditioning works – discovers the baby, its eyes closed, its pulse jumpy, and when she touches the tip of its wrinkled nose, its heat almost scalds her finger.

Hurriedly draping her dupatta over the bundle, Mrs Chopra carries the baby inside, sits down at her desk, pulls her chair closer to the aircooler and when she peels away the towel's layers, she almost cries out aloud as if she has witnessed a miracle unfold.

For, this is a boy.

Only the second boy in the orphanage – there are seventy-eight girls – and a boy with no visible disability, a fact of no small import since the only other boy in Little House is Sunil, no last name, five years old and still unadopted because he has Down's syndrome.

The new baby begins to cry.

~

'Let me look, Didi, let me look,' says Asma Khatoon, the janitor, running, almost tripping over the bucket of Dettol water she is mopping the floor with. '*Masha Allah*,' she says, wiping her hands on her sari, torn in too many places to count, 'so beautiful is this child, may I hold him?'

'No, no, nothing doing,' says Mrs Chopra, 'your hands are

wet, we can't let anything happen to him. He doesn't look more than a day old, look at the red patches on his head, the skin peeling off his fingers. You go tell the day nurse to prepare some milk, God knows how long he's been unfed, we need to clean him up, we need to fill him up with water. Imagine, this poor child, left alone in this heat. What if a dog from the garbage heap had scented him out, attacked him last night.'

According to the rules of Little House, Mrs Chopra's first task is to report this new entry so she walks to the director's office but not before she has recorded a clip of the baby on her phone, the blink of one eye, the slight wiggle of one toe, and checked the boxes in the form: 'normal, male, infant'.

~

In his thirteen years as director of Little House, Rajat Sharma – Indian Administrative Service, 1988; MPA, Kennedy School, Harvard, 2000 – has never seen a 'normal male infant' being left on his doorstep.

'Who lets go of a boy, Mrs Chopra, tell me who? Which mother has done this? And, that too, in so killing a heat wave? Which father's heart is so hard?' says Mr Sharma, himself the father of a son. 'Let's immediately get his files in order, I want all paperwork done before I leave for home today. And if we get this right, Mrs Chopra, I, you, all of us, will be on TV. English, Hindi, all channels. Boy deserted on the hottest night since Independence. I can already see the ticker: "Breaking News, Coldheart Mother Dumps Baby In Record Heat".'

'Of course, sir,' says Mrs Chopra. 'What name should we enter in the file?'

'Name?' He pauses but only for a second. 'Call him Orphan. That's it, Orphan. It's an unusual name, that's what TV people want.'

'Yes, sir,' says Mrs Chopra.

'Also, it's a common noun,' says Mr Sharma, 'like a blank. Like "Baby". Any family which adopts him can fill in their own, whatever name they like.'

~

Over the next hour, Orphan is fed, changed, washed, all the while lying next to the red towel he has been found in.

'This must carry the smell of his mother,' Mrs Chopra tells Asma, 'until Kalyani the night nurse comes, this will help calm him down.' And help it does. His hunger fed, his thirst quenched by milk and water spooned into him, his body cooled by a sponge-wash and wind from the aircooler through which running water gurgles like a stream, the sound of a lullaby, Orphan slips in and out of sleep, his head resting on the red towel left behind by his mother.

Where is his mother?

Where's Bhow, that first eyewitness?

The dog has watched it all and although, in the normal course of things, her little head and heart should not register any of this, they do, and so she finds a cool corner in the garbage heap to sit where she sheds a drop of dog-tear that no one but herself can see.

WOMAN

OLD CHILD

I SPEAK so softly I wonder whether my words carry to you. Up the stairs, so weak, do they slip under your door, climb into your bed, reach your ears? Because if they don't, please let me know. I will retell this story, of the giant, the very tall woman.

~

Last night, I hear nothing. I am in bed, tired, my legs hurt, my eyes begin to close, I hear neither the door knock nor the window rattle. Or the sound of her footsteps up the stairs, her fidgeting with the lock, her walking into the house, all 12 feet of her. She knows where I am, she knows where everything in my house is because she walks without disturbing a thing, no tripping, no stumbling, she walks into the bedroom, to the edge of my bed from where she lifts me up, she carries me out of the room, she walks with me and the strange thing is that I am not aware of any of this because I have fallen asleep, I don't know when exactly, and it's only when my eyes open that I realise I am not in bed, the floor is at least 9 feet, 10 feet below me and it's clear this is the woman you asked me about that winter afternoon thirty years forty years ago.

She is here.

The woman, at least 12 feet tall.

~

The last time I am lifted so high off the ground, it's on the Ferris wheel in the park with you and your father. We are on our way back from the Zoo. You are six years seven years old, I get so dizzy I close my eyes. Your father laughs, look, she's so scared, he says. That dizziness returns last night although I have no reason to be afraid: she holds me firm, my chin rests comfortably on her shoulder, I smell the cotton fabric of her sari, bright yellow, I feel her hair, black and glossy, brush my face. I wish to see what she looks like, for that I need to turn my head but I prefer to stay still. Once, twice, she bends, tries to avoid grazing the ceiling. I try to speak but fear, like

13

someone or something, has pushed its way into my mouth, caught my tongue between its fingers. So, my lips part but no words come as she pats me on the back like I am a baby she is trying to help fall asleep.

~

Close your eyes, she says, close your eyes.

Her face is inches from mine but her voice comes from some place far away like the rolling of distant thunder, cold and wet.

Let's go out, you need some fresh air, she says, stooping to walk through the door, the weight of her palm gentle on my back.

I pretend I am asleep, her heart beats against mine. I feel the street below, through each of her footsteps, precise and heavy. I am fully awake now, perched on her, my entire body tense.

What do I look like if somebody sees us?

A bug in the rain that flies into you, by accident, clasps your dress and then doesn't let go.

My head so close to the tops of trees, I hear telegraph wires sing, crows flap in their nests as they begin to wake up, wait for the first light of day. There is no one out at this darkest of hours except the boldest of fireflies and with nothing to constrain her movement, she walks upright now, no crouch, no bend. A light wind has begun to blow, it fans my face. She walks as if she knows this neighbourhood, all its lanes and bylanes, its open hydrants, the tar of the street long gone, baby pigs playing with trash, dirt-tracks that twist in and out of empty plots with half-built houses.

How long she walks I am not sure because my eyes close again, on their own, and I never know when I go back to sleep or when she turns to walk home, when and how she places me back on the bed until the morning when I wake up to see, for the first time, that pillows are propped up on either side of me.

Exactly as I do with you.

There are scratch marks on the ceiling where her head must have scraped the plaster. And a strand of her hair, more than 6 feet long, lies on my bedspread. Like a line drawn with a felt-tipped pen.

~

She may return, maybe by the end of this night.

She knows where I live, I think she has marked me out. The next time, instead of placing me back in the bed, she may take me away to where she lives, where giants live, in hiding in this city. Where there will be others like her, young and old, tall and very, very tall, who will play with me.

Your mother, this old child.

They will pass me, as loving adults do with a baby, from one pair of hands to another. And although I never thought I would tell you this – no child should ever have to hear this from her parent – I have to tell you: I am afraid.

That's why I won't sleep, I won't switch off the lights tonight.

MAN

FLYING DOG

DIWALI evening, there is a terror alert across the city: security agencies suspect an attack by the Lashkar-e-Toiba, a spectacular hit, say the men and women on TV, bigger than the 26/11 Mumbai attacks, this time they may come by air, breach the no-fly zone, glide down from the sky in parachutes filled with poison gas. The alarming word has spread, he sees policemen at every street corner, they prop themselves against lamp-posts. In dirty brown uniforms, they look like straggly plants in clay flowerpots. He wants to walk up to them, tear their limbs, pluck their leaves.

One by one.

~

He, Sukrit, Arsh and Aatish. Four friends and one dog, too. Black-and-white. The dog is a bitch, teats swollen but pups missing.

Brave Dog.

Homeless in this city, day and night, Dog hears trucks thunder by, she hears the cough of the sick and the old, she breathes exhaust, in and out. But that evening, the Diwali fireworks reduce her to a scaredy-cat, make her stray into Apartment Complex where fountains and sparklers whistling from earth to sky, hissing rattlesnakes on fire, twinkling lights strung across balconies force her to squeeze herself flat under a blue Porsche Cayenne (Rs 1.2 crore) in Visitors' Parking. Right next to a sprawling concrete quadrangle fringed by five apartment towers that glow in the night sky, towering lamps of glass and steel.

(They love this game, putting the price of everything they see in brackets.)

He stands and watches as, crouching on all fours, craning their necks to see under this car, Aatish and Sukrit dangle one Kentucky Fried Chicken leg each (Rs 119 for half a bucket). Part chewed, mustard-ketchup-mayo smeared like ointment on an open wound. Dog is frightened but she is hungry, too.

She trusts the four, so she crawls out, even lets Sukrit clamp her jaws with both his hands, lets Arsh grip both her front legs, lets Aatish lift her tail, tie four rockets (Rs 245 for a packet of six) to it with a plastic string.

Dog lunges for the chicken leg which has fallen to the ground now but Arsh kicks it away, Aatish pulls her tail hard, she pulls, she pushes, she strains against hands and fingers that hold her down, she tries to wriggle out but with her jaws forcibly shut she can only twitch, muffle her bark.

In one deft flick, Aatish lights the four rocket wicks with his cigarette lighter. The first sparks sputter, they let Dog go, they watch.

Flames leap, saffron, green and white, a bit of blue, colours of the flag.

Dog makes a sound.

~

It is a sound he has never heard before. It comes from Dog all right but it is more than just sound, it has a shape and texture too, hard edges that scrape his skin like a knife. He smells flesh burn. Dog runs but she can go only a few yards before she trips. One by one, each of the four rockets rips the plastic string, embeds into Dog's back, a jet of fire that gouges a hole in her black fur, mats its fringe with charred skin and blood. Three clear holes, the fourth one bleeds into them.

Dog crumples like a balloon, its gas draining out.

~

My turn, says Sukrit.

He opens Dog's mouth, parts her jaws, she offers no resistance, he lights a chocolate bomb and drops it inside. This is how they do it in Iraq, Sukrit says, they do this to people, with real bombs, I watched it in a documentary.

Arsh flicks his cellphone (Rs 41,245), records the explosion, its aftermath. Seventeen seconds.

Bitch, Arsh says.

Like the dogs in *Amores Perros*, Sukrit says.

They like movies, they run backwards, Dog pieces raining on all four.

~

Past midnight.

He showers and scrubs with a Body Shop seaweed sponge he bought as part of a special Diwali hamper (Rs 5,657), he stands under the shower, steams Dog's singed flesh and fur out of the pores of his skin, coats himself with Buriti Baby Body Butter (Rs 795), and lies down. He switches the air conditioner (Rs 62,550) on although it is cold but he wants to shiver under his blanket. He tries to sleep but can't, he wonders what Sukrit, Arsh and Aatish are doing.

Lying in bed, he turns around to look at the sky through the window, thick with smog. Most of the revellers have gone home, there is a no-fireworks midnight deadline set by the court to cut down on noise levels and pollution. But fireworks are still going off far away, their noise, from a distance, soft and muffled, the sky coughing its smoke-filled throat.

~

He cannot sleep so he gets up, walks onto the balcony and when he looks up, he sees Dog, with flesh-coloured wings, flying into the moon, her jaws open so wide she may soon swallow a star or two, her tail a plume of fire, slashing the night sky.

A shooting star.

Wish, wish, he tells himself.

And he wishes for all that he will never have before he goes to sleep.

The Metro announcement wakes him up. It's Gitanjali Aiyar's voice, the woman who read the news on TV once upon a time.

Next station is Race Course, she says, doors will open to the right.

CHILD

KALYANI DAS

FOR a newborn without a mother, Orphan is the least demanding baby in Little House. Which is the best thing that can happen to Kalyani Das, trainee nurse.

~

Kalyani is the only one from her family who graduated from school when they migrated from their village in West Bengal to New City. Each day, her mother works as a maid in four homes; her father drives a cycle rickshaw for sixteen hours; her brother, Bhai, does the day shift as a gardener's assistant in Apartment Complex; and her sister, Pinki, ten years eleven years old, works as a nanny to a four-year-old boy. They live in a one-room, one-lightbulb house with tarpaulin as door, a sheet of tin as roof.

Shelley Madam, Kalyani's teacher at nursing school, where she takes morning classes, has told her that, just like her daughter, if Kalyani works hard, if she takes a CL exam (Commission and Licensure nursing exam but the words are too big for her to remember), she can move to America or England. Where they pay more, where they don't treat you like a maid.

She needs to prepare for the exam at night so once Kalyani discovers that Orphan sleeps long hours, uninterrupted, she promptly signs up for permanent nightshift at Little House. Of the twelve hours of the shift, she gets, on average, ten hours free. Only once, maybe twice, Orphan wakes up, needs to be cleaned and fed, then he goes right back to sleep. A miracle, say the nurses, for a baby so young to keep so disciplined a schedule.

Kalyani uses her abundant spare time to either sleep – waking up at 5 a.m. every day to help her mother with the housework, she's drained by the time she starts her shift – or take a practice test from a used Kaplan guide Shelley Madam gave her as a gift.

~

The only one at Little House who has a sense of Kalyani's ambition, who has noticed her reading, writing at night is Dr Neel Chatterjee, the night resident doctor. The son of a VVIP, he has recently returned from some kind of a medical course in Paris. Who this VVIP is no one knows but whispers in Little House say Dr Chatterjee's father is only a couple of places below the Chief Minister herself and can, therefore, order the Little House director around.

Maybe his father's clout has set off a rebellion in his heart, who knows, but Dr Chatterjee fancies himself a free-thinking liberal, even a Marxist, and sincerely admires how Kalyani Das, twenty-four, poor, working class, is using The Wretched System to her benefit. Many a night, Dr Chatterjee drops by to say hello to her and, less than 5 feet from a sleeping Orphan, they talk, he in a chair, she leaning against the wall or sitting on the floor. He tells her about Paris, open-air cafés, people sitting down to dinner at tables laid out on cobbled pavements. How on winter evenings, cold and clear, his favourite restaurant drapes a blood-red blanket, warm and soft, on the backrest of each chair. He tells her about bread, freshly baked, that he can smell from fifteen houses away, his walk along the Seine, a river so small, so clean it looks as if it were hand-drawn in a picture. On his phone, he shows her a clip of tourist boats gliding down this river. The crowd at the Eiffel Tower, a man go by riding a horse.

Kalyani watches, she listens, she rarely speaks.

One day Dr Chatterjee asks her why and she says, 'You have so much to show me, sir, what can I say.'

~

So Dr Chatterjee is surprised one night when she suddenly seems to step out of her shell and tell him about her plan to go to America. She mentions the names of cities, New York, Pittsburgh, Boston.

'What if you don't get through?' Dr Chatterjee asks.

'What do you mean, I won't get through? Maybe not America right away but one day I will go.'

'How do you know that?' Dr Chatterjee leads her on.

'Shelley Madam told me that nurses will always be in demand because no one, other than your parents, can take care of you the way they can. Even your wife or husband will have problems once you are very ill. Who is going to clean you up when you wet your bed?

'I will do it, I will do it very well, because I am learning not to smell the smells. I will clean up, give pills on time, do the laundry, scrub the floor, work twelve, fourteen, sixteen hours, and I will smile all those hours. Sir, it doesn't matter if I do this here or in America because shit, piss, sweat, blood, they all look and smell the same wherever you are, whoever you are. So why not work where I make more money?'

Kalyani has never spoken so much at one time. She is suddenly aware of this, so is Dr Chatterjee. An uncomfortable silence follows which Dr Chatterjee rushes to fill: 'What about your family, can you leave them here?'

'Forget family, sir, my family only needs to see me happy and earn so much that my father doesn't have to cycle the whole day, Pinki can go to school, Ma doesn't need to work in so many homes.'

'Where do you live?'

'From here, I change two buses and then take the Metro.'

'Tell me your address.'

'What will you do with my address, sir? You can't come and visit me there.'

'Why not?'

'People like you don't come there. There is no house, it's just a row of rooms.'

'It doesn't matter, I may get you a few books that will help you in your CL exam.'

'Bring them to the hospital, Doctor, but if you really wish to get your shoes and trousers dirty, let me write this down: take the bus from here to AIIMS, take the Metro to New City, get off at Sikanderpur. Once you are there, call me on my phone, I will guide you through the lanes.'

~

Kalyani tears a slip of paper from her notebook. Dr Chatterjee wants to tell her that it would be easier if she calls him from her phone and he can save her number but he decides against it because he wants to watch her write. She is unsure about holding a pen, he thinks, for all her fingers are pulled into a fist, clenching, straining hard, as if she's bracing for a fight when she is writing, the pen her weapon. He looks at the way her hair falls over her face – neatly cut, as if by a professional, she must have saved money for this – he notices her lips move as she writes, maybe she is reading her number to herself, slowly, like a child.

'Here's my number,' Kalyani says. 'I am here each night Monday to Saturday but on Sundays when I am at home, I put the phone on silent by 9 p.m. because everyone sleeps early, we all have to wake up when it's still dark. That's the only time when there is no crowd at the community tap where we live, when we can bathe and fill our buckets before anyone comes.'

'I won't call you so late,' he says.

Dr Chatterjee hears Orphan cry, their talking must have woken him up.

'See you,' he says as he turns to leave. Kalyani doesn't say anything in reply, her back turned to him as she stands next to Orphan's cot, reaches down to lift him up, to tell him a story to lull him back to sleep, fragments of a dream which she has once seen.

About The Mall in New City, across the street and the Metro tracks from her slum, about babies who walk through doors made of glass.

MEANWHILE

BABIES WALK THROUGH DOORS
MADE OF GLASS

FAR, far away from Little House, in Apartment Complex in New City next to The Mall, the largest mall in the country, there are scores of apartments, minimum four-bedroom, hall, kitchen, where, unlike in Little House, there are no orphans, where babies live with their parents, each one safe and happy.

~

Once upon a time, there is a power-cut in Apartment Complex right in the middle of the night.

Fans drone to a stop, air conditioners click, go silent.

There is full power back-up with a row of generators in the basement but something's wrong, maybe diesel has run out, maybe the night-shift technician is drunk, he cannot be woken up.

It is July.

Very, very hot.

~

In one apartment on the top floor, in a room where each wall is painted a different colour, the ceiling like the sky, Baby gets up, drenched with sweat.

He climbs down from his bed, walks out of his bedroom.

Baby is confident. The way he walks down the steps, one by one, you would not guess that he has just learned how to walk.

Baby reaches the door.

He drags a stool, gets up on it, stands on his toes, slides the bolt open.

Through the open door, a light night wind enters the house, fans his face.

Baby walks out.

~

In the house, in the room upstairs next to Baby's, his parents are fast asleep. So deeply that the power-cut and the heat do not wake them up.

Baby's father spends fourteen hours at work, in the office, the mother the same time at home.

~

The lift's working, it has emergency power.

Baby calls the lift.

Baby is now tall enough to reach 0 on the panel.

He presses 0, Ground Floor.

Down and down goes the lift.

Ground Floor, lift doors open.

Baby steps into the lobby.

It's dark.

~

Baby walks out.

Security Guard cannot see Baby because he is out in the garden, looking up, catching cool waterdrops from the long line of air conditioners along the wall.

Into his mouth, into his dry lips. He is thirsty.

Drip, drip, drip.

~

Step by measured step, slipping into the shadows when he's afraid he may be noticed, Baby walks out of his building, out of Apartment Complex – and is now on the street outside.

Fifty steps later, Baby reaches The Mall.

To his left, the first shop is Weekender for Kids.

Baby sees clothes coloured red, green and white.

Jeans, shirts, plastic pails, plastic spades. For the seashore that's more than 1,300 kilometres away.

Next shop: McDonald's.

On an iron bench, sits Ronald McDonald, his plastic lap a seat into which Baby crawls.

~

Look, look, what can you see? On the street, more babies.

Because when Baby woke up, let's call him Baby One because he's the first one to wake up, he is the one the story begins with, maybe he sends a thought-message to other babies. This message wakes them up, too, and all of them tiptoe out of their homes, their parents fast asleep.

And they walk towards The Mall.

Big babies, small babies, boy babies, girl babies, sleepy babies, wake-up babies.

Babies like you, babies unlike you.

They are all here.

To lie down on the steps right at the entrance to The Mall.

~

And, then, a strange thing happens.

All the babies stand up. And, led by Baby One, they walk through the glass door of The Mall.

Like light, like sound.

Like the night breeze that blows the heat around.

They are inside The Mall.

All lights are out, all shops are closed but so powerful and so big are The Mall's air conditioners that even after they have been switched off for more than six hours, the air inside is still cool.

The babies feel it in their face, in their hair, and they smile.

The babies are happy.

~

'Hush,' says Baby One. 'Let's get to sleep without making any noise, no talking, the security guards are asleep.'

They lie down, one by one, on the cold, tiled floor.

'I will stay up,' says a baby who cannot sleep. 'Because I slept in the afternoon.'

'OK,' says Baby One, 'then you be our Alarm Clock Baby. When the power's back, when you see the streetlights switch on, you wake us up.'

'Sure, that sounds wonderful,' says Baby Who Slept In The Afternoon who now has a new name, Alarm Clock Baby.

'I will wake all of you up so that we can return to our homes before our parents wake up so that they do not need to worry,' says Alarm Clock Baby.

'Yes, yes, yes,' all babies sing in a chorus.

'Hush,' says Baby One.

The babies sleep.

The Mall sleeps.

Alarm Clock Baby is the only one up.

Goodnight, The Mall.

Goodnight, babies.

WOMAN

NOBEL PRIZE

ON the way here, you don't say a word, your eyes are closed, you sit still, you only move with each shudder of the taxi van as its wheels spin, lurch over the broken road. Your head rests against the window pane smudged with dust, hot to the touch. Your arm is draped over your suitcase, pressing it hard as if you are trying to stop it from growing wings and flying away.

What do you have in that suitcase? You can show me later.

I sit next to the driver, I keep turning round to look for hints of the past, immediate and distant, in your face. In the way your hair falls over your forehead, straight, in the way only two of your nails are stained with half-moons of red polish, the faint smudge below your eyes marking, possibly, the line of your tears.

The rest of you is a puzzle with a million pieces that I neither have the skill nor the time to put together.

~

When you walk into the house, breakfast is ready.

The cook, who comes in once a day, made egg curry, your favourite. I have told her what you like to eat. But the food remains untouched as you sleep right through whatever is left of the morning, the afternoon, evening, even a bit of the night.

You are awake now, I think, because I hear you cry. Let me know if you need anything, an extra blanket or something.

It's so clear how helpless I am, how useless. All I can offer, after all these years, to you, my daughter, are the assurances of room and board. I am little more than a motel, old and rundown.

~

A few days earlier, I get your call.

'I need a place to stay for a while,' is the first thing you say.

A million questions tie my tongue.

'Ma, are you there?'

'Yes,' I say.

'I need to visit you, can I come over? Just for a few days, not more than a week.'

'Of course,' I say.

I move the phone away, I am crying, I don't want you to listen to the noises I make.

'On one condition, Ma. Are you OK with that?'

'What condition?' I swallow my tears, I steady my voice.

'You don't ask me anything. No questions.'

'Where are you calling from?' I ask.

'I am calling from New City.'

'What kind of a name is that, where is this place?'

'I told you, Ma, no questions.'

'OK, fine.'

Of course, it's not OK, it's not fine, but what else can I say?

'Can I, at least, ask when you are coming? I need to put some things in order, prepare the house for you.'

'Ma, is there a room for me?'

'What do you mean?'

'A room, where no one will disturb me?'

'Of course there is, no one will disturb you.'

'I need to rest. Is it quiet?'

'From your room, all you see is an empty field, barren at this time of year. There is the highway but the windows keep out the sound of traffic.'

'You have someone to help you?'

'You don't worry, you don't have to do a thing. I told you there's this woman who cooks and cleans. Her son is Neel, a bright boy, he wants to be a doctor. He helps me with errands, you will like them.'

'Ma, are you still teaching at the school?'

'No, I left the school, I retired, I am very old, you know.'

'You stay at home the entire day?'

'Yes, but I won't get in your way.'

'Are you sure? Or are you just saying that?'

'You don't worry about me, my students gave me a beautiful farewell gift, a set of three books. They told me, ma'am, you don't know how to use the Internet so we have ordered them for you. Three books written by Nobel Laureates, each for a very important year in my life. The first one is by Henri Bergson, Nobel, 1927, the year your father was born. I was born in 1945, the year it went to Gabriela Mistral, so the second book is a book of poems by her. You were born in 1973, that's the year for Patrick White, the third book is a novel by him. You should read them too.'

'Ma, I am not interested in the books you have, I have no wish to read. You read, I am not coming there to read a book.'

'I was just telling you...'

'Bye, Ma,' you say. 'See you at the station.'

You are rude but, no, this isn't the time to tell you that.

Indeed, this isn't a time to ask you any of the questions I want to ask:

Why haven't you called me all these years?

What have you been up to?

Why does a smart young woman want to return home?

Are you hurt? Are you ill?

Is there something, someone you are running away from?

No, I don't ask any of these questions.

'Have a good trip,' is all I say instead. 'I will see you soon. I will get a taxi van if you have luggage.'

I speak to the dial tone.

~

So let it be your way.

I will ask no questions.

We are two people in 1 billion plus if you take this country, 7 billion if you take the world, and, of course, whatever happened to you, my child, whatever happened to me, your mother, whatever happens to us from now on doesn't matter to anyone except us. Because look around, near and far, everywhere else, outside this house, beyond its darkness and its tears, its walls, its floors, and you will see the healthy, the happy, the young, the old, the quiet and the noisy live on, unaware that we even exist. You will see traffic move down streets, the sun rise up in the sky. Trace your finger on a globe, close your eyes and stop – if it's land you can be sure that if someone is crying there, someone is laughing as well.

That's why, my child, the only thing that matters is my love for you even if I have made such a mess of it, even if I don't know who you are now or what secrets you have dragged here with you.

With this as comfort, I will try to drift away to sleep, to the sound of tears, yours and mine, to the rustle of strange creatures that wake up some nights in this house.

If we are lucky, you may see some of them.

Funny little dogs with flesh-coloured wings pinned to their backs.

Rainbirds that fly through thick sheets of falling water, the rest of the time they sit on branches, their wings closed and dripping.

Fireflies that enter your head, through your eyes. To light up the darkest of your dreams.

MAN

GOOGLE MAPS

HIS three friends are lucky.

Sukrit Sharma is in Singapore (Orchard Road), Aatish Patil is in New York (Park Slope), Arsh Pervez is in Paris (rue du Bac). He explores their neighbourhoods on Google Street View, cursor-walks up and down their cross-streets, right and left. Zooms in to examine a store, patch of pavement. Each one's neighbourhood is far far superior to his, there's absolutely no comparison.

He doesn't have a florist as in Park Slope, its rows of peonies, lilies, dahlias, red, white and purple, under the azure Brooklyn sky, waterdrops like pearls sitting on petals; golden-skinned women pushing strollers, pregnant; hearts, newly formed, beating under blue dresses.

There's no river beside his street, as in Paris, no beautiful Algerian woman wrapping oven-fresh croissants in butter paper, no tiny cars scurrying around like bugs in picturebooks, no evening light dappling the tall glass windows.

There's no manicured rainforest as in Singapore, leaves draped over flyovers like thick green curtains. Spotless quadrangles on Orchard Road, odour-free toilets in Sentosa, a little corner to wash the sand off your feet. Women, slender, in beige and black, their skin smooth and white as steamed fish, the scales removed.

What's here, instead, outside Apartment Complex, in New City?

Garbage the size of a hill.

Six giant sewer pipes, waiting for almost a year to be installed Godknowswhere. These serve as homes for mothers and babies who sleep after their day's work at a nearby construction site.

There are six security guards huddled at the gate, forced to wear long-sleeved shirts and ties in this heat. Two are from Bihar, the other four from Uttar Pradesh, all leaving behind fathers with cancer, mothers with TB, wives with uterine cysts, children who have dropped out of school, all waiting for Rs 4,000 to come every month.

They carry disease and death, grief and rage.

Yes, there is a florist, right next to The Mall, but the shop is wet, you walk through mud to reach flowers that wilt. The man who prepares the bouquet sprays his hollow cough on the plastic wrap.

No florist, no river, no rainforest.

But his is the biggest house of them all.

~

Six rooms (6,275 square feet carpet area, Rs 5 crore cost price, market value Rs 12 crore, $2 million). Great community, peer comfort, barely a mile from The Leela, the seven-star hotel (rack rate for Single Deluxe Suite: Rs 32,540 per night, drop-off and pick-up from Indira Gandhi International Airport in a BMW 6i), half a mile from The Mall (4.3 million square feet of retail space). The apartment is his, he owes nothing to no one. He

33

spent Rs 1.5 crore on its interiors, double-glazed Fenestra windows imported from Bangkok, false ceiling for air-conditioned vents, rafters for special energy-saving fluorescent lights the contractor said he got from Belgium. He spent so much because they pay him so much. Why, he doesn't know. He has stopped asking this question. What does he do to get paid so much? He once knew but now isn't sure. What he knows, for sure, is that he is going to kill – and get away.

~

Because quite a few get caught these days. Even the rich ones because you can no longer buy your way out of everything. Because there's no stopping the lynch mob, hungry and thirsty, fed and watered by TV. He has seen their victims, checked towels covering the face, herded into Tis Hazari Court by dirty cops in dirty uniform. Chased by reporters. There's one reporter he loves to look at. Every time she comes on, he spreads her legs inside his head, he pushes the microphone deep inside her, switches off all the lights, lies down on the sofa to listen to her spasm magnified through his home theatre. He saw her first when she was reporting on the Rahul Malhotra case: Malhotra, the grandson of a former chief of the Air Force, visiting home from Stanford, driving a Ferrari on his way home after a party, ran over six people sleeping on the street, got away because the witnesses turned hostile, one by one. One said it was a truck that ran them over, not a car; another said the car had wings and flew away.

Malhotra was convicted, let off on good conduct.

He isn't Rahul Malhotra, he can't pull strings, he knows no one powerful.

His father is a simple man.

Like the man in that Gieve Patel painting, the old man wearing old glasses, in the rain with bread and bananas.

~

Race Course gone.

Next station Jor Bagh.

Next station INA.

Only two other passengers in his coach now.

An elderly man with a woman, much younger, both with their eyes closed as if in invitation, to let him look at them. Perhaps, a father and daughter, he thinks, but the way her head rests on his shoulder, their fingers lock, they may be man and wife. For a moment, he's tempted to sit next to her, smell the heat from her hair, but, no, he won't because he likes standing, the train rocking him, the knowledge that he, and steel and glass, and these two lovers on board, old and young, are all hurtling, together, through the blackness beneath the city.

~

Next station is AIIMS. Doors will open to the left.

11.49 p.m.

This isn't his stop but he steps off the train.

~

All India Institute of Medical Sciences.

1.5 million patients, 100,000 surgical operations a year, over a thousand doctors and nurses, tons and tons of white cotton wool. Bloodstains, cancer, tumours, trauma, tubes, monitors, oscilloscopes, MRI plates against light frosted white, beeps, blood, IV drips, men, women and children, some newborn, some dead, some dying. He walks towards the hospital, the heatwave so thick it's like walking through sludge. At the entrance, right next to security, there's a girl selling a red balloon, with a woman, apparently her mother.

The balloon stains the night like a drop of blood on a slide.

Albert Lamorisse, 1956, Paris, *Le Ballon Rouge,* he bought the movie DVD via Amazon.com, got it delivered to Aatish's apartment in New York, Fedexed to him on his birthday. His favourite is the last scene in which a cluster of countless coloured balloons carry the boy across the sky above the city.

~

He asks, 'How much?'

Balloon Girl and her mother walk towards him.

The night is silent except for the light fall of their footsteps. He sees wary smiles in their eyes, trusting in the dark.

Looks like Red Balloon is leading the girl on.

'Only ten rupees,' says Balloon Girl.

CHILD

CITY ROUTE

ORPHAN'S first day out is planned as an event, carefully choreographed by Kalyani Das and Dr Chatterjee, that begins with an email the doctor drafts and redrafts, at least six times, before sending it to the director, Mr Sharma, requesting that he be allowed to take Orphan out for an hour or so.

Sir, with all due respect, may I suggest, in the spirit of freedom that you have so carefully nurtured in Little House, that Orphan be allowed to choose the route we take on his first day out? Let's give him a map of the National Capital Region, let's give him a pen, let Orphan trace a line, a curve, whatever. And that's the route we shall take him on.

Three days later, comes the reply:

Dear Dr Chatterjee, normally I wouldn't say this to a staffer but you are a student to me, you are learning. So let me tell you that rules in the government are like lines drawn in stone. All children here are in our custody as per a solemn, binding commitment to the honourable court. So, just like everybody else, Orphan has to wait until we plan a field trip for his cohort but I am going to make an exception. I like your innovative idea of letting him choose his route. Such things build individualism, something for which we have so little regard in our culture. In other words, you may start planning. I would like to be there when Orphan chooses his route.

Dr Chatterjee's first instinct is to doubt Mr Sharma's motive behind this acceptance: is he trying to reach out to his powerful, influential father, the VVIP friend of the Chief Minister, who, once he knows that Mr Sharma has been nice to his son, may pull wheels and levers, move cranks and shafts in the government's machinery to help Mr Sharma move up? From this sinecure at an obscure orphanage to the rarer echelons of the State Secretariat? Maybe yes, maybe no, but so what, Dr Chatterjee tells himself. Mr Sharma has approved his request, cleared the trip, that's all that matters.

'*Sir, thank you so much, I will always be grateful,*' he replies.

～

At exactly 5 p.m. – an hour before he begins to wind down, turning in for the day – when Orphan is at his most alert and agile, he is brought to Mr Sharma's office and seated on his desk. Mr Sharma, Mrs Chopra, nurses and attendants watching silently, Dr Chatterjee spreads the map of the entire National Capital Region, all its twelve flaps, prises open Orphan's little fingers, gently wraps them around a pen.

Twice, the pen slips out; once, it falls to the floor.

'Here, give it to me,' says Kalyani, and she holds Orphan's hand, guides him to the exact spot on the map where Little House is.

'This is Little House, this is from where we start,' Kalyani says, 'now I am letting go, Orphan, you move the pen.'

The child's hand moves.

From Little House, down the road, past the garbage heap at the entrance, onto Ring Road in a winding line that curves sharply, the pen takes a sprawling arc that cuts across the southern part of the city, becomes straight again for what seems like six kilometres or so, loops around the railway station, zigzags across the forested Ridge, heads for the highway where it meanders towards New City, comes to a stop right at the city's border, where the highway touches The Mall.

It's there that Orphan lets go of the pen.

'Thank you, Orphan,' says Dr Chatterjee. 'Quite a long route, the entire thing will take many days, so let Dr Chatterjee choose which section you will take.'

Everyone cheers.

The noise makes Orphan cry.

The gathered crowd tries to make sense of the scrawl Orphan has left on the map.

'Very adventurous,' says Mr Sharma.

Mrs Chopra says, 'It looks like the city's Metro map, Yellow and Blue lines.'

A nurse, in charge of laundry, says it reminds her of a hair-ribbon blowing in the wind.

The transport supervisor says it's similar to the route taken by two Delhi Transport Corporation buses, Route Nos. 414 and 527.

~

Late that night, the first part of their mission accomplished – the route plotted – and Orphan fast asleep, Kalyani and Dr Chatterjee sit together and look at the line that the child's pen has drawn.

'Look, sir,' says Kalyani, 'it ends very near where I live. We can take him to The Mall.'

'A mall is no place for a baby. His line also touches the railway station, that's a much better place for him to spend the day,' says Dr Chatterjee. 'We will arrive early, get a place on the overbridge from where Orphan can watch the trains, porters, passengers.'

'Yes, weighing machines with coloured spinning dials, blinking lights. We can buy a ticket and board a local train, travel up and down three or four trips, give Orphan his first view from a train window,' says Kalyani.

'In the afternoon, we will take him to Platforms 12 and 13, from where the Rajdhanis leave, show him their red-and-white coaches, some imported from Germany, with their sealed glass windows. Ticket examiners in black coats.'

'But have you seen, sir, how Orphan's line, before it travels across the city, takes a break just outside Little House? A short gap. Means there is someone outside Little House he wants to go with? He wants to spend some time at the entrance?'

'Don't be silly,' says Dr Chatterjee, 'you are reading too much into this line.'

~

And so they go on, into the late hours, trying to make sense of this child's drawing, how and why it curls around the highway before it enters The Mall, why it goes this way and not that, how it shows a steady hand and a uniform pressure that you do not usually see from fingers so small and so young. Both unaware, of course, that Orphan, in that ink scrawl, may have actually foreshadowed the route he will take, not with the kind nurse and the good doctor, but, yes, with someone else when he leaves Little House for the world outside – in search of his home.

WOMAN

HENRI BERGSON

YOU may ask me when you wake up, Ma, why did you put all these soft toys in my room, cluttering my bed? I am almost forty, Ma, you may say, I don't need these to go to sleep, but look carefully, you may very well ask me, where did you get such an amazing variety of toys? Not at all like when I was a kid, when I had only one bear. Brown and shapeless, stuffed with cotton wool that leaked in many places, its whiskers so hard they pricked like needles, its skin painted yellow that ran with each wash until it turned grey, then white.

But look at these, Ma, you will say, there are giraffes with hats, mice going to school, with bags, lunchboxes, water-bottles. Bears with umbrellas, elephants with scarves. Are all of these for me?

I will then tell you, yes, there is a little plan behind these toys.

I don't know if it will work but it's an idea I got reading the book by Henri Bergson I told you about.

~

Henri Bergson. Born in Paris, 1859. Very strong in mathematics as a child, he first works as a schoolteacher, then goes on to teach philosophy in college. He writes many books, even on religion, the appeal of Christianity over Buddhism, but the one I am reading is about what happens inside our heads when we sleep.

It's called *On Dreams*.

There is a strong link, Bergson says, between what we see, what we touch and what we hear when we are awake and what we see, what we touch and what we hear when we are dreaming – between our self and our dream-self. He says that, when we are awake, 'we live outside of ourselves' and it's only when we sleep, that 'we retire into ourselves'. So when we close our eyes, right at the moment of falling asleep, the coloured spots and moving forms that we see are the ones that consolidate into the outlines of objects and people we then go on to see in our dreams. Bergson calls this the 'visual dust' that fabricates our dreams. This visual dust is fed by memory and sensations. Memories stored deep in our unconscious. And the sensations we feel when we sleep: external sensations like the touch of the pillow, our feet against the sheet, the hard bed; internal sensations like the heart beating inside us, the blood coursing through our veins. All these combine to become the content of dreams.

~

That's where the idea of using the toys came to me. Not just the toys, my child, look around and you shall see. There is so much more.

41

I sprinkle visual dust all around.

I set up your bedroom before you arrive.

I buy toys, put them in a line right next to the windowsill, so that you will look at the animals before you fall asleep. I get an air conditioner on rent, only for you, install it in a place so that its draught covers the entire bed. I change the mattress, get one that's stiff, that stays firm, so that when you lie down, your back doesn't strain. I get a bedsheet the colour of water, a thin blanket the colour of grass.

So if Bergson is right and if your hands brush against the toys or the toys are the last thing you see before you close your eyes, maybe you will dream of a forest. With happy animals in it, all brightly coloured. You will dream of a yellow mouse going to school, a giraffe in a hat, a bear with an umbrella. You will find yourself lying down on a bed of soft green grass. In your hair, there will be a cool wind. And because the room is so cold, the forest floor will be covered with snow.

MAN

HOUSE GUESTS

'ONLY ten rupees,' says Balloon Girl.

~

Red Balloon must have been filled recently since it tugs hard, wants to fly away into the night, so the girl has tied its string around her wrist – looped it over several times – which she now thrusts at him.

'Only one left,' she says. 'The last.'

'Come home with me,' he says, 'there is food, I will give you a bed to sleep in, I will give you some money, there's no work that you have to do.'

His heart's racing so hard he can hear it. He's never done something like this before, he is amazed that he has said what he has said.

Balloon Girl smiles, looks at her mother who looks at him.

The mother, too, has never before heard anyone say this to her.

Once, not very long ago, a woman rolls down her car window and says, 'Why are you and your daughter begging? Why don't you come and work in my house? Bring your daughter along, I will pay you.' Before she can reply, however, the lights change, the woman's car drives away, she never sees her again. Another time, there's a man in a car who gestures to her to come closer, puts his hand in his pocket to make it seem he's taking out money to give to her but when she walks up to him, stands right next to his window, his hand darts out and, in full view of everyone, he grabs her breast.

But this is the first time someone's telling her, come home with me, I have things to give, none to take. He looks young, he doesn't look so strong. If he tries to do something funny, she can hit him, there are two of them against the one of him.

~

'Whatever you have to give, give us here, we are not going anywhere,' the mother says, drawing her daughter close to her, Red Balloon half covering her face.

'There's nothing to fear,' he says. 'I will drop you back right here.'

She doesn't answer, she walks away. He counts her steps, one to twelve. He watches her talk to her daughter.

'Tell me quickly, I can't keep waiting,' he says. 'I am going for a walk, I will be back in five minutes.'

~

That's an act he's putting on. For, he is wary now. A hospital security guard is looking at him. He can't arouse suspicion, he walks towards the hospital's main entrance, looking straight ahead, trying hard to appear normal, as if he is a patient or a visitor. He turns around to look at her, makes that turn as casual as he can. Sees she is still talking to the child. What are they discussing? The mother needs the daughter's advice? Will she call someone? He isn't sure. These days, everyone has a cell-phone, even those who go hungry. Does she have one, too? If she has, won't that be a problem? He's barely yards away from the Emergency entrance when he turns again to look. If she doesn't respond, call out to him, in the next one minute, two minutes, he is going to keep walking, he will walk out of the hospital and never return because he doesn't want to be stopped, questioned by anyone although he knows that's unlikely given the crowd of visitors even at so late an hour.

The next time he turns to look at her, she nods her head.

Mother and Balloon Girl agree.

He calls a taxi.

He opens the rear door for them, slips into the passenger seat in front.

Apartment Complex, New City, he says.

Let's go, says Taxi Driver as he looks at the woman and the child in the rear-view mirror.

~

They stand in the centre of his 800-square-foot bathroom, Mother and Balloon Girl, casting shadows on the white onyx tiles on the floor, holding each other, fearful the walls will

44

close on them and the spotless, smooth floor will move away from underneath their bare feet.

'Nothing to be afraid of, both of you are so dirty,' he says, knowing that he should put it more politely but aware that he doesn't need to be polite, there's no one in the room listening to him except these two.

'I am going to leave you in the bathroom alone, I have clean clothes for you here.' He points to a brown wicker chair in the corner where he's put two bathrobes, one for the mother, one for the child.

Their empty eyes follow his.

'You wear them like this,' he slips on a bathrobe over his clothes, ties its belt at the waist. It reaches just below his knees, it will cover her ankles. 'It's like a towel,' he says, 'it will soak all the water, dry you up.'

His movements are awkward, he hasn't done anything like this before.

Neither mother nor child says a word.

'Take this,' he says.

He hands Mother and Balloon Girl a fresh soap each, pink for the girl, blue for the mother (Shea Soap, Rs 175 each). Each gets a Bath Lily (Rs 200).

'Use this to scrub the dirt off,' he says. 'But you need to wet it with water first.' He shows them how, switches on the fan in the bathroom, turns it towards the bathtub.

'Sit in there, here are two buckets, I will mix the water for you, hot and cold,' he says.

Two buckets full.

'I am right here' – he leaves the bathroom, closes the door behind him –'you take your time, let me know if you need anything.'

~

45

It's a little after one in the morning, most lights in Apartment Complex are out. He pours himself a drink, drops an ice-cube into it, hears it crack, hears the water splash in the bathroom, hears Balloon Girl and Mother talk, laugh, the shower curtain rustle. He hears the tap run.

'Be careful,' he calls out, 'keep checking the water otherwise you may burn yourself.'

He isn't sure if they know blue is cold, red is hot.

He doesn't want an accident.

So far things have progressed smoothly: he brings them here by taxi, Red Balloon between them, touching the taxi's roof. Sit on the floor, he whispers to them when they are about to enter Apartment Complex, to avoid the closed-circuit TV cameras at the entrance. Taxi Driver couldn't care less, he's not even looking. In case Security Guard at the entrance to his building stops, asks him, sir, who are these two, he knows what to say: they are my new maids, they were stranded since they missed the last Metro and I had to go and pick them up.

But when they walk in, Security Guard isn't there.

He tips Taxi Driver extra for not speaking throughout the ride, for not asking any questions.

~

Mother and Balloon Girl step out of the bathroom, dripping, both in bathrobes half-wrapped, half-open, their old clothes in a soiled heap on the floor. He has kept food for them on the table.

Warm bread with butter and jam already spread, for Balloon Girl. Boiled egg. Breakfast at night. For the mother, there's fried rice and chicken leftovers from the meal he ordered in from the Chinese restaurant at The Leela the previous day.

They don't want to sit at the table. They eat, sitting on the floor, their bathrobes wet against the wall. He leaves the room, lets them eat in private.

He returns to pour them water in glasses, chilled. He shows them the guest room where they can sleep where the AC has been on the entire evening, the room cold like in winter.

~

Balloon Girl is fast asleep. Mother, too. The girl has tied Red Balloon to the armrest of a chair in the room, some of its gas has leaked away, it hovers above her face, above her hair, black, cropped close. He doesn't want them to know where he lives, he has to drop them off before sunrise but he will let them sleep for a while because he likes to watch them sleeping.

Watch Balloon Girl's bare legs, her mother's feet. He can do anything with them now and no one will know.

~

In their white bathrobes that fall open so that he can see their skin, Mother's breast and Balloon Girl's ribs, they look like giant white canna lilies strewn on his bed. Like the women in the Diego Rivera print he has framed on his wall. He takes all the time in the world to move, step by careful step, as if he's walking on jagged glass, so that they are not disturbed. He gets into bed, lies down, his back pressed against the wall, in a position so awkward he isn't sure how long he can stay that way.

Next to him, Mother and Balloon Girl move in their sleep.

He can't get his heart to slow down, he's afraid its beating will wake them up. He is still, his body tense, his muscles taut. He can smell them, soap, water and dinner. Water from their hair has stained the bedsheet in two shapeless patches of wet. In the night light, he can see Mother's feet, her nails ingrown and chipped. Countless crevices crack her hard heels,

47

skin peels on the soles of her feet like earth gone dry. Balloon
Girl's feet, in contrast, are soft, she must have stayed in the
water for a while because the tips of her fingers and toes are
still wrinkled.

He touches Balloon Girl's heels, she doesn't move her leg,
he lets his hand rest there and he closes his eyes, setting the
alarm clock inside his head for an hour so that he can wake
them up in the dark, get them to change back into their
clothes, give them some money, drop them back at the
entrance to the hospital.

And if Balloon Girl doesn't mind, he will keep Red Balloon
which bobs in the night air in the room, drowsy, not far from
the sleeping child and her mother.

CHILD

ENTER BHOW

IN her broken English, which she is trying to mend at free
classes an NGO offers two days a week to domestic helps,
Kalyani reads Orphan stories from books donated to the Little
House library. She sings him Bengali songs she's heard from
her parents, nonsense rhymes; she tells him about days when
she herself is a child in the village who hears the April nor'-
wester whistle through mango trees, chases dragonflies as they
flit, from leaf to leaf, across the surface of the pond unbroken,
still as glass, just before the skies open up with rain. She tells
him how she goes to the city one day to see the trams. Like
trains, but smaller. Only two coaches that go so slow you can

hop on, hop off without the tram stopping. The first circus her father takes her to where a man rides a motorcycle spinning himself up and down the sides of a spherical cage. She includes bits from her biography: about her brother, who works as a gardener, and her sister who would love to play with him. She tells Orphan about how her father and mother don't have any money to buy her dolls when she is a child so she makes her own. With paper, shreds of cloth, broomsticks, coloured glass from broken bangles. Of course, Kalyani knows that Orphan is too young to understand any of these stories, that her words sail over his head but, she knows this, too, that the words, wrapped in the warmth of her voice in all its cadences, its sings and its songs, lull him to sleep.

~

There's one story that's her favourite.

And Orphan's, too, for this is the one he responds the most strongly to, in which he follows each move of Kalyani's eyes, hands and lips, tracks her every gesture. So Kalyani makes this part of her daily routine with him, right at the end, just after he is fed, washed and ready for bed.

Carrying Orphan, she walks with him down the long hallway of Little House.

'Today, we will look at three of your friends and see how each one of them came here. Look, there is Sunil, you know how Sunil came here? He came here in a big car that drove right up to the gate.' Through a window, they can see the street outside and Kalyani points Orphan to a car passing by.

She moves to the next child.

'Look, there is Pooja, you know how she came here?

'One day, a wind blew a little cloud from the sky into her house. Pooja wanted to fly so she jumped onto it and Baby Cloud flew across the city. Over streets and cars and buses and vans, between buildings, it passed all the big clouds in the sky, Mother Cloud, Father Cloud, and landed here on the roof of Little House. Pooja climbed off Baby Cloud and walked into her room. She was wet with water from the cloud and we had to dry her with a big white towel.'

Kalyani tells Orphan to look up at the sky and always there is at least one wisp of white. 'That's the cloud that brought her,' she says.

'Now there is Neha. A big black bumblebee, sitting on a big, beautiful yellow sunflower, saw Neha sitting on a leaf and picked her up, carried her from flower to flower, leaf to leaf and then came here. Dropped her, gently, on her bed.'

She points to a fallen leaf.

By now, Kalyani reaches the end of the hallway from where they can see the main entrance to Little House. She walks up to the gate, stops just a few steps short – taking a child out of Little House, without the director's clearance, is forbidden – and from where they stand, they can see the dog. 'You know how you, Orphan, came here? You came riding on the back of that dog, can you see her?'

She points to the biggest dog in the group, a black-and-white mongrel with a coat unusually clean for the mess she is sitting in: vegetable peels, plastic, paper cups, filth, all the waste from Little House.

'That dog's name is Bhow,' Kalyani tells Orphan. 'Bhow brought you here. You sat on top of her, she was like your horse, you came here riding across the city, like a little prince.'

Kalyani sits down on the floor, Orphan can barely support himself on his feet so she props him up against herself to help him get a better view, his hands on her shoulders. And they sit there, for ten minutes, fifteen minutes for him to look at Bhow. Not knowing, of course, that it's Bhow who watches Orphan being abandoned, who watches his mother drive away in that summer night, and it's only when Orphan has had his fill, when his eyes begin to close, that Kalyani lifts him up and, humming a tune, walks slowly back to his bed.

This has become their ritual: choosing three children each day, listening to how each one came to Little House and then ending up with Bhow, who never leaves the garbage heap.

~

One such evening, after their walk down the hallway during which Kalyani tells him how one child has come to Little House in a flying chair, one in a boat that sails down the water running from the tap, and a third is blown in by a wind, after she has shown him Bhow, when she's adjusting the pillows around him in bed, smoothening his blanket, the child reaches out and touches her face.

Orphan's little fingers brush her cheeks and her eyebrows. At first, Kalyani thinks this is an accident but this is a movement, planned and plotted inside that little head, ruled by that little heart, because moments later, Orphan does it again, his hand reaches out to touch her, his fingers close around her hair, he says something that sounds like Ma. Tears flood Kalyani's eyes, the first time since she has come to Little House, she quickly wipes them away.

'You go to sleep,' she says.

~

'Watch what you tell him.' Dr Chatterjee stands right behind her, making her jump with a start. 'He likes you.'

'I didn't tell him anything, sir,' says Kalyani.

'Maybe behind all this talk of becoming a nurse and running away, you want to be a mother.'

'Don't be silly,' she says. 'What will I do with him? There are so many families in this city wanting to adopt him, everyone wants a son. Why shouldn't Orphan live like a prince? Now, leave us alone, it's time for him to sleep.'

Turning her back to him, as she pats Orphan to sleep, her fingers tremble, her head begins to spin, she doesn't know what has come over her.

MEANWHILE

TWO LOVERS ON-BOARD
THE NIGHT METRO

YOU are late, she says.

Sorry, I couldn't get an autorickshaw, he says.

I don't like to wait here.

You never told me this.

I don't like this apartment, this bed, I don't like this mattress, the walls, this paint. The AC here makes so much noise.

This is the only place I could get without answering too many questions. The man who owns this lives in New York, he isn't here to bother us.

I know.

You said we needed a place of our own. Neutral zone, no hotel room.

I know.

I could change the mattress?

The mattress is all right. Just waiting here, by myself, I can't stand.

Next time, why don't you wait outside and we both walk up together? I will call you when I am a minute away.

You know you can't do that. He checks all my calls, received, missed, every call.

Why do you let him?

He's my husband.

~

My son's not well, she says. Must be the heat, he had fever last night, I hope it isn't dengue.

Dengue breaks out late October, this is only July. You could have stayed home.

I wanted to see you.

Sit down, you make me nervous, the way you stand there, looking out of the window.

He asked me, Ma, where are you going? I said, I am going to the doctor, I will be back very soon in about half an hour, with your medicine. He said, Ma, stay at home, I am frightened. I told him, I have locked the doors and windows, nobody can come in. Pull the blanket over your head, I said, think you are inside a tent.

Where's your husband?

On tour.

So who's with the child at home?

The maid.

~

You are trembling, he says.

No, I am not, she says.

Give me your hands.

You know a year before my father died, he fractured his ankle, he was in hospital for five days, in a lot of pain and when he would fall asleep, I would sit by his side, hold his hand. I realised I had never held his hand since I had been a girl so in that hospital room, I held his hand as long as I could. One day, I think I held it for almost an hour.

~

You know something, she says, anyone who holds your hands won't know how old you are.

What do you mean?

They aren't hard, rough.

Must be because I have done no manual labour.

I like your hands.

You were born when my daughter was six years old.

You keep doing this arithmetic.

No, just wanted to let you know.

Where is she? You never talk about her.

She left.

Means?

I don't know where she is.

Have you tried Googling her?

I have.

And?

And, what? Nothing.

~

You are crying, he says.

I don't know, she says, for more than an hour last night, his temperature was 104.

Let's go see the doctor.

So late?

Emergency is open the whole night.

What do I tell the doctor?

Let's listen to what he says, he may give us some medicine, ask for some tests you could get done first thing in the morning.

OK.

~

He locks the door, follows her down the stairs.

Heat rises from the tarred street as if a furnace smoulders below their feet. The night sky is cloudless except for stray flecks of white that squat low on the new skyscrapers, the promise of water glinting on glass and steel, reflected in the neons that spell out the names of offices where men and women work, day in, day out, at call centres, looking at clocks in all places except their own.

Convergys, PricewaterhouseCoopers, Ericsson, Nokia, Sapient, Lucent.

Each with its own colour: blue, orange, so many shades of white, green. Down below, the fluorescent Metro sign glows, yellow against night black.

They board the train, the coach is empty at this late hour except for a young man standing in the corner. Thin, his wrist so slim that his watch slides halfway to his elbow when he raises his hand to brush his hair. He looks at her, she looks away.

~

This is so much nicer than the flat, she says, this Metro coach, as she leans into him, the train's air-conditioned draught fans her face. He tilts his head to touch hers, to listen to the voices inside her head, to breathe in the day's heat and sweat tangled in her hair. Her hands cover his, their fingers lock, and she knows all is well with him by her side, that she's going to pick up the medicine, her son will wake up soon and his fever will be gone.

They close their eyes, the young man in the corner turns to look.

WOMAN

KINDERGARTEN TEACHER

WHAT would your father have done tonight?

He would not have been sitting downstairs like I am: all alone, waiting for you to wake up, wary in my own house, unsure of my own child.

No, not your father.

He wouldn't have let himself be bullied into accepting your terms like I have. That I can't ask you any questions. He would have laughed the whole thing off, said what kind of a silly condition is that, walked up the stairs, got you to open the door, got you out of bed and walked you down the stairs. Got you moving, got you living, just like he does with me when I first move to the city forty-five years, fifty years ago, the wife of the youngest professor in his college.

~

The day is long, so are the hours after he leaves at 10 a.m. I have never lived in a city so big, I have never been alone in a house for so long on a single day so when your father's away, I search for empty spaces to fill. Chairs, table, windowsill, the balcony floor between the flowerpots. After the maid has left, I take a little towel, wipe away imaginary dust from tabletops, the frame of our bed, the Philips radio.

At the window, I see a group of women, all older than me,

sitting, in a circle, on the low terrace of the next house, knitting, talking. One is oiling another's hair. They smile at me, one invites me to join them.

In a few months, I get tired of this routine and I tell your father.

Thank God you told me this so soon, he says, I thought you would spend ten, twelve, fifteen years like this before telling me that you were bored to death waiting for me every day. I have an answer, he says, you get ready tomorrow morning along with me, we are going to meet someone.

Who will do the morning chores, I ask, who will iron your clothes, pack your lunchbox, and he says, forget all of that for one day, I will wear wrinkled clothes, I will buy some fruit on my way to college, there's no need for a lunchbox, what we will do tomorrow is much, much more important. You have a bath, wear a nice sari and be ready, I need you to get a copy of your college certificate.

What certificate, I ask, I am not going to go to any university. And what college certificate, I have one but is it even worth anything? BA in Home Science, cooking, stitching, who needs all that?

I heard you, your father says, let's not talk about it until tomorrow morning.

That night, I can't sleep. Lying next to me, your father senses this, he doesn't tell me anything. Only once, he asks me, are you OK?

I can't sleep, I say, I don't know where you are taking me tomorrow.

Relax, he says, you don't need to worry.

~

The next morning is a blur.

Your father wakes up, reads the newspaper, goes to the

58

market to get the day's groceries, the maid comes and starts her cleaning, scrubbing, I tell her to go home early because I want her out of the way. By the time your father is back, I am bathed, dressed in a sari I have worn only once before. I still have that with me, I will show it to you tomorrow morning. It's sky blue, little white stars sprinkled all over, it will look very good on you given how slim you are.

Your father looks at me and says, look at the new teacher, every child will wish to be your student.

~

St Aloysius Day School for Boys and Girls.

Your father and I wait in the lobby of the principal's office under a giant photograph of St Aloysius. A frail child, his hair cropped close, he holds a wooden crucifix. I read the legend typed on a piece of paper pasted on the wall next to the picture. I remember it to this day:

'St Aloysius died at twenty-three, he helped hundreds of sick people when the plague struck Rome.'

Will they ask me about the saint? The plague? Rome? I know nothing, I am nervous, your father holds my hand underneath a file that holds my certificates.

We wait until someone from the principal's office calls me in. By name, it's funny, I have not heard someone say my name like that.

I get up, wait for your father to join me but he doesn't.

You go inside, he says, answer their questions, answer whatever they ask you and tell them what you know. If you don't know the answer to a question, say I don't know. If you don't like it inside, get up, say thank you to her and walk out, I am here, I am not going anywhere.

~

The principal's name is Sister Agnes Consuelo.

She speaks slowly, softly, she speaks only in English. She begins with simple, direct questions, easy, to which I answer confidently with a yes or no.

Your husband said you are new to the city, do you like it so far?

You live near the school?

You have a BA degree?

That's a nice sari you are wearing, she says, where did you get it?

My parents gave it to me, I say, and she says, I like my teachers in saris.

Tell me about your day, she asks, and I tell her exactly what I told you earlier, how I wait for the maid to leave and then dust the rooms again, listen to the radio. I am afraid she may ask me something about the news on the radio which your father listens to every night but she doesn't, she stands up, smiles and says, see you tomorrow, I will introduce you to the Kindergarten Class, KG, Section A, the students are waiting for you. We will help you become a teacher, she says.

She takes my hand in hers. Welcome to our school, she says, your husband is right, you will make a good teacher.

Thank you, I say.

The meeting's done, about fifteen minutes, it seems like five.

~

Evening comes, your father and I are children, talking non-stop, he's back home early, we go shopping because he says all women who work in the city need to carry a bag to keep pens, keys, handkerchief. Bag bought, we go to Bata to buy a pair of shoes. No harm if it has a little bit of heel, he says, begin wearing them right now so that you get used to them before morning, as he gets the cashier to pack my old shoes in the box while I slip into the new ones. This way you won't get sores tomorrow, he says. It's evening, surely you can't cook dinner now, he says, and so we go to a South Indian restaurant. He orders masala dosa – let's have something you do not cook at home – and we return home around nine at night.

I have never been out so late since I came to this city.

~

Lying in bed, the fears return. What did your father tell Sister Agnes? What has he promised her about me that I am neither aware of nor capable of? What will happen tomorrow morning? How will I stand in front of forty children, boys and girls, what if they keep shouting and I cannot do anything, what if I start crying?

Go to sleep now, says your father, you need to get up early, I will drop you off at the school before I go to college. As if he has heard the voices in my head, he says, even I had no idea what to teach, how to teach when I walked into college the first day. You learn, just like your students. All you need to know and all you need to keep telling yourself is that you have seen and done more than the boys and girls in the class, you have more stories to tell them than they have to tell you.

The next morning, I begin as a kindergarten teacher.

~

That's what your father does to me and that's what he would have done tonight, he would have said, baby, write down your problems, all the questions that you have in your head. Make three boxes, one that says 'Can be solved today', one that says 'Will need some time and help', and the last one that says 'Will never be solved'. Let's see which problem goes into which box.

That's your father. I wish he were here today.

Who knows, he may drop by. Because, some nights, he does, like that woman, 12 feet tall, he slips into this house.

MAN

NEW CITY

BALLOON Girl and her mother have been quite neat. This must be their first time in a bathtub but they have followed his instructions to the last one because hardly any water has spilled out, there are only two damp patches on the floormat where they dry themselves, their towels in two crumpled balls on the floor. There are some smudges in the tub, along its sides and its lip, footprints and handprints, large and small, but these aren't much of a problem, he turns the shower on for the water to wash these stains away. Maybe he will get it scrubbed clean later, scoured and disinfected. He may need something strong to get rid of the clump of hair that sits in the drain. They live on the street near the hospital, you never know what germs they might carry.

~

He takes out a fresh pair of latex gloves from a box Arsh got him as a gift the last time he was here.

'This is the only thing you will like from Paris,' Arsh says. 'Maybe you can get these here too but I have got you top quality. Twelve boxes, each with fifty gloves, that's six hundred, will last you a long time.'

He thinks so, too, but he's down to three boxes – and it's been just over a year since Arsh left.

He slips on a pair, sprays Dettol on his hands, ties a fresh, ironed handkerchief around his mouth and nose. A dank warmth radiates from the pile of their soiled clothes as if someone alive, made of flesh and blood, is sleeping under them. The mother's yellow sari, orange blouse, two of its four hooks missing. A shred of a towel. Balloon Girl's dress is a grey frock, the colour of street; a sleeve torn, frayed around the neck. Her underwear is a pair of boy shorts with a string.

Five pieces, all cotton.

Washer and dryer are in the bathroom, installed as one unit, front-loading, next to the bathtub. Someone may hear at night, he worries, he will muffle the sound by closing the bathroom door. He drops the clothes in, pours liquid detergent, double of what's needed, adds fabric softener, switches the machine on.

Should take an hour, at the most.

He will drape them over the air conditioner for faster drying.

~

It will be nice if Balloon Girl wakes up, he thinks, because he can then show her the washing machine. He will tell her to sit down on the floor and, through the machine's circular glass window, watch the clothes spin and tumble. Slow first, then so fast that it looks like a fan, making the clothes disappear into a blur. He will show her how streaks of water slide down glass, like tears; the red light glowing in the display panel in the dark. He will tell her to place her hand on the machine, feel its movement. He has so much to show her. From his wrap-around balcony, more than a thousand square feet, he will point out to her the road they took when they came from the hospital, that heads to Jaipur and then farther south and west to Mumbai where the sea is. He will show her the office building, across the street, that's shaped like a ship, its top like a mast, its terrace converging on a point in the night sky just under the stars. They are under the flight corridor and he will show her planes, big ones landing or taking off, small ones very high up, moving between the moon and the stars, bound east or west for cities he hasn't seen.

He will show her his city.

New City, that's still not ready, that's being built as they watch, freshly laid tar on its streets gleaming, all its buildings scrubbed and polished, from their iron gates to their red-and-yellow barricades with red lights blinking, as if all the parts of the city have been bought in a box, from a shop that sells cities, and is now being unpacked, the different pieces laid out across what was once a thousand villages. He will show her the Town & Country Resort, the new club they have just built, he will take her to the edge of its shimmering swimming pool, ask her to look down and see, below the water on the floor, a magnificent cockroach unlike any creature she has seen before.

He loves New City. Especially at this time in the night, especially from this height, because then he cannot see a single imperfection. It spreads below him, dark and flowing, like the sky itself, dotted with stars on the ground, lights, the diffused glare of the traffic below, points of light that move, and, in between, a wisp of smoke rising, from an oven in the slums across the Metro tracks.

There is so much to show, should he wake her up?

It's still night, he walks to the bedroom to check.

~

Mother and Balloon Girl sleep, each one has drawn the bathrobe tight around herself like a quilt. The mother's right arm is draped around the girl, holding her close.

He will let them sleep.

The room is cold, he raises the temperature 5 degrees. Five beeps but no one wakes up. Which suits him fine since their clothes, he can hear, have only now started their spin cycle.

He will wait. So he sits on the floor, next to their bed, watches their two chests rise and fall, listens to two hearts beating.

CHILD

CAMERA INDIA

THE very day Orphan receives his Certificate of Abandonment under the Juvenile Justice (Care & Protection of Children) Act, 2000, and is, therefore, legally free for adoption, Priscilla Thomas, forty-two, the country's most famous TV anchor, single, announces her wish to start a family in a dramatic moment at the end of her weekly show, *Camera India*, when she looks into an estimated 10 million or so pairs of eyes, and she says words to this effect:

'Ladies and gentlemen, 65 per cent of the children adopted in this city this year were girls because, one, there are more girls out there abandoned, helpless baby girls crying in the dark. If they haven't already been killed in the uterus, that is. Two, everyone wants to be politically correct. That, quote, we don't kill baby girls, we bring them home and take care of them, unquote. And, three, we all know, and I know my feminist guests on the panel will disagree with me, that daughters are more kind, more loyal, more sacrificing than sons. So getting a girl home means you get an adopted daughter who will always be grateful to you.

'Well, enough is enough, I say. You have seen me, you know me, I never ever blurred the line between my personal and my professional, ladies and gentlemen, you know that, but not tonight. Tonight I want to tell the nation that I am going to go out and get myself a baby.

'A boy, yes, a boy.

'Because, in all our big talk of being an emerging power, we, as a people, as a nation, blind ourselves. We refuse to see facts and the fact is: when a helpless, homeless baby lies abandoned, whether it should have a home should not depend on, pardon my language here, what's there or not there between those legs.'

There's no controlling the studio audience.

Some jump off chairs, one falls off, another closes his eyes in prompt prayer, others run up to Ms Thomas and ask for her autograph. On their arms, their necks, one man lifts his T-shirt, points to his heart, says, please sign here, Priscilla, please. Special guest for the evening Miss Universe 1992 Sushmita Sen, with her adopted daughters, walks up to Ms Thomas and hugs her so hard her microphone falls down, its wires get tangled, its electronic whine pierces the studio and living rooms across the country but no one cares as Ms Thomas, one arm around Ms Sen, the other wiping a tear from her eye, shouts out her signature line: 'Thank you, India, thank you, we will be right back.'

~

Mr Sharma watches this and knows instantly that this is the right time and the right place to do the right thing for Orphan, for Little House and for himself.

Three birds and he can hit them with one stone that has fallen from the heavens above.

Orphan could be the TV baby and have, as his mother, Ms Thomas, the most famous woman – now mother – in India. Mr Sharma himself will become a star. His only appearance on TV so far has been a twenty-second clip on child welfare on a news channel whose owner, a realtor, is in prison for raping his marketing assistant. This could make him a national figure, Mr Sharma tells himself, and, who knows, thanks to YouTube, he will even go bacterial, viral, whatever is the word they use these days.

So that night, after his wife and his son have gone to sleep, Mr Sharma sits down to write an email to Ms Thomas – why wait for tomorrow, if you want to do something, do it right now, at this very instant, that's always been his motto – and to ensure that it catches her eye from among the countless that must choke her inbox, he tries to be evocative in the subject line:

MAMA THOMAS, FROM YOUR SON, SOON TO BE

~

Dear, Respected Ms Thomas, writes Mr Sharma.
Tears fill my eyes as I watch your show tonight but once I wipe them, I can see clearly. I see a little boy just down the hall from where I sit and I know you are his mother.
Here he is, speaking to you in his own voice:
My name is Orphan. It's an unreal name. I have been waiting in Little House for a real home, for a real mother to give me a real name. I will be the least trouble, everyone here will tell you how quiet I am, how disciplined in my habits. In your house, it will be as if I am not even there.
You say, displaying rare courage, that you wish for a son.
That's why I sleep tonight, a happier and a more hopeful baby boy, because I have seen my mother.
I wait for your reply.

It's 2 a.m. when Mr Sharma hits Send.

At 2.03 a.m., comes Ms Thomas's reply:

Mr Sharma, see you in your office at Little House, 10 a.m. today.

Mr Sharma wants to wake up his wife, his child, switch on all the lights in the house, read aloud his email.

He calls Mrs Chopra.

~

'Did I wake you up?'

'No problem, sir, not at all.'

'I usually don't call so late in the night but this is very important,' says Mr Sharma.

'Yes, sir.'

'Priscilla Thomas...'

'Yes, sir, Ms Thomas, the TV woman.'

'Did you watch her show?'

'No, sir, I was in the kitchen, my son returned late in the night.'

'Ms Thomas is coming to Little House tomorrow at 10 a.m. to look at Orphan for adoption. This could be our moment, Mrs Chopra, the day we have been waiting for. At last, the world will get to know the wonderful work I, you, we, all of us, do at Little House. And Orphan gets a super home.'

'Very good, sir, that's too good.'

'You were the one who picked up Orphan first, I want you to be there in case she wants to interview you.'

'Sir, of course, I will be there an hour early.'

'And on your way, please get pastries, samosas, cold drinks, Coke, that we can offer her and her crew.'

'Shouldn't we prepare him, sir?'

'Prepare? Who?'

'Orphan?'

'Prepare him means, Mrs Chopra?'

'His mother may be coming tomorrow, that he will be leaving us shortly. The child needs to be prepared for what is going to happen to him.'

'Don't jump the gun, Mrs Chopra, no need to think of the chicken before the egg. Let's see how this goes, the only preparation I want is that Orphan should be bathed, dressed well, he should smell good, put some nice talcum powder behind his ears. Ms Thomas may want to hold him and you know how important first impressions are, especially if her camera is running. Orphan smells, or wets himself, she will say, let me go to Mumbai to get a boy. Or even Kolkata, to the Missionaries of Charity.'

'Sir, what about Kalyani? She is his nurse. She is always with him, shouldn't we tell her?'

'What about her? We call her a nurse but she is little more than a maid, why do we need to tell her? She doesn't need to know. Let's keep this between us. Strictly professional.'

'Of course, sir, thank you.'

'Goodnight.'

~

Back in Little House, it is quiet. All the babies sleep.

Sitting on the floor, her back against the wall next to Orphan's cot, Kalyani has nodded off. She is tired, her chest hurts, she feels the first flush of a fever. Her nursing exam guide slips to the floor and makes a noise which no one hears. During the night, on his rounds, Dr Chatterjee comes in to check, finds her curled up, like a child. He gets a sheet and covers her with it, up to her neck.

Kalyani doesn't move even the slightest, so deep has she fallen asleep.

WOMAN

YOUR BIRTH

I REMEMBER, like every mother does, the first touch of your skin against mine, damp and soft, when they wheel you into my room in the nursing home after they measure you, weigh you, clean you up. I have some stitches which hurt as I hold you in the crook of my arm, sized and shaped to make you a perfect fit. When you cry, they take you away to feed you because I am not ready with milk.

Through the night, I slip in and out of sleep.

~

I remember the day before and the day after your birth, my three days of doing nothing; of having, at my service, three nurses, two attendants, two doctors, from wake-up to sleep time. My legs massaged, my back kneaded; my heels, cracked in several places, dipped in warm water from where steam rises, fragrant, then dabbed dry, gently, with a warm towel and then, in the end, softened with cold cream. My first manicure, my first pedicure, I learn these words in the hospital, someone else cutting, filing my nails to a perfect shape – all edges rounded, dead skin removed.

An attendant escorts me to the bathroom, holds my hand, like I am a little girl. I tell her, you don't have to, she says, no, we have to be very careful, there is someone inside you now.

The bathroom floor is dry, I stand under the shower. The

nurse tells me to undress, I am awkward, she says, no one's looking, don't worry, I am going to close the door.

I watch water run down my body, there's a mirror in the bathroom in which I see myself, through the shower's frosted door, my shape and, inside it, yours.

The bath soap is liquid gel, so soft in my hands it slips between my fingers, drips to the floor, mixes with the water there, foaming a puddle around my feet. The towel Jincy, the nurse, gives me is so large it wraps me in its folds, one, two, three, half a four, almost like a sari, white in colour.

Take two towels, Didi, she says, one for the shower, one for the hair. And drop them in the bathroom, leave them there, we will clean up.

They give me a blue gown, buttons in the back.

You don't have to wear anything underneath the gown, she says, matter-of-fact.

That night, I latch the door, step out of my gown, walk around in my room, I have never done this and so I do it again and again. I stand at the window and look down at the street. At people walking by, trams, buses. I wait for a crowd to gather, to point to me and say, look up, look, there's a naked pregnant woman at the window, is she crazy?

~

It's like I am on vacation.

There's no waking up in the morning looking at the clock, no dragging myself to the balcony to light the oven, clear last night's ash, no choosing the right-sized pieces of coal so that they catch fire quickly, no putting wood or paper to help the fire spread, no closing eyes to keep the smoke out. No ironing clothes, no cooking in the kitchen, no sitting on my haunches, no sweat trickling down my back. The nursing home has a generator so there's no preparing for the power-cut every evening, cleaning lanterns with ash, no making new wicks from old clothes, no pouring kerosene oil. So I don't wake up once I fall sleep. Except, of course, when they bring you to me twice or thrice in the night when you cry. Even then, I just hold you close and my big sleep drags your small one into its folds.

Breakfast is cornflakes and milk in a white ceramic bowl cool to the touch. They check on me every four hours, lunch you won't believe: three kinds of vegetables, two pieces of fish, chicken too, bread so soft, so white, so warm I don't want to eat it, I want to show it to your father. Rice is poured onto the plate compacted, shaped like a bowl, steaming fresh with fragrance of herbs I have never smelt before. Glass of milk, chilled in the fridge; orange juice, and, on top of all this, ice cream. Strawberry one day, vanilla the other, they ask, would you like a cup or a stick, choose, we can give you both if you wish. And towels, big and small, rolled up, warm and cold, whatever feels good at that time, for the forehead, for my face.

All this because of you.

~

My stay at the hospital must cost a lot, these three days in the nursing home, but your father never mentions the expenses.

When I ask him, he says he told someone at college to recommend a nursing home and that's what led him to this place. He says they have a bed in the room for visitors and he can sleep at night but he says, no, you stay by yourself, I won't stay the night because knowing you, you will start worrying about me, what will I have for dinner, what will I take for lunch to college, are my clothes ironed, every silly little thing, and I don't want you to worry about these things because this is our first child and the child, you, and I, all three of us, deserve the best. Even if the best is, like this room in the nursing home, something we can afford for only three days.

~

The last night in the hospital, I cannot sleep. You have been crying a lot and although I am feeding you now, that doesn't help.

You give her to me, says Jincy the nurse, try to get some sleep. I will take care of her until you wake up.

But I don't sleep, I find myself standing by the window looking out at the street, quiet at this time, and I picture this city without your father in it. He must be asleep at home or reading something for his classes the next day but for a moment he disappears, he is not there, he will never come back. As this image begins to fill out, I feel fear strengthen its grip, the entire night sky enters the room minus the stars and the moon, just its darkness, nothing else. Clouds drop down as fog, slip and swirl into the room through which I see the nurse walking towards me holding you in her arms. I shout at her not to bring you into this blackness, to keep you outside where there must be light, where there must be people. But she hands you over to me and it's then that I realise, for the first time, that, along with you, I have also been born, as a mother, and, very much like you, I am clueless in the dark.

MAN

HIGHWAY MYNAHS

HE needs to get Balloon Girl and her mother into his car without Security Guard seeing. That should take him five minutes, six minutes during which he needs Security Guard out of the way. So he needs to set up a little distraction. Silly but effective.

~

'Where were you when I walked in a few hours ago?' His voice is cold, amplified in the silence. As if he's reading from a script.

'Sir, I was right here,' says Security Guard.

Unquestioning submission in his voice, in his eyes, in the way his shoulders droop, pull his head down, make his arms wilt by his side.

'No, you were not here, I didn't see you.'

'I must have gone to the toilet, sir. Only for two minutes.'

'Two minutes or two hours, you know that you are not supposed to leave this place and, if you have to, you need to get a replacement.'

'Sorry, sir.'

'I can complain to the security manager.'

'Yes, sir.'

'I can get you taken off duty.'

'Please don't, sir, it will never happen again.'

'You should never leave this place. Your job is to guard the building.'

'Yes.'

'There's something I would like you to do.'

'Yes, sir?'

'I forgot, I left a bag just outside my door, can you get it for me? I will wait here while you are gone.'

'Of course, sir, I will take the lift, be back in a few minutes.'

~

It goes exactly as per script.

There is no bag, of course.

As soon as Security Guard steps into the lift, he calls out to Balloon Girl and her mother. They are hiding in the shadow, on the first-floor landing.

'Get into the car, quick, both of you,' he says, 'sit down on the floor, not the seats. Exactly like when we came from the hospital. You don't want anyone to see you because they will call the police. Not a word until we are out on the street.'

They do exactly as told; he starts the car. They avoid Security Guard. He will tip him a few hundred rupees tomorrow.

They are crouched on the floor, he smells detergent from their clothes, lavender from the soap. Balloon Girl's hair is short so it's almost dry but her mother's is still wet, dripping thin trails of water on her shoulders, across her blouse.

'Careful now, we are leaving, lie low and quiet. There are cameras at the gate, we have to be very careful.'

It's before daybreak, the darkest hour.

~

Of course, there's nothing illegal in what he has done, he is sure of that, but to be doubly sure, he runs through the sequence of events in his head. He invites them over, he asks them clearly, in Hindi, at the hospital, do you want to come home. She says yes, the mother, an adult. No coercion there. He gets them home, he asks them to take a bath, no, he merely suggests they take a bath which they agree to. He provides them with soap, cream, the kind he uses, bathrobes, the use of his bathroom, living quarters, all for free; he even washes their clothes for them, he gives them food, now he will give them some money and he will never ever see them again. Yes, he does touch the child and the mother but there's nothing irregular, out of place, about the touches. His fingers do brush the mother's breasts when he adjusts her bathrobe but that was accidental and, anyway, she is asleep when that happens, he is sure of that. There is no camera in his room that would have recorded anything.

He is safe, he rolls down the car window.

'We are all clear,' he says, 'you may get up from the floor and sit next to the window, the wind will dry your hair.'

But the mother doesn't move. In his rear-view mirror, he sees Balloon Girl looking out, the wind in her hair, yellow neon lights, from the street outside, dappling her face.

~

He will take Ring Road, he decides, because traffic is thin at this time of the night although these days they have police everywhere with speed guns and breathalysers. He hopes no one stops him but if they do, he has his story ready, the same one from last night. They are his maid and her daughter and he is taking them back home. He will drop them off in Yusuf-sarai Market, at least two traffic lights before AIIMS, near Green Park Metro Station, Rhythm Restro Bar, closed at this time, at a place where no one is looking, where there is no police van. Then he will keep going straight, take a left at the next light and get onto the highway via the Dhaula Kuan exchange. They don't know how to open the car door so he will have to do it. Sitting in the driver's seat, he will reach back and click the door open. Close it as soon as they are out and then there will be no looking back.

'Here, take this,' he says, one hand on the steering wheel, the other extended behind him – with the cash, 5,000 rupees, in 500-rupee notes.

'You can get change from any shop.'

The mother's fingers brush against his.

She is cold as ice.

Balloon Girl is fast asleep.

He will wake her up when the time comes.

~

Drop-off is perfect.

He closes the door, doesn't wait to see which way they go.

~

On the way home, traffic has surged. A long line of cars is backed up at the highway toll gate. Sixteen lanes, all full, he slips into the Tag Only lane but even that's choked, bumper to bumper, but today he's fine with the waiting because there's nothing to worry about any more. Relief washes over him, from his head to the tips of his fingers. There's a strong whiff of detergent in the car, he must have poured a lot more than needed, just five pieces of clothing he should have measured more carefully. He will tell Driver to wash the car, maybe take it to the carwash. He lowers the four windows to let wind come in, blow away all traces of Balloon Girl and her mother. He has done nothing wrong, he is sure of that, but as extra caution, he should get the seats and the floor wiped clean. Disinfected.

All fingerprints removed, too.

Still not moving, to his left, in the next lane, he sees two mynahs, both the birds hopping between two cars, pecking away at something he cannot see in the dark.

These are brave birds, so close they move to the cars' wheels. Even when the vehicles move, these birds don't fly away, they hop a few steps back, to the left or right, resume pecking at something invisible. Maybe dead insects, traces of food dropped from cars? Chips, gum? There is another one he can see, a third bird; yet another one, a fourth, and, three cars farther down, he sees a fifth. A little flock of mynahs has landed and is looking for food in the lanes, between the traffic. He has never seen this before.

Where have these birds come from? There are no trees along the highway all the way up to the airport, all were cut, so where do these birds live? Perhaps, in the rafters high above, underneath the sprawling roof that covers the thirty-two lanes in two sweeping arcs. Maybe the lights from the cars and trucks have confused the birds. He watches them more carefully. The yellow beak, the yellow splotch around each mynah's eye is the colour of the cones placed on the road to mark the lanes, their wings the colour of the carpet he has at home in the living room, the carpet he doesn't let Balloon Girl and her mother step on because it's invaluable, he paid so much for it he doesn't remember.

His car inches forward, he watches one mynah hop back, stand still, this one so close to his car that he can see its feathers, silky and brown, moving in a faint rustle in the gust of the exhaust from the car.

He wants to open the door, reach out and touch the bird, run the tip of a finger in its soft down.

Let the bird nibble at his finger, but traffic clears, the line is moving, it's his turn.

~

He drives up, waits for the all-clear beep as the toll sensor reads his tag, lifts the barrier to let him pass.

Up ahead, the sky stains red with the first light of day and, behind him, the cars begin to move, the mynahs flutter, rise from the road and fly up, looking for their perch.

CHILD

PRISCILLA THOMAS

'YOUR email strikes a chord, Mr Sharma, it calls out to me. I have a million-and-a-half followers on Twitter and no message I receive after the show can match the power of yours. That's why I am here, alone, no camera crew. This is a meeting off the record because today I am here as a prospective parent, not as anchor of *Camera India*.'

Priscilla Thomas is in his office.

He cannot believe this, he looks again.

Yes, Priscilla Thomas, across from him, he can reach out and touch her. So close.

~

Mr Sharma wishes he could record this so that he could show it to his wife who keeps telling him she has no idea what he does at work, to his son who rather than doing his homework keeps playing with his mother's cellphone, to all his friends who will never believe that the same Ms Thomas, who walks waist-deep in the waters of the tsunami, dragging a corpse, the same Ms Thomas who walks the streets as a prostitute to expose the city's seamy side, the same Ms Thomas who gets actor Katrina Kaif to dance with the Army chief as a Happy New Year gift to the nation, the same Priscilla Thomas is sitting in his office in Little House.

'Thank you, Ms Thomas,' Mr Sharma says, 'I knew that someone as sensitive as you would respond. I am going to, very briefly (he has learnt, watching her on TV, that her attention span has no time for anything longer than ten words), tell you what the rules are. The rules which we shall fast-forward for you, obviously.'

'I appreciate that, Mr Sharma, I do. What's the process, in short?'

There is no camera – the absence of a TV crew has surely disappointed Mr Sharma although he doesn't show it – but he behaves as if there is one, as if she's interviewing him. He takes a long, silent breath, lifts his face an inch so that his double chin doesn't show, counts the steps off on his fingers.

'It's simple, Ms Thomas.

'One, you register yourself with us since we are also a certified adoption agency.

'Two, we do a child study report, a report on Orphan, his health, mental and physical, his social, emotional development.

'Three, a home study of the prospective parent which means a study of your background, of your place of work, your financial details, two letters of recommendation, a bank reference, we assess your capability to take care of the child, then after the home study has been accepted by us, four, we submit the papers to the court and inform the Child Welfare Department. Then the match-up, we see whether your background matches the child's needs. Fifth and final.'

Has she heard all this, he wonders?

Because Ms Thomas is texting, tweeting, retweeting, Facebooking, he isn't sure, raising her head only twice to acknowledge Mr Sharma, without looking at him, and hardly has he finished when she asks:

'How long will the whole thing take? Guesstimate?'

'Normally, four to six, eight months but in your case child study is done, for home study you just fill up the form. We all know who you are, your reputation precedes you, the match-up you are already doing today. I can have Orphan in your house in less than a month. Three weeks, if we are lucky.'

'Don't break rules for me, Mr Sharma,' she smiles, still texting.

'No, no, no, Ms Thomas, no breaking rules. Every day in your news show you issue a clarion call to this benighted nation against corruption, how can I break the rules for you? Just a little adjustment.'

'I like adjustments, Mr Sharma.' Ms Thomas gets up from the chair. 'Come, let's go see Orphan. What a strange name, very matter-of-fact. I get a good feeling about this kid.'

~

'There he is, look, in the corner. The boy sitting all by himself at the table, let's walk up to him.' Mr Sharma points to Orphan in the activity room, crowded with children, all girls.

'Let's not disturb him right now, what's he doing? What's a map doing in front of him?' says Ms Thomas.

'Ms Thomas, that's a very interesting story. Our doctor, a very bright gentleman, had this idea that Orphan should draw a line on a map of Delhi and that's the route they would take on his first day out. Since then, he loves looking at maps, drawing lines.'

'What a story, Mr Sharma, you should have told us that day itself, we would have sent a reporter and a crew. Meet the orphan who charts his own course.'

'Excellent headline, Ms Thomas,' says Mr Sharma, 'but I decided against publicity at that stage. You know that would have harmed the child.'

'Quite the contrary, Mr Sharma, publicity never harms, it only helps. The public gives you publicity. Ordinary strangers who lead dull, ordinary lives, whose existence you've been unaware of, start talking about you, you give them a story to get excited about. That's why I think if we had done the story then, about a lonely kid plotting his route on a map, Orphan would have, by now, found a home.'

'But he's found one now, Ms Thomas,' says Mr Sharma, 'he's found yours.'

'You have only one boy?' Her response is like a whiplash. Sharp, quick, entirely unexpected.

'No, no, Ms Thomas, we have another one but he's much older, about five, his name is Sunil but...'

'... but what?'

'He has Down's syndrome, even that would have been fine but his is a severe case, there are other complications too, he has a defective heart, also leukaemia. In fact, Ms Thomas, his days are numbered. Our medical board has given him one to two years at the most.'

'Where is he?'

'He's sleeping, I think,' says Mr Sharma. 'He always is, but, of course, we can see him if you wish.'

~

Five minutes later, less than a minute after Mr Sharma shows Ms Thomas the sleeping Sunil, a white blanket covering him right up to his neck, the rasps of his breath the only sound in his room, Ms Thomas leans into him and whispers, 'He's my son, Mr Sharma, I have found him. Let's go to your office. Sunil is my son, I have decided. Please start the paperwork.'

She doesn't give him any time to respond.

'I know what's on your mind, Mr Sharma. You wish Orphan to be my child, yes, Orphan is a great story. A healthy boy abandoned by his mother on the hottest night of the year, a boy who may not know how to sit yet but sure knows how to read a map, he will be my new baby, it's a great story, but trust

82

me, I am not looking for a story here, Mr Sharma, I am in search of a son and Sunil is my son. Someone will come and take Orphan away, he's a bright, normal kid, but no one will adopt Sunil. After gender, disability is our new cancer, Mr Sharma, I have done so many shows on this subject. I have carried people in wheelchairs to and from my show but they can't even build a ramp in my office, forget streets and pavements. I want Sunil, I am coming with my camera, my producer and the entire crew, we will go live from Little House. We have a story, Mr Sharma.'

'Just one thing, Ms Thomas,' says Mr Sharma. 'As I said, Sunil doesn't have long to live. Two years maximum.'

'That's exactly my point, Mr Sharma, that's why he needs me more. I have been childless for so long, after two years I will be childless again, it doesn't matter. What matters is that a mother would have done her duty. Two years later is two years later.'

So breathless, so unanticipated is the pace of events that Mr Sharma is left reeling. Little House is his domain, this is where he has worked for over fifteen years and now this woman waltzes in, takes over, as if this is her stage, her studio, while he, Mrs Chopra, all the staff and all the children are passive members of her audience whose only job is to applaud on cue.

No.

He, Mr Sharma, IAS, Harvard, will stand up to her, he will tell her that no one can choose their child, that right belongs to the State, to Little House. He will tell her that she cannot broadcast from Little House because it violates the privacy of all children there, he will tell her that he will have to process her request for Sunil just like he would do for anybody and he cannot give her a day and a time when she can take the child home.

Absolutely no short-cuts, he will do due diligence on her,

so what if she is the most famous anchor in the world's largest democracy.

But, of course, Mr Sharma doesn't say or do any of this.

'I understand and appreciate your sentiment, Ms Thomas,' he says, when he walks her to her car. 'You fix the date for the shoot, I will get all of Sunil's paperwork done, it's been a pleasure and a privilege.'

~

'You were right, sir,' says Mrs Chopra when Mr Sharma tells her what happened. 'To tell me that night not to tell Orphan or Kalyani anything. How would we have told him that he had been rejected by the first mother who came to see him. You were right, sir, one hundred per cent right.'

'It's experience, Mrs Chopra,' says Mr Sharma, 'only experience.'

~

A fortnight later, in a two-hour special show preceded by a day-long telethon advertised on billboards plastered across the city, sponsored by Mothercare, Reliance Petroleum, Tata Motors and Life Insurance Corporation of India, Priscilla Thomas becomes a mother to Sunil, a Down's syndrome child.

The State Chief Minister and the Union Minister for Child Welfare are the chief guests. A panel of experts discusses Down's syndrome, the public apathy to disability, the need for a new law, they all agree that *The Amazing Adoption of Sunil Thomas* – as the show is now titled – will do wonders in raising public awareness and sensitivity not only to Down's syndrome, in particular, but to disability in general.

A scientist from Brisbane, on live hook-up, quotes a new study in Australia that shows life expectancy for people with Down's syndrome is steadily going up – his remarks are welcomed with thunderous applause and further close-ups of Sunil who has gone back to sleep.

As for Mr Sharma, he gets as many as 420 seconds on TV, spread across six appearances, in which he is told – by Ms Thomas's assistants – to talk about how and why Ms Thomas's move is a 'landmark decision' in the history of child welfare in India.

~

Orphan, too, appears during the broadcast – in one frame in which the cameraman, capturing the 'feel' of Little House, this home of hope, as Ms Thomas calls it, gets him lying on his bed, quietly, playing with a yellow car, one wheel broken, Kalyani by his side. Orphan is in the frame for exactly two seconds.

Maybe appropriate given that he's not the story today, maybe a little unfair because now he is the only boy left in Little House.

MEANWHILE

THE MAGNIFICENT COCKROACH
IN THE SWIMMING POOL

ONCE upon a time, at the bottom of the swimming pool in the Town & Country Resort, the most upscale club in New City, less than six kilometres from Indira Gandhi International Airport, lives a cockroach. Not your usual cockroach, half-a-middle-finger long, scuttling in the dark across the floor underneath the kitchen sink when you switch the lights on.

This cockroach is 18 inches long, just under 10 inches wide, the size of a small cat, its body coated with an extra special secretion that keeps it waterproof.

So special is this creature that it even has a name: CR, for 'cock roach'.

Like *ER*, the American medical drama once big on TV.

Or like Emaar, the construction company whose huge neon sign near the airport is the first thing you see as your plane begins to descend, purrs its landing gears open, kisses the roofs of the slums just yards off the highway.

'We Are Building The New India,' the sign reads. '7 malls. 6 Special Economic Zones. 3 Villa complexes, Andalusian, Mediterranean, American. 2 Greg Norman golf courses.'

Once they start construction, there will, inevitably, be cockroaches. Not like CR, of course.

Ordinary 1-inch ones. That dart in and out between bags of

sand, crawl under tattered mats on which women workers sit and feed their babies. Or rest their heads which carry cement, stonechips the whole day. From machine to site, machine to site.

~

CR sits on the floor of the swimming pool.

He is glorious red in colour. Fine wine in dim yellow light. Eyes, brilliant yellow half-moons.

Antennae, almost 2 feet long, delicate and beautiful. Like fronds of some alien plant that fell down to earth.

Once a fortnight, when they empty the pool to scrub its floor, CR crawls underneath a raised cinderblock that covers one of the twelve drainage filters set in two rows of six.

For food, CR never has to struggle. Because he nibbles on dead skin and salt that water scrubs off swimmers. These give CR the calories he needs. There's another, more reliable source of food. Evenings, the club rents the poolside for dinners, office parties, birthdays. At these gatherings, something falls from a raised fork or from an outstretched spoon into the water. A drunk guest trips over his shadow, his plate crashes down, some food slips in.

Crumbs float down to CR.

Butter naan, pasta, palak paneer, vegetable spring roll, chicken Manchurian.

~

This is a healthier diet than what CR gets, on average, when he is human. When he is the third of five children of a farmer, one of the five hundred farmers who have to sell their land to developers to make way for the club and nearby Apartment Complex.

CR is the only one who tells his father not to sell.

'This is all we have got, Father,' he says, 'this is where we live. The money you will get will run out, what do we do then?'

'That's why I keep telling you that you should study, do well in school, but you never listen,' says his father, brushing him away as if he were a cockroach.

CR turns to his mother hoping she will step in and help but she sits silently, clueless, as she almost always is.

~

July, 47 degrees Celsius outside, 27 inside the pool.

Sheela is swimming. Her swimsuit is red. It has tummy control, halter neck.

Sheela wants to pee.

The club's rules are clear, she should use the women's rest room. But she is lazy, there's no one in the pool, she thinks, no one will notice, let me pee, it's water anyway, I pay so much for membership, she tells herself, why can't they clean up after me? And who will object? The only person she can see is a janitor, he doesn't even speak English – Sheela is sure that, if he objects, she will shout him down. How dare he tell her what to do.

So she keeps swimming. Lets her pee and water mix.

CR notices.

Because CR feels a warm, weak, yellow trickle that flows into his eye, his antennae quiver as they sense change in his waterworld, making him swim upward. He climbs up the pool's wall while Sheela is still inside, clambers over the edge, slips on the thin film of water that covers the marble tiles and once he's out in the open, he crawls to the deckchair where she has put her towel, under which lies her duffel bag. Maybe it's her pee, its smell acts like a homing signal, a beacon that guides him straight into her bag.

The fierce sun on his back, CR feels the sudden temperature change and crawls right inside, burrows underneath Sheela's towel, under her change of clothes, a red T-shirt and blue jeans, fresh underwear, lace, slithers over the Kiehl's moisturiser and sunscreen bottles to sit at the bottom. Under the spare towel. Big blue, as soft as a cloud.

And CR goes home with Sheela.

~

Home is in Apartment Complex.

Home is where the heart is.

Her heart, the one Sheela chose to give away to Sukrit Sharma, investment banker, who is, at this moment, sitting in a restaurant on Orchard Road in Singapore waiting for his client. Sheela and Sukrit will get married in winter and she will move to Singapore.

The first time she visits him, she falls in love with Changi Airport, the clothes stores in the city, designer and knockoffs at Vivo City Mall and Bugis Junction.

'One year, honey, I am not doing anything here except loving you and shopping,' she tells him.

'Of course,' he says, he holds her close.

She tries out the short gingham skirt with the banded waistline and the belt loops, she tries out snug turtleneck crop tops. She doesn't like what she sees in the mirror: fat drips down her sides. That night, looking through the hotel-room window at the blinking lights on Sentosa Beach, she can't hold back her tears.

'I have six more months to go for the wedding,' she says. 'I will join the gym, I will swim a kilometre each day so that I lose all this weight.'

'I love you,' says her husband, 'even if you don't do any of this but, yes, swimming is great, both cardio and stretch, and don't they have a wonderful pool at your club?'

~

Sheela has lunch, tells her maid to clear up, decides on a nap.

~

CR loses his argument.

The size of their landholding is so small, his father says, the harvest yields nothing. Builders are offering a high value, everyone else is selling. We can use the money to buy cheap land elsewhere, we will have a lot to spare, use some of it to help you learn some skills so that you get a job. Maybe you can open a shop in the village.

But CR says, 'No, I am going to go on a fast unto death to protest against the sale of land.'

'Don't be silly,' says his father, 'who do you think you are? Anna Hazare? No one will care and even if they do, it doesn't matter. Look what finally happened to the poor old man, the next time he will get a crowd is only when he dies.'

The father is right.

CR stops eating and drinking, sits in one corner of the house and because he is the only one protesting, no TV cameras are switched on, there is no breaking news, no one gets to know, and on the twenty-fourth day of his fast, under a full moon, CR, looking like his shadow, breathes his last. Meanwhile, for these twenty-four days and twenty-four nights, his mother keeps constant vigil praying to all the gods, so ardent her prayers, so deep her fervour, that exactly one hour after CR dies, the gods, who sit in golden chariots and move heaven and earth, shower the mother with petals from the sky and grant her two wishes.

She wishes: One, let my son be reincarnated as someone who should live on this land. Two, he should change back into a human being the day he's touched by someone very special, someone who loves him and lives, with him, on this land.

Yes, yes, the gods say to both.

And so CR is born, in his afterlife, as an unusually long

cockroach who lives in the swimming pool that comes up on the land his father once owned.

~

Sheela's maid is cleaning up in the kitchen when CR crawls out from the bag she has left in the lobby, climbs the stairs, follows the fragrance of her trail, slips into her bedroom, shivers since the temperature there is below 20, climbs onto the bed, slips in under her thin blue sheet.

Sheela hears a faint rustle, feels something moist, soft and hard at the same time. But she is tired, she doesn't open her eyes.

CR's antennae touch her face, she thinks it's her hair.

CR's legs rub against hers, she thinks it's the edges of the pillow cover. Or something in her dream. She turns, her arm moves, her fingers come to rest on the yellow half-moon of CR's eyes. It causes him some discomfort but he likes the chill of the room blending with the warmth of the woman beside him, beautiful and lonely, in yellow shorts and a white T-shirt, without sleeves, some of her fat already cross-trained and treadmilled away.

CR lies absolutely still, feeling love for the first time in his life, waiting for her to wake up and kiss him so that his mother's second wish can be fulfilled.

So that he can become human again, grow up, go looking to find out what happened to his father, his mother, his four siblings, find out where they are now, what they did with the compensation they got for the land. Do they ever visit the swimming pool? Does one of them stare into the water where he once lived? While Sheela and Sukrit Sharma will go ahead and get married this winter, live happily ever after in Singapore, which, according to World Bank, is the best country in the world to start a business.

WOMAN

VILLAGE OPAAR

ONE minute, that's all the train will stop here for, your father says. We are travelling to his village, the first time since you were born. We need to show her to all the elders, we need to get her blessed with their love, he says. Your grandparents are no more but you have uncles and aunts, nephews and nieces I haven't met. You are four months, five months old, winter has begun.

The train, scheduled to arrive at 10 p.m., is four hours late. The ticket examiner looks at you, bundled up, says, don't worry, I will alert you a few minutes in advance, you gather all your bags, wait at the door. I will help you with the luggage, he says.

As the train pulls out of the station, it begins to rain.

~

Rain I have never seen before. It begins as a shower, very slight, on the cold afternoon we leave the city. At first, I don't even think it's rain, so light and spidery it is when it hits my face. Instead, I think, it's a passenger a few seats ahead. Maybe she's rinsing her hand, emptying her water-bottle of its last few drops which the wind tears, sends flying our way.

But, no, this is rain.

Rain that soon swells to fill every space there is. It forces passengers to close windows, stuff handkerchiefs, towels, sheaves of newspaper pages into the red, metallic slats of the shutters to prevent water from gushing in, flooding the seats. It's rain bent on wringing out all the water the entire sky, the moon and the stars can hold, so fierce I am afraid it will push the train off the tracks.

Don't worry, says your father, the train is faster, it will soon overtake the rain, will take us to a place where it's dry.

~

He's wrong, rain follows us to our station. It drums its asbestos roof, runs down its ridges to flow in streams onto the platform, creeps towards the bench where we sit waiting for your uncle who is supposed to pick us up. I hear an electric scream, I cover your ears, there's another train coming, each of the million drops of rain lit by its blinding beam. This train thunders by so fast it makes the rain look weak, its coaches flashing streaks of red and white. From where I sit, I see the station's exit, past the station master's lime-yellow room. Next to it is a flight of steps that lead to a narrow dirt-track where a bullock-cart rests like a child's see-saw, abandoned, its tyres half-hidden under water.

You can close your eyes, rest for a while, says your father. I think my cousin got stuck in the rain, he says, he should be here any time now.

~

Funny name our village has.

Opaar.

Means, in Bengali, the other side, more than a thousand kilometres east of where we are tonight, at the end of a straight line that passes through towns and villages I have never heard of. Some I know, like Panagarh and Chittaranjan, towns which the train passes when it's light but, as evening falls, slips into night, the places grow progressively unfamiliar, their names on yellow boards meaning nothing but etching themselves so hard in my mind I still remember some after all these years.

Didori, Pili, Lohta, Koilak, Karmauli, Siho, and then Opaar.

~

Where have we come to? How long do we have to wait here? It's getting cold, my shawl may not be enough to keep you warm. I hold you close, cover you completely, feel the rush of your breath against my neck, your lips moving in sleep. Your father stands underneath a broken awning, looking at the empty road, waiting for the rickshaw or whatever it is that will take us home. The only brightness on the platform is from the one 60-watt lamp above the timetable, written in chalk on blackboard, and from a long, fluorescent tube strung in between the rafters that stammers light white and yellow.

Everyone in Opaar is waiting to see our baby, to bless our baby, says your father, speaking aloud so that his voice can carry to me. What he says next I cannot hear because a sudden clap of lightning lights up the entire station, sends a rainbird flying in circles, screeching, its wings dripping, and then it's dark again, the bird is gone, the roll of distant thunder muffles all sounds, even that of falling rain.

MAN

BALLOON GIRL

WHEN he walks into his building in Apartment Complex, Security Guard says he's been waiting for him. It's been almost three hours since he left with Balloon Girl and her mother.

'Sir, I didn't find your bag,' says Security Guard.

'Did you look carefully?'

'Yes, sir, I rushed back to tell you but Main Gate told me you had already left.'

'Maybe I kept it somewhere else.'

'Sir, one request, please do not complain against me to the supervisor. If I lose this job, where will I go?'

'You should be careful, more responsible.'

'I will, sir, I will. Please.'

'Now get back to work.'

'Anything I can do, please tell me, any time.'

'I am tired, I am going to sleep for a while, do not allow anyone to knock on my door, not even the maid. Tell her it's her day off today.'

'Of course,' says Security Guard, 'I know your maid. I will tell her to come tomorrow. I will tell her you are not feeling well.'

'Don't tell her anything like that, just tell her I am not at home.'

'Yes, sir,' he says, 'please don't complain to the supervisor.'

He gives Security Guard a 500-rupee note.

'No, sir, this isn't necessary.'

'Keep it,' he says.

~

Security Guard feels the crispness of the note between his fingers. Quite generous, that's three days' salary. Every month he gets Rs 5,000 – to feed himself and his family of four. Three children, one wife, who he has left in the village, all wait for the first week of each month to receive money that he sends. One of his children, the youngest son, is doing very well in school. His teacher says, you are lucky, maybe he is the first one in the family who will go to college. He told him last week, Father, get me a new pair of shoes. Maybe this 500 will help.

~

He wants to sleep in the bed in which Balloon Girl and her mother slept. He undresses.

The two damp smudges on the bedsheet are still there. One big, one small. Like two clouds in the summer sky. He lies down, one side of his face pressed against mother smudge. He switches his cellphone off, removes its battery, just in case anyone's tracking. He unplugs the land phone, too, lowers the air conditioner's temperature to 9.

Because he wants harsh winter in the room, the opposite of what it is outside.

He falls asleep.

~

Balloon Girl and he are flying over the city, above the scattered cloud cover, each has one arm outstretched, the other holding the string attached to Red Balloon. A sudden wind pushes them down into a free fall through the clouds. Balloon Girl shouts with excitement and fear, pointing out the city, spread out below like a puzzle. There is the hospital, she says, from where you picked us up last night. He marvels at her telescopic sight, wonders how she can identify that cluster of buildings, but she is right. There is the AIIMS Main Building, the flyover exchange where six roads cross, loop into each other, between them the sprawling patch of manicured grass punctured with steel pods that glint in the sun. There's the population clock, its numbers ticking, a billion plus, the digits in so many places he loses count. The wind has changed, they are flying upwards now, farther away from the ground, the street and the grass below beginning to blur as clouds swirl around their feet. They are next to an aeroplane, the wind blows them right up to its windows. Look inside, he tells Balloon Girl, this is the first time she is looking into a plane, they see passengers getting ready for a meal, breakfast, dinner, he's not sure, the seatbelt signs are off, stewardesses walk up and down the aisle, each one with a French wig, a deep blue skirt. Both he and Balloon Girl knock on one window and wait for the passengers to notice them but no one does.

The plane is below them now, he can see the flaps of the wings move, the red light blink. When he looks down, his head reels, he is so high up that descending safely no longer seems an option. He wants Balloon Girl to drift down slowly, to let her land somewhere near AIIMS, she can find her way to her mother, leave him in the sky above the clouds because he is frightened of what he wants to do to her. To do with her.

'Get away from me – I will hurt you,' he says.

'I can't hear you,' she says.

'You leave me, you go down,' he shouts above the roar of the aeroplane engine. 'I will hurt you.'

'You will never hurt me,' she says. 'Mother and I came to your house, we took a bath, we slept, you washed our clothes, you fed us.'

'That doesn't matter,' he says, 'that was last night.'

'Just as you told us to do, I will never tell anyone about last night, you will not hurt me, you will never hurt me.' She holds his hand tighter.

'Get away from me,' he says. 'I am telling you, get away from me.'

He shouts, almost screams, but the wind is hard, it whisks his words away from Balloon Girl as she looks down, smiling one moment, laughing the other, at what she sees below her.

'We are over the Zoo,' she says, pointing out three elephants in their pens, a man preparing to feed them.

They are descending now, flying so low they can see the bird cages, the lion enclosure, the hippopotamus, dustbins shaped like a monkey and a penguin. A wind lifts them up over the ruins of a fort, over the lake where boats, brightly coloured, wait for passengers.

'That tickles,' she laughs.

His fingers are in Balloon Girl's hair, soft after last night's bath with the scrub and the special butter soap. He smells her smells.

Winter cream and red wool, girl skin and shampoo, one night old.

He wants to swallow her lips, so small that just one gulp will do. She will bleed and he will then move up, up her face, over her nose, her pencil-line eyebrows and her eyes, each one half his little finger long, across her forehead, into her scalp. He will enter her, as gently as he can, in the sky, under the clouds. No one will see because the aeroplane, with its passengers, has gone, and down below no one has the time to look even if her blood drips, mixes with the rain, long overdue in the parched city, its red will slide down the double-glazed windows in Apartment Complex, turn brown as it will clot throughout the day and merge with the mud.

He wakes up. The room is cold. He gets himself a quilt, pulls it over his head and this time when he closes his eyes he slides into the calm of dreamless sleep.

CHILD

THE SEPARATION

KALYANI Das walks up to Little House director Mr Sharma and hands him her resignation letter written, with help from Dr Chatterjee, on a sheet torn from her exercise book. She says, in her letter, that she's got a job at a bigger hospital that will give her more money – and she needs more money. Also, two nurses from this hospital, she tells Mr Sharma, went to America last year and the head of the nursing section has told her that she, too, stands a chance because they value those who have worked in an orphanage.

Mr Sharma tries hard to persuade her to stay on, promises to waive her one-year traineeship period, a significant concession given the rigid rules of the Child Welfare Department. He offers – don't quote me to anybody, he says, because I am not supposed to say all this but I am saying this because I like you – to help her go abroad.

'I am respected in international circles, my word carries weight, I will give you a very strong recommendation at the end of your training period,' he says.

When none of this works, Mr Sharma gets Mrs Chopra to speak to her as well – 'Talk to her as if you were her mother,' he tells her – but Kalyani has made up her mind.

'Mrs Chopra, you will understand because you are a mother,' she says. 'It's very difficult at home. My mother has to work in at least four homes, my father drives a cycle rickshaw the whole day, I need more money.'

'What about Orphan, Kalyani?'asks Mrs Chopra. 'Who will take care of him?'

'I think of him all the time,' says Kalyani, 'but better to leave now when he is so young, when he won't notice that I am gone, that someone else has replaced me.' She cannot hide the quiver in her voice.

'Look, Kalyani, you said I will understand because I am a mother. Yes, I am a mother of two sons,' says Mrs Chopra, 'and I know when a child is lying, I know you are not telling me the real reason.'

'No, Mrs Chopra,' says Kalyani, 'that's the only reason, I need to make more money.'

'What about Orphan? I am sorry if I am asking you again, why are you leaving him so suddenly? He may not be able to speak but he will be affected, deeply, trust me.'

Mrs Chopra sees Kalyani's eyes fill up, she doesn't press further.

'As you wish then, all the best,' she says. 'But stay in touch, let me know if you need help with anything.'

Kalyani doesn't reply, she quickly turns, leaves the room, she can no longer hold back her tears.

~

Does Orphan miss Kalyani?

No one in Little House knows. A day after she leaves, Mr Sharma calls in Mrs Chopra.

'Orphan was always with Kalyani, night and day,' says Mr Sharma, 'but he is a baby, he has not bonded with anyone yet. Let's completely change his circumstances. The change in setting will help him overcome her absence.'

So Orphan is moved up, from infant to toddler section. From one nurse (Kalyani) dedicated to him full-time, here there's only one nurse, working eight-hour shifts, who has to look after twenty-five children. Orphan moves from his own cot to one bed that all these children share. A long bed, with pillows lined up to mark each one's space. Any other baby would take time to adjust to this drastic change but here, too, to the surprise of the staff, Orphan follows the same schedule as he had with Kalyani. He's the first one to eat when the big dinner bowl is wheeled in and the cereal poured out in cups. While it's always a challenge to get most of the other children to eat, Orphan crawls to his bowl with a clear sense of purpose, as if, at the beginning of the day itself, when he wakes up, a magical clock inside him has been set for the next twenty-four-hour period and has taken over all his physical movements. The new nurse, too, helps reinforce this order and discipline. She chooses Orphan as the first one to be fed, cleaned, bathed, dressed, she lets him go to bed and lie down where they have marked a corner for him, farthest from the door and in the quietest section of the hall so that he is least likely to be disturbed by the noise created by the other children.

If he misses Kalyani, Orphan doesn't let it show.

~

As for Kalyani, she cries a little for Orphan every night.

Her reason for leaving Little House is not the one she mentions in her resignation letter. She wishes to keep it a secret, at least for now. It has torn her up, wrecked her heart, but her only comfort is her belief that she is leaving Little House because that's the only way she can protect Orphan.

WOMAN

IRON & ICE

THERE is Iron Man and there is Ice Man, there is a memory of hot and a memory of cold.

~

You are six years seven years old, we can afford only one set of school uniform: white skirt, white top, white socks. You return every afternoon carrying the entire school's dirt with you, on you: chalk dust and mud spatter to grass stains and lunch, the trail of the journey back on the crowded bus. Evening, before I enter the kitchen to start cooking dinner, I wash your skirt and top, hang them out to dry on the balcony. By late night, if there is electricity, I iron them so that we are not rushed in the morning. Your skirt has pleats, each one needs to be ironed very carefully. Some evenings, however, when the clothes haven't dried – when the air is humid or there is no wind that night, or I am too tired – I leave ironing for the morning. Those days, I get up early so that I can iron your clothes before you wake up. But at least once, twice a week, there is a power-cut. And then your father says, give me her clothes and he places them, the skirt, the top, even the socks, within the folds of the morning newspaper. We need to use today's newspaper, he says, because it's the cleanest. Give me my handkerchief, he says, because I need to keep myself dry, we cannot have my sweat dripping on her clothes, and he goes looking for the Iron Man who has a stall by the roadside, against a broken wall, in which he fires his coal oven to heat his iron.

Your father returns by the time you are finished with breakfast, he has brought your clothes right on time for you to put them on. The skirt and top, neatly folded in places where the creases should be, covered on either side by the newspaper, the pair of socks folded, placed on top. You are ready to slip into your uniform, spotless, stainless white. Perfectly straight, each pleat in perfect place.

Look at my little princess, says your father, as he walks you to the bus stop.

~

Ma, you tell me one day, there is a girl in my class, her name is Priya, there are ice cubes in her water-bottle, it's wrapped in canvas, that prevents the cold from getting out. Every morning, she takes me to a corner of the classroom, lets me dip a finger into the water and touch the ice. Even by lunch-time, the ice hasn't melted and she lets me drink some of that cold water. Ma, why can't I have some ice and I tell you that Priya probably has a fridge at home and that's why she can get ice cubes every morning and we don't have one and you ask me why and I say we need to wait until your father has saved up enough money.

You don't accept this explanation and you begin to cry when your father enters the room and he takes one look at you and says, what's wrong with my little princess and I tell him the ice story and he says we need to quickly get some ice to freeze those tears.

~

Give me my handkerchief, he says, and goes out looking, this time for Ice Man, and in an hour, he walks in, a small block of ice wrapped in his handkerchief, covered with sawdust. Quick, quick, my little princess, go get a bowl of water, he says, we need to clean the ice, wash all the sawdust away. You are so excited that you laugh, you cry, you shout as if he's got a puppy wrapped up in that handkerchief. The sawdust gone, I use a steel cup to break the block of ice into smaller pieces, one of which darts across the floor leaving a cold trail of water for you to chase.

You try to pick the ice piece from the floor but it keeps slipping from between your fingers. We cannot play with ice, let's make a nice drink, says your father, as he takes out a bottle of squash he has bought along with the ice. We mix water and squash in a big pitcher, drop all the shards of ice in it.

You drink two glasses, you say you want to keep some for the water-bottle that you will take to school tomorrow and your father says, it will not stay, the ice is already beginning to melt. I will get some more this weekend, he says, from the Ice Man, and we drink all of the squash until we are full and the floor is cold where the ice was and sticky with sugar and water.

MAN

KAHINI'S CLOTHES

THE bathrobes that Balloon Girl and her mother wore are washed. He is going to put them back in the wardrobe. In The Room, the most special place in his house, deep inside, farthest from the door, a place he doesn't enter until he has to.

Like this morning when he has locked himself in, told Security Guard not to let the maid disturb him. The Room is where his past lives, a past in which there is Kahini, a woman he loves, and the faint promise of their child.

That's why in one corner, propped up against the wall, there is a wooden easel with double-sided magnetic boards, black-board and whiteboard. There is coloured chalk on the floor, erasers, wooden shapes, the letters A to Z from a brightly coloured magnetic alphabet with pictures. Strewn around, for little hands and feet to push and kick in the course of play. Yellow tennis balls, red footballs fill up a wicker basket in the centre of which stands upright, like a prop in a school play, a child's red-and-yellow umbrella, open, planted in the middle. The basket on the floor and a butterfly mobile hanging from the ceiling, blue and white, with a wingspan of three feet, create the two bright splashes of colour in The Room which is, otherwise, painted in silent colours, its walls and ceiling in office white, drab but spotless. Across the easel and the black-board, against the wall, is a shoe rack where in neat rows of black, brown and a dash of red-and-blue, are Kahini's shoes. All worn, the leather veined on the heels, softened by her feet, but each one gleaming, as if freshly dusted and polished.

Then there is the wardrobe. Its veneer is light oak, it has two mirrored central doors behind which is a hanging rail on which are her clothes. Saris, salwar kameez, jeans and shirts, long skirts, trousers. He pushes the clothes to one side, makes space on the railing on which he hangs the two bathrobes. The air in the wardrobe is musty, he needs to let the sun and the wind touch the clothes so he leaves the mirrored doors open, walks across The Room to the easel, picks up a wooden letter from the floor, lets it drop down. Its weight kicks off motes of dust from the carpet. In the mirror, the white-hot light from the summer sky bounces back to hurt his eyes.

He walks to the window, pulls the blinds down because he likes the dark, he likes everything in The Room to be wrapped up in puddles of their own shadows. Like he himself is right now, cold and naked.

CHILD

WALL COLLAPSE

'WE have breaking news coming in,' announces Priscilla Thomas to the soundtrack of cymbals clashing, drums rolling, a globe spinning across the blue screen, the map of India scattering stars in its wake.

'If you live in the capital and if you have looked outside, you know the weather is playing up. Playing up rather seriously. After the very, very hot days, so hot that people died in the heat, we have a thunderstorm, we have news of walls collapsing, streets flooding, trees falling, people getting killed.

'Reporter Payal Wadhwa has braved the weather to send us this report. Payal?'

~

'Absolutely, Priscilla,' says Payal Wadhwa, standing under an umbrella embossed with the *Camera India* logo.

'The dust storm we have seen in the capital today was very much in the forecast for the last two days, not just here for Delhi but for Punjab, Haryana, western Uttar Pradesh as well as Rajasthan. But when it hit today, it surprised even the Met Office which says that the wind speed and severity of the storm were much stronger than anticipated. But the storm is unlikely to continue until tomorrow which means this respite could be short-lived.

'The reason behind the dust storm and the wind is an upper-air cyclonic circulation that lies over Haryana with another western disturbance lying over Pakistan adjoining the state of Jammu and Kashmir. Some showers have been seen here in the capital accompanied by thunder and lightning and more rain is expected through the day. As far as the maximum temperature is concerned, it was 44 degrees yesterday and today it's come down by more than 12 degrees to 32, temperatures in the entire north are expected to come down.

'Along with this good news, Priscilla, is some not so good. At least five construction workers have been killed and ten are feared trapped when a building they were working on in the centre of the city collapsed in the storm. Local residents say the disaster could have been averted but builders violated the construction plan cleared by the municipal corporation. Four floors were approved but workers were building a fifth floor. That's not the only rule flouted. Police sources have told *Camera India* they suspect the use of poor-quality raw material to be responsible for the wall collapse, but so far no action has been taken against the authority which gives the final quality certificate to the builder for the material they are using.

'There's a report of another wall collapse but this is a minor one, at a place called Little House.'

'Of course, I know where that is, that's where we broadcast live from just the other day,' says Ms Thomas.

'Absolutely, Priscilla, the very same place. From where you welcomed that wonderful boy, Sunil, into your life. I have received a video from one of our viewers who captured the scene on his camera phone and we will play it for you a little while later. It shows that a section of the wall of Little House has been broken. There are no reports of any casualties but authorities are checking how and why this happened. So far, one child, yes, one child, is reported missing. We will send you an update as soon as we get one.'

'Thank you, Payal,' says Ms Thomas. 'It only goes to show the shocking state of our public infrastructure, one freak storm and so much damage – that will be the subject of our debate later in the evening. We shall play that video Payal has got and we will get Mr Rajat Sharma, the director of Little House, on the show, too.'

MEANWHILE

MR SHARMA'S SON
AND THE CAMERA PHONE

MY name is Aman Sharma, I am eleven years old, my father says I am too young to own a cellphone of my own. It's not about money, he says, because my father can afford one, he is director of Little House, it's an orphanage. He was on TV recently. He is always on his phone, his secretary is Mrs Chopra and he keeps calling her to check who has called him in the office.

My mother has a phone, too, not a smartphone, but it has a very good camera. When I am done with school homework, when her phone is charged, she allows me to play with it. For forty minutes, forty-five minutes every day, slightly longer on Saturdays and Sundays.

She has set five conditions.

One: I can only use the phone when she is at home.

Two: I can only use the phone when she gives it to me. I cannot pick it up even if it's lying unattended.

Three: I cannot make any calls except in an emergency. Emergency means if there is a fire in the house or if I find her unconscious. Something as serious as that.

Four: I cannot answer any incoming calls.

And, five: I cannot give her number to any of my friends in school.

Yes, I say, I will follow these rules. Which is quite easy since I am not interested at all in any of these things. I don't have any calls to make, I don't have any friends I wish to talk to. All I am interested in is the camera. Because whenever I get the phone, I go straight to camera, options, choose video.

And I film.

~

I know all camera options on my mother's phone, video format: high, normal, basic. Scene mode, night or auto. How to record camera sounds, even add text. I know that the best time to film outdoors is before sunset, that you should try to keep the light behind you so that there isn't too much shadow. I cannot download the video and edit it outside the phone so I use the phone camera itself as an editor. Recording and pausing, recording and pausing. Sometimes, I record black or white between scenes. That's my fade-in and fade-out. I keep deleting much of what I have recorded because there is not enough space on the phone. There are a few films I like which I have not deleted.

Nothing very special, but for some reason I like these films.

~

The first is called *Lunch*.

It's about my mother warming lunch for me when I am back from school. She takes the portions out of the fridge one by one, rice, chicken, dal. She puts each back on the gas. Its flame is blue and yellow. Then she serves them neatly, on the white china plate that's my favourite. Speaking clearly and slowly, naming each item, I record that as voice-over. The last scene: my lunch on the table, my mother washing her hands.

~

The second film is called *Mynah Bird*.

It's about a mynah, drenched by the rain.

It flies onto our balcony, finds its perch in a tiny space where the wall meets the roof. I have never seen so wet a bird; so much water drips from its feathers that it can hardly sit or balance itself. There's a wind and the mynah trembles. Behind the bird, you can see the sky, dark and grey. I switch the camera to night mode, record the rain, its sound, the rustle of the mynah's feathers as they scrape the wall. The bird is so frightened that, even when I bring the camera to just about 10 inches from its beak, it doesn't fly away. I get a tight close-up, I am able to film that funny sound the bird's feathers make as they rub against the wall.

~

I tell my mother I need a camera, I really need a video camera. A small camera. She can set a hundred, a thousand, a million conditions and I will follow each one. My mother says, you aren't doing well in school. Wait for a year, two years and if you do well, I will tell your father to get you a camera. Two years? That's such a long time, I tell my mother, hundreds and hundreds of scenes will pass me by, unrecorded, but she doesn't listen.

I want to – but I cannot – tell her that every day in school all I think of is what to record when I get my own camera.

For example, when Sharmila Ma'am is teaching history, my eyes record her lips. Red. Her eyes, her glasses, their steel frame. Chalk in her hand, dust on her fingers, some on her sari. The shape of our exercise books in her red bag. Her shoes, her toenails also painted red. I fail the history exam. Not only because I don't listen to what Ma'am says but also because I don't like memorising dates and numbers.

'Mrs Sharma,' Sharmila Ma'am tells my mother at the

parent–teacher meeting, 'you need to sit down with your child. He needs help with history. He is bright but he is very distracted, he keeps looking at everything except the blackboard.'

'Of course, I will,' says my mother.

~

My mother is nervous. She is waiting for my father to return home. I know when she is nervous, she plays with the ring on her finger as she is doing now. Taking it off, putting it back on.

Late night, my father is back.

I am in the next room, awake, with her phone.

'Why can't we give Aman a camera? We can buy one of those small digital ones. He wants it so much, even we can use it,' says my mother.

'He's failed an exam and you want him to have a camera?'

'I think it will help him. I will set down conditions. You should see some of the things he has recorded on my phone.'

'Every kid these days does that, everyone is recording.'

'He is special.'

'He has failed an exam, the only one in his class.'

'I will help him with history, I took it in college.'

'Why didn't you help him all this while?'

After this, I cannot make out what they say except that each one is talking in a loud voice.

~

I am outside their room, right next to the door which is open, offering me a chink through which I record.

I film my father, my mother, their audio, their video.

My father slamming the door as he leaves the house, the sound of his footsteps as he walks down the stairs. My mother, playing with the ring on her finger.

WOMAN

WITCHES DANCE

RAIN continues to fall. It floods the platform, makes the water creep towards the bench where I sit, you cradled in my lap. Your father has kept our two suitcases on the bench. We don't want those to get wet, he says, while he himself, standing at the entrance looking into the night, is drenched to the bone. He has covered his head with a handkerchief which is now soaked with water that drips down his neck over his collar all across the back of his shirt.

I can get a towel out from the suitcase, I tell him.

No need, he says, let's wait for my cousin to come, let's reach home and then I will dry myself, what's the point when we are going to get wet again.

I see a light, he says, that must be for us.

~

It's a bullock-cart.

Your father's cousin has come to pick us up. Had this been morning and you awake, you would have seen the bull, each horn wrapped in a red cloth held in place by yellow threads, a tiny bell lost in the folds of its neck. The bullock-cart has a fresh coat of white paint and a canvas shelter rigged into a tent with bamboo frames. To protect us from rain and any immodest eyes that may look at this time of the night at me,

Opaar's new wife, new mother, newly arrived from the city.

We set out, swaying, lurching along the dirt-track that meanders from the station to the village. Rain, which is now a drizzle, streams down the sides of the cart. You wake up crying, your father tells his cousin to stop, to let me change and feed you, and then we resume our journey.

The only sounds I hear are the raindrops and the cart's wheels creaking. Like an old wooden door opening and closing in a steady wind.

Your father falls asleep, his head rests at an awkward angle but I don't want to wake him up, he has had a very long day. He had to go to college hours before we boarded the train, he said there were some students who needed something explained.

His cousin, the man who is driving the cart, shouts out to the bull, nudging it back on track everytime it goes off course into the slush by the side of the road.

I, too, fall asleep.

~

In Opaar, it's still dark when we arrive. They are waiting for us, many of them carrying lanterns, so many I can neither count nor estimate. There are your father's brothers, their wives, his nephews and nieces; your father's uncles, aunts, their children; his sister is also visiting with her husband and their children. Young and old, child and adult, men and women all talking to each other, their noise like chatter of birds in trees.

It wakes you up as I climb down from the cart onto a wooden platform someone has placed next to the wheel so that I don't have to step into the mud. The men move away from me, crowd around your father. They are asking him about the train, the delay, the rain and the city.

It's my first trip here after my marriage so the women break into song, a coconut is broken, rice grains are sprinkled on my head, earthen lamps are lit. You begin crying. Two girls, perpetually giggling, take you from me and begin rocking you. She is so beautiful, says one of them, she's like a doll.

My heart misses a beat with you gone but I am reassured with your father by my side, the crowd of smiling faces, all unfamiliar but all welcoming, so I let the girls keep you for a while.

And then it's like magic.

We are led to our one-room house your father says he built with his savings. It's one of the few in Opaar made of bricks, stones and some cement; most of the other houses in the village are thatched huts with mud walls and floors. By the light of lanterns, in less than an hour, an army of volunteers, visible and invisible, children and grown-ups, gets to work. Their shadows dance on the walls as doors are opened, the room is swept, the bed is made, an earthen pitcher is filled with water, a mosquito net is strung over the bed, the windowsill is wiped clean, the floor is mopped, someone brings a hand-fan, someone else lights two kerosene lanterns – there is no electricity in the village – someone brings two buckets of water and puts these on the porch outside, someone fans your face, two clean towels are brought and hung from pegs hurriedly hammered into the wall.

By the time they are gone, you, your father and I have every conceivable comfort possible and, as we lie down to rest, you fast asleep, we see dawn breaking.

~

Three days and three nights we spend in Opaar. I am the Queen, our house is the Palace and you the Little Princess, so special is the treatment we get. A group of girls have been deputed to serve as my attendants. They make tea for us in the morning, warm milk for you, bring water for my bath. The bathroom is a thatched enclosure with no roof, one door missing, so they stand guard as I quickly pour the bucket of water over my head. One girl oils my hair, another braids it, others bring their school books and friends and they all sit around me in a circle and ask me to teach them English.

In the evening, one of them brings a lantern, another gets water and they escort me to a clearing behind the house, across a field and beyond the pond, to the toilet. The embarrassment of doing it in the open for the first time is only fleeting as the girls laugh, tell me stories of how they got caught, how they now know all the best places to do it where no one goes, where the ground is flat and hard, where your feet don't sink in the mud, where grass doesn't tickle you when you sit down. They teach me tricks: how to squat, each foot on a stone – chosen carefully so that it doesn't wobble – to increase the clearing between myself and the earth.

On our second day in Opaar, there is a thunderstorm shortly after lunch and girls come running, each one carrying a wicker basket on their waist like a baby. The wind whistles through mango orchards across the paddy fields beyond our house. That's your orchard, they tell me, it belongs to you and your daughter and your husband.

I stand in the porch with you, the cool water-laden wind blowing so hard you close your eyes. Palm trees bend like thin sticks in the wind, children run, skip across the mud, to catch the mangoes as they fall. That evening, the girls return with three big raw green mangoes. They cut thin slices, rub burnt chilli paste and salt on each slice dipped in mustard oil and we eat, all of us, one by one, until we are full, the chilli so hot that we sit, our mouths open, blowing air to cool our tongues on fire.

~

At night, the girls tell me about the witches in Opaar.

Who slip out of their homes under the cover of blackness and head for the pond where the village ends, where the railway tracks are, where no one lives and no one goes because big black cargo trains with no lights come thundering by at night, they follow no schedule, they travel without warning. To appease the spirits that give them magical powers, each witch has to sacrifice a child, preferably a baby not over three months old, and that's why, the girls say, all parents of babies in this village have to be extra careful. Sometimes these witches sacrifice their own babies. They drown them in the pond by holding their heads underwater, smear their tiny bodies with mud they collect from the riverbank, wait for it to dry. Once the dead babies are caked with mud, the witches light earthen lamps which they arrange in a circle around each corpse. Then they dance through the night to the flickering light of the lamps, their giant shadows flitting in the trees.

That's why whenever a baby in the village falls ill, the girls are now speaking in whispers, we have to find out if it's under a witch's spell because then we call the witchdoctor who comes with a broom he beats the witch with, shouting at the spirit to leave her body. He hurts her, she begins to cry but the fact is that she is not crying, it's the spirit inside her crying and only when she is bruised so hard that she begins to bleed does the spirit leave her body, she crumples to the floor.

~

I want to tell them there is nothing like witches or spirits, I want to tell them that a sick child needs a doctor, not a witch-doctor, but watching their eyes gleam in the dark, I let it be, I let myself slip into their world and although one part of me has decided to listen so that I can retell these stories to you when you grow up and want stories that scare you, another is deeply drawn into these tales until I am one with the inky blackness outside, the sound of crickets chirping, the wind whistling in the trees, the sudden report of a raindrop falling, the hulking grey shadow of the mosquito net on the wall, the chill of these fears reinforcing the warmth of the familiar. That these men, women and children in Opaar have, even if it is for the moment, decided to embrace us as their own, giving up the little they have. Unmindful of their own hardship, they have joined hands to throw a protective circle, of trust and love, around us and placed us at its centre.

~

Days after your father's funeral a few years later, some of the same men, women from the village come to visit us. They tell me to bring you to the village so that you can play in the open. In the city, there is no place to play, they say, she can join other children collecting mangoes that drop from trees in a storm. She can swim in the pond, she will make so many friends. There is also land that's in your name, they say, come and claim it, we will get a lawyer from the District Headquarters to help you with the paperwork.

But with your father gone, so is Opaar.

Everyone we met there was there because of him. You and I were his and, therefore, Opaar's.

With him no more, I worry what kind of a welcome we would get. Would they call you the one who brought bad luck to the family, the daughter who took the father away? Would they say, look at her mother, she doesn't wear white after her husband's death? Or maybe I am mistaken, there is still a place there for you and for me. Perhaps you would like to visit the village now that you are all grown-up, see how the village has changed, get our house opened once again, aired. Lie down under the mosquito net, watch the shadows on the wall, listen to the wind in the trees. Keep your ears open for witches dancing in the dark, big black cargo trains tearing down to nowhere.

MAN

PROTEST RALLY

GRIDLOCK on the highway, his car hasn't moved an inch in almost an hour. He tells Driver not to switch off the engine because he needs the air conditioner at maximum, the temperature set to less than 20 degrees because outside it's more than 40. The car seems to have plunged into a lake on fire and even if the windows are rolled up, it doesn't matter because heat flows in, through the tiniest of spaces. It bakes the seats, scorches the surfaces, from the dashboard to the inside of doors, the entire inside of the roof. It snakes through the collar of his shirt to wet his back and chest, trickle into his shoes, between his toes.

The city police – egged on by angry judges of the High Court – banned dark sun film on vehicle windows after incidents of rape in moving cars. Take the covers off, they ordered, sunlight is our society's best disinfectant, let everyone see what's going on inside. To cut the glare, therefore, he rolls down the window on his side, drapes a newspaper's double-spread over the glass, then rolls the window up making a temporary curtain of newsprint that offers him shade.

That done, he pushes back his seat, adjusts it to flat, lies down, puts his headphones on to shut out all the noise, the AC, the fan, the rustle of Driver's clothes, the scrape of Driver's fingers, hard and calloused, against the steering wheel, soft and plush.

It's still hot inside; he reaches out to turn the temperature knob down – and it's then that he sees the first face.

~

The face looks him straight in the eye. A man's face, forty years, forty-five years old, sweat, stubble, hair cut cheap, skin pocked, shirt smudged, one button undone showing hair on chest, trousers grey, the colour of perpetual dirt. The face says something, his mouth opens and closes, the tongue darts in and out, licks the upper lip between words he cannot hear. He is standing four cars and a bus ahead. Next to him is a boy, little more than a child, ten years eleven years old, echoing the man in shout and scream but more restless, fidgety, running from one car to another. Behind them are others, men, women and children, he can count at least a dozen. All angry faces, there are no placards so he cannot make out what they are protesting for or against. Beyond them, there are more, and beyond them, even more. One face for each car on the highway, it seems, oblivious to the heat that flows down from the white sky above. One of them carries a stick he begins to beat the cars with. Gentle tap at first with the clear threat of something stronger.

Tap tap against this trunk, tap against that door, tap on this tyre, tap on that window, tap tap on that bonnet. A light brush against his windshield.

They have now found a clearing ahead, a space between the vehicles large enough for six or seven of them to gather, for one of them to hold an effigy of someone who looks like the

Chief Minister, a woman with grey hair, a fawn-coloured sari, hideous, teeth drawn like those on a skeleton. The sari is dipped in kerosene, set ablaze, its smell wafts into his car despite the closed window, along with the smoke, the shouting gets louder, the air around the burning effigy shimmers like in a mirage.

He tells Driver to find out who these people are, what they are up to, what they want, why the police haven't come yet. But leave the engine running, he says, I want the air conditioner on. He switches on the TV in his car, flips through the news channels, reads one full cycle of the crawl at the bottom of the screen, there's nothing as yet on what's happening on the highway.

The crowd gets bigger, more sticks dance in the heat, there are women, too, in brightly coloured saris that remind him of Balloon Girl's mother, a cluster of them standing, another sitting between the rows of cars, straddling the broken white line that marks the lanes, where just hours ago, under the reflected haze of neon lights, he had seen mynahs, in the dark.

~

Driver is back with a report:

'Sir, there is no water, there is no power in their old city for three days, they say they don't have water to drink, they are protesting, they are waiting for the local MLA or MP to come, give them an assurance that power and water will be back by this evening. And until that happens, they are not going to allow us to move.'

~

A woman steps out of her car in the adjoining lane, squeezes herself between his car and hers, the folds of fat on her arms press against his window so hard he can see the pores of her skin, feel her through the doors and the metal. Where does she think she's going?

He wants to get out of the car, stop her from going anywhere and, in full view of everyone, commuters, motorists, protesters, highway staff, even the police who will be here any time, he wants to hold her, bite and chew on some of that fat, swallow some, along with the fuzz on it, later clean it from between his teeth. He knows he will retch, he will throw up the fat into the fire that the protesters have lit, wait for white smoke to rise so that he and Balloon Girl can ride the plume, holding on to Red Balloon, above this stationary traffic, over the cars and the angry men, women and children.

Into the sky above the city.

Driver is speaking: 'Sir, I don't think this will clear soon. I have a suggestion.'

He doesn't say anything.

'You see that woman, sir, she's walking to the exit, you could do that, too. In ten minutes, in the direction we came, you can get off the highway, take The Mall exit. You will find taxis there.' A little stone hits his windshield.

There's no damage except a smudge, like bird-dropping, which Driver reaching out with his rag wipes away. 'There may be violence, sir,' he says. 'The police may come, I think you should leave.'

It's been almost an hour but none of the news channels has anything on the highway jam, there is a rerun of some discussion from the previous night involving five men and a woman who looks nowhere like his favourite reporter, the one he wants to listen to at night, to the sounds her body makes. He flips channels: markets are down again.

'Sir, you want to stay in the car until the road clears?' Driver asks.

CHILD

ORPHAN ESCAPES

'I AM standing right outside Little House' – Ms Priscilla Thomas is reporting live –'where I got Sunil, my baby boy. This is the place where the wall broke in the thunderstorm last night, and, as you can see, behind me, there is a hole in the wall through which, it is suspected, a little boy called Orphan crawled out.

'He was the only boy left in Little House. Officials and staff here have no clue where this child is. Some say he may be trapped under debris, others that he may still be on the premises, hiding somewhere. But why should a child, little more than a baby, to be precise, hide? And for so long? In the other wall-collapse across the city, where five workers were killed, we know how the building contractor violated the construction plan and used substandard raw material. Here, it's too early to find out what exactly happened but you know I was here recently, along with the Chief Minister herself, and because of this place, I am a mother now and a child has a home. A safe home, where walls don't collapse because there is a thunderstorm.'

~

Cut to video of Sunil smiling in Ms Thomas's living room, sitting on the floor, the morning sun streaming over his left shoulder, the cool shadow of a gulmohar tree playing on his face.

~

'Ladies and gentlemen, I have a confession to make,' continues Ms Thomas. 'When I was here the first time, I did see Orphan. Officials at Little House told me, and I will not name them to protect their identities, because they were breaking the law by pushing one specific child, they told me I should adopt Orphan because he was the youngest one, his transition would be easiest. I watched him play, I was struck by his intelligence, how delicate he was, how strong at the same time.'

~

Cut to video of Orphan lying on his bed, playing with a yellow car, one wheel broken, Kalyani by his side.

~

'I said, no, I am not going to take Orphan because he is normal quote unquote, there is nothing wrong with him and he is going to find a home. Sunil is ill, Sunil's days may be numbered, he is the one who needs a home more and now look at the irony, the paradox, call it what you will. It's Orphan who has gone missing, he is the one who is homeless. Imagine how things would have panned out had I adopted them both, Sunil and Orphan, they would have been brothers, safe in my house. The fact is we have left too many of our children to the force of chance, to the luxury of luck. And, when we do that, as a nation, we, the people, undermine our future, we destroy our demographic dividend.'

~

Cut to Sunil, Ms Thomas feeding him with a bright yellow spoon.

~

'Let's listen to the person who was the first one to find Orphan, abandoned at the doorstep.'

'I cannot believe this,' says Mrs Chopra. 'He can hardly stand on his own, let alone walk, he hasn't even learned how to talk. The night nurse was asleep when the storm came, the resident doctor had the day off. The strange thing is there is no other damage, not one branch has fallen off the trees in the yard. Just this wall that opens next to the street.'

~

Cut to broken wall, heap of stones, street outside, the garbage heap.

~

Mr Sharma orders a thorough search of the entire premises of Little House, top to bottom, room to room, floor to ceiling. Each nook, every corner, the turn of every passageway, storage shelves and cupboards are investigated, undersides of beds and tables, sinks in all the rest rooms, sinks in kitchen, bathrooms, water tanks, even the cobwebbed store room where all broken furniture is kept, pending government auction and disposal. Teams of staff scour the neighbourhood, all along the wall, intact and broken. Asma Khatoon, the janitor, is told to look in the garbage heap as well. Who knows, says Mr Sharma, an infant can stumble and fall, hit his head against something hard and lie there, calling for help. She looks amid plastic and paper, glass and bottles dry and wet, but there is nothing, no sign of Orphan, and when it is established beyond doubt that Orphan has, indeed, gone missing, the local police are called in.

Mr Sharma wants to record an FIR, a First Information Report, against unknown people, include charges of trafficking and kidnap, but the policemen say that that would drag him and Little House into big trouble. There is no cognisable offence established yet, they say, so why not settle for a general station diary. Mr Sharma relents. This is the first missing child under his watch and it suits him that the police avoid taking any step that could, sometime in the future, lead to legal proceedings and, in the process, taint what he thinks is his impeccable CV.

~

Leaving for home that evening, Mrs Chopra goes to Orphan's bed to check for any sign, any clue that could help find him, but there is nothing.

His sheet is spread taut, the small pillow neatly fluffed up, not even a wrinkle to show that a little head had rested here once. It's as if Orphan had never been here, the boy she saved that morning with her own breath and the beating of her heart.

On her way out, she stops to say goodbye to Mr Sharma who is standing by the window.

'I know it's difficult to accept but we have to look ahead,' he says without looking at her. 'I liked that boy very much. I am sure he will find a nice home.'

'I don't know,' Mrs Chopra says. 'I don't know where he is, sir, all I know after working here so many years is that an orphan remains an orphan. Once abandoned, always abandoned.'

WOMAN

FATHER'S STUDENTS

ON weekends and on some weekdays, too, especially during exam time, our home becomes an open house for your father's students. At least six or seven, sometimes even ten, walk in for a study session – over days, weeks, months and years, an endless stream. That expands our little house to accommodate a classroom where they sit in a circle. With Sir, that's what they call your father, in the centre: he is their sun, they are his planets, each one shines off him, bright and dazzling. The first time I am tempted to go and sit in that circle, I tell your father this and he says, of course, why not, but then quickly adds, I think you will get bored in ten minutes, it's too technical.

Over the next few days, therefore, I steal glances at the books they use. He is right, it is too technical, the book they use the most is about Magadhi language and its formation. This is the language in which the Buddha preached two thousand years ago, in which his edicts were written on iron pillars in the kingdom of Ashoka. The book is about its rules of grammar and syntax, how its verbs and nouns draw from Sanskrit.

~

His students are respectful to me although I don't think I am that many years older than them. They stand up when I enter with tea for all of them – the men in the room are awkward, the women rush to take the tray from my hands and begin passing around the teacups. One of the women is named Krishna and she says, Ma'am, you don't have to do this, I could have made the tea. Another woman asks me about my school and my teaching and she says she wants to be a teacher, too, once she is done with college. This is small talk, polite talk, their way of trying to include me in their circle and my response is to smile and say, now you people go back to your studies, I have some work to do, and I withdraw from the room.

The rest of the afternoon or evening I am on my own.

If I have brought work from school, like grading papers or looking at worksheets, I get busy with that. Otherwise, I lie down, listen to the radio or just sit and look out of the window.

When you come into our lives, you keep me busy. Some days, after I have cleaned you up and fed you, Krishna takes you away, says, leave her to us, you can forget about her for a few hours. You are then part of this study circle, carried from one pair of hands to another, a joyous bundle of novelty and distraction.

These sessions make your father so happy that it seems it's only through teaching that he can draw strength and sustenance. He says, the more I teach, the more I learn. You should hear how the students talk about him. Sir is the best, they tell me when they help me rinse the teacups, he's the only one in the faculty who has so much time for us. Sir is the only one who listens to us, the only one who gets us to ask questions even when we do not know what to ask.

Sir, Sir, Sir, they keep going on.

~

All of them, the men and the women. Including the man in glasses, with hair almost to his shoulders. He is one of your father's students, his name is.

I cannot bring myself to say his name.

Well, not yet, maybe later, not until I have told you things that need to be told.

Like how he's been with me the last thirty years, forty years.

Like how I have never told you about him until tonight.

Like what he did when your father died.

Like, we are in love.

There, I have said it. It's not so hard to speak the unspeakable when there are so few left to listen.

MAN

WATER CANNONS

NO, he decides, he won't leave the car because how long can this traffic jam on the highway last? One hour, three hours, four? He shall wait, Driver has no reason to complain, he will get paid for overtime, quite generous, beyond 6 p.m. at the rate of Rs 100 per hour.

~

Protesters block the lanes heading towards Delhi, leaving the other side – the lanes that lead to Jaipur and Mumbai – free where traffic is moving, even if it is slow. Suddenly, the car in front of him, with a man in the back seat, takes a sudden swerve to the right and heads for the divider cutting across a line of stationary cars. A policeman and an employee of the Highway Customer Service office, both in uniform, appear from nowhere, move the traffic cones, push the barricades to make a clearing for this car, letting it take a U-turn, cross the divider to the other side and then drive away.

Other cars honk, two drivers get out, shout at the policeman, who shrugs, who couldn't care less.

'Special case,' he shouts, 'emergency,' and walks away because he knows how this works. The man in that car must be a VIP: politician, judge, newspaper owner, TV anchor or maybe he knows someone who knows one of these VIPs. That someone makes a call to someone else who then calls the local police to say, a friend of mine is stuck in the protest rally on the highway, he needs to get out, it's very important, he needs to be somewhere and he's already late and please will you help him get out of this terrible jam and then a call goes out on wireless to the police van parked closest to the highway which then sends a policeman to the Highway Customer Service office, passes on the message to the manager or whoever is in charge who, in turn, gets someone to go, identify the car, move the barricades, break the lane for the car to get out of the gridlock. The calls are then made, in the reverse order, until the VIP gets a call and says, thank you very much, you didn't need to go through all that trouble only for me but thank you very much, see you soon.

That's how it's done in this city.

Strings are pulled, puppets are moved, there's some shouting, there's some cursing followed by the silence of resignation.

~

He watches this little drama and it fills him with rage, he wants to stop this, turn all the wheels back in time and space but all he can do is push his seat back, tilt it to flat and lie down, close his eyes. As long as the engine runs, so does the air conditioner; the windows are rolled up, he is fine. Last week, a three-year-old died in a car closed, engine running, but that was in a parking lot in The Mall, asphyxiation by carbon monoxide in a closed space. But he is safe, he is no child.

As extra precaution, he tells Driver to lower the window once in a while for fresh air to come in.

~

To help himself fall asleep, he can ask Driver about his home and his family. Because once Driver starts talking, it is almost always a sad story, son failed his exam, daughter is sick, wife has a blood test, all this lulls him to sleep. But he is a good driver, efficient, he picks things up fast. Like the time he told him, please use a deodorant and wear fresh socks each day because I cannot have you driving my car if you smell like this and from that day on, he never has to complain, not even once, not on the most humid, sweltering day of the year. For, Driver is always fresh, lime fresh.

Like Balloon Girl, after bath.

Fresh, washed, clean, flying with him in the sky.

It's not even been twenty-four hours since he dropped her and her mother off and he wishes to see Balloon Girl again. He can wish her into appearing, he only has to close his eyes and she will be there, he has to choose the setting. Does he want her standing on the pavement, outside his car? Or sitting at his dining table at home, her small fingers around a cool white porcelain bowl of milk and cornflakes? Does he want her back in the sky with swirling clouds and flying aircraft? Balloon Girl will be there, wherever he wants her to be. Right now, he wants her in the car with him and the moment he closes his eyes and imagines her, there she is, Balloon Girl, sitting in the back seat, her clothes as clean as they were when he handed them to her this morning, and she is smiling at the way Driver sleeps, how his head leans back, his mouth open.

He begins to show her what the knobs and buttons on his car's dashboard do. Turn this, the car gets colder.

Flick this, TV switches on. Press this, red light blinks.

This one is for automatic lock, this one plays music, arrow up is louder, arrow down is softer, this one is the wiper, press this, he says, and she presses it hard, leaning across Driver whose head has come to rest against the window.

Water hits the windscreen.

With an impact so shuddering Driver wakes up with a start.

Balloon Girl is gone, water streams down the windscreen hard, the glass has turned opaque.

'Water cannons, sir,' says Driver.

That's what the police are using.

Tata trucks, each fitted with a water tank and motors, enter the highway from the other side, the one that's relatively free, into which the VIP car was allowed to turn. Police have set up fresh barricades, Driver rolls the window down, hears the police on the megaphone telling the crowd to retreat, go home, the local MP has arrived.

~

'Ladies and gentlemen, I hear you,' says the MP, standing on the divider, water cannons behind him.

'I listen to you, I understand what you are going through. From here, I am going directly to the Chief Minister's office and I promise you I will not leave that office until I have come up with a solution, until you have power and water back.

'The problem is there are people with unauthorised connections and they are drawing more power than they should and we have to speak to them. My request to all of you, with folded hands, is please call off this protest here, the highway is blocked, it has inconvenienced thousands of people.'

The crowd is angry, these words hardly have any effect, the MP hurriedly climbs down and is escorted off the highway into his car.

No one has heard him and even if they have, they haven't listened.

Police switch the cannons on, jets of water arc across eight lanes of traffic to slam into the protesters. Someone in the truck, in a yellow helmet, is navigating the jet, spraying the stranded cars as well.

One protester, a boy, barely in his teens, takes off his shirt. Twirling it around his head, he runs towards the cannons when a jet catches him full in the face and neck, throws him off his feet into a giant puddle that's spreading across the lanes on the highway. He hears the crunch of the boy hitting the road. Someone lends him a hand, helps him to get up, the boy is hurt, pain twists his face. Clear water from the cannons turns black and green with dirt on the highway, trash thrown from cars. Drops of water slide down his window, too, he catches them in his fingers, cool to the touch.

Like Balloon Girl's face in the clouds.

CHILD

TRAFFIC SIGNAL

'LET'S go,' says Bhow, 'there's no time to waste.'

Bhow is a dog of few words.

She is the only eyewitness to Orphan's arrival at Little House and it's only appropriate that she is the only one who watches Orphan crawl out through the hole in the wall created by the storm.

This is their first meeting so she can tell him about how exciting the world is outside, how the days and nights stretch from the wretched doorstep of Little House to that glorious place where sky meets the city. She can tell him about that scorching night when she sees a woman leave him. She can tell him about the blood-red towel in which he was wrapped, how Mrs Chopra picked him up in the morning, but Bhow is a practical dog, more prose than verse, so she skips all this drama and the first thing she does is lick Orphan clean.

Starting from the toes of his bare feet, moving up his ankles, his small knees, up his chest, his neck and his face, down his arms, hands, in between his fingers, his little nails.

Her tongue tickles; Orphan laughs, sort of.

'Not too loud,' says Bhow, 'careful, we don't want anyone to hear us. We have to remove every Little House smell from you because they will get sniffer dogs, give them your pillow, your clothes, ask them to smell their way to you. And then they will bring you back here.'

Orphan listens.

'Done,' says Bhow. 'Get on top of me, no one's looking, it's still dark, let's get out of here before the sun comes out.'

And they set off, dog and child, into the city.

~

The storm has cooled the night.

Orphan, drenched with Bhow's licking, shivers in a slight chill. Bhow has neither leash nor collar and Orphan is too small to be able to control her movements. He cannot hold onto her tight, curl his legs around her, so Bhow walks slowly, the infant's hands on the thick, matted fur around her neck. There's little traffic at so early an hour except for call-centre Toyotas that dart from light to light, discoloured and broken trucks carrying stone chips and iron rods, gleaming ones carrying Maersk shipping containers geometrically arranged, bound for shores across the ocean – each passing vehicle sets off a wind that threatens to knock Orphan off Bhow's back.

So she keeps her ears open to catch the faintest rumble of an oncoming vehicle long before the child can hear or see, pulls over to the left, waits for it to pass and then begins walking again.

Clearly, Bhow has taken charge with a plan that seems meticulously crafted well in advance, step by careful step. Every half-hour, Bhow stops at a secluded spot, maybe a patch of pavement against the shuttered door of a shop, or in the corner of a blind alley off the road at the end of a lane, where she sits down, curls herself up around Orphan to help him sleep.

As day breaks, they are off Ring Road, walking the leafy streets of neighbourhoods in the southern part of the city, quiet before the morning rush-hour. The occasional schoolbus passes them by, they watch guards waiting for the shift to change at the iron gates of houses hidden behind walls. They pass drivers washing cars, maids headed to work. Some strays bark at Bhow, one even comes running right up to her but she doesn't react.

'Let's keep walking,' she says, 'keep looking straight. Just a few hours more and then we will be home.'

~

Home for Bhow is off the national highway next to a traffic signal beyond the toll gate where the thirty-two lanes veer off into a network of streets that twist and loop like petals of a giant flower and make up New City. One goes towards The Mall, another to The Leela Hotel, barely one mile from Apartment Complex.

MEANWHILE

AN EVENING IN THE LIFE
OF KALYANI'S SISTER

IT is past 11 p.m., Ma is cooking dinner, Baba's bath is over, he is drying himself, the crowd at the community tap cleared only at 10 p.m. Pinki has finished dusting the floor, Bhai's lying down. Kalyani has quit her job at Little House, she is washing the dishes, getting the house ready for dinner.

'What happened to all of you today?' asks Baba, water dripping down his back.

Each one gets to tell a story from the day that's just ended. Tonight, it's Pinki's turn.

She will tell, they will listen, sitting on the floor in a circle of sorts.

~

'Around 5.30 p.m., Dada Babu comes back from work, Didi says it's very hot today so we won't have dinner at home, let's all go eat out at The Mall. Wash your hands and face with soap, she tells me, scrub hard, we are going to a restaurant. She sprays some of her perfume on me. Also on Krish, the baby. I clean up Krish, he is in no mood to go, he keeps crying, rubbing his eyes. Dada Babu says he must be tired, let's stay at home, we can order in some food, but Didi says, no, I am tired of staying at home. And if Krish is tired, he can always sleep in the stroller.

'When we step out, it is already six, we have to return home by eight, Didi tells me. On our way to The Mall, we walk under the Metro tracks, Krish points to watch the big yellow digger that they are using to lay the road. He has got a small one at home exactly like that. I stop so that Krish can watch but Didi says, let's keep walking, we want to finish early when the restaurant is empty, let's be the first ones in and out.

'She is right, there's no one in the restaurant except us, it's cold and very dark inside although there are lights along the wall, lights on the ceiling, some even on the floor. A man comes up to us, he is wearing a black coat, he takes us to a big sofa and a table. We all sit there. Krish has fallen quiet.

'The man brings two books, gives one to Didi, one to Dada Babu. That's the menu, Didi says, it has everything the restaurant can serve this evening. What do you want to eat, she asks me, and I don't know what to say so I tell her, Didi, I will eat whatever you order.

'Across from our table is a big glass tank along the entire wall. It is full of water and it has fishes. Red, yellow, blue, black, white. With small trees, rocks and coloured stones, like marbles.

'Didi tells me she needs to talk to Dada Babu for a while so can I please take Krish right up to the tank so that he can watch the fishes? There is a toy frog sitting at the bottom of the tank blowing bubbles. There is a little turtle, too. In fifteen minutes, Krish falls asleep, Didi tells me to take off his shoes.

'Food has come to the table, I can see that Didi and Dada Babu are talking but I can't hear what they are saying. I stand there, watching the fishes.

'Pinki, you leave the stroller here, we will take an hour, Didi says, Krish has fallen asleep. Why don't you wait outside? If he wakes up I will call you, we will get your food packed.

137

'The man who had taken us inside shows me the way out, tells me where to sit a few steps away from the restaurant's entrance, on a bench. You sit here, he says, if they need you, I will come and get you, don't go anywhere.

'OK, I say.

'This bench is next to the playpen where Krish and I go every weekend. They have slides, cars, bridges. There is a tree house as well, with a toy kitchen. Made of green plastic. They charge Rs 150 for one hour, they give a ticket we need to stick on Krish's back. His favourite is the red car which you move with your feet. I like the blue slide but I haven't tried it, these things are only for the children, not for us.

'This evening, there are only two or three children in the playpen. I know the girl who works there, she's also from West Bengal, her name is Durga, she's at least four years, five years older than I am. When Durga sees me, she tells me, why are you sitting there on the bench, come over to the playpen, no one's looking, you can try out the blue slide and we can talk. She is talking aloud.

'I say, no, I cannot go, what if Didi calls me, the waiter has said that he will come here to look for me.

'Come over for just five to ten minutes, Durga says, we can see the waiter if he comes out. I am frightened because when Didi gets angry, she gets very angry, but then Durga is right, there is no crowd in the playpen, Krish is deep in sleep, I don't think he will wake up so soon, this is also his sleep time.

'So I tell Durga, OK, but only for five minutes. I go up and down the blue slide so many times I lose count, I climb into the tree house, I enter the toy kitchen, I play with the toy oven, the toy cups and plates. If Didi catches me playing, I can always tell her I am trying to see what new toys have come to the playpen so that I can help Krish play with them but Didi doesn't come out, she is busy with dinner with Dada Babu.

138

They take a long time, about an hour, and by the time they are done and step out of the restaurant pushing Krish's stroller, I am back on the bench.'

~

'Did they give you some food at the restaurant?'asks Ma.

'They packed it, Didi said she has kept it in the fridge, she will give it to me for lunch tomorrow,' says Pinki. 'I will bring it home for all of you.'

'No, no, not at all, never,' says Baba, 'you eat it at their house itself, that's your share, no need to bring it home.'

Ma has heard it all, she begins serving dinner, a drop of sweat rolls down her forehead to the tip of her nose and as she wipes it with her sari, she wonders when has Pinki, not even eleven years old, grown up so much.

WOMAN

THE ACCIDENT

SISTER Agnes Consuelo, the principal, should not be here, she should be in her office. Instead, she stands at my classroom door, looking in, and then, without saying a word, walks in, right up to the blackboard where I stand. Children, please stand up, welcome Sister Agnes, I tell them, and they say, in a chorus of fifty-one distinct voices, good afternoon, Sister Agnes, welcome to Kindergarten Class, and they all stand up, boys and girls tired and drained because it's 1.15 p.m., barely fifteen minutes away from the end of day.

I tell them to rest their heads on their desks, close their eyes. No talking.

Sister Agnes holds my shoulder; she has never held me like this. She leans into me, she wants to tell me something in confidence, she doesn't want the children in the class to hear, she is so close I see the charts on the softboard – of the solar system, the sun and the planets, black and blue – reflected in the curve of her glasses.

Some children promptly go back to resting their heads on their desks, eyes closed, mouth shut, just as I have instructed. Others talk, open, close desks, pack, unpack bags, tie shoelaces.

Sister Agnes has her back to them, I raise my finger to my lips to tell them to be quiet.

Sister Agnes says she wants me to go with her to the office.

She says she has asked her assistant to come upstairs and supervise the children until the end of the class.

'Please take your bag,' she says, 'you don't need to return to the classroom.'

The chalk slips between my fingers, I pick it up, I dust the blackboard.

I am about to tell the children that I will be going downstairs and I will see them tomorrow when Sister Agnes says, 'Let's go.'

We step out of the classroom, my fingers smeared with chalk dust, my eyes blurred, Sister Agnes holds my arm as if I am learning to walk.

~

I am in her office.

Sister Agnes steps out, leaving me alone, I hear her talking to someone, a man, but I cannot make out what they are saying, she mentions my name, she mentions your father's name.

She walks in.

'Your daughter is on her way, we have sent someone to get her. You please sit here for a while, can I get you a glass of water, there has been an accident,' she says. 'Your husband.'

MAN

PARIS WALK

THE water cannons work, the protest is broken, the protesters — forty, fifty of them, men, women and children — begin to disperse. Gone is their rage as, flanked by policemen, they shuffle towards the ramp that exits the highway, defeated, drenched and dripping like crows caught in rain.

'Now, traffic will begin to move,' says Driver, smiles as he hears engines all around switch on, indicators blink, rear lights gleam, reflected in water on the cars and on the highway.

He tells Driver to go ahead and wait at the next exit, he wants to check on a little something. He steps out of the car, out of the fierce noon day on the highway in New City into early morning, breakfast time, in Paris.

~

He finds he is on rue du Bac, a sign on the wall says this is the 7th arrondissement, this is where his friend Arsh lives. Number 100. He will drop by, give him a surprise but, first, he wants to go for a walk.

How the hell did you come to Paris, Arsh will ask, why didn't you tell me in advance, I could have planned something, but now that you are here, I am sorry, I cannot do much, I have to go to work but here is the key to my house, help yourself to whatever is there in the fridge, make yourself comfortable, I will try to come back early and then we go out at night.

He wants to see the Seine, Arsh has told him it's a short walk from his house.

He looks around, he's at 15 rue du Bac, right across from him is a café, Le Gévaudan. It's yet to open, a man is cleaning up inside. Four chairs sit outside under a red awning so wide it covers almost the entire cobbled pavement.

Next door is a restaurant, Artisan Boulanger. This is also shut. There is a wine shop, Nicolas, again closed, he must have come very early, what time is it? Let me walk for a while before the shops open, he thinks.

He is hungry, he hasn't had anything since his drink last night when Balloon Girl and her mother were asleep.

A woman in a tan coat, which reaches to her knees, throws a cigarette into a drain.

Their eyes meet.

~

Two men walk past, talking to each other, he walks through them, in between. To his right is Galerie Verneuil: a CD, DVD shop, it sells posters and postcards too, it's open but it doesn't draw him in, he keeps walking. Up ahead, there is the office of CB Richard Ellis. It's a familiar name, he has to interact with their India office at work. He pitches real-estate projects to them which they offer to banks which, in turn, offer these projects to their private clients as high-return investments. Projects in New City, commercial and residential, mainly luxury, off the highway where his car stands now.

It's cold, he is the only one on the street in just shirt and trousers.

An old woman peers through the glass window of Du Bout Du Monde, he stops to look but cannot make out what kind of a store it is, it looks like a bar with a stage against the wall, some kind of a theatre.

Every second shop on this street is a gallery of some sort.

Montres de Prestige et de Collection, 34 rue du Bac, is he walking in the right direction?

He wants to see the river first before he meets Arsh. He knows from his Google walks that streets in Paris are short. He will walk down a few blocks, if there is no river, he will turn back. An Eric Kayser is open from where he smells bread, freshly baked, and coffee, should he stop and have something to eat before the walk to the river? He decides against it, crosses rue de Verneuil, heads east towards the sun climbing the sky in front, between the grand buildings on either side, with their arches and gabled windows, walks down the narrow road squeezed in between, perpetually in shadow.

One shop has a sign in English: 'Farrow & Ball, Manufacturers of Traditional Paper and Paint'. He imagines a workshop in the basement packed with rolls of wood pulp, vats of boiling water, drums of glue, dyes of different colours extracted from flowers.

Two trash bags, tied at the mouth, are propped at the entrance.

~

The wind is stronger, colder, it must be from the river, he crosses rue de l'Université, keeps walking down rue du Bac, that's what Arsh has told him, the river is a short walk from my house straight down and there it is, he can see the narrow road open up into a sprawling intersection. Past rue de Lille, rue du Bac ends and merges into Pont Royal from where he can see the Seine.

Flowing, in full spate, it must have rained the whole night here.

He crosses the street, he is along Quai Anatole France, steps into a puddle, he is beginning to shiver, his teeth chatter but there are too few people out at this time for him to attract attention. He will borrow a blazer from Arsh, in his pocket he has a handkerchief that has trapped some of the heat from New City. He wears it around his neck like a scarf, covers his ears, but that brings little respite.

Maybe if he walks faster it will be warmer so he breaks into a light jog, runs along Quai des Tuileries, the Seine to his left, the river he has been dreaming of.

He reaches a bridge where a man and a boy have parked their bicycles and are looking down at the river. The water is clear, the strong wind rakes its surface setting off little eddies, the early morning sun is to his right so his shadow falls across the bridge onto the water where it trembles with the ripples. The man and the boy sense his presence, turn to look, the boy smiles at him.

Arsh has told him the weather can abruptly change, he looks up at the sky, there is a big cloud but the rest of it is a clear blue. He wishes to sit outside, have breakfast at Eric Kayser, then walk back on rue du Bac, along the river, take the Metro because up ahead he sees a sign for the station, half a mile down from Musée d'Orsay: Concorde.

From there, it's just three Metro stops along the Yellow Line, he knows all these by heart, Line 1 towards La Défense. Past Champs-Élysées, Franklin D. Roosevelt, George V and then Charles-de-Gaulle Étoile, that's where the Arc de Triomphe is, the monument for soldiers, it looks so much like India Gate.

He wishes Balloon Girl were there, they could take Line 6 to Bir-Hakeim and then the Eiffel Tower, from where he will show her how cities don't look so different from high above.

~

They are at the India Gate red light.

A young man with a camera knocks on the window. 'Sir, a photograph?'

'Do we look like tourists?' Driver shouts at him as the lights turn green.

He wakes up.

'Sorry, sir,' says Driver, 'these men don't listen until you shout.'

'Keep driving, I am not going to work today,' he says, before closing his eyes again.

CHILD

CITY LIGHTS

HOME for Bhow, and this evening for Orphan, is a patch of concrete, dug-up, broken, over-run with weeds and trash, under the highway between two pillars, next to a traffic intersection. So tired is Orphan that the moment he gets off Bhow, his legs buckle, his eyes close. Bhow curls up around the child, adjusts herself so that her shadow falls on Orphan's eyes, shields him from the fierce red of the setting sun about to roll off the highway.

~

The strays of New City, Bhow's friends and family, wake Orphan up.

He feels their eyes and ears, fur and tail, whine and scratch, bark and growl as they lick him all over, their tongues and their bodies a blur of brown and black, white and grey. One dog has her tail chewed off, another has a limp, a third has an ear missing. Bhow tells them to back off, leave Orphan alone as he rubs his eyes to find that he is drenched with light. From the blue-white, red-and-yellow billboards at The Mall. There is Zara, Debenhams, Beer Garden, the glittering sign of The Leela as wide as a city block – all emitting a glare his eyes have never seen before as he wakes up for the first time not in Little House, but far away from its familiar shapes and smells, from his corner in the bed against its wall.

Orphan begins to cry.

'Let's help him wash,' says Bhow, using her nose to point out to Orphan a pipe that runs down the pillar from which water gushes through a crack. 'Licks and kisses won't fill his empty stomach.'

Bhow helps Orphan undress, pulls down his shorts with her jaws, pushes him ahead with the tip of her nose until the child, half walking, half crawling, comes to sit down under the pipe. Water runs down his head, slips into his ears, over his nose and his lips. He gulps, swallows, he drinks the water, shivers in its sudden cold splash. Bath done, Orphan stands up, clumsy on his two feet, water crawls under him, up, between the legs, wetting some crusted blood from early this morning when he fell once, water stinging the bruise.

He sees the lights of The Mall through the water in his eyes, bent and refracted into the colours of a rainbow. Like through the kaleidoscope Kalyani had once brought to show him how easy it is to split light from the sun.

WOMAN

LAST RITES

YOUR father is home.

They take him off the stretcher and place him on a canvas sheet someone has spread on the floor, they bring blocks of ice, speckled with sawdust, that they press against his body, push smaller pieces of it between him and the sheet, under his neck and between his legs, around his feet. In the heat, however, the ice begins to melt into fingers of chilled water that draw puddles across the floor, send wisps of steam into the air.

They say it was an accident, the bus was crowded, he was standing on the footboard when he slipped and fell, was run over by another bus but where are the marks?

A bus hit him, he fell onto the street, and I see not one scratch on his face. Where is the blood? The injury? Instead, he is dressed in the calm and peace of sleep, his glasses are off. His blue shirt is unruffled, neither smudge nor tear, there are thin grey streaks on his black trousers as if he only leaned against a dirty wall. Lying on his back, his hands by his side, the palms are open, upturned towards the ceiling, again no marks there. There's nothing to mark that this is his end.

~

You whisper into my ear, wake him up, wake him up. You step into the puddle, you walk from me to him, you leave footprints on the floor. You touch his fingers, you hold them like you do when you go for a walk with him. You feel inside his shirt pocket to check if there is something inside, a gift he never told you about.

You whisper into my ear, wake him up, wake him up.

Then you tell him, wake up, wake up, you begin to scream so loud I am afraid you will stop breathing. I hold you, I promise I will not cry in your presence, that's the least a parent can do for her child.

~

Krishna says she will take you to her house, she will help you wash, change your clothes since you are still in school uniform. She will give you dinner, she has two nieces your age, you can play with them, she says. Ma'am, she is very young, she doesn't need to be here any more, I am taking her with me,

I will be with her throughout, don't you worry, I will bring her later in the night, after the cremation. When Krishna picks you up, you have fallen asleep, I see you leave the room, your head resting on her shoulder, your face streaked where the tears mixed with water from the ice.

I don't want to see you go, I want to hold you until your father comes back from the dead.

~

They undress him, bathe him, ask me to pour water on him.

They dress him in white, give me his blue shirt and his black trousers. They tell me to stay at home. They say women do not, should not, go for the cremation.

No, I say, I will go.

They send the priest to talk to me, I send him back. There is sudden disquiet in the room.

'Are you sure?' asks Sister Agnes, 'are you sure you want to go?'

'Yes,' I tell her.

MAN

PENGUINS, PELICANS

NO, Balloon Girl isn't waiting at Charles-de-Gaulle Étoile Station. Maybe she doesn't like Paris, maybe she finds it too cold and wet, the brisk wind from across the river, so she flies, on her own, halfway across the world to warm Singapore, where his friend Sukrit lives, waiting for Sheela to join him once they are married. So when he steps out of the station, he finds himself at Changi Airport from where he takes a cab to Orchard Road, takes the Metro to Boon Lay, a bus to Jurong Bird Park.

And there she is.

In the crowd of tourists in Penguin Coast, the park's most popular attraction, right at the entrance, 1,500 square metres of a climate-controlled enclosure, its interior flooded with a blue-white light meant to simulate cold sun glinting off the ice cap. The observation deck is an almost full-scale model of a Portuguese galleon, complete with a mast, wooden beams and timber floors. It moves under your feet to make you believe you are watching the penguins from onboard an ancient ship sailing the stormy sea.

'I knew you would come to see me,' Balloon Girl says, slipping her hand into his, her face bathed by the cold blue light.

She takes a step back so that they are now both in shadow, no one is looking at them, everyone's eyes are trained on the penguins.

He can do anything to her, with her.

Blood-rush floods his head, the tips of his fingers tingle, he has to close his eyes to steady himself.

No, he doesn't want to hurt her but he doesn't trust himself so he wants Balloon Girl and himself in the open, in the hot humid bright sunlight, where there are people, where everyone's watching, where he cannot do what he wants to do, where she will be safe.

He holds her hand, turns to leave.

'No,' she says, 'let's wait, they will feed the penguins now, I want to watch.'

She lets go of his hand, runs down the ramp leading from the deck to where the glass is, walling off the enclosed den in which the penguins are. Her face is inches away from the wall. A penguin swims under the surface, coming straight to where she is as if her breath is a homing signal, it touches the glass wall and swims away, splashes out of the water, clambers aboard the rocks on one side of the tank. It's a Humboldt Penguin, small, a black horseshoe band on its front, a white stripe on its head.

'Look,' she says, 'it's so much smaller than me.'

The small penguin is up on the rocks, with the entire flock of its family, more than a dozen penguins, small and big. Balloon Girl points to King Penguin, almost as tall as her, its orange ear patch gleaming like fresh paint.

'I want to watch how they eat,' she says, her arms outstretched, inviting him to lift her up so that, raised, she can look at the man, in scuba gear, who has entered the tank and is throwing fish, from a pail, into the penguin crowd.

He lifts her high over his head, he can smell the detergent on her, clean and fresh although it's been seven hours, eight hours since she put on the clothes he washed. He holds her at the waist, firmly, her neck is inches away from his face. Her skin, soft and brown. He smells the soap in her hair from last night, his arms begin to hurt but he keeps holding her until all the fish in the man's pail has been fed to the penguins, until she wants to get down and go see the lories.

'I want to feed birds,' says Balloon Girl.

~

So they take the boardwalk that leads from Penguin Coast to Pelican Cove, passing a lake so crowded with pelicans, white with big yellow beaks, the water looks like a sprawling green meadow covered with flowers with long bulbs, many moving, many still; some even swooping down across the sky to plunge in. Past Pelican Cove are the gliding swans on the way to Lori Loft, its gigantic net draped over a huge enclosure, almost 9,000 square metres.

From a counter where they show their tickets, he and

Balloon Girl pick up a cup of nectar each, the bird feed, and walk down a swaying wooden bridge. Scenting the feed, lories and lorikeets fly down, unafraid, perch on her head.

Three birds feed from her cup: two sitting on her arm, the other walks up and down, from the elbow to her wrist. She laughs, the noise makes it fly away.

'Quiet,' he says, and the birds return.

One sits on her shoulder and pecks at her earlobe, the other on the rim of the nectar cup. The birds are a blaze of colour around her face and her arms. Yellow, red, blue, black. Stripes, bands and patches. He watches the birds begin to peel her skin, tear her earlobe away. He watches her blood mix with the feed in the nectar cup, he hears her cries for help mingle with the birds' ceaseless chirp and chatter. He wants to put his mouth there, where she bleeds, drink it all in, feel the wind from the flutter of the birds' wings in his face.

CHILD

UNCLE, AUNTY

'HEY, kid, don't finish all the water, leave some for me.' It's a woman's voice shouting out to Orphan over the roar of water gushing from the pipe.

'Relax, Aunty,' says Bhow, 'you will have enough water to wash your baby's bandage. Let him clean himself.'

'Look at this,' she shouts to an imaginary audience, 'a dog telling me about being clean, a bitch who lives in the garbage heap.'

With a one-year-old baby girl, Aunty shares living quarters with Bhow's family. Home for her is under the tarpaulin sheet she has draped on pegs hammered into pillars that prop up the highway above, the sheet held down with bricks. Who the baby's father is, where she has come from – is she even the mother? – no one knows, no one asks. Each day, before rush-hour begins, Aunty wraps the baby in scraps of clothes she has picked up from the trashheaps of neighbourhoods in New City across the highway. Torn, unwashed, the dirtier the better. She wraps white cotton gauze around the baby's fore-head, wets it with a red dye she's procured from no one knows where. Props in place, baby is ready. Looking injured, bleeding: a spreading red stain across her forehead, her face pinched and pitiful under the cruel white.

When the traffic lights turn red, Aunty rushes to the inter-section, chooses a car with at least one woman in it, knocks on its window, presses the baby against it so that she is level with the passengers. Sometimes, she goes down on her knees and raises the baby skywards as if in prayer. At other times, she suddenly breaks into a startling scream, her mouth agape, tears flow down her face, mucus from her nose.

Regular passengers who drive by this traffic intersection know Aunty's trick, they don't even bother to look, they only raise the window, turn AC or music on, wait for green. Some give her money to ensure she doesn't dirty the car.

~

With Aunty, there are others who live and work around the traffic lights. Orphans all, like the ones in Little House but with no roof, no bed.

There is Uncle, who has neither arms nor legs. He is only a head, a torso, a waist and four stumps where the limbs should have been. Pushing himself from his waist, he crawls from pavement to car every time the lights turn red, then back to the pavement. He and Aunty work in tandem: if she targets one car, he does the next. He shares some of his daily collections in return for food she cooks.

~

There is a boy–girl duo who show up in the morning and leave by sunset. Girl does cartwheels, boy cleans windshields. No one knows where they come from or where they go. They both claim they are ten years eleven years old but each one looks much younger, much smaller.

~

There are vendors, at least a dozen of them, who flit in and out of this intersection from sunrise to sunset. One sells coconut slices, another car dusters and phone chargers, plastic helicopters, magazines and bestsellers in shrink-wrap. Men, boys who know how to strike a bargain between a traffic light's red and green.

~

'Where have you come from, you little prince?' Aunty asks Orphan. 'I have never seen Bhow and his family so protective, so caring about anyone.'

Orphan cannot talk.

Wet and naked, he shivers.

'Let him wear his clothes, Aunty,' says Bhow, 'you want him to catch a cold or fever?'

'What a nice, quiet little boy, he's so shy,' she says. 'I will help dress him up and he can also help me with my act.'

'He's doing no such thing,' says Bhow. 'He's just a child, a baby. And this is only temporary, he won't stay here.'

'They all say the same thing when they come,' Aunty says,

walking back to her tent outside which an aluminium pot simmers on a bed of burning coal. It's her dinner: rice, salt, half an onion a truck driver drops into her palm.

She returns with a scrap of red cloth with which she towels Orphan dry, wraps it around him and then puts his clothes back on.

'You are a handsome boy,' she says.'Wait for about half an hour, I will give you something to eat. I will mash some rice for you.'

Orphan can only cry in reply.

'Don't waste your tears, little man,' says Aunty, 'learn a lesson from me. In this city, do not cry when no one's looking.'

MEANWHILE

MRS USHA CHOPRA
BABYSITS IN MUMBAI

MRS Chopra of Little House has two children, Elder Son and Younger Son.

Younger Son's wife, Lata, has had a baby and she has to return to work since her ninety-day maternity leave is ending but their nanny has to go back to her village because her mother is ill. Lata cannot extend her maternity leave since the Mumbai asset-management company she works for has named her lead fund manager for a real-estate fund it's launching as markets are climbing back, the US job-loss rate is tapering off faster than expected.

There is Deepa, the cook, who is efficient, but she can't take care of both baby and kitchen. Lata's mother cannot come, she is full-time carer to Lata's father who last week slipped in the bathroom in their Bangalore house and sprained his back.

So Mrs Chopra gets a call from Younger Son.

~

'Ma, you work too hard at that orphanage of yours, take some time off, come and spend some time with your grandson,' he says.

'Of course, I will, maybe in the winter when it's freezing here.'

'Ma, I am sorry, we cannot wait that long,' he says, 'we need you here, it's kind of urgent, there's no one to take care of the baby. I have sent you the air ticket for tomorrow.

'Tomorrow?'

'I know, Ma, that's too short notice but I was very busy. I am sure you will get leave if you tell them it's a family emergency, I am sure they will understand.'

'I am sure they will,' she says.

'I have sent you a business-class ticket, Ma,' says Younger Son. 'If you want to rest, you can adjust the seat to make it flat. My driver will wait at the airport, he has a cellphone, I will message you his number.'

'You didn't have to spend so much,' she says. 'I could have taken the train.'

'You don't sound happy, Ma.'

'Of course I am happy, I can't wait to see all of you,' she says.

~

Elder Son lives with his mother, he is five years older than Younger Son, he didn't do as well in school or college, he works as a medical representative, pushing new drugs to old doctors.

'How selfish of him to just call and order you around. And what a silly time to choose for the flight, 7 p.m., that's peak office hour,' he says that night. 'I will drop you off at the airport.'

'If it's trouble, forget it,' says Mrs Chopra. 'I will take a taxi.'

'I will drop you off.'

'I will be away out only for a few days until their nanny is back. I can cook something for you, leave it in the fridge.'

'Ma, I can take care of myself, don't you worry.'

~

That night, she packs her suitcase in the living room. There's only one bedroom in her house which she has given up to Elder Son. She spreads a sheet on the floor in the living room in the clearing between chairs. When she lies down and switches the lights off, she likes to look at the sky through the small window in the wall, turn her head until she can catch a star.

Elder Son works very hard, he leaves at 9 a.m. and is back only by 11 p.m., six days a week, going from hospital to hospital, doctor to doctor. This is his fifth job in as many years, he doesn't make much beyond the commissions and so if sales are down, that adds up to hardly anything. She has told him, money isn't a problem, we have my salary too. All along the windowsill in the living room, he has lined up gifts he gets to distribute to doctors: little rubber toys, decorative penholders, paperclips in the shape of frogs and alligators, paperweights that tell the time of day, the temperature in the room.

Elder Son was married once but that lasted barely six months, he moved back in when his wife left him. With him around, Mrs Chopra likes to wake up every morning because he has given a sense of purpose to her day. She likes watching the sun rise over the park across the street; she likes boiling two cups of water for two cups of tea, one for Elder Son, one for herself; she likes getting his breakfast ready. They have tea together as he flips through the morning newspaper that sits between them like a third member of the family. She asks him where he is going that day and he gives her answers vague and uninterested. She packs his lunchbox and it's only when he's left for work she cleans his room, makes the bed, dusts the sheets, gets his laundry done, then takes the Metro to Little House.

On her return, she cooks dinner, watches TV as she waits for him, for the doorbell to ring, arranges and rearranges his room. He is back when most of the lights in the building are out, some nights she smells drink on him but she never mentions it, although it feels as if someone, with very cold hands, has grabbed her heart. His father drank himself to death and she wonders whether he still lives in a corner of his son's head. She says, you get ready, wash, I will give you chapatis, fresh off the gas, he has dinner and then he says he has to get up early, so he goes to bed.

She stays up an hour or so and only when he is asleep does she turn in for the night – looking at the star in the night sky framed by the window.

~

'Mrs Chopra, we are about to land.' The stewardess wakes her up, her hand on her shoulder. 'You didn't even have dinner, you must be tired, can I get you something? Tea?'

'No,' she smiles. 'I don't need anything.'

At the airport, Younger Son waits in the lounge with a uniformed driver. On the way, he tells her about the TV and DVD player in the car's back seat, how Baby loves it, keeps staring at it. He tells her about airbags and why he needs them because with Baby now the car needs to be safer. He shows her Baby's car seat.

'In America, this is compulsory,' he says, 'it keeps Baby safe. Also, Lata doesn't have to keep holding the baby, she can do her own thing.'

~

It's 8 a.m., Younger Son and Lata are leaving for work and Mrs Chopra is in the living room with Baby in her lap.

'Ma, we are very actively looking for a nanny, we have three

159

or four candidates and will decide very soon,' says Lata. 'It's just for a week or so and you can ask Deepa to help you with whatever you need. I know you need to get back soon.'

'You don't worry,' she says, 'I am here until you find someone.'

~

There is nothing to do the entire day, Mrs Chopra walks from room to room. She's happy that Younger Son has all this. She's happy that he has a car seat so that Baby is safe, she's happy that he has the kind of house she only sees on TV, its glass walls washed so clean it seems they aren't even there, its kitchen as big as her two rooms put together, with equipment she has never seen: a giant oven with yellow light inside and numbers flashing on the counter, gas stove with six burners, fridge that spreads across one entire wall.

'This is the best kitchen in the building,' says Deepa, who navigates all this with an ease so familiar that Mrs Chopra finds it odd, even surprising.

'Didi is very nice,' Deepa continues, 'she takes very good care of me. She works for fourteen hours a day but when she comes home, never once does she lose her temper or shout at me.'

Most of the time during the day, Baby sleeps, but when he wakes up, they take turns holding him.

Mrs Chopra keeps checking her cellphone but Elder Son hasn't called.

Where is he? Has he had lunch? What did he eat when he left home today? Is he waiting in the lobby of some hospital?

~

They sit down for dinner. Baby has gone to sleep.

'I can't get through to your brother,' she tells Younger Son, 'will you please check.'

'I did try to call him twice today but both times it says his phone is switched off. I have sent him an SMS, too,' he says. 'Ma, how's his work going?'

'Fine, he works very hard.'

'Is the money he makes sufficient?'

'I think so.'

'You know, Ma, he can always ask me if he needs anything, he can call me anytime.'

'I have told him that but you be careful with your money now that Baby is here. You didn't have to buy me business-class tickets.'

'Ma, that was just so that you could be comfortable on the plane.'

'I slept the whole way.'

'You must have slept very comfortably then.'

'Of course I liked the way I could push the seat back until it almost becomes a bed. I didn't know how to do it, there was a woman in the seat next to me and she showed me how.'

There is not much to talk about.

She sits at the table as Lata and her husband talk about work, about things she doesn't understand, words that don't mean anything as they float over the table, hover over the precious china that Deepa took out today, before they get sucked away by the cool draught from the air-conditioning ducts concealed behind the false ceiling. Mrs Chopra waits for them to finish, the food dries on her fingers.

She looks around the table, at all that will go back into the fridge. There's fish in the bowl, just the kind Elder Son likes, steamed. Has he had dinner? Is he still outside some doctor's office? Or is he drinking with his friends? Why didn't he call? Didn't he check his phone? Has his SIM card run out?

Baby wakes up.

Mrs Chopra is glad he does, it lets her get up and leave.

'You go on with your dinner,' she tells Lata. 'I will check on the child.'

She goes into the guest bathroom to wash her hands and she hears Younger Son from the dining table. 'Don't worry, Ma,' he says, 'I will call him right after dinner, he must have returned home.'

But the call doesn't get through.

~

That night she cannot sleep. She looks at the alien Mumbai sky through the glass wall in the guest room and assures herself that it's the same sky, with the same moon and the same stars, that drapes her other son in another city, that will guard him until her return. She wants to be able to somehow speak to the night and the sky, maybe ask them to send her child a message. That she misses him, that she will soon be on her way back. That she hopes he is fine.

She turns on her side and tries to sleep again, this time falling back on a device she has used many times in the past, thinking of the children in Little House, and going down the list of their names, counting them in her head, by name.

It works and by the time she reaches Orphan, just when she begins thinking where he could be, is he alive or is he dead, who took him away that night, where did he go through that broken wall, she falls into sleep.

WOMAN

DRINKING WATER

NO one wants me to go, no one will let me go because I am a woman and I have no place at the cremation ground, they say, because there will be wood, there will be fire, there will be smoke, because all the rituals will be performed by men, that's the way it is, where's the need for you to be there? You do not have a son, so your husband's cousin who lives in the city has been called to light the pyre, they tell me. But I am not giving in, I will not let them remove your father's body unless they let me sit next to him in the truck they have hired to take him away.

The priest is livid. Who does she think she is, he mutters under his breath, a mutter clearly meant for my ears too. This hasn't happened in all the years I have lived in this city, he says, in the hundreds of funerals I have taken care of, can someone please make her understand? That's what happens to these city women, he says, especially those who work: they forget what needs to be done, they don't care about what should be done.

The sun has set, the ice has melted, the truck has arrived.

One by one, teachers from my school leave for home. Sister Agnes is still there, standing in a corner. She walks up to me, tells me to let your father's body go but when I say, no, she says she understands. I have no idea why they don't let you go, she says, let me speak with them.

Your father's colleagues from college are there, too, but they only stand there, in loose clusters of grief. They are waiting for the body to be loaded onto the truck, they will go to the crematorium with him. Your father's students have taken charge. I don't have to do anything, they make all arrangements. From getting the priest to arranging for the death certificate, booking a slot at the crematorium, buying the countless items they need for the funeral: cloth, wood, incense sticks, camphor, rice, sandalwood paste, earthen pots, tulsi leaves, flowers, ghee, a coconut.

~

The stand-off continues until he arrives. He, your father's student, the one I have told you about. He walks up to the priest and asks him, why is the body still lying in the house? The priest points at me and says, ask her, she is the one who says we cannot take him unless she comes with us too.

So? he asks, and in a voice so loud that everyone can hear, he says, ma'am will go. If she wishes to go, she will go, nobody should and nobody can stop her. I will ensure that she goes. She is his wife. There is silence in the room, everyone's looking at him and at me. Everyone fidgets, uncomfortable, but there is no denying the wave of relief that's suddenly come crashing into the room. Someone has spoken, the deadlock broken.

He walks up to me, holds my hand and says, let's go.

You must be thirsty, he says, then goes inside, he knows where the kitchen is, he has been here so many weekends for your father's classes, he pours a glass of water for me. Drink this, he says, if you want I will get you another glass, I am sure you haven't had water since you came back from school. I met your daughter on my way here, he says, she is with Krishna, she has had dinner and she has gone to sleep.

When I raise the glass to my lips, my legs give way, I slide along the wall to the floor, he holds me by the arm and he helps lift me up.

~

I hear something in the room, do you?

Isn't it exactly like the noise your father makes when he returns home from college? The same sound of the door closing behind him, the chair being dragged along the floor for him to sit in as he takes his shoes off.

Is he here? Maybe he knows you are here and he has come visiting.

I hear him walk into the kitchen, I hear water being poured into a glass. I think he has come to listen to me because until now I have never said any of these things to anyone, about what happened to me and you after his death.

The curtains move.

I feel him sit on the sofa I am sitting on but when I put my hand out into the space next to me where I think he is, there is nothing except the humid air and the night. He gets up, I see the sofa cover, stretched taut over the seat, move as he perhaps brushes the dust off before he walks away. Has he gone, up the stairs to check on you?

MAN

BREAKING NEWS

'CHILD RAPED, KILLED, MOTHER SEVERELY ASSAULTED, BODY FOUND NEAR AIIMS, CHILD RAPED, KILLED,

MOTHER SEVERELY ASSAULTED, BODY FOUND NEAR AIIMS', he reads it the second time it crawls at the bottom of the TV screen on the dashboard of his car, he wants to press Pause, realises he cannot, needs to wait for the ticker to complete its cycle, there it is again, 'CHILD RAPED, KILLED, MOTHER SEVERELY ASSAULTED, BODY FOUND NEAR AIIMS', did Driver see him read this? Doesn't look like he did, Driver's eyes are fixed straight ahead, they have left India Gate and are now driving down Shanti Path, a ribbon of black laid out on the green, embassies on either side. No, this news cannot be about Balloon Girl and her mother, he dropped them off safely, he remembers the blue light on her face, the smell of soap in her hair, how they stared into the aircraft, dead children do not watch penguins, he closes his eyes but there's no escaping the ticker, 'CHILD RAPED, KILLED, MOTHER SEVERELY ASSAULTED, BODY FOUND NEAR AIIMS', it cannot be, his heart races, they have got it wrong, he wants to call the station, ask for the TV reporter, the one whose spasm he wants to hear on his home theatre, he wants to tell her how to get her facts straight, not put out such falsehood, 'CHILD RAPED, KILLED, MOTHER SEVERELY ASSAULTED, BODY FOUND NEAR AIIMS', maybe they are speaking of another child, another mother, there are so many of them near AIIMS, in the evenings when he is stuck in traffic there, he sees them, children and their mothers standing outside shops selling household appliances, TV, fridge, microwave, blender, utensils, non-stick, what if a husband or father has done it, his heart slows, he breathes deep, it's so cold inside the car that he gets gooseflesh on his arms, on his back under the shirt, he is hard again, he turns to adjust himself in the seat, his eyes are open under the dark glasses, Driver keeps driving, neither looking left nor right, there is an ad on TV, for some kind of cement that doesn't crack in the heat, the ticker keeps crawling, 'CHILD RAPED, KILLED, MOTHER SEVERELY ASSAULTED, BODY FOUND NEAR AIIMS', he switches the TV off, closes his eyes, tells Driver, let's go to AIIMS. If Balloon Girl is dead, raped and killed, shouldn't she be in the AIIMS mortuary? He needs to check on Balloon Girl and her mother.

These days, you cannot believe what you read in the papers or watch on TV, he needs to find out for himself.

CHILD

THE MALL

FROM the website of The Mall, the largest mall in India:

The Mall is an apogee of lifestyle distinction, it offers not only unprecedented scale in terms of its size but also an experience of unparalleled retail mix combined with entertainment and leisure attractions that have changed the concept of shopping mall experience. With the best location, a flat '0' km from south Delhi and a 16-lane approach on the national express highway. The Mall offers a wide range of facilities including premium international and domestic retail brands, anchor stores, hypermarket, seven-screen multiplex cinema, restaurants and coffee shops, food court, car showroom, fitness and meditation centre, beer garden, bowling alley, ice-skating rink, simulated golf course, kids' play zone and recreational zone.

The Mall is the largest operational shopping mall in India, with 1 kilometre of shopping experience on every floor.

~

One kilometre of shopping experience on every floor translates into 208 stores. Their break-up by type and number:

Anchor stores (one brand name but selling several kinds of goods including Debenhams, Next, Big Bazaar, Reliance, Timeout, Marks & Spencer): 11
Books, Toys, Cards and Gifts: 7
Entertainment and Services/Speciality Stores: 16
Footwear/Leather/Luggage: 18
Kids' Wear and Infant Care: 3
Men's Apparel and Accessories: 19
Spa and Salon: 4
Sunglasses and Optician: 2
Women's Apparel and Accessories: 21
Apparel Unisex: 33
Electronics: 12
Food, Grocery and Confectionery: 26
Home Furnishing and Accessories: 12
Lingerie/Inner Wear: 1
Personal Care: 6
Sports Wear: 6
Watches and Jewellery: 11

~

With state-of-the-art facilities for shopping, entertainment, food, fitness and luxury-brand shopping, it is a true Destination Mall that remains open for most of the day and night.

With three basement levels, The Mall has more than 2,500 car-parking spaces and offers amenities such as wide atrium spaces, high-speed elevators and escalators, multiple entry/exits.

~

It is through one of these multiple entry/exits that they will slip into The Mall tonight. Men, women and children from under the highway. They will enter a few hours after the last movie show, after all the bars and the restaurants have shut, lights and escalators are switched off except the emergency lights, of course, and when most of the security guards have gone to sleep. Exactly how many of them no one knows but there will be Aunty with her fake-blood Bandaged Baby, Uncle without his arms and legs, there will be Bhow's kith and kin, dogs big and small, quick and slow, dogs who know how to squeeze themselves through narrow openings in the door, babies who can walk through glass. There will be street vendors, adept at using their ten fingers to display at least twenty items, there will be Windshield Wiper Boy and the Cartwheel Dancer Girl, he with his mop, she with bright red ribbons in her hair.

And, of course, there will be Orphan, the youngest and the newest member of this family.

~

What will they do in The Mall?

Two hundred and eight stores, there's so much to do.

WOMAN

LECTURE NOTES

I WILL read aloud your father's college lecture notes, I will keep my voice low. If his ghost is here, he will listen. I think he will be pleased because I never did this when he was around. I will read a few paragraphs to give you a sense of what he loves, what he teaches.

~

Language, says Joseph Vendryes in his 1921 classic Le Langage, does not exist apart from the people who think and speak it. Its roots go deep into the consciousness of each one of us. It's from there that it draws sustenance enabling it to blossom into speech. Language exists on the lips of common people. Spontaneity is its life, it has a sort of elasticity natural to life. But this isn't the case with literary language. It develops from spoken language but grammar imposes a certain invariable order.

~

Your father's notes are in three exercise books.

I smell the paper and ink, the touch of his hands, his fingers, the years.

He uses blue ink. Every night when he sits down for dinner, there is a blue smudge below his nail on the side of the middle finger of his right hand. The pages, though, are spotless: there's no scratch, no streak, no smudge. No sign of any faltering.

~

Spoken dialect may be compared to a flowing stream constantly changing and literary language to a canal that issues out of it. In the latter, the flow of currents is checked by dams in the form of grammatical and other formal conventions, causing the water to stagnate. Vendryes compares literary language to the formation of a film of ice on the surface of a river. 'The stream which still flows under the ice that imprisons it is the popular and natural language; the cold which produces the ice and would fain restrain the flood is the stabilising action exerted by the grammarians and pedagogues; and the sunbeam which gives language its liberty is the indomitable force of life, triumphing over rules and breaking the fetters of tradition.'

~

I find the exercise books years after your father's death when I am cleaning up one day, brushing away dust mites in the cupboard, chasing out the silverfish from his books, watching them dart across the pages. On one page of his notes, in the margins, there is a pen sketch, very neat and elegant, of a tiny house by the banks of a river on which is a boat with its reflection. There are mountains behind the house between which a sun sets and birds fly. Does he draw that for you?

~

A time comes when a literary language, because of its highly conventionalised structure, becomes lifeless, artificial and colourless. It ceases to be intelligible to the people and then it is discarded and becomes dead. The need, then, is felt for the creation of a new language. One may naturally ask when and at what moment the course of linguistic evolution takes shape as to warrant the creation of a new language.

Marcel Cohen is of the opinion that the transformation of a language can be rapid. A period of a thousand years suffices for the accomplishment of the thrust from one language to the other. The history of the origin of Sanskrit, Prakrit and the Modern Indo-Aryan languages illustrates the law of birth and death of literary languages.

~

Is your father's ghost listening? He must be because he is so quiet, I can't hear him move as I do on certain nights when I cannot sleep.

The curtains are still, I cannot hear the windows creak.

Is he in your room? If he is, I hope he lets you know that. Maybe it's easier for you to tell him stuff that you cannot tell me. So look for new creases in your bedspread.

If they appear and if they move, that means he is there. You may switch off the air conditioner for a while because he may be cold, he's not used to it.

~

Magadhi is a Prakrit language which evolved from Sanskrit. To understand the relationship between these two, let's look at a simple parallel. Indo-Aryan speech comes before us in the shape of three portraits. Sanskrit is a portrait of a boy of ten years; Prakrit of the same boy who has turned fourteen while Modern Indo-Aryan is one who has turned into a man of nineteen. In the life of language, our one year is almost equal to a century.

~

I press the notebook's pages against my face. Each word your father writes crawls into me through my eyes and my mouth, I swallow your father's words, I feel them inside me, next to my heart. The notes get progressively difficult, I cannot read them out loud to you since there are mathematical symbols, technical terms that describe the formation of the language, its verbs, adjectives and tenses, the thousand-and-one rules of its grammar.

Of course, there is someone who can help me understand all this.

You know who I am talking about but I can tell you more about him only when your father's ghost leaves the house because I don't want him to hear, I want this to be our secret.

MAN

TRAIN FEAR

WILL he find Balloon Girl in the AIIMS mortuary?

Instead of an answer in his head, all he feels is fear. Like he has never felt before.

No, that's wrong, he has felt fear like this only once. Long ago, at a railway station.

He sits in a train, next to a window. He is a boy, he has both parents.

~

He is nine years ten years old. His father, his mother and he are on a train to where he doesn't remember. What he remembers is that his father cannot pay for air-conditioned or first class so they are in the general compartment, all windows open, his nose pressed against the bars, the iron-red paint peeling off in flakes, the heat from the engine and the fierce noonday sun floating inside, into his hair and his eyes.

The train has stopped at a station. They have run out of drinking water. Father gets off the train to fill the pitcher with water from the station's tap. Through the window, if he leans his head, he can see a row of taps and a very large crowd, passengers waiting, jostling, to fill their pitchers, bottles. His mother tell his father to hurry up because the train stops for just one or two minutes.

His heart begins to race, what if the mighty train with twenty, thirty coaches, two giant black engines, drivers with oil smeared on their faces and hands, as they lean out of their cabins, begins to move? The guard will wave his green flag, blow the whistle, there will be no one to stop the train.

His father has disappeared in the crowd at the tap.

He will lose his father.

Mother, I don't want water, he says, I will go thirsty, please tell him we do not need water, please tell him he should return soon, the train will start to move.

Mother laughs, you are not a baby any more, she says, you are a big boy now, why are you worried?

He cannot see his father, the vendors are pushing their trolleys away from the train, he hears the piercing whistle, that's the guard, he must be waving the flag. The train begins to pull out.

The sun blazing in the sky disappears, falls off the edge of the earth, day turns into night, blackness enters the coach through the window, cold and dark, he will never see his father again.

The train is gathering speed, the platform is now a living thing, pitch black, spread out all the way to where the sky meets the trees and the earth, heaving, rising until it curls up from the ground to the clouds, looks at him with many eyes blazing, many tongues in a mouth which is now as big as the night sky itself, opening wide as it descends, moving along with the train, as fast, until it's right in front, it snaps, bites off the bars of the window, enters the coach, swallows him and while he is travelling inside this monster, the only sound he can hear is of the train moving and his mother saying, you are not a baby any more, you are a big boy now.

~

That boy who is not a baby wants to kill his mother although he doesn't know what killing means. He wants to push her out

174

of the running train, he wants to watch her head roll down the tracks, her body get cut by the iron wheels, into two, three, four pieces, each piece tumbling, falling, and then speeding away like the trees and the ponds and the dirt-tracks that thunder past him, backwards, like in a stampede in reverse.

Why are you crying, Father asks, sitting next to him, the pitcher at his feet, full of water, and he turns, buries his head in his father's chest.

~

That fear is back as the car moves towards the hospital, that same cold blackness in the middle of the white-hot day.

This time it's the road that has become a living thing curling up into the sky, then coming down to break his car window and swallow him. He can hear his mother's laughter in his ears, her words, you are not a baby any more, you are a big boy now.

'We are almost there,' says Driver. 'Do you want me to stop at the hospital?'

CHILD

NEEL CHATTERJEE

'STEP on the bricks,' says Kalyani, 'one by one, don't worry, they won't move, you won't trip.'

'I know that,' says Dr Chatterjee as he stands at the edge of a puddle of dirty water outside her house, unsure how to cross. It is afternoon when the slum is deserted except for the very young and the very old, those who cannot work and those who can only play. Bhai, Ma, Pinki and Baba are all out at work, Kalyani is at home.

She has a fever, not high enough to worry but it makes her body ache, in the knees, in her head and heels. She is lying down when she hears his voice call out her name.

~

'What happened to your phone? I try calling but it's dead.'

'I had to give the phone back when I left Little House, I will get one soon.'

'How have you been?'

'I am fine, Doctor, just a mild fever.'

'Have you seen any doctor?'

'It's nothing, it will go away, please sit down.'

She shows him to the only chair in her house. Sunlight drips through the crack in the tin roof, stains the wall, falls into a pool of shadow on the floor.

The bed is rolled up neatly along one side of the wall next to the kerosene stove and the lantern.

He takes his shoes off before he steps inside. It's so hot that he reaches out to switch on a stand fan in a corner.

'That won't work,' says Kalyani, 'a few minutes ago, the power went off.'

'That's fine,' he says, 'no need.'

'All well, sir?'

'Yes, I have some news.'

'What happened?'

'Orphan left.'

'Left means? Has he found a home?'

'I hope so.'

'Hope?'

'He ran away.'

'How can he do that? He hasn't even learned how to walk.'

'They found a hole in the wall and he wasn't there, it was the morning after the storm, they suspect the wind broke the wall, someone came inside and took him away.'

'Where were you when the storm came?'

'I didn't go to work that night.'

'I don't believe this. Maybe he's hurt and he's still somewhere there in Little House.'

'No, no, they looked everywhere, Orphan's gone.'

'Then someone must have come and taken him away, he can't walk away on his own.'

'Mr Sharma is very angry.'

'I can imagine that.'

'They even suspect you since he went missing after you left Little House. They say you may have come and taken him away at night.'

'They can come and check my house. Have they sent you to do that?'

'No, Kalyani, never. And even if they do, I will never do that. I know you will never hurt Orphan.'

~

She lights the little gas stove to make some tea for him. He watches her move, the turn of her wrists, her fingers, as she opens a plastic box to spoon out the tea leaves, measures out the sugar, pours the milk from a small steel cup, adjusts the heat, leans back to see if the gas is right, so precise, as she pours out the tea into the cup a wisp of steam rises to touch her face.

~

Power is back, she shifts the stand fan to direct its draught towards him.

'Where do you think Orphan is right now?' she asks.

177

'It's been more than a week now,' he says, 'you think he's alive?'

'Please do not say such a thing.'

'What thing?'

'About the possibility of Orphan not being alive, let's not even mention it.'

'No, I am not so sure if he is safe.'

'Where do we look for him in this city?'

'They have put his name out on TV with a picture.'

'But what about those who do not watch TV, what if they are the only ones who know where he is?'

~

Tea is over, Kalyani sits on the floor, her back pressed against the wall, her eyes are closing, the fever must be coming back. It's time for him to leave.

'I came to ask you something,' he says.

'Yes?'

'I have been thinking about you.'

'Yes?'

'I don't know how to say it but I think of you a lot. After you left Little House, it's been, how do I say it, very empty there.'

'I had to leave, I need more money.'

'I can give you money.'

The words tumble out on their own, he doesn't want her to hear them but he cannot take them back.

'No, no, I don't want your money,' she says.

'No, that's not what I meant, I am very sorry.'

'Here, let me take your cup,' she says.

He hands her the cup and saucer, both still warm from the tea.

Their fingers do not touch.

178

'I will get going now,' he says, 'I need to be back at Little House for the night shift, you know how it's like.'

'It was nice of you to visit me,' she says, getting up to see him off at the door. 'And tell me about Orphan. I hope he's fine.'

'You should go see a doctor today,' he says.

'I think I should be fine by tomorrow,' she says.

'Let me know when you get a phone.'

'Sure, Doctor,' she says.

And he knows then that what he so badly wants is not meant to be. He steps on the same stones on his way out. The puddle has shrunk in the afternoon heat, and when he turns back to look, Kalyani is gone, the tarpaulin door still as in a painting.

MEANWHILE

REPORTER FROM LITTLE HOUSE
AT HER CHILD'S NURSERY SCHOOL

'WELCOME, parents, my name is Devika Bhattacharya, my colleague here is Megha Tripathi. We are class teachers of Nursery, Section E, New City International School, ranked first in Education World Survey for three successive years, 2011, 2012, 2013.

'Congratulations. As you know, more than two thousand children applied for thirty-five seats in this class. You are the lucky ones, we are delighted to have you here today as we embark on a journey to your child's future.

'First of all, please fill out the forms you received in the Admission Packet you picked up at the entrance, we will have an interaction. After which the principal and the director of the Primary Section would like to share a few words with you, thank you very much. If you need any water, the cooler is in the hallway outside.'

Payal Wadhwa has filled out her form.

'Nature of Work: Reporter, *Camera India*'.

Then, questions and questions, so many she loses count.

Are you a working mother? If no, why not? If yes, what are your hours in the office?

What is your favourite activity with your child?

What are the values you want your child to imbibe at school?
What do you do when your child misbehaves?
Which books did you last read with your child?
What's your view on children from the economically weaker section studying in the same class as your child?

She knows these answers by heart, an honest mishmash of some fact, some fudge.

She turns the form in, looks out through the window into the playground, a 7-foot-high wall with barbed wire that runs all around. So different from the crumbling wall she reported on yesterday, at Little House, the orphanage, after the freak thunderstorm, where a child went missing, a child, they say, younger than hers.

She looks around her, in the classroom.

So this will be where her son, her baby boy, who she has left at home since it's his sleeptime, will play each day five days a week over the next year, five, ten, twelve years. This is what he will see from next week: stickers of starfish, sea anemone, crab, oyster and coral, all with smiling faces. Sea creatures in a city over 1,300 kilometres away from the sea.

Payal closes her eyes to find herself at the bottom of the ocean where these sea creatures live, miles of water pressing her from above. She doesn't wish to swim back to the surface.

'Thank you, ladies and gentlemen, now we begin the interaction segment of today's programme. We would like you to share with the class an anecdote about your child. Please introduce yourself and mention your child's name.'

~

'Hello everyone, my name is Vanshikha, my daughter's name is Zara. She is all ready to start school next week, I am sure of that. How am I sure? Well, yesterday, when I came home from work, she told me, Mama, you keep telling me that if I go to school, I can study and become whatever I want to be and then I can go to office in the morning, have my own car, come back every day just like you and Papa. Yes, I said.

'To which she said, Mama, I start school next week. So when can I go to office, where is my car, where is my driver?'

Some laughter, some applause.

'Thank you,' says Devika, 'that's a very nice story, next one, please?'

'Hi, my name is Natasha. Three months ago, we moved from Boston where our son, Aryan, was born. We lived there for three years. One day, soon after we arrived here, he asked me, Mum, why is everyone's hair black here? In Boston, he said, it was white, gold, red, yellow, so many colours. I said, that is America, this is India, people in India are different, their hair is black. He said, Mum, we should buy colours for people in India because their hair is only one colour.'

~

Two more parents stand up and say something.

~

Payal buys a goldfish bowl for her son's third birthday. With a pair of goldfish, fish food, a plant and a little plastic frog that blows bubbles. She sets it all up so that he can see it first thing in the morning. He's delighted, he sits on the floor for one full hour, rapt, looking at the fish. The second night, she finds they have died. Both float up to the surface of the bowl, the water is clouded with dirt. She calls up the store and the man says, I am sorry, ma'am, maybe it's the temperature change, at night the water may have turned cold. She empties the bowl out, washes the pebbles and the frog, wraps it all in newspaper and keeps it away. The two fish go into the trash can in the kitchen. When he asks her about the fish, she says, they came for your birthday and now they have gone to their mother who lives in the sea.

~

'Let's all begin moving to the auditorium,' says Megha.

'There will be a short presentation. Refreshments are kept at the entrance.'

The auditorium lights hurt Payal's eyes. There's a giant screen that shows the first page of a PowerPoint presentation.

'The school joins with parents and community,' the principal starts, 'to assist the students in developing skills to become independent, self-sufficient adults who will succeed and contribute responsibly in a global community rooted strongly in the values that define Indian culture and family.'

The overhead lights are now switched off. The auditorium is dark. For the first time this evening, Payal feels a calm descend on her. Like what it feels under the ocean into the depths of which she swims down, the voice from the stage a rumble in the waves. 'At this school,' the principal goes on, 'the learning process is seen as one that is both challenging and enjoyable. Our students are encouraged to develop sound ethical values...' She gets up and walks out on tiptoe, closing the huge door behind her.

~

A group of teachers are huddled in the hallway.

'Can I help?' one of them asks her.

'Which way is the restroom?' asks Payal.

They show her the way.

She walks out of the school to her car parked three blocks away. She thinks of her child, not yet four, fast asleep at home, her husband at work, the school starting next week, six missed calls from her TV station, they must be asking for a follow-up to the story about the orphanage and the missing baby. As she approaches her car, she can see, between her and the vehicle, her child's years stretching ahead of her, Nursery, Class 1, Class 2, Class 3, Class 4, Class 5, Class 6, Class 7, Class 8, Class 9, Class 10, Class 11, Class 12 and then four years of college – and she wonders how she will pull through.

Without an ocean to dive in and sit on its floor, without the light streaming in through the miles of water above her, without the shoals of fish swimming past her eyes, the two goldfish searching for their mother, the coral tangled in her hair.

WOMAN

SHAVING BLADE

YOU will ask me when you wake up, Ma, why is this man, this student of my father, so important? You will ask me, Ma, why is he so special? Just because he says you can go to Father's cremation, offers you a glass of water, helps lift you up when you slip down?

That's why I need to tell you who this man is, how he is the only one who walks up to me when your father's lying on the floor, the only one who stands by my side to tell everyone there that there's nothing wrong in me wanting to go to the crematorium, that no one should stop me. He is the only one who offers me his arm, the arm I hold as he helps me get up from the floor. He is the one who sits next to me in the truck, next to your father's body, holding the ends of the wooden cot with both hands as the truck lurches and sways. He waves the incense smoke away from my eyes, he is the one who is with me when they lower your father down from the truck, place him on a raised cement platform, begin piling wood on him. He is the one who gives orders to the priest, checks the papers, pays the fee, arranges the flowers, he is the one who lights the pyre with your father's cousin, with whom I watch the flames, the smoke and, in the end, the embers. When a wind carries smoke and ash into my eyes, he moves a few feet in front of me to block them both.

He escorts me to my empty home.

He is the one who opens the door when Krishna walks in, carrying you, fast asleep. She says you woke up in the night saying you want to be with your mother and your father. She gives you to me, you sleep with your head on my shoulder. He says, I will hold her, you go and wash.

~

In the bathroom, your father's shaving brush rests on the sink exactly where he left it, with the blade he used this morning, foam flecked on the razor's edge. The soap he used is still wet. I sit on the red-tiled floor, pour water over myself, I cry.

MAN

NEWS TICKER

'CHILD RAPED, KILLED, MOTHER SEVERELY ASSAULTED, BODY FOUND NEAR AIIMS', the news ticker should move to the next item but it doesn't, it continues and he cannot believe what he's seeing but there they are, the letters, the words, 'IF THIS IS TRUE, IT RAISES A FEW QUESTIONS TO WHICH WE HAVE NO ANSWER YET AND UNTIL WE HAVE AN ANSWER, WE CANNOT PRONOUNCE ANYONE GUILTY, THERE IS RULE OF LAW AND DUE PROCESS IN A DEMO-CRACY, THE WORLD'S LARGEST, SO LET'S HOLD JUDGEMENT UNTIL ALL THE FACTS ARE IN, WE WILL TAKE A SHORT AD BREAK NOW, RETURNING TO THE MAIN STORY OF THE DAY.'

~

He switches off the TV but the news ticker is now streaming in a straight line, across the white-hot sky, like the trail of a jet plane, hard and unbroken, bending down in an arc to crawl across the windshield of his car, slide down the bonnet onto the road, then curl up to ride the trunk of a taxi in front, enter that vehicle, into the cellphone its passenger is using.

~

BECAUSE IF THIS ACTUALLY HAPPENED, HE SHOULD FEEL IT, HE SHOULD HAVE SIGNS, SYMPTOMS ON HIS BODY AND INSIDE HIS BODY AS WELL BECAUSE JUST AS THE VICTIMS, BALLOON GIRL AND HER MOTHER, CARRY EVIDENCE OF ALLEGED RAPE AND ASSAULT AND KILLING SO SHOULD THE PERPETRATOR BECAUSE IF HE DID RAPE, HE SHOULD HURT BECAUSE HE FORCED HIMSELF INTO HER, THERE SHOULD BE TRACES OF HER BLOOD ON HIM, CRUSTED SEMEN ON HER, THERE SHOULD BE SKIN, TISSUE UNDER HIS NAILS

~

Can Driver see this ticker that's crawling everywhere?

He can read English but can he read this hurried stream, its blue-white letters, cold and electronic, on his skin, warm and dark? Small caps that leave no trace once they come and go.

~

IF HE DOES RAPE HER, IF HE DOES KILL HER, HOW DOES HE RAPE HER? HOW DOES HE KILL HER? HE DOES NOT USE A GUN BECAUSE HE DOES NOT HAVE ONE, DOES HE STRANGLE HER? DOES HE CHOKE HER? AND WHILE HE DOES ALL THIS TO HER, WHERE

187

IS THE MOTHER? SHE IS NOT SITTING THERE QUIET, SHE WILL SHOUT AND SHE WILL SCREAM, SHE WILL CLAW AT HIS FACE, SHE WILL BITE, SHE WILL SCRATCH, BUT THEN WHERE ARE THE MARKS, THE CUTS AND THE BRUISES? UNLESS HE BEATS HER UNCONSCIOUS, SEVERELY ASSAULTS HER, BEFORE HE RAPES AND KILLS BALLOON GIRL, IMPOSSIBLE

~

Have we reached AIIMS? he asks.

Driver takes the Shah Jahan Road radial exit, past the florist at the corner of the road leading to Khan Market, heads south, takes a left on Ring Road, crosses one red light, passes Jor Bagh Metro Station, towards the hospital, the ticker runs across the leaves of the gulmohur trees that line the road.

~

HE DOES NOT USE A GUN BECAUSE HE DOES NOT HAVE ONE, DOES HE STRANGLE HER? DOES HE SIT ATOP HER, PINNING THE LITTLE GIRL DOWN, AND ALTHOUGH HE IS THIN, SHE IS A LITTLE GIRL NO MATCH FOR HIS WEIGHT, DOES HE GAG HER? WITH A PILLOW OR WITH A TOWEL? SO WHERE IS THEIR SMELL? THEY BOTH SMELL STRONG, THAT HE RECALLS DISTINCTLY, THAT'S WHY HE USED THE SOAP, WASHING MACHINE AND THE BATH. THEIR SMELL SHOULD BE ON HIM, THERE SHOULD BE EVIDENCE IN HIS HOUSE, ON THE BED, IN THE SHEETS, IN THE WASHING MACHINE? OR DID HE DO IT AFTER THEY SHOWER? BUT HE FEEDS THEM AFTER THE BATH, BREAD, ORANGE JUICE, RICE, HE ASKS THEM TO LIE DOWN IN THE GUEST ROOM

~

Slow down near the entrance, he says, as they pass the hospital, there is no Balloon Girl, no Mother, no one selling any balloons. Just an endless stream of patients and their crowd of visitors, with plastic bags carrying food from home, fruit, medicine, large X-ray envelopes. Shuffling, standing, walking, waiting. Behind them, another crowd, this one better dressed, many in doctors' white aprons, with placards. Another protest rally, his second of the day, this one against the government's announcement to reserve seats for backward-caste students.

A young woman shouts, 'No to Quota, Yes to Merit, No to Quota, Yes to Merit.'

Driver stops. A policeman says, keep moving, no parking here, no stopping here.

The news ticker moves on the crowd, its words breaking over the faces.

~

IF HE HAS DONE THIS, HOW DOES HE TAKE THEM DOWNSTAIRS INTO THE CAR? YOU MEAN TO SAY HE CARRIES BOTH OF THEM, ONE BY ONE, DOWN THE LIFT, HE BUNDLES THEM BOTH INTO THE CAR, WHAT IS SECURITY GUARD DOING AT THAT TIME? HE DRIVES DOWN THE HIGHWAY, ACROSS THE CITY, CARRYING A BODY AND A SEVERELY ASSAULTED WOMAN AND THEN HE OPENS THE CAR DOOR AND DUMPS BOTH OF THEM NEAR AIIMS? SURELY YOU MUST BE JOKING

~

They have crossed the hospital and are at Yusufsarai Market.

All shops are open. Pressure cookers, LCD TVs, microwaves, OTG, LG, Samsung, IFB, Bosch, Sony, Sanyo, Videocon, cellphones, the new Gurdwara, hardware stores, tiles, pipes, Karnataka Restaurant, Indian Oil Corporation Building, its business development office, for globalisation, for petrochemicals, for exploration and production, Gujarat Fisheries, Green Park Metro Station, Rhythm Restro Bar. No balloon, no girl, no mother.

Of course, he hasn't done anything. He loves her, didn't he restrain himself in the Bird Park, among the penguins and the pelicans? How can he ever hurt someone he loves so much, he tells himself, and the rest of the words are gone, the original ticker is back on his TV:

'CHILD RAPED, KILLED, MOTHER SEVERELY ASSAULTED, BODY FOUND NEAR AIIMS'

~

You go home, he tells Driver, I will drive, I don't need you now.

And he takes a U-turn at the next red light, heads back to AIIMS, he needs to check the mortuary.

CHILD

NIGHT PLAYGROUND

LIKE children, restless and excited, out on a school trip to a magical park for the first time, that's how they walk: pressed along one side of The Mall that faces the road, sidling against the Plexiglas billboards of the Ralph Lauren man in red, a black-and-white Priyanka Chopra in Guess, they walk under awnings, draped in shadow, towards Gate 12. This is the last gate to remain open because this is the one customers use when they are headed for the seven-screen cinema multiplex where the last show ends at 1 a.m., at least three hours after the last store in The Mall closes for the day.

It is minutes after 3 a.m., most of the guards have gone to sleep.

They know where to go, they know what to do – all of them except Orphan, of course, for whom this is the first night.

He sits on Bhow's back, fresh after being bathed and fed and having slept.

Whether Gate 12 is open or its guard is asleep or whether they glide through glass isn't clear, what's clear is that, one by one, they are all inside The Mall. Unseen and unheard. Even if their footsteps make a sound, no one hears that above the clatter of traffic that thunders up and down the highway.

~

They know where to go – all the spaces.

One kilometre of shopping on each floor means countless bends and corners, sharp and gradual, alcoves and clearings, corridors that abruptly branch out or gradually meander away from the main atrium into spaces out of bounds for people during business hours. The small space in front of one of the service lifts, for example, tucked away around a corner, used only for garbage cans that go up and down, to and from the parking lot. Or, the tiny hallway behind the Baskin-Robbins store's main display case, accessible through a small sliding door that has no lock. This is where they keep empty ice-cream cartons during the day, but at night, you can squeeze into that space and lie down. Then there are the big spaces waiting to be occupied, which fall vacant when an entire shop moves out, when its shelves, ceilings, lights all are torn down. When one tenant's checked out and the other one hasn't moved in. At least a thousand-plus square feet of prime commercial real estate, the entire floor gouged out. Italian vitrified tiles or wood flooring, all ripped off to expose mud and earth in which grows a forest of dead wires, walled in on three sides by smudged glass marked by crosses in chalk and draped under endless rolls of tarp. There are many such spaces in The Mall in which stores are born and die.

Then there is Food Court on the third floor: twenty-six stores, only five of them restaurants with their private areas, the others share a sprawling dining hall packed with chairs and tables still littered with leftovers from last night waiting for the cleaners later in the morning. The counters are there to be climbed over so that the cooking areas, the gleaming steel ovens and sinks can be explored. Or chairs and tables joined to make beds for the night.

And, of course, there are the stores — after all, that's what The Mall is all about.

Stores, stores and stores.

Right and left, up and down.

Big Bazaar and Debenhams, Zara, Marks & Spencer, Kidzone, the children's play area, almost half a floor, Next, Reliance, Westside, Mothercare, Promod, Vero Moda, Nike, where you enter and hide right through the day if you know where to hide. Each has a trial room, some of these have sofas and chairs, ideal to crawl under. Each floor has toilets, too. Stalls, sinks, tissue dispensers, liquid soap gel, automated sprinklers, and optical sensor-run flushes.

Spaces to play, places to hide.

And all of these, at this time, dark or dimly lit, by emergency lights switched on after midnight, adding to the shadows that help them hide.

~

If they know where to go, they know what to do – each one his or her own thing, sometimes alone, sometimes in groups, each night something different, so endless are the possibilities.

Depending on what you need.

If you are tired at the end of the day and you want to rest, even sleep, you lie down in one of these spaces. Choose a spot in an emptied-out store, right next to its glass wall if you wish to fall asleep watching the sky and the stars. If you are not too particular about a bedroom with a view, it's easier. Pick any of the hundreds of spots all over The Mall, behind the ice-cream display case, in front of the service lift, even next to the escalator. Or in the children's play area where there are bouncies to lie down on, small tree houses, dolls' houses to move into; a Thomas railway train, each coach so big it can serve as a bedroom.

If you are hungry, head straight to the Food Court and on the way, keep looking inside trash cans. Most of them are cleared by late evening but an entire set is kept for the morning shift that starts at 8 a.m. You may strike gold in the ones next to Kidzone, where the carousel and the jungle gym are. Because food isn't allowed in the play area, many parents who are new to The Mall, who buy food, have to discard it before they are allowed to enter. So on some days, the trash cans here are Leftover Heaven. You will find sandwiches barely nibbled, Cola glasses half drunk. And because of the air conditioning, chances are the food hasn't gone bad.

If you wish to wash, slip into the bathroom. Get up on the sink, get into the sink, each is sturdy, squeeze liquid soap and wash your hair, armpits, between the legs, all the areas you cannot wash when you live on the highway. Dry yourself with paper towels in the stalls. On some nights, like tonight, when it's very hot, you don't need to dry yourself. Many nights, Aunty walks around dripping, her wet hair plastered across her face. She says it's cooler this way, to let the water from your skin evaporate and take the heat away.

Then there is play, this is what they do most of the time. Mischief, but harmless.

All the while ensuring that nothing is damaged, no guard wakes up, no one is caught because one wrong step and they will tighten security, keep them out for ever.

So Uncle will crawl into the display window of Tommy Hilfiger (Men's), Windshield Wiper Boy and Cartwheel Dancer Girl will pluck clothes from one of the mannequins and wrap them around Uncle, prop him against the wall so that you cannot make out that he has neither arms nor legs, place a tweed cap on his head, a woollen scarf around his neck. Sometimes they will pick up a shopping cart from outside Reliance Store and give Uncle a ride in it, up and down the hallway, fast and slow, and he will say, his eyes gleaming like a child's, I wish I had this with me on the street, so much easier to be pushed to the cars – when the light turns red – in a shopping cart than to crawl on the road keeping an eye out for phlegm and spit.

Aunty will undress, take a shower at the sink in the Ladies' Rest Room, and, holding Bandaged Baby in one hand and her wet clothes in the other, she will run down the hallway, naked, she will squeeze into a clothes shop and try out everything she can in whatever time she has. From jeans, blue and black, to underwear of all colours, from saris to jackets lined with fake fur. She will take Bandaged Baby to Mothercare, get her to try out the brightly coloured onesies, soft woollen caps and socks with little bows around the ankles. She will tell one of the dogs to stand outside and keep a watch just in case a guard wakes up and comes to check.

Kids head for Kidzone where they ride the carousel, its music and lights switched off but the big wheel turning.

Many of them stand there, press their noses against the glass wall and look at New City spread before them, cars and trucks on the highway, and because they are so high above they can point to where they live on the street, to the exact patch on the pavement.

Some nights, when there is a power-cut in the neighbourhood, other children walk into The Mall to sleep in the atrium under the giant glass roof, some of them are the rich children from Apartment Complex that's a mile away, children in night clothes, matching shirts and pyjamas, and they all lie down and look up at the night sky. On other nights, when they are more adventurous, they race each other in the atrium, play with the dogs and the children from under the highway, shout, hear the echo of their voices bouncing off steel and glass.

And then the hours pass and they begin to yawn wherever they are, in the trial room of a store, on the counter of a kitchen or next to a trash can, and as the first red-white light of day smudges the night above the highway, reflects off the sweeping glass exteriors of The Mall, they begin to leave. Aunty and Bandaged Baby, Uncle and Windshield Wiper Boy, Cartwheel Dancer Girl, all vendors and dogs, back to the traffic intersection where they came from. To face the next day, to seek out the kindness of strangers at the traffic lights, between red and green.

~

Tonight, as they leave, there is someone in The Mall who is watching them, someone who doesn't need to slip out like them because she lives here. Very few have seen her, no one knows how old she is. Her eyes, wet and teary, catch the first light of day as she watches them from a window in Europa, the biggest theatre in the multiplex.

Her name is Ms Violets Rose – yes, two flowers in one name, a tiny bouquet, if you so wish.

WOMAN

JOHNNY'S MOVIE

ONCE you are up, I would like us to watch a movie together, a short film, no more than ten minutes long, there are no actors in it.

You tell me when you call me from New City that you don't want to watch movies or read books or listen to any of the rubbish I say but maybe you will change your mind when you wake up, unpack, settle down in this house.

Because only when you are ready to sit in the same room as I – we do not have to talk – can you and I watch the movie together.

Give it five minutes, if you do not like what you see, walk away, do something else. I won't, I will watch the entire movie because it seems new to me every time I watch it.

~

There's a little story about this movie. The man who made it is a boy I taught in kindergarten at St Aloysius.

One evening, a year or so ago, just after dinner, I am preparing to go to bed with the Nobel book I told you about, it's the one by Patrick White, when the phone rings and I wonder who can this be at this time, and when I pick up the phone, a man's voice mentions my name and says, 'Can I speak to her?'

And I say, 'Yes, this is she.'

And he says, 'Ma'am, do you remember me?'

'Sorry, I do not,' I say. 'Who is this?'

And he says, 'My name is Maheshwar Agarwal. My nickname in school and at home was Johnny, you were my teacher at St Aloysius Day School. I got your number from the school.'

I am flustered, I am very embarrassed that I do not remember anyone called Maheshwar or Johnny, maybe my memory is failing, but I do not wish to appear rude so I say, 'Yes, yes, I remember, how are you, Johnny?'

He's a bright kid, he senses the hesitation in my voice.

'It's perfectly all right, ma'am, if you do not recall me, because I do not expect that you will. You had so many students. I didn't do particularly well for you to remember me and I never was in touch. In fact, I didn't do well in school at all, I used to skip school to watch movies. I failed twice in my Board exams and then I somehow passed. I took some kind of a course and now I work in a TV station, ma'am.'

This time, I do not lie: 'I am sorry, Johnny, I do not watch a lot of TV.'

'Ma'am, I am calling,' he says, 'to tell you I am sending you a movie I made.'

I want to know why he is sending it to me but I don't know how to ask this question or whether I should ask it.

An uncomfortable pause which he rushes in to fill.

'Ma'am' – I can hear his nervousness –'you are the only teacher I still remember from my school.'

I let him speak.

'My wife says your KG teacher is the one who knows you best because she knows you when you know nothing, she is the one who teaches you how to read, write, count and I never got to say thank you to you. That's why I want you to watch my first movie and tell me what you think.'

He says this all in one breath.

'Of course I will,' I tell him. 'When are you coming to see me?'

'I do not live in your city, ma'am,' he says, 'let me send you the DVD.'

'Sure,' I say and I give him my address and Johnny keeps his word.

The movie arrives in two days, just a DVD, no note, no sender's address.

~

The most interesting thing about the movie is that it is all from existing material. There is not one image Johnny has photographed or recorded, not one chord of sound he has created. He has taken two days of TV news and commercials, almost eighteen hours of video and audio, mixed them all up, cut and spliced images from these to make a film that lasts barely ten minutes.

It's about a boy, ten years eleven years old, who builds a ship near a city called New City and then drags it to the sea, hundreds of kilometres away, from where he sets sail, down the coastline along Orissa, Andhra Pradesh, around Sri Lanka, across the Indian Ocean, up to Africa, south south south to Antarctica to get some ice for his dying father.

Where does he get his remarkable images from? Well, that's the mystery of the film and you and I will try to figure it out.

I can guess some. Like, I think, he gets the image of the ocean from a news item on an oil spill in the Pacific; the morning mist from a shot of the smoke-filled sky after a bomb explosion. These are what strike me the first time I watch the movie, before I remember that summer afternoon your father went in search of ice.

MAN

FOUR BODIES

'DO you have a name for the patient?' asks the AIIMS Mortuary Man.

'A girl with a red balloon and her mother. They live somewhere here, they were here last night.'

'I am not so sure, I have four bodies,' says Mortuary Man, '500 rupees to view each body. No haggling, fixed rate.'

'I will give you 700.'

'Not more than one or two minutes each body.'

'I will try to be quick.'

'Half the money now, balance when you leave.'

He counts the 1,400.

'You have a handkerchief?'asks Mortuary Man. 'Cover your nose.'

The sun has set, post-mortem time is over. He hears the noise from the anti-quota protest rally, the whine of a police car, the shouting of slogans. By men and women.

'What are you waiting for?' says Mortuary Man as he pushes him inside. 'Get in quick, finish your business, do you want me to lose my job?'

~

He steps into a swarm of flies, grey and black, moving like a shadow in the thick, stale air of the mortuary. They fly into his face, buzz in his ears, stain his shirtfront, crawl down his fingers. One nibbles at his nails. As if he himself is a fresh, new body that's walked in. One hand covering his nose with his handkerchief, he uses the other to swat them away but the flies, having explored the bodies in the room, have nowhere to go. Above their buzz, he hears the sound of someone crying.

An elderly man squats in the corner on the cement floor, below a platform on which lies Body 1, a woman's body. Next to him is a white plastic bag, its mouth open. She is on her back. Her thin legs are splayed, the skin peeled from below her right breast all the way down to her knees to reveal bone, fat and muscle. White, yellow, red, but death has drained all her colours to a burnt black-brown lit by one electric light bulb which hangs from the ceiling right above her body.

The room is windless but the bulb swings in a tiny arc. Maybe it's the breath from the crying old man. Who is she? His wife, daughter, sister? Her head has been battered in, blood has matted the hair, her forehead is crushed pushing the entire face down, like a balloon, its air run out.

Body 1 is not Balloon Girl.

~

Body 2 and Body 3 are covered, each on a stretcher under the hospital's regulation blue sheet pulled over the head. Must be deaths in the hospital. Post-surgery, pre-surgery, disease. Each one at least 5 feet tall, head to toe, so neither is Balloon Girl, neither can be Balloon Girl.

But he will check just to be sure.

Body 2 is a man, his eyes open. There is a cut across his chest freshly shaven and it's now stitched, the heart must have given way.

Body 3 is a woman so fat her stomach drips, like tallow, over either side of the stretcher. She reminds him of the woman who waddled out of her car on the highway.

Not Balloon Girl, for sure.

~

Body 4 is no girl, she is a woman. Beautiful.

She makes his heart ache, she makes everything in the room disappear so that now they are alone, she and him. Gone are the flies, the stench, the old man crying. Her hair is black, silk, cropped close, her skin the colour and smell of lavender. The handkerchief is off his nose as he bends to look at her more carefully. Is she really dead, he wonders, because he feels the fullness of life rise up from her, envelop him like a warm wave.

She is on her back, like the other bodies, but her face, flawless, is turned to his side, her eyes closed, her arms straight, on either side of her body. He touches her below the chin, on her black mole, his finger traces her lips, there is a faint wetness, he slips the finger in, feels her teeth and gums, runs the finger all along the edge of her right shoulder down to her breasts. He looks to his left and right, no one's watching, the old man is gone, he can hear people outside, the sound of talk and tears, but he cannot see anybody means nobody can see him so he quickly bends, kisses the hollow between her breasts where he thinks she is still warm.

He is very hard, he wants to undress.

No, he will not hurt her.

He only wishes to lie down next to her, keep looking up at the ceiling, and as and when they shut the mortuary, switch off the lights, he will close his eyes and sleep. The platform on which she lies is narrow so he will need to adjust himself, snuggle against her, but he won't disturb her at night. Before he climbs up onto the platform, he wants to breathe her in so he places one hand on each of her knees and begins to part her legs, slowly, as if she were sleeping and he doesn't want to wake her up, all the while looking at her face.

A fly sits on her lips, he swats it away. He lowers her head when he hears her: 'What do you think are you doing? Let's go.'

~

'Let's go, let's go,' shouts Balloon Girl. 'Someone's coming.'

She stands at the entrance, she gestures to him to get out.

He turns away from Body 4, breathless, breaks into a run.

When he exits the mortuary, it's already dark. Street lights are on, so are the lights in the hospital's rooms and wards. OB vans from TV stations crowd the entrance, filming the protests where a new group of students has taken over from the previous one.

'Where's my balance?' shouts Mortuary Man. 'You took such a long time, I was sending someone inside to check on you. Did you find what you were looking for?'

He doesn't register a word. 'You found the body you were looking for? Is that body in there?'

'No, it's not,' he says.

'That's good news then, whoever you came to look for is alive,' laughs Mortuary Man.

Balloon Girl is standing next to him, pulling at his arm.

'Don't waste any time, let's go,' she says.

He pays the balance and turns to walk away.

'Or maybe the body you want hasn't been released by the hospital, come back tomorrow, I will be here. Half-price, only 250 rupees.'

Mortuary Man laughs again, he can see the gleam in his eyes, has he seen him with Body 4? No, too late to worry about such things as he walks, runs, to his car, Balloon Girl by his side. If she hadn't been there to warn him, he could have been caught. So he turns around to thank her for looking out for him, for coming to get him out of there, but Balloon Girl's gone.

CHILD

VIOLETS ROSE

BHOW barks once, twice, to clear her throat. She needs to speak.

It's past midnight, Bandaged Baby is asleep, so is Orphan, both on the same tattered quilt, like siblings united.

Seven consecutive nights of play in The Mall and they are all tired so today they will sleep early. It's late on Sunday, traffic is thin, the traffic lights are set to constant blink mode. Uncle tries his luck, crawls to the occasional car that slows down but no one even stops to look. All windows are rolled up for air conditioners to run at maximum efficiency because there is no let-up in the heat – the night sky is cloudless, black and fierce.

'Come back, Uncle,' says Bhow, 'I have an announcement to make.'

They sit in a circle, the dog in the centre.

~

'I know we all need to sleep so let me come straight to the point, this is about Orphan and what we should do with him because the time has come for me to take my leave. I need to go back to Little House. A dog has her turf and if she leaves it, she loses it. I am the one who brought Orphan here and I think it's unfair on my part to leave him here, to expect that all of you take care of him, that I give you one extra mouth to feed.

'There's another thing. Orphan is the youngest of us all, a mere infant, someone has to teach him to walk, someone has to teach him to talk. Aunty is the only one who could have helped but she is busy with Bandaged Baby. I cannot leave him alone since I have seen his mother walk up to the steps of Little House and leave him there, I have seen tears in her eyes.'

'Why not take him back to Little House, Bhow?' asks Aunty. 'At least someone will take care of him there – they will feed him better food than we can give, teach him what he needs to learn.'

'No, he isn't going back, Aunty. His mother has left him, his nurse has left him, his doctor, too. And that morning after the storm, I see Orphan crawl out through the hole all by himself. Something, someone pushes him out and so, no, he cannot return, that will be against his wishes, against his best interests. But he cannot live here, on the pavement under the highway. Sorry, no disrespect to any of you, but he is a human child and I got him here, he's my responsibility. So he will move across the street.' Bhow turns around to face The Mall. 'He will live there with Ms Violets Rose, two flowers in one name, a tiny bouquet, if you so wish.'

~

'You mean the cinema woman, the one who lives inside the theatre?' asks Windshield Wiper Boy. 'Have you met her? Is she willing to take him in?'

'I haven't talked to her but I can tell you one thing,' says Bhow, 'she remains largely invisible but ever since Orphan has been coming with us to The Mall, I see her every morning, looking at us as we leave.'

"How do you know?"

'I turn to look back and I see the day's first light bouncing off her glasses.'

'Can she take care of him?' asks Uncle. 'Isn't she too old?'

'That's exactly why she can, Uncle, she is older than New City, she has the wisdom of ages, she can take care of him,' says Bhow.

'Why doesn't she come out and talk to us, Bhow?' asks Aunty. 'I hardly see her.'

'Don't get her wrong,' says Bhow. 'For so long has she lived in the dark that she doesn't want to step out into the light. Maybe her eyes hurt. But I will tell you one thing, she likes the fact that we come to play in The Mall at night, it makes her feel less lonely. She likes to hear the noises we make.'

'How are you so sure that she will take him in?' asks Aunty.

'Let's find out,' says Bhow. 'I will take Orphan to her, right away. He is sleeping, so now is the best time to carry him. You don't have to come with us, you all need rest. And we do not want to create a crowd, we do not want to frighten Ms Rose.'

'We will miss Orphan,' says Cartwheel Dancer Girl. 'He never says anything but I am beginning to like him. I can take care of him.'

'You are an angel,' says Bhow. 'I am sure you will take good care of him but he needs to be away from here. And he's not going far away, he will be across the street and I am sure once he learns how to speak and walk and run, Ms Rose will send him to play when you go visiting The Mall.'

~

Orphan's eyes are closed in sleep as they all help place him on Bhow, adjust his legs on her back, rest his head against hers.

Watched by all, Bhow waits for the road to clear before they cross the street, climb up the embankment that separates the lane leading to The Mall from the highway, walk along the wall, slip into Gate 12, which leads to the Europa cinema theatre where Ms Violets Rose waits in the dark.

MEANWHILE

A DAY IN THE LIFE
OF KALYANI'S MOTHER

'IT'S your turn tonight, Ma,' says Kalyani.

'I am not well,' Ma says.

'Tell us what happened to you, that will make you feel better,' says Kalyani.

~

'All of you know the house where I work for Didi. In Apartment Complex, right at the top, on the 20th floor, so high that although it's been more than a year I've been working there, I still get dizzy every time I step out onto the verandah and look down. One day, a friend of Didi's told me the view from the verandah is like when you look out of the window of an aeroplane. They have one lift in the building only for us. I don't know how to read but it's written on a poster on the wall next to the lift's button. In English: the lift is for servants and pets.

'Before I sweep and scrub the floors, I wash the dishes. Above the kitchen sink is a window that opens out onto the verandah. Standing there, I see green as far as my eye can see; the tops of trees, just like in our village, and beyond that, the highway. But this morning, when I look out, my head begins to spin. I think it's the height but soon, my legs, shoulders and arms all begin to hurt.

'I need to take breaks during which I sit down on the floor of the kitchen, close my eyes, that seems to reduce the pain. Didi walks in, asks what is wrong. I don't wish to hide anything from her so I tell her that my body hurts. She says, forget the dishes today, just do the floors and go home. Don't forget to take some medicine from me when you leave because there is a party at home tomorrow. At least eight to ten people have been invited, we will serve them snacks, drinks and dinner so there will be a lot of work to do, many dishes to wash. I want you to be here tomorrow and the day after, that's why no need to tire yourself out today. Don't forget to take the medicine when you go.

'Twice, I feel I am falling down. After the floors are done, when I tell Didi I am going home, she gives me a banana and says, eat this because you should not have medicine on an empty stomach. She makes me take two green capsules. Rest for a while, sit down on the floor, leave after ten, fifteen minutes, says Didi.

'The capsules work like magic. Ten minutes, the pain is gone.

'Don't forget, says Didi, as I leave, tomorrow is a big day. Tell people at home that you will be returning late tomorrow night. Take this capsule for the morning, she says, have it just before you come.'

~

'I hope you are feeling better, Ma,' says Kalyani. 'If not, I can go to Didi's tomorrow and help her out.'

'The capsules have worked, I will be all right, I feel better already,' says Ma.

After dinner, she washes the dishes, empties out the coal oven. The ceiling has sprung a tiny leak, a thin stream of water from the tank on the roof scurries down the wall, collects into a puddle from where it darts into the cracks on the floor. Kalyani puts a bucket against the wall to collect this water.

'We will have to fix it tomorrow,' says Baba, 'before the rains.'

~

They live in one of a row of rooms, small rectangles cut out of brick and mortar, each with a tarpaulin sheet as a door, the tin in the roof beaten, cracked in many places. These rooms are owned by a slumlord who comes once a month to collect the rent. Many families who live here are from Bangladesh, all illegally migrated, who have, to escape detection by the local police, changed their names from Muslim to Hindu. The police know this, the owner knows this, both use this information to threaten, coerce and extort. You complain about water leaking, you should be lucky I am letting you stay here, the slumlord will say if Baba goes to complain. At least once every six months, there is pressure from higher-ups – usually following a debate in the press or a security threat – to crack down on the migrants. Suddenly, platoons of policemen show up, in helmets and with riot shields just in case bricks and stones are thrown. Bulldozers run through homes, what's inside – pots and pans, clothes and boxes – is thrown outside. Some residents are picked up, taken to the detention centre in the city. But most are out at work where they stay until they get news that the police have left. Some families get split, wife is arrested, husband hides, children are picked up, some tears are shed but within hours, it all settles down, the police are paid off, the slumlord raises the rent saying his risk has gone up.

~

The children are sleeping, Baba's eyes are closed, too, one arm over his face to shut off the light that slips into the room through the gap in the door.

Ma imagines Pinki playing on the blue slide in The Mall. The capsules have helped ease the pain, banished the fever, but not the heaviness she feels almost crushing her forehead. She tries to distract herself with new questions, new concerns.

What will Kalyani do now that she has left the orphanage? Why did she leave? Why does she look so drained?

We don't need her money immediately, all of us are earning, so she can take some time off. She says she already has a job at a new hospital. What kind of a job is it?

They all need voter-identity cards otherwise they will have to keep paying the police; they need ration cards; they need to save money; they need to find a husband for Kalyani.

She worries about Pinki after she heard last month that a thirteen-year-old girl, a few rooms down, ran away with a twenty-five-year-old good-for-nothing boy, returned after two weeks, pregnant. What if something like this happens to Pinki? And Bhai? Someone has talked to her about a girl for him, time to get him married so that his wife can come and help you, how long will you run this house but, no, Bhai is still a boy, let him grow up, let him earn, save some money.

She hopes Baba doesn't fall ill, how will he pull that cycle rickshaw? Even when he is healthy, his legs, his arms are so thin, so weak. Their savings, all of it in a tin box, underneath the blanket, will be gone once they have to see a doctor.

She has heard frightening stories in the neighbourhood, of an entire family's six months' savings gone for just a few blood tests, an X-ray, two visits to the doctor.

Fear swirls like floaters, brightly coloured, in front of her eyes as they close to the drip of water from the roof into the bucket. She times the drips, roughly one a minute. When the bucket is full, it will be time to wake up.

WOMAN

SHORTEST STORY

THE shortest love story ever told is when a parent tells her child that she loves a man who is not her father. Because that's all she needs to say.

There is a man, he isn't your father, he loves me and I love him.

Whatever else she says, by way of explanation, serves no purpose because, for the child, this new love is always a kind of betrayal.

~

That's why I will keep this short:

Yes, your father's student and I love each other.

And as I say this, I can see them come, the fireflies in the dark, ready to enter our heads, light the darkest of our dreams.

MAN

THE FLIES

A FLY from the AIIMS mortuary slips into his car and sits on his dashboard. He tries to swat it away, he turns the fan

on to maximum, rolls all four windows down but it doesn't
leave.

~

He cannot avoid the flies just as he cannot avoid the poor.

Wherever he looks, wherever he goes, they are there, many
many more of them than there are of him. They stalk him,
look him in the eye. Whether they stand or sit, crawl or
crouch, cry or laugh. Or, even when they make love, as he sees
them once, in the middle of the road in the middle of the
night, they keep looking at him. At traffic lights, they tap and
claw at his windows. Leave trails on glass. Of sweat and slime,
like the dead do in movies. They even look like the dead,
many of their faces half-eaten by disease. Some have noses
missing, their lips chewed off. Some have black hollows where
once there were eyes, stumps where once were limbs, wounds
and sores where once was skin.

They speak the language of those whose tongues are twisted
beyond repair. They use few intelligible sentences, theirs is a
rambling, an incoherent garble of beg and beseech. Some fall
to the ground and stay there, sniff at his trouser-legs, rub
themselves against the heels of his shoes. Like lonely dogs do,
when in heat. Others sprawl on pavements, their legs splayed,
their heads thrown back as they sleep.

So many of them crawl out at night that he fears he will trip
and fall right into them, into their mass, damp and dark. Like
the basket of bait, fresh worms, grey and slimy, he sees at the
fish market. Once they suck him in, their faces will touch his,
his fingers will slip into their mouths, their lips and tongues
will meet. They may even make love to him, rape him, and if
he's lucky, they will let him do whatever he wants to do to
them in return for money.

That's on the road.

~

Off the road, at home, when he sits down to dinner, they stand outside his room, looking in.

Like mournful pets kept out, they stare at him through the window or the door. If either is made of glass, he can see them. All standing in line, young and old, big and small, looking at his hands as his fingers pick up food and drink, their eyes following each movement from plate to mouth, from glass to lips.

They don't spare him even if he hides in a place they cannot see. Because they know he is there, they smell him out, like dogs, they pound the wall, scratch at the plaster, crack the cement. Like bawling infants who do not have words to either express or explain their hurt or anger, they sometimes hit their heads against the wall. Hard, harder, hardest, until they bleed. Until blood, thick red and brown, flows down their faces, mixes with their drool and sweat, loops back to enter their mouths through their parted lips.

Most shameless are mothers with children. Like the one he sees when he stops under the highway, next to the traffic lights across from The Mall. She shows him her tongue, her nipples, once she shows him her vagina when she lifts her sari all the way to her waist and before the lights turn green, she shows him her bandaged baby. The sight of the baby makes him hard, she makes him throw up as well. Then there is a man at the same signal, who is only face and chest. He crawls up to the car and smiles at him. Give me money, he says, mocking, give me money and ask me anything in return, I will do it. I will show you how I shit, how I pee and how I fuck. You want to see that? Given that I have no legs, no arms, do you wish to see how I hold my woman?

~

On National Geographic, he watches the close-up of a fly.

It's washing itself, rubbing its front legs, the voice-over says it was resting, minutes earlier, on a trash heap near an open sewer in the city.

The camera slows down.

He sees the brown, black flakes of filth that the fly so lovingly caresses, its compound eyes glistening. The fly stops moving, balances itself on its front legs and cleans its hind legs, both up in the air. Then back to the front legs which it uses to clean its face, its eyes, all the while trembling hard, rubbing against each other, he can count the bristles around its eye, one, two, three, four, five, six, looks like hard black hair, and then suddenly, there's the sound of something like an explosion, a flash of light, and the fly is on its back, its legs flail, convulse, and then it's dead.

Someone swats the fly.

That's how he wants to kill these flies, one by one, night after night, he wishes he could stop those legs from moving. Because they frighten him, they become blades that carve him open, slice right through his head and his heart. Empty out whatever is inside him. Like a butcher cleans a chicken, they wring his neck, let his entire blood drip, take out the nerves, the skin, the fat, all the insides, all that's not edible.

And then they begin to fill him up, every space there is – between the arteries and veins, in between the bones – with guilt, big and black, fresh and bleeding.

~

He doesn't want to meet the flies, he won't go home tonight.

CHILD

FLICKER, TREMBLE

FROM the evidence so far, Bhow is a dog who not only has a strong sense of fairness but one of duty as well and that's why as soon as she finds a little clearing in the shadows inside The Mall, just a few steps away from Europa, Bhow stops, looks left, looks right, smells no one coming, goes down on all fours, gently eases Orphan off her back, rings herself in a protective curl around him, and tells him the story of Ms Violets Rose.

How much of it Orphan understands isn't clear but one thing is: his eyes and ears remain open as long as Bhow speaks.

~

'Deep inside The Mall, not far from where you and your friends from under the highway play, inside Europa, the most fancy of the seven cinema theatres in the multiplex, in a space which no one can see, lives Ms Violets Rose. Funny name that is, two flowers in one name, a tiny bouquet, if you so wish. Indeed, she looks like a plant because she is always in a green cotton dress dappled with leaf-patterns; her arms and legs so thin that it hurts looking at them, they resemble slender stalks and stems in the way they move when she walks. Look carefully and you will think Ms Rose has uprooted herself from a flower bed, brushed the earth and mud off, walked out of a garden in the morning – the brooch in her white hair glinting like dew, freshly fallen.

'How old is she no one knows. Some say she is a hundred

years old, in human years, some say two hundred, but, obviously, that's an exaggeration. You may, if you do not know anything about Ms Rose but only see her in a crowd, not even look at her twice. You will think she is an old woman clocking the hours until the very end with nothing left to do.

'Because in New City, where six out of every ten people are under thirty, where lights shine bright with hope and ambition, life and leisure, there is no place for someone as ancient as her, someone who, at first glimpse, is little more than a shadow, pale and bloodless, resting in a forgotten corner, a mere flicker of light, a tremble of the theatre's curtains.

'However, Ms Rose is anything but. Her eyes have a perpetual gleam, each step a spring in the dark. Because this, Europa, is her home. She knows this place. She knows The Mall's multiplex inside out, left, right, centre. For this is her home long before The Mall is even a drawing on a sheet, long before glass and steel begin to line up in the sky.

'This is her home when it is all farmland here, when wheat and mustard grow on either side of dirt-tracks, hard and unbroken, under a constant cloud of dust kicked up by a scorching summer wind that blows in from across the desert to the west. When Ms Rose is a young woman, when she and her father and her mother watch the first prospectors arrive, begin buying land around their farm, plot by plot, day by day. She watches cranes and excavators trundle in to gouge out holes in the earth so big they look like they have been made by something that's come hurtling down from space. Each hole then becomes home to a foundation which, in turn, props up an entire building, ten, twelve floors, four apartments to each floor, three rooms to each apartment, each room like a cell in this creature called New City that grows bigger and bigger with each hour, day, month and year. Until they start working on The Mall, brick by brick, steel rod by steel rod, glass by glass, day by night.

'So when her parents die, suddenly, leaving her nothing because they sell the land and there's no inheritance for their daughter, Ms Rose decides to make her new home in Europa, the premium theatre in the multiplex, because it's the one place where she can hide since it's always in the dark, where the seats are deep and large, where Ms Rose knows how to squeeze herself into spaces most unusual just as we, dogs, do under parked cars, between rickshaws, on top of garbage heaps.

'She knows which spaces exist where inside the theatre.

'Between two adjacent seats. Between one seat and the other in front. Underneath a seat, on the steps, pressed against the handrail. In the margins left uncovered by the carpet. In the wedge between an armrest and its seat, even in the hollow meant for the coffee cup or the drink. Under its curve.

'Sometimes Ms Rose may lie down underneath a seat if she is tired, curl up and go to sleep. At other times, she may sit behind the cinema screen on the main stage or even hide in the wings. Or walk into the folds of the heavy red curtains once they are drawn.

'When there are many vacant seats – this usually happens during the first show of a weekday, early morning – she waits for the lights to be switched off, for the previews to be over and just before the feature presentation begins, when all the lights are dimmed, she slips out of her hiding place into one of the empty seats.

'She likes to keep moving: So F14 one day, Row F, seat number 14; the next day C3, C27; the day after M18 or L9, a new seat number each time.

'This is her world, all of this and only this, the cinema theatre in the dark. During shows and in between. Rumour has it that she knows a trick or two and only you, Orphan, can tell us whether this is true. I am not going to go by what others tell me, I will leave it for you to discover.'

~

Orphan is half-awake as Bhow carries him towards the theatre and when she reaches its entrance, fringed with drapes in deep blue velvet, she barks once, clears her throat, calls out to Ms Rose who appears instantly, as if she has been waiting all this while, at the door, for a dog to show up with a child on her back.

'Ms Rose,' says Bhow, 'this is Orphan, Orphan, this is Ms Rose.'

'Thank you, Bhow,' says Ms Rose as she bends down to lift Orphan from Bhow's back, and carries him inside.

'Welcome, my child, it's still dark, this is no time for a child to be awake,' she whispers in the gentlest of whispers, each word half-stern half-soft like leaves in spring.

'Let's help you sleep.' Her fingers, like petals, drum his back and for the first time since he left Little House, Orphan falls asleep in the embrace of a human, warm and close.

~

As for Bhow, with Orphan safely delivered into Ms Rose's hands, deep inside Europa, she tears down the steps, her tail wagging into a blur, her bark bouncing off the glass walls of the stores, the noise magnifying into a swell that floods The Mall but this time she doesn't care whether there's someone who sees or hears, so happy she is.

WOMAN

DIARY ENTRIES

I KEEP writing to your father after he's dead. Nothing long, just words and some sentences, fragments of sentences. Just in case his ghost wishes to read one day or night. I am going to read some aloud, some of the entries from the early years.

In no particular order.

I hope you are listening.

~

I use your pen. I take it to school. Every day. And like you, I, too, have a constant ink stain on my index finger.

~

How do I make it easier for our child? Do I wait for her to forget you? Maybe I should begin to hide some of your things so that she isn't reminded of you. Like your books, your clothes, your spectacles.

~

I realise how little you have. Three shirts, three pairs of trousers, two pairs of socks, one pair of shoes. Two vests, two pieces of under-wear. That's all. It all fits in one suitcase. Sometimes, when no one is at home, I put the suitcase on our bed and I lie down next to it. I hear voices from inside – of you and your students.

~

Yesterday, cleaning the house, I come across your handkerchief. The big blue one, the one you get the ice in. It's washed and folded, smells of soap, I don't remember washing it. It was in your pocket on the day of the accident.

~

They give me your shoes and socks. I don't wash them, I won't wash them. Yesterday, I pick some dirt from one sole, I eat it.

~

What if, just like you, I am hit by a bus? What happens then? Have you thought of that?

~

Yesterday is the first day I don't think of you.

~

We have the two ticketfoils. For the first and the only English movie we went to, Ben-Hur. *I keep them in that suitcase.*

~

Your daughter, our daughter, needs you more than I do.

~

You push me to speak up, you push me to go out and work, you push me to do the interview, you push me to stand on my own feet. Why don't you push me to learn how to live without you?

~

I miss you the most in the morning.

~

I am not going to change the newspaper you have used to line the bookshelves. I want to find out how long it takes for newsprint to turn brittle, crumble to paperdust.

~

They never find out who the bus driver is who hit you. Some nights, when I cannot sleep, I think of him, the driver. Where is he? Is he sleeping? It's possible that one day I may board a bus the same man is driving.

~

Did you visit me last night? I hear someone talk, just like you, I feel someone get into bed. My eyes close, I reach out to touch you but you are gone.

~

Some nights, our daughter frightens me. Because she says she can see you even if we all know you are dead.

MAN

THE LEELA

HE decides he will not go home tonight, he will check in at The Leela, the hotel so beautiful, so clean it clears his head. Free of the flies who rub their legs, stalk him day and night with their sour smell of damp. He loves how the hotel gleams at this time of the day when it's past twilight, how its countless glass eyes, its windows, polished, unblemished, reflect the red from the sky, blue and white from the neons of The Mall, yellow from the traffic on the highway backed up on the thirty-two lanes at the toll gate. Exactly where he was last night, with the mynahs.

Maybe, if he's lucky, he will watch the birds again tonight. In the windows of his Single Deluxe Suite. Bent and blurred, as if seen through tears. The Leela will send a BMW 6i to pick him up from wherever he is but, no, he will spare them the trouble.

He drives up in his own car which carries the remains of the day: streaks on the windshield, marked by water from police cannons; smudges left behind by flies – the fat woman on the highway, the VIP who jumped the line. In the car, there's the smell of Balloon Girl and her mother. Laundry and lavender, sweat and street. On his clothes, he smells formaldehyde from the AIIMS mortuary and feels the warmth from the bodies on their backs, cut open and stitched closed. He shivers, a bit of the Paris wind that ripples the surface of the Seine is caught in his hair. On his fingers, between them, and on his wrists, the lories of Singapore have left the farm-odour of their feed.

He will wash all these away tonight.

Two cameras blink red and yellow as they scan the surface of his car at The Leela entrance. Two men in cheap black suits smile as they request him to open his door so that they can run a hand-held sensor over his dashboard.

All is clear, he hands them his keys, walks into the hotel, it's the hour when The Leela rests because the late lunch crowd has gone, evening has just begun. Most of the rooms lie in wait, beds made, fresh and cold.

In the lobby, in the centre of an atrium that soars into the sky, a fountain gurgles around a sprawling Japanese garden.

~

The woman at reception who checks him in has fuzz on her arms, gold in colour in the light. His bill comes to almost Rs 50,000, including taxes and breakfast.

'I can walk up with you, sir, do your check-in right in your room,' she says. 'You don't have to stand here, would you prefer that?'

'No need, please do it here,' he says.

'I will show you to your room, sir,' she says. 'Any baggage?'

'None,' he says.

They take the lift to the 10th floor, which is, in fact, 15, since five floors are The Mall.

'Welcome,' she says, opening the door to his room, waiting for him to step in.

He wonders if she can smell the smells on him.

He lets her step inside first, she says, thank you, he notices the nape of her neck ringed by the collar of her black blouse.

Her sari glitters, she is wearing a fragrance, cheap.

~

Single Deluxe Suite is an entire apartment, 1,200 square feet.

Living room, bedroom, fully equipped kitchen with an entire cooking range, silverware and a china set for at least a family of ten. There is a 54-inch television screen, he switches it on, Priscilla Thomas is interviewing a woman who is crying, he mutes the TV, waits for the ticker to complete one loop to check if there's any update on Balloon Girl, if there's anything on the child raped, killed, mother severely assaulted, body found near AIIMS but there's nothing. He switches it off.

There are so many things in the room, his eyes glaze over, but what takes his breath away is the glass wall. He has seen its pictures in the hotel's promotional brochures stuffed into his mailbox but nothing prepares him for this. Seemingly endless, the wall starts from one end of the living room, goes all the way round, wraps itself around the bedroom and ends in the bathroom. The entire glass in one sweeping, seamless curve, spotless. The bathroom and its rain shower are in an alcove also encased in glass that juts out, like a balcony, from the rest of the suite so that when he steps inside it's like he is suspended in mid-air. Standing under the shower, when he looks down, he can see the tops of cars on the highway, the glass floor the only thing that protects him from the sheer drop to the street, almost a thousand feet. The setting sun bathes the suite in a glow that flits across the glass wall, changing colours that swirl from red to yellow like northern lights he has once seen on TV.

He cannot let anything come in the way between him and this.

So he undresses, takes out Laundry Bag from the cupboard, stuffs it with his vest, shirt, trousers, socks, underwear, his shoes, calls Reception Woman, tells her he has put the bag out, he doesn't want anyone to come inside. He asks her to take everything away, wash, iron and send back, and don't disturb me, he says, don't ring the bell, drop a note through the door, leave the clothes outside on a clothes rail, please. I want it quick, very quick, I need to go out later in the evening.

'Of course, sir,' she says. 'My pleasure.'

~

He smiles when he hangs up and steps into the rain shower in the glass room.

My pleasure, her pleasure.

The shower jet drums his body. The sky, the setting sun, the clouds are just beyond the glass wall, almost within his touch, it seems. Can anyone see him? Someone from a plane above? Someone looking up from below? No, this glass has a special protective sunscreen film that keeps the outside

outside. He is so high above and so clearly can he see the traffic below him that his head reels when he looks down, forcing him to close his eyes, sit down in the shower, prop his feet against the wall and let the water run, hot and hard.

My pleasure, her pleasure, my pleasure, the words ring in his ears.

His pleasure will be when he calls Reception Woman to his room, when he will shave her fuzz, he will be gentle, he will use the woman's razor in the bath and the liquid soap, to show her how beautiful is the skin she conceals underneath, the skin that's the colour of light in the room. His pleasure will be when he gets rid of that shine on her sari, when he asks her to take it off so that he can pluck the glitter out but that may take an inordinate amount of time. Better if he just asks her to undress and, as she waits in his bed, the Tommy Hilfiger quilt wrapped around her, he will put the sari in the oven – why do they have an entire cooking range in the suite? – set the temperature to 450°, 500°, wait for the fabric to melt, there must be some nylon in it, switch it off before the smoke sets off the alarm in the room.

He looks down, imagines a hole in the floor through which his bathwater drips down onto the highway, people may mistake it for the rain they have been waiting for.

His pleasure will be when he presses her face against the glass wall. To see how the light dapples her body now that it's free of hair.

When he asks her to point out to him where she lives.

She will then tell him, between her screams, that one reason she wears that sari which he does not like, one reason her arms are unshaven is that there has been no water and no power in her home for the last three days. He will ask himself is she lying, saying this to save her skin? Because as Reception Woman at The Leela, she may not make a lot of money but, certainly, she makes enough to go to a beauty salon and get herself waxed or threaded or whatever women do these days for men like him. But he will like her answer. Because he will be able to connect that, instantly, with reality. Because he can see her neighbourhood, he can see it through glass, far away, a grey smudge on the horizon, as he stands in the rain shower. He has seen the anger, he is an eyewitness to the protest rally on the highway. He has seen the water cannons, the police, the bedraggled men, women and children trooping back home, wet and spent.

That's why he will understand her when she sits on the floor of this Single Deluxe Suite and breaks into tears, when she begs him to let her go.

He will let her go, he won't harm her at all, he can restrain himself, but his pleasure will be when he asks her to step into the shower.

If you have had no water for three days, if there has been no power for three days, how have you been cleaning yourself, he will ask her. With a towel soaked in water from a glass? With tissue paper, wet? Or do you sneak into a room at the hotel, when no one is looking, and take a shower? She will say, no, in the building in which I live, we store water in a Sintex tank on the roof and we store extra water in buckets and I use that to take a bath every day but by then he has pushed her inside the shower.

He tells her to undress, he says I will turn the other way, I won't look, so you don't have to feel embarrassed, and he hears water flow down her and along with that noise, he hears the sound of her crying hard, her breaths, she shouts, let me go, please let me go, my parents, my brother are at home and he says, of course, I will let you go, who do you think I am, I just want you clean and smooth, all the needless hair gone from your arms, and because this is the best shower I have ever used, I wish to share it with you, and above the sound of these words in his head, he hears an unusual sound, he sees a blur. A shape moving fast.

Who is this hovering in the air, tapping at the glass wall of the shower, drawing lines where steam has fogged the glass?

CHILD

CINEMA THEATRE

WHEN Orphan's eyes open, all he sees is the dark. He has never seen such darkness before. Not at Little House, where light always streams into his room from the hallway – sunlight during the day, lamplight at night. From the nurses' station where Kalyani sits, from the overhead 60-watt bulbs. Or the glare from headlights of passing cars that slips in through the window to spray arcs of yellow and white across the walls.

Never such darkness before.

Not even on the pavement, under the highway, his home for these few nights. Where even in the darkest hour, just before the first light of day, everything is lit by neons. From The Mall, up above, from the traffic, down below, and from the streetlights in between, suspended in air.

Maybe one day, when he has the words, Orphan will be able to tell what this is like, this sudden dark. This seeing without seeing. Where the eyes are open, waiting for light, and then catching nothing but black.

If Orphan doesn't cry, if he shows few signs of fear, perhaps it is because in the dark he has the assurance of things solid.

Like Ms Rose's soft shoulder on which his head rests.

Strands of her white hair that brush against his face.

Her arms, which are wrapped around him, one patting him gently below the neck, the other holding him straight, behind his small knees.

And, of course, her voice. That, like a slight wind, floats in and past his ears. With words he doesn't understand but senses, exactly, what they mean: that he is safe.

~

Bhow is right, Ms Rose knows her way in Europa. A mere wisp in the dark, she carries the child like a plant carries its flower. All the theatre's lights are switched off but she walks briskly down the steps as if her feet can see, veers suddenly to her right to enter Row O (maybe O for Orphan).

She then heads straight for Seats 12 and 13, right in the centre.

Carrying the child, she sits down, adjusts her seat to recline. And then she stays there, gently rocking Orphan, her eyes closed, her lips moving as if in prayer. She holds him like she's holding a gift she has been waiting for and which has finally arrived. The only sound in the theatre her breath, the rocking of her seat, a long, slow creak, noise the wind makes with a solitary window left open in an empty house.

It lulls Orphan to sleep.

Ms Rose gets up, holding the seat so that it doesn't spring back because in the almost complete silence in the theatre, that would make a sound that could wake Orphan up and she doesn't want to take any chances. With one hand tucked under his head, she lowers him into the seat next to her, adjusts him so that he is deep inside, his head safely resting against the back, his feet at least 6 inches clear of the edge so that even if he moves, there is no risk of him rolling off the seat.

She need not worry because she will find out in a few hours, just as Kalyani does in Little House, how little trouble this child is.

As if the fear of being abandoned has given him qualities that make caring for him a much simpler task than expected.

~

Orphan in deep sleep, Ms Rose plans for his food.

If only Bhow had told her a day in advance, she would have made all the arrangements. She can still, she can walk into Food Court, choose a stall, cook something for Orphan, or walk into Mothercare to pick up a change of clothes and shoes. She has noticed that his feet are bare. But she is not sure how long can she leave him alone in Europa.

What if he wakes up in the dark, begins to cry? Or moves, rolls off the seat and hurts himself against the armrest or falls down to the hardwood floor even if it's carpeted?

No, she cannot leave him for more than five minutes, ten minutes.

Which is all that she needs to walk into the multiplex's café next door, right across the lounge where the posters and the big LCD screens are.

There is nothing in the display case, chairs are upturned on the tables. She looks for a sandwich, a brownie, some bread which she can mash into paste and feed him but there's nothing. A fistful of popcorn lies scattered on the floor of the machine but that's no food for a child. In a corner on the display counter is a stack of cups and in a wicker basket, there are sachets of dairy creamer. She picks up a dozen of them and a cup. Moving with a speed and efficiency that belie her years, Ms Rose gets warm water from the sink in the washroom, sits on its tiled floor – spotless after being mopped by the night-shift attendants – and she empties the dairy creamer out, sachet by sachet, into the water to prepare a feed for Orphan, his first cup in Europa of almost-milk.

Surely, she tells herself, this is no way to welcome a child into her world but she can do little.

How hungry Orphan is she doesn't know, all she knows is that it will be hunger that will, most probably, wake him up, make him cry. And for that she will need something ready, something at hand. So Ms Rose returns to Europa holding the cup full of dairy creamer and water, freshly mixed. Some of the powder has got on her nails in flecks of white. All her ten fingers are wrapped around the plastic cup, also white. That and the milk in the cup, for a moment, bring light into the dark. White in the black. Orphan hasn't moved when Ms Rose is back.

He is exactly where he was when she left him, his hands and his legs still, as if in a picture. As if he has stilled himself to sleep just so that Ms Rose is relieved when she returns. So that she discovers that this child, who has been handed over to her, can be relied upon, that he is not much of a bother.

It hurts her back but Ms Rose bends down, brings her left ear close to Orphan's face and smiles as she feels the warmth of his breath.

She settles down into her seat and, holding the cup in her hand, looks straight ahead at the red curtains behind which, she knows, lie Orphan's new homes.

In Europa, she has so much to show, so much to tell.

MEANWHILE

A DAY IN THE LIFE
OF KALYANI'S BROTHER

'I TWISTED my ankle today,' says Bhai, Kalyani's brother.
Tonight, it's his turn.

~

'We have to tend to the trees in Apartment Complex, trim dead
branches, clear fallen leaves. This morning, when we walk in,
Estate Manager is waiting for us. He's shouting, I can hear him
from three blocks away. Look at the trees, he says, each one is
covered with insects I have never seen before. Hundreds and
hundreds. Since morning, my phone's been ringing with residents complaining the trees are being destroyed. And you know
what this means? Apartment Complex is the only one in New
City which is so green, it has so many trees, that's why in January, even migratory birds, on their way south, land here. That's
why people pay crores to buy a flat here, crores, do you understand what a crore means? It's what you would make as salary in
two hundred years, can you imagine that?

'He is right about the insects, none of us has seen such
things before. From a distance, it looks like someone has taken
chalk and marked all the trees with dots and when you get
closer, you see each dot move.

'Deepak Das, the head of our group, the supervisor, picks

up one of these white insects. It doesn't fly, it crawls down his finger, across his palm.

'So tell me what can be done, says Estate Manager, the residents say it's my fault that I hired people like you who know nothing about trees. We need trained gardeners, they say, not manual labour freshly arrived from villages.

'We are silent, we stand listening, what can we do? I am a little frightened because I know he's right, I don't know anything about trees except that they need light and water.

'Find a way out, says Estate Manager, we must have these insects gone as soon as possible. Otherwise, I don't know what answer I will give to the residents. If you can't clean this up, I will have no option but to call your contractor, tell him that it's over, we don't need your services.

'Don't worry, I will find something, Deepak tells us when Estate Manager has gone. I have some medicine, he says, and if that doesn't help, I know someone who knows more about this than I do. I will go meet him this evening, maybe get him here tonight, show him these insects. In the meantime, let's try to remove as many as we can, he says, with our hands.'

~

'He gives each one of us a black plastic bag – he says, this will help you see the insects clearly, white on black – and tells us to pluck and pinch. Walk from tree to tree, pluck the insect, pinch it to death, drop it in the bag, leave the tree only when there is no insect left, not one. Each tree takes at least an hour.

'Pick, pinch, drop, pick, pinch, drop.

'My plastic bag soon turns white. Some insects fall in my hair, one drops on my face, I try to brush it away, trip over a brick on the pavement, twist my ankle.

'By lunch, I have only finished two-and-a-half, three trees, there are so many I cannot count. We are all drenched in sweat, this makes it easier for insects to stick to us. We go down to the basement parking lot to have our lunch because that's the only place where there is shade. All of us, like the trees, are now covered with white dots.

'Be careful, says Deepak, these insects look like rice, don't let any fall into the food, it will be very difficult to pick them out. We will tell Estate Manager we ate them all.

'He makes some of us laugh.

'After lunch, it's back to work, tree by tree, insect by insect. By evening, we finish clearing all the trees that line the driveway. We have at least a hundred more trees to clear, it will take us this whole week, maybe the next one too. When the bags are full, we take them to a corner and set them on fire. The smoke is white and thick. Smells like human bodies at the cremation ground, says Deepak.

'When we leave for the day, Estate Manager comes and says we have done good work but he isn't sure if the insects are gone. Maybe they have left eggs behind, he says, let's hope they are not back tomorrow.

'I ask Deepak what if we cannot get rid of the insects and he says, don't worry, this Estate Manager gets angry all the time and blames us for everything. Why can't he, instead of just standing there and shouting, help us? We aren't educated but he is. He can read and write, he can talk to someone who knows. Anyway, I am going to get some medicine tomorrow from my friend.

'I hope that works because none of us knows what to do.'

~

'I got one of the insects for you all to see,' says Bhai. 'It's dead.'

He opens his palms and they crowd around him in a circle, Ma, Baba, Kalyani and Pinki. They cut off the light and in the dark, the insect glows white, a pale dot of lifeless light.

WOMAN

NIGHT LAUGH

IT'S four months, five months after your father's death. Winter has come, we are in the last term of school and you ask me, at least once a week, when is Father coming back? To which I have no answer except to look into your eyes, try to search for a clue beyond our tears.

~

One night, the noise of something falling wakes me up. The alarm clock on the bedside table shows 3.16 in the morning, I am so precise about the time because both clock hands are together, I remember looking at the clock and wondering where the hour hand had gone. The room has turned cold, I must have left a window open. You sleep next to me, curled up under your quilt. This must be some noise from outside, something in the kitchen sliding, falling over under its own weight. Perhaps, the broom propped up against the wall. I try to get back to sleep but hardly have I closed my eyes when I hear you get up, the flick of the light switch. I know you cannot reach there unless you stand on a table so who has switched it on?

I am scared, I don't open my eyes because I think it is a dream but, no, there's no mistaking your movement. I open my eyes and see you climb down the bed, let the quilt fall to the floor, walk towards the door. I try to call out to you but I cannot speak. Every time you wake up in the middle of the night to go to the bathroom or to drink a glass of water, you wake me up, you want me to be with you but this time, I see you walk out of the room on your own, like someone grown-up trapped inside a child.

I lie in bed, my eyes follow you. You don't walk towards the bathroom or the kitchen, you walk towards the balcony.

~

I trail you at a distance, I am on tiptoe. You have dropped the quilt on the floor, you take a detour to the dining room, you walk up to the table, stand there for a while, you look at the chairs. I am at the door, pressed against the wall, looking in, and I see you pull a chair out, drag it by its legs. The chair is heavy but you hold it as if it's a toy, where do you get that strength from?

I am your mother, I should stop you, ask you what you want, I should switch on all the lights in our little house, shake you hard, make you snap out of whatever state you are in, help you get back to bed and fall asleep again, but I cannot do any of these things, all I do is to watch you in hiding.

~

You push the chair to the edge of the balcony, climb up. The balcony has an iron grille your father got installed so I know that you are safe, you won't fall. You hold the iron bars with both your hands, press your face to the grille, you look into the night.

There is nothing to look at except black, a dirt-track, empty fields, the tops of trees but you stand on the chair looking straight ahead. I do not want to say anything lest it startle you, make you turn to look at me, fall off the chair. So I stand behind you, at least 6 to 7 feet away, and watch you stare into the night. For a full ten minutes, a cold wind rustles the leaves and your hair.

I cough, clear my throat, to get your attention, but you don't hear me.

Suddenly, you raise your right hand and you wave at someone. I do not know who that is in the dark. You begin to laugh. You laugh like when you are playing, you laugh like someone is tickling you, you laugh as you laugh with your father. Your head thrown back, your eyes closed tight, the laugh makes your face glow in the dark. You peer down the balcony and keep laughing, keep waving, without saying a word, so loud is your laughter I am afraid you will wake people up.

~

I help you climb down from the chair but you are not even aware that I am there.

You keep looking into the night but this time you are crying. I ask you what happened but you don't say a word. I ask you to tell me who you are waving at, who makes you laugh so much, and you look at me with a gaze so empty I can fall right into it.

~

You push me away and you walk back to the bed, you pick up the quilt and you cover yourself with it. I hear you cry yourself to sleep. When I am sure you are in deep sleep, when I can hear your breaths, long and deep, I walk back to the balcony, I get up on the same chair and look into the night. There's nothing to see except your fingerprints in the dust on the iron bars, the night stretching endless. I peer down just in case there is someone or something but again I see nothing except the fog that is beginning to roll in. Which, by the end of the night, smothers the entire city. Grounds trains and planes, pushes the air temperature to just a few decimal points above zero, brings frost in the neighbourhood.

~

It's the next afternoon that you come running to me, jumping commas, skipping breath, and you say, Ma, may I ask you something, may I ask you something, and I say, of course, baby, you may ask me anything and it's then that you ask me about the woman, 12 feet tall.

MAN

GOOD ADVICE

WHO is this hovering in the air, like a fly but beautiful, tapping at the glass wall of the rain shower, drawing lines where cold air has fogged the warm glass? Who is this who has found his room and has a message for him, who else can it be but Balloon Girl?

He gets up from the bathroom floor with a start, quickly wraps a towel around his waist because, no, he cannot let her see him like this, she is just a child. He tells her to wait for a few minutes so that he can step out of the shower and dry himself, slip into his bathrobe, but she has walked through the glass wall into the room and although there is no Red Balloon with her, she floats, gliding in and out of the furniture in the suite's living room, her feet inches above the floor.

'We do not have time,' she says. 'I have something very important to tell you.'

~

And then she breaks into speech which he doesn't interrupt, which he can't interrupt to ask anything, because the words flow thick and fast, like water in the shower.

'Taxi Driver knows,' says Balloon Girl, 'Taxi Driver knows. He is the one who brought us to your house from the hospital. He has seen your face, he has seen our faces. He doesn't know anything right now but he will watch the news this evening and he is going to put two and two together and he will wonder where we are, my mother and I, and he will ask questions. But, right now, as I am in your room, he is at the taxi stand, waiting for passengers. His evening shift has just begun.'

But why should he be worried, he isn't guilty of any crime.

There she is, Balloon Girl, standing right in front of him.

Where is the child raped and killed?

Where is the mother severely assaulted?

He plans to call the TV station and tell them to take that news ticker off.

He is about to tell her that when she says, 'What are you waiting for? I have told you where he is. You need to take care of him, bring him here before he speaks to anyone.'

And then she is gone, leaving prints of her small lips, small feet on the glass wall.

~

She is right, he tells himself, Taxi Driver is the only one who knows.

He is the last witness, a witness to what exactly he doesn't know but he hopes he will soon find out. He will get him into this room because Balloon Girl says so and until now, Balloon Girl has never been wrong.

By the time his clothes are sent up, washed and ironed, it's shortly before dinner at The Leela.

On the way out, he sees Reception Woman behind the counter. Working at her terminal, signing a new guest in, in the same sari. She smiles at him. Relieved that she is still safe, that he is fresh and fragrant, he steps out into the evening to get Taxi Driver home, to the Single Deluxe Suite at The Leela.

Balloon Girl will tell him what to do next, how to take care of him.

~

'Sir, may I get your car?' The man in the suit asks him for the keys again.

'Yes, please,' he says. 'I will wait.'

CHILD

TUBERCULOSIS REPORT

THE reports have come in. Of her blood, her sputum samples, the X-ray of her chest. There are cavities in her lung field, the presence of bacilli is confirmed, Kalyani Das is diagnosed with tuberculosis.

~

'Six to nine months of medicine,' says Doctor, 'she needs to have lots of fruits and fish, milk and eggs. Proteins.'

Ma begins to cry.

'No use crying, we will start with an injection. Your daughter is a nurse, she knows the drill. Streptomycin injections for at least three months.'

Yes, Kalyani has read this in the nurses' handbook.

A set of six – or is it seven pills? – every morning after breakfast. She knows their names: Rifampicin, Ethambutol.

'Collect the pills from the TB centre downstairs,' says Doctor. 'You don't have to pay anything, the government pays for this. She cannot miss a single day. Who all are there at home?'

'The three of us. And her sister and brother, five people in all,' says Baba.

'Can you put her in a separate room, just for a few weeks?'

'We don't have one, we live in one room, Doctor.'

'Then you have to be very careful because there is always risk of infection. But keep the windows open, let there be air and sunlight in the room.'

'We will do that, Doctor,' says Baba.

'And, you, you cover your mouth when you cough,' Doctor tells Kalyani. 'It spreads through the air but no need to be worried. If all goes well, if the medicine starts working, and I am confident it will, she should start feeling better in two weeks.'

They get up, Kalyani holds Ma's shoulder as they walk. Baba clutches the plastic bag – which carries all the reports – as if it were a living thing. As if all the incomprehensible letters and words typed on those sheets that confirm the disease also spell out, if rearranged, the secret to its cure which will heal his daughter, his eldest child and the one he, secretly, loves the most.

~

Baba gets his rickshaw to the hospital, today he will drive them home.

Ma holds her close, one arm around her, just like when she is a little girl in the village. Baba drives cautiously, skirting the bumps and potholes on the street.

'You drop me off and you both go to work,' says Kalyani. 'I will take my medicine. Anyway, I will sleep most of the time.'

'Shut up,' says Ma, 'if I don't go to work today, nothing will happen. I have told Didi that I need to take you to the doctor.'

Baba sees a fruit cart by the side of the road and pulls over. He buys two apples and two bananas, almost half a day's earnings.

As he walks back to the rickshaw, he wants to think only of his daughter. How she has become so thin he can see her ribs through her blouse. He wants to think of what he can do to help her recover. He wants to think of what he can do to save her because she is his baby, his firstborn, and although, in the village, everyone says it would have been better if he'd had a son, he falls in love with her the first time he holds her in his arms. He wants to think of how she pulls through when she is a child, every time she is struck by disease. Through malaria, typhoid, so many bouts of high fever that he has lost count. Once, everyone gives up on her, when she is eight years nine years old, but she recovers. And this when he or his wife don't pray as much as the others. In fact, he doesn't tell anyone but he doesn't quite believe that prayers make a difference. So it must be something inside his Kalyani that keeps guiding her to safety, that makes her the only one in the family to finish school, all twelve classes, that makes her read and write, even English. He is proud of her and he wants to think of that pride as he drives her home.

But all what enters his head, above the noise of traffic, the creak of his rickshaw's wheels, the jangle of its chain, the laboured breathing of his daughter, is the thought of money.

All the money they have saved since they moved to New City.

About Rs 45,000, accumulated rupee by rupee, month by month, from the earnings of all five. Even from Pinki, his youngest, who should not be earning. Some of the money he keeps in a box under the bed, the balance he has kept with the rickshaw owner, tells him that he will take it when he goes to his village.

He has big plans for these savings: to add to them each month; to use them for, first Kalyani's and then Pinki's marriage; to move to a two-room house; to buy a TV, because he doesn't like that on some evenings his wife and children have to stand outside their neighbour's door to watch TV. He wants to save more so that he can buy some land in his village because that's where they will return to when they are old, when the three children have married and left to live in their own homes, he will need to go back to the village because that's where home is, under the bright sky, not in the shadows of this little house in New City.

But now Kalyani cannot work, for at least a year, that's 7,000, 8,000 gone every month. Doctor says six to nine months but she will need at least three more to recover fully. There will be more tests. The medicine he can get for free thanks to the slip Doctor has given him. He needs to show that at the TB centre every time he needs to pick up fresh stocks of the pills. But he has to buy fruits and eggs and fish.

He and Ma don't have to eat fruit, they don't have TB. Even Bhai, he is an adult now, he will understand. But Pinki is a child, how will they keep her away from the fruit? Maybe once a week he will get some for her, that much he can afford. But that is only if all goes well, if Kalyani is cured in six months.

What if she is not?

What if she has the kind of TB, which, Doctor says, takes two, even two-and-a-half years? Then there is also a kind of TB that doesn't get cured. He knows three people in his village who died of TB but, no, he will not think of that. They were all old, older than him, much older than Kalyani.

His daughter cannot die.

~

Baba's off on his rickshaw, Ma goes to take a bath, Kalyani sneaks out of the house to go to the local phone booth and calls up the hospital she is supposed to join in a few days.

The operator keeps her on hold for more than ten minutes and then, after two wrong connections, puts her through to the human resources woman who interviewed her and offered her the job.

Kalyani tells her she is ill, she needs to take medical leave. She knows what the answer will be.

'How long?' asks the HR woman.

Kalyani knows she cannot say six months, that's too long.

'At least a month,' she says, 'or two.'

'I am sorry, Kalyani,' says the HR woman, firm but polite. 'You haven't even joined us so you don't get any leave, but let me tell you something. Please get in touch with me once you are well and then check if there is a vacancy. All the best, you take care of yourself.'

She doesn't ask Kalyani about her illness.

On her way back, Kalyani needs to sit down at the bus stop to stop her feet from flowing away from her body like water.

~

That evening, Kalyani is the first one to have dinner. Alone, in a corner. Egg curry, some rice, a slice of fish. And an apple, later.

Pinki watches her eat.

'I don't need both eggs and fish, Ma, either will do,' says Kalyani.

'That's fine,' says Ma, 'we have both today and I made this for all of us. Pinki, come and help me, let your sister eat.'

Kalyani knows, however, that from tomorrow, this special dinner will be only for her. They cannot afford this every day, she has done the arithmetic.

~

That night, after they have all had dinner, Ma says, 'Do not tell anyone about this, do not tell anyone that Kalyani has TB. All of them will tell us to stop working and if word gets around, no one will hire us. Pinki takes care of a child, I wash dishes, they will not want us around.'

'Will I also fall ill, Ma?' asks Pinki.

'No, no,' says Ma, 'we will keep the window open, we will let air and sunlight come in.'

Kalyani hears all this.

~

Kalyani's eyes are closed but she isn't sleeping, her back is turned towards her family as she faces the wall. She knows she will become, if she hasn't already, a burden on her family, a burden that each one will have to carry and because of its weight, she knows, they will stumble and fall. That's why the least she can do is not to let them know that she has heard what Ma has said. She will also not tell them that she has a secret of her own.

~

That she first spits blood when she is in Little House, that she wakes up with the chills next to Orphan, she suspects she has

243

TB, she checks and the nurses' handbook confirms this so that's why she leaves Little House because she doesn't want Orphan to catch the disease. Has she done the right thing? She is not sure. Because Orphan leaves Little House – that wasn't part of any of her plans – and now no one knows where he is, so it doesn't really help, does it? By not revealing her condition early, has she infected others in her home already? Has she made matters worse for herself? Well, no one in the house has any symptoms yet. Should she have told Doctor this morning that she has had symptoms for a while? How would that have helped? She is not sure. She isn't the kind who keeps secrets inside her because these weigh her down, because she craves lightness.

So why is this happening to her? This web of lies and half-truths, these secrets, this illness that threatens to consume her. She hears everyone settling down to sleep, Baba switch the lights off, and she cannot hold it any more so she lets the tears flow, she coughs to cover her crying.

WOMAN

PATRICK WHITE

YOU say you have no interest in what I read but I need to tell you about a woman named Theodora Goodman because, I think, we have a lot to learn from her. Both you and I. She is the central character in *The Aunt's Story* by Patrick White, one the three books they gave me as a farewell gift because White was awarded the Nobel Prize the year you were born. The book is in three parts and when it opens, Theodora is as old as I am when your father dies, as young as you are today, give or take a few years.

I will read some lines to give you a sense of how the book sounds.

~

She thought of the narrowness of the limits within which a human soul may speak and be understood by its nearest of mental kin, of how soon it reaches that solitary land of the individual experience, in which no fellow footfall is ever heard.

~

Theodora lives in Moreton Bay, in Australia, and we meet her the morning her mother has passed away. The coffin – *the shiny box that contained a waxwork* – is in the room which was her mother's bedroom. Theodora waits for her sister, her very beautiful sister, Fanny, and Fanny's husband, Frank, to come down from Sydney for the funeral.

Once upon a time when Theodora is in school, she and Frank are attracted to each other but nothing comes of it except a few awkward moments of tenderness. Theodora, who has taken care of her mother all these years, realises that she is free now but she doesn't know what to do with this freedom. She cannot even cry like her sister Fanny. For Fanny, emotions were either black or white. *For Theodora, who was less certain, the white of love was sometimes smudged by hate. So she could not mourn.*

~

Fanny has three children, two boys and a girl. The girl's name is Lou, Theodora loves Lou. As the adults talk, the children play with a strange toy called 'filigree ball' that Theodora's mother, their grandma, brought from India. Indians, Theodora tells them, fill this hollow brass ball with fire and roll it downhill.

Why do they do it, Aunt Theo, Lou asks Theodora who replies that she doesn't know.

'I have no idea,' she says. *'I have forgotten. Or perhaps I never knew.'*

~

As she waits for the funeral, we get to know about Theodora's childhood, her growing up in a house called Meroe which has deeply affected her. She loves – and she remembers – its trees, its rose garden from where, every morning, *roselight* enters her room and colours the wall. There's a creek near the house which dries to white mud in the summer. Meroe is where she first meets Frank, Meroe is from where she goes to school and where she meets a girl called Violet Adams and they become the best of friends. For Theodora, Meroe is where *the pulse of existence quickened, where she ran into the receiving sun.*

Meroe is where her father dies.

~

After her mother's death, Theodora moves to Paris where she checks into a hotel and runs into a cast of characters so strange it's hard to know who is real, who is not. They have funny names, there is Sergei Sokolnikov, a general from Russia; Madame Rapallo, an American adventuress, rumoured to be the mother of a princess. They both have been guests in the hotel for years. There are twins Marthe and Berthe who walk around the hotel discussing war and language. There is Henriette, neither young nor old, who works in the hotel, whose body smells of *nakedness and sun.* There is a girl called Katina who is both white and black.

Theodora befriends them all and, soon, the general starts referring to her as his sister Ludmilla and Theodora plays along. They go for long walks during which he tells her stories of his life. Day by day, she, too, begins to settle down in this hotel.

~

Then one night, a night *thick with quiet stars*, there is a fire in the hotel. Theodora watches the flames, the smoke as everything burns, including the black beetle in the wood, the cockroach in the cold consommé. It's the last part of the book that's my favourite. I am not going to give the story away because, who knows, you may wish to read the book when you wake up.

~

Australia to Europe to America.

After the hotel burns down, we find Theodora on board a train in America that's headed for California. There are cornfields as far as her eyes can see; houses and towns pass her by like notes of music that she can read. Abruptly, she gets off the train and finds herself in a small town where a stranger suggests she walk towards a guest house to stay for the night.

Between pines and firs, she walks. In her handbag, she finds aspirin and eau-de-Cologne, pictures of children, sticky lozenges, strips and sheaves of tickets she bought in New York. She tears all of these into small pieces and she walks on.

She is taken in by a family, who welcome her, make her a bowl of noodles and ask her to stay. When they ask her her name, she says she is Pilkington, her name torn out by the roots, just as she had torn the tickets from her handbag. *This way perhaps she came a little closer to humility, to anonymity, to pureness of being.*

~

She walks away from this house, too, her feet leading her to a thin house which is empty, where there are things old and broken. It's here that she meets a man called Holstius. She says, I have seen you somewhere at a railway station or in a hotel.

Possibly, he says.

He seems to give voice to her thoughts, she can touch him if she wishes.

She begins to live here and what happens later is something I will get you to read. To find out what happens to Theodora Goodman, who is all alone.

Until:

They will come for you soon, with every sign of the greatest kindness, they will give you warm drinks, simple, nourishing food, and encourage you to relax in a white room and tell your life.

MAN

FREEZE FRAME

HE will take care of Taxi Driver.

That's what Balloon Girl says he should do, that's why Balloon Girl helps, she makes the entire world stop so that he is the only one who can move, so that the crowds don't slow him down.

~

That's why when he stands on the steps of The Leela and waits for the parking attendant to get his car, he realises everything is still and he's walked into a painting whose canvas is limitless, stretches from sky to sky, glass to glass. Behind him and in front, above and below.

All movement has stopped.

The giant revolving door is an unmoving blur wrapped around three women, one in a sari, one in a black dress, another in something blue. And one man in plain trousers and shirt. All four, lit by yellow lamplight. Like insects caught in amber.

Two guards crouch holding metal detectors like boys at play hold paddles. In front, two guests stand, their arms outstretched, following orders in a drill. In a corner, on the pavement, someone cups a frozen flame to light a cigarette. The fountain in the lobby has stopped in mid-air, its water now shards of glass undecided, unsure if – and when – will they fall.

All hotel staff wear smiling masks.

A baby, in her nanny's lap, sitting on a Queen Anne chair, wears a weeping mask.

A red leather suitcase falls, is held up by air.

Two young women stare into each other's phones, their peach faces lit by screen blue, their four shoulders bare. One wears heels, her left shoe inches above the ground.

There is a wedding reception in the hotel. One wall is decked with flowers, three petals have fallen off, they dot the air in points of an invisible triangle over the heads of an overweight, almost obese, couple, their fingers sparkling with jewelled rings.

Gift boxes scatter in flecks of coloured paint. Little boys in suits lean against the escalator like dolls propped up after they have fallen. Little girls show their small midriffs in small adult clothes.

He closes his eyes.

He wants to undress the little girls, pluck the sequins from their hair, wash away the make-up and polish from their faces, lick them clean, restore them to childhood.

At the bakery at one end of the lobby, a child's face is pressed against its glass display, a cone in one hand, an ice-cream drop on his lower lip. Far away, beyond the steps, across the driveway into the hotel, over the heads of people, he can see the row of cars waiting to enter. Bumper to bumper, each one waits for Security. The first has its trunk open, on which streetlight slashes a yellow line. A hulking, black Mitsubishi Pajero sits in the hotel driveway, its doors open, three men out, three men in, all frozen in mid-step.

Lobby clocks stop measuring time in New York, London, Paris, Dubai, Delhi, Singapore, Beijing, Hong Kong and Sydney.

He raises his hand, just an inch or so, to check if he can move.

Yes, he can. So how does that affect everything else?

No, it doesn't, because thanks to Balloon Girl, he isn't part of this painting.

~

So he lets his fingers rise, drop, rise again, he draws lines in the air.

He takes a step forward, he takes a step back. Nothing moves except him.

No one's looking at him, no one looks at him as he jumps, like a child on a trampoline. He falls, he jumps again, flails his arms, he shouts, the painting goes on. No one listens, no one sees.

The next time he jumps, he sees his car. It's the fourth one.

He begins to walk towards it. On the way, he passes the Mitsubishi Pajero, the driver has a frightened look on his face.

~

There is no one in his car. His keys are in the ignition. The parking attendant must have stepped out before all this happened. He gets in, he smells the freshness from his clothes, the shampoo in his hair, the bath gel he used. He and his car are the only things moving through this painting. He turns the wipers on, even they move, he sprays his windshield with water and soap, the dirt clears, he can see the evening sky through the glass now, in vivid black and blue paint. In strokes and brushes.

Oil, watercolour on canvas, on paper, charcoal sketch, line drawing, everything mixed, still.

Taxi Driver will be at the stand, Balloon Girl says, he is waiting for his night shift to begin.

~

He is on the highway now, Balloon Girl loves him so much she has ensured he keeps moving in his lane. Uninterrupted, no one behind him, no one in front, the rest of the traffic stationary, like it was this morning, the painting goes on. The highway itself is pencil-black, he can see each individual line in the shade, cross-hatches, lanes marked as white broken lines. The trees on the divider are still, green paint of their leaves drips down the wire mesh put to prevent people from walking across the highway.

He steps on the gas, he is driving at 80 km per hour, standard speed, he goes up to 85, the lane is clear, it has opened up only for him, he is at 90 now, moving towards 100, 110, 120, that's the speed on the autobahn, he can see the exit sign coming up, 'Airport, Dwarka, Dhaula Kuan, Vasant Vihar', the letters clearly written by hand, the arrow a white smudge on the green.

He will take the Dhaula Kuan exit, turn on Ring Road, go all the way to AIIMS, no crowd, no nothing, he should be there in less than twenty minutes. Balloon Girl will be there to help him, he wants to listen to some music, turn the dashboard TV on, but just when he leans to his left to reach the switch, there it is.

Right in front, a huge, hulking shadow in the sky, black on black.

He slows down to 75, 65, 60, down to 40 now, no, it's not black, it's white, he needs to stop, there is no one in his lane.

He gets out of the car and looks up, looks in front to see a giant Boeing 747, Lufthansa, coming in to land, from Munich, maybe Frankfurt, the plane stationary in the air. It spans both sides of the highway, its nose pointed towards the runway less than a kilometre above. He can see the aircraft's windows lit by warm yellow cabin light, faces looking down on him, each one painted with so much care and beauty. The plane is so close he wants to climb up onto his car and touch its undercarriage, feel its wheels, the air sliced by the turbine blades.

But he decides against it.

No, there should be no disturbing this stillness.

He cannot digress, he needs to see Taxi Driver. So he continues to drive straight ahead.

Unhindered, undisturbed, the world standing still, he is guided by Balloon Girl, his only compass.

CHILD

BLOOD RIVER

KALYANI is in the centre of the room, she coughs blood. It stains her dress, drips down her legs to the floor where it fans into a red-brown delta, runs into the cement cracks before it begins, right in front of her eyes, to collect, like rain water rising, lapping against the edge where the floor meets the walls. She covers her mouth with her palm to dam the flow but her blood breaches the embankment her fingers make to gush through, gurgling, sputtering, so thick so fast that all she can do is to give herself up to this raging torrent from within. She stands, her arms flopped by her side, her chest hurting so hard she is afraid it will split her open. She wants to close her eyes but she finds she cannot because it seems someone has removed her eyelids and when she tries to blink, she does not feel the familiar touch of eyelash against eyelash, the lid gently shutting down, like a curtain, over the eye. Instead, it's as if someone wants her to keep looking. At her blood as it now covers the entire floor, begins to creep up the walls. It slips through the crack under the tarpaulin sheet onto the verandah outside, spills over, begins to flow into the street.

~

'May I speak to Mrs Usha Chopra?'
　'Mrs Chopra speaking.'
　'This is Kalyani, Kalyani Das.'

253

'Kalyani, how have you been? Such a long time, I thought you had forgotten all of us, how's your new job?'

'I am not well, Mrs Chopra.'

'What happened?'

'I am ill, Mrs Chopra, I have TB.' She doesn't know any other way to say this.

She hears silence in which she can hear Mrs Chopra breathe. She doesn't know what to tell her next. She doesn't know why she dialled the number. She wants to hang up.

'Have you seen a doctor, Kalyani?'

'Yes, I am under treatment, I called to ask you, have they found Orphan?'

'We haven't heard anything, the police are still looking for him, I think. How do you know?'

'Doctor Chatterjee told me that he is missing.'

'You need some help, Kalyani? I can send you some money.'

'No, no, Mrs Chopra, I will tell you when I need something.'

'Who's with you now?'

'I am with everyone, with my family. Ma, Baba, Bhai and Pinki.'

'Don't be alone.'

'No, I won't.'

'When did you find out?'

'A few days ago.'

'TB is very normal, follow the course of the medicine. Do not slip up.'

'Yes, Mrs Chopra.'

'Call me when you need something. Call me any time.'

'Yes, Mrs Chopra.'

'Anything else?'

'No, nothing.'

The phone booth, its table with its Formica top, its glass

door, spins around her in circles of colour. Hot and cold, fast and faster. The street begins to move, too, under her feet. She reaches out to hold on to something, she slips, her fingers claw at the air. She stands still, a bench floats towards her which she holds, she lowers herself onto it. The man who runs the phone booth offers her water to drink. You are not well, rest here for a few minutes, she hears him as if he's speaking into a long hollow tube, the length of a Metro train, and her right ear is pressed at one end. Her fingers wrap around the plastic cup, this helps her steady her hand.

Call me any time, Mrs Chopra says.

And Kalyani wants to keep those four words, wrap each one of them in cotton wool, soft, clean, warm and white, and hold them close, not let even one slip away.

~

Her blood is now on the street. In swirling puddles first, small, underneath cars, parked and moving. As she looks, it thickens, clots, coming into touch with air and water. It spreads, a limitless stain, covering the entire yard in the middle of the slum, forcing children to stop playing and start shouting. Neighbours appear at doors and watch the red flow by, smooth at first, then congealing into clumps. Pieces of trash ride its current, plastic bottles and newspaper wrap, vegetable peels, fish bones. It's now beginning to smell. First, a bit like iron in a scrapyard, and then the stench grows to include other smells. Her smell, the odours of her insides, sick and wasting. Then, that of the garbage heap outside Little House on hot days. She hopes for a wind that will blow this smell away but the leaves are still, the sky a sheet of metal, hammered straight by the sun, staining in one corner, near the horizon where it touches the highway. Her blood has now begun to climb to the heavens.

~

'You have reached Neel's phone, please leave a message and I will get back to you.'

'Doctor Sir, this is Kalyani. I have been trying to call you but no one picks up. This is my third call.'

She heads back home.

~

She can see Baba swim in the stream of blood, his rickshaw a hundred pieces of rubber, twisted metal and plastic. She can see Orphan, in a boat, being steered on its own, in the river of her blood. He is as small as she remembers him to be and he is looking at her now, his eyes glint in the dark, his hands reach out to touch her. In one hand, he holds the black pen she and Dr Chatterjee gave him to mark the city's map. With crumpled pieces of cloth, with her hands, and with the end of her sari, Ma tries to plug breaches in the wall to keep the blood out. Pinki screams, the blood rises up to her waist. Bhai is nowhere to be seen.

~

Evening falls like a sudden stone, cracks her nightmare open, wakes her up.

The house is empty, a wisp of smoke enters from a coal oven outside. Pinki will be the first one to come home, followed by Bhai, Ma and then Baba. That's how it is every evening and Kalyani clears the room, switches on the light but today she is so weak she cannot get up.

Sweat has drenched her when she was sleeping, her clothes stick to her. She wants to take a bath but this isn't the time she can go to the community tap. She wants to stand under water, cold and hot, the kind of shower she once saw in a hospital room where her nursing teacher had taken her to show her around. She turns to face the wall, her back hurts lying pressed against the floor so long.

What if the TB carries on living inside her? What if weeks become months become years? What if it's the other kind of TB, the one that may never be cured? What will happen when Baba's money runs out? What will happen to her plans to take the nursing exam? How many more days and nights of being a burden to everyone? Each question rattles, shakes the house of dreams Kalyani has built for herself, she doesn't know how long before it begins to crumble.

MEANWHILE

WHERE WAS RED BALLOON
BEFORE BALLOON GIRL?

ONCE upon a time in a shop that sells balloons wholesale, in one packet of a hundred balloons, Made in China, exactly a hundred, lives a red balloon. Red Balloon is bright and sharp as most things red should be. Like apples and blood, the setting sun, or, Mars, the planet. But Red Balloon is always unhappy because it is shy, its colour is against its nature, it wishes it were Grey Balloon.

Dull, easy to miss, last to be picked up.

That's why whichever way you hold the packet, upside down or downside up, Red Balloon will always find a way to slip to the bottom. Where it comes to rest underneath the flashy balloons. The blues and yellows, the greens and golds.

That's how Red Balloon lives in the shop.

Until one day, a thin, tall man with long grey hair walks in and buys the packet whole.

~

This man's name is Kailash Sahu and there is only one thing he loves to do.

No, make it two.

He loves to blow up balloons, some with his breath but most with helium so that they can fly. And he loves to push his balloon trolley all around the city, stop at places where parents bring children. There is an iron hanger rigged to his trolley to which he ties the balloons. So when he walks, the balloons float over his head, cover his face and, from a distance, it appears as if balloons are pulling the trolley across the city.

~

Red Balloon is nervous, a little.

Because gone is the comfort of the shop, the safety of numbers. Now, it's in Kailash Sahu's trolley and it's out on the road. It doesn't know who it will go to. Red Balloon is a very observant balloon. So while other balloons gossip, chat, tell tales about imaginary adventures, Red Balloon keeps watching the sliver of sunlight that slips in. He watches it change colour – blue to white – as the sun climbs the sky. As Kailash moves from National Railway Museum to Nehru Planetarium, Zoo to India Gate where he drops anchor for the day after he has sold a dozen balloons, each for Rs 10.

But Red Balloon stays in the box.

Evening turns to night, the last tourists leave, the man with the two dancing monkeys packs up his props, Kailash takes out Red Balloon, fills it with gas, ties it to the trolley and begins his long walk home.

From India Gate, left on Shah Jahan Road, down Prithviraj Road, where the VVIP bungalows are, left on Ring Road. Nobody stops him to buy a balloon. Rich children want Mall balloons, sealed mechanically, which come in all kinds of shapes, aeroplane, Mickey Mouse, Nemo, these stay afloat for days while his balloons, tied by hand, last two nights, three at the most.

By the time he nears AIIMS, it's well past 9 p.m. Red Balloon knows its end is near.

At the entrance, Kailash sees a girl and her mother. The girl smiles when she sees Red Balloon, Kailash cannot hear her but he can see her talking to her mother, pointing to the balloon.

He pushes the trolley right up to them and stops.

'How much?'asks the girl.

'No,' says her mother, 'let him go, we cannot buy it.'

'Take it,' says Kailash, unties Red Balloon from the trolley hanger and ties the string to the girl's wrist.

'How much does it cost?' asks Mother.

'Ten rupees,' says Kailash, 'but you can have it. This is the last one and I am headed home.'

The girl runs in circles around her mother, Red Balloon at least 3 feet above her head in the night sky.

'Play with the balloon,' says mother, 'but if someone wants to buy it, we can make Ten rupees.'

'I don't want to sell it,' says the girl.

~

Barely two hours later, around midnight, when the crowd at the hospital's entrance has thinned, a man walks up to the girl, a thin man, his wrist so slim his watch slides halfway to his elbow when he raises his arm, points to the balloon, and asks, 'How much?'

'Only ten rupees,' says Balloon Girl, as she thrusts her wrist towards him.

Red Balloon sees itself reflected in the man's empty eyes.

WOMAN

ASIATIC LION

ONE winter morning, just before you leave for school, you tell me, Ma, I need to prepare a chart on 'My Favourite Animal' for my class and I have chosen the Asiatic Lion, *Panthera leo persica,* and I want to watch the lion, Ma, how it moves, how it walks and how it sits, and I say, of course, that's a great idea, that's the best way to do this chart, your method of enquiry, observing things for yourself before you start putting them down on paper. And, who knows, I add, that little board they have outside the lion's enclosure may have details you may not find in any book, you could take that down. Like where it has come from, which year was it born. Ma, you ask, may I meet the man who feeds the lions? I can watch him, I can ask him questions, too. How much meat does a lion need for lunch? I can put all these in my chart.

Of course, I say, you can do all that, we will go this weekend.

~

I call him.

I call him because it promises to be a beautiful winter morning, the newspaper says the sun will melt the previous night's fog. This is the first trip out for all of us and I call him because I want him around you and me, I want him in the space your father left behind.

He says I don't need to worry about anything. He tells me, you just ensure that Saturday night she sleeps early so that she wakes up fresh, wide awake when we set out. Let's beat the rush, try to be at the Zoo ten, fifteen minutes before it opens so that we can be right in front of the line at the ticket counter. It's a Sunday, it's winter, there will be a very big crowd, he says, we do not want to get caught.

What about lunch? I ask.

I have everything worked out, he says, not to worry, you relax.

That's his favourite, most frequent line to me: *not to worry, you relax, I have everything worked out.*

He says this first at your father's funeral.

~

The next morning he is at our door with a red cloth bag, lined with newspaper and towels to keep the heat in. I have got sandwiches for her, the kind she likes, with eggs and tomatoes, he says. I have samosas and tea for us, hot milk chocolate for her. And because they will not let us carry food inside, I have hired a taxi for the day, we will keep all this in it and at lunchtime we will step out, eat, and then go back inside. Along with the food, he has brought a new drawing book and a box of crayons, unopened, because I have told him about the chart you have to make.

She can sit in front of the enclosure and draw the lion, he says, with the moat and the cage and the grass and the trees.

~

We are in the taxi, in the rear seat. You sit between him and me. The bag with the food and the drinks is on the passenger seat in front. The drawing book is in your lap, the box of crayons balanced on your knees.

That's when it happens.

The taxi lurches to a stop at a red light, the box of crayons slides down, flies open, pencils spill out into a bright puddle of colour on the black mat on the taxi floor. Some roll under the seat in front.

He bends down to pick it up when the drawing book falls too.

You are crying.

I see your tears, I see your shoulders shaking but I do not hear anything. He is crouched on the floor of the taxi, picking up the pencils and putting them back into the box.

What happened? I ask.

You scream in reply.

~

Ma, you say, breathing deep, in and out, in and out, I tell you, yes, please tell me, tell me what's the matter, did something, someone hurt you, tell me, I am listening, and you shake your head, you ball your fists and start hitting the seat in front, you knock the box of crayons from his hand. I don't want this, Ma, throw this out right now, you say, the lights change to green, the taxi driver asks me if he should pull over, I say, no, keep driving, we will sort this out, and I know right then that I have made a mistake, that I should never have said that because you take my words, *we, will, sort, this, out*, and you throw them back at me, loud and hard. Ma, you cannot sort this out, you say, I do not want to go to the Zoo with him, and you point to him sitting next to you holding the drawing book and looking at you, at me with not one expression on his face. I don't want him in the taxi, Ma, you say, get him out, get him out of the taxi, I do not want anyone in the taxi except you, except Ma and Papa and I know that Papa isn't dead, Ma, you know that, too, don't you, you know that very well, he isn't dead. I am not going to say a word because I need to let you speak, I need to listen to you. So I sit there, my eyes on yours, my ears catching your words as they rush headlong down a slope unchecked, gathering speed, cutting, bruising themselves as well, and you say, Ma, you know something?

Papa comes to our house almost every other night.

I am sleeping, Ma, we are sleeping when I hear him knock on the door, I hear him walk downstairs, some nights I run to the balcony and he is there, waiting for me downstairs. And he waves to me, he makes funny faces, Ma, he makes me laugh, you say this with tears streaming down your face.

Ma, I tell him to come inside the house and he says, no, I cannot come in any more and when I ask him why, he says, you ask Ma because Ma is with someone else now and when I ask who, he says, you ask Ma.

Last night, Papa had come again, he told me, you are going to the Zoo with Ma and I will also come with you, and that's why I don't want him in the taxi, Ma, and before I can say anything, he taps the driver on his shoulder and asks him to pull over, he gets out of the taxi and comes to my side of the door, waits for me to lower the window to tell me that the taxi has been paid for, that we can keep it as long as we want to.

Standing in the street, cars honking for ours to give them the right of way, he shows me where he has kept the sand-wiches and the chocolate milk and then he smiles at you and says, draw a nice lion, have a great time at the Zoo, do not forget to ask the man what he feeds him.

And he is gone.

It's only then that you calm down.

~

All this happens so fast that, at first, I am not even sure whether it's happened. And then I see he isn't there in the taxi, we are moving, you are looking out of the window, your face marked with tears. I see scratches your nails have left on the taxi seat. On my arms, in little red lines of blood. Your words, which had tumbled out in a fury unrestrained, now sit in my ears, in a little painful pile.

I don't know what to do with them.

Right now we are going to the Zoo, you have a lion to watch, you have a chart to make.

~

We rent an electric trolley, tell the driver to drop us off where the lions are, no stopping anywhere along the way. We are the first ones to reach the enclosure. It's empty, the lions are inside, two of them, male and female. A Zoo employee passing by stops and tells us that we have come right on time, we are lucky, breakfast is ten minutes away, that we should be able to see the lions eat.

You are so excited you cannot stand still.

I want to see the lions, Ma, you say, I want to see them right now.

Quiet, says the zookeeper, let's not disturb them.

~

The Asiatic lions walk out of their cave: the male, Sheroo, followed by Durga, the female. Both are old, frail, their faces sunken, but you don't notice that. This is the first time you are watching real lions and you stand rooted, as if the slightest movement will scare them away. Your eyes follow them as they walk, majestic even in each tired step, across the grassy ground that separates their cave from the moat, from one end of the enclosure to the other and then back again.

Slowly, inch by inch, you lower yourself so that you sit down on the ledge that runs parallel to the railing. From your new vantage point, you get a better view, you watch them, your lips parted, your eyes sparkling with awe. And then you open the drawing book and the box of crayons we got from the taxi. You take out two coloured pencils, black and yellow, and as you begin drawing, I look at the pencil in your hands, the drawing book in your lap, the things he got for you with so much love, and I try to smile but I have to turn away from the lions, away from you because I don't want you to see the tears in my eyes.

Behind me, I hear the lions walk and the scratching sound your crayons make.

MAN

TAXI DRIVER

THERE he is, Taxi Driver. Exactly as Balloon Girl says, leaning against the tree at the taxi stand. His night shift has begun.

And, then, Taxi Driver is gone.

And all he remembers are five scenes in between. Sight and sound and, of course, the smell.

~

First, Taxi Driver's smell.

Human, male, unwashed after fourteen hours in the sun, more than twelve of those sitting in one position, his back pressed against cheap leather, shirt soaking rivulets of sweat, clouds of dust caught in cheap cotton, worn for the third night, fourth day in a row. The shirt in which he sleeps as well. Its collar, once blue, now grey, marked by a thick black line that grime has etched all along the inside. The collar that smells of last night's drool, now dry, that dripped down his chin during the short sleep he snatched from waking.

His hair traps some of the blazing sun, smells charred. Like Dog smell on that Diwali evening. Taxi Driver's trousers are agape at the waist, their zip down, broken, pressed on either side by the two ends of a needless belt. From here, another smell rises. Maybe drops of urine spattered in the underwear, musty odours of slow discharge from the penis, sweat near the anus.

He breathes all this in, tells Taxi Driver, who shows no signs of recognition, I need you for the entire evening, I don't need your taxi, drive a mile from the stand, leave it in a Metro parking lot, come with me in my car to my hotel, have a drink and dinner, I will drop you back.

He protests, sir, I cannot leave the taxi like this. He smothers the protest with promise of money – 20,000 rupees for the night, that's more than a month's salary, this leaves no room for any negotiation.

Taxi Driver smiles and says, of course, sir, let's go.

~

Hot water cold water, very hot, steaming, very cold, ice, jets, spray, red, blue, blue, red, turn dial left, turn dial right. Steel hose, shower head, white porcelain, cold. Different settings: drizzle, heavy rain, drum, massage, pressure jet, a million drops knead his tired back, the skin below his shoulders is splotched.

I am done, Taxi Driver says, to which he says, no, stay inside for at least half an hour, I will clean all of you today. Bend, sit, spread your legs, soap the inside of your thighs with this blue shower gel, he says as he pours shampoo and conditioner, bottle after bottle, counts a dozen in all, down Taxi Driver's head, chest, back, penis, pubic hair, armpits until the drain clogs with hair and dirt, water backs up.

Pick it up, he says, we will flush it down the toilet.

It's done now, says Taxi Driver, I am cleaner than clean, this is like when I was born.

No, not done yet, he says, just stand there underneath the shower and let the water run, run, run; run for ten, twelve, fifteen, twenty minutes, there is no hurry, let it run uninterrupted over your head down the neck, shoulders, chest, back, legs, toes, turn around, let the water run down your face, open your mouth, let it clean there as well, and then shave. You know how to shave, don't you?

Yes, sir.

Here, take this razor and soap and shave yourself clean.

Yes, perfect, it looks very good, it looks very neat, now let the water run again, there are flecks of soap under your ears, let the water wash them away and while the water runs, look through the glass wall, the glass floor, look down at the highway, at the cars, their lights, look at New City, how beautiful it is, have you ever seen something like this?

No, sir, never.

So keep looking, he says, look up at the stars and the moon, if you are lucky you may even see an aeroplane flying. And when the people in the plane look down, they will not be able to see you because the glass will be fogged, they may see your shape, like a little animal kept in fluid in a jar. Taxi Driver doesn't understand this, he only smiles, his eyes closed, water running down his face, hot, cold, red, blue.

He makes him shave a second time, brush his teeth, wash himself all over again.

Until Taxi Driver begins to tremble.

~

No, I don't want to eat anything, sir, I already had dinner, no, I don't want to drink, I am on duty, but if you insist, sir, I can, anything you give me, favourite? No, no, nothing like that, sir, whatever I can afford, there isn't much to spend at the end of the month, some nights we drink, OK, very nice of you, sir, to bring me here, to give me this, yes, some ice will be nice.

First drink.

I am married, sir, I have a wife and one child, she is three years old, yes, yes, that's why I brought them here from the village so that I can send her to school, not now, she is very young, but yes, in a year or so, there is a school near where we live. Yes, sir, you said the right thing, daughter has to go to school, she has to study, she has to work. I can't go home during the week, I meet them only on Sundays.

Second drink.

If you insist, sir, I can have some rice and dal, nothing else, do they have that here, thank you, that was very nice, sir, how about you, you are not eating anything, you are not drinking anything, this is the first time I am in a room in such a big hotel, if you hadn't brought me here, I would never have seen all this. There are so many lights here, this is like a cinema hall, sir.

Third drink.

Balloon Girl is in the room, she has floated in through the crack in the window, she is up on the ceiling, looking down at both of them.

Fourth drink.

Last night? Yes, yes, now that you say it, sir, I remember, I remember last night. Yes, you were there, I dropped you off, sir, with that girl and the woman, both were your maids, and then I went home. No, no one came to me today, no one has come asking me anything, you were the only one who came just when my night shift began. No more drinks, sir, I am all right, no more, I have had four, I think, they are checking now at the entrance to the highway, the police stand there with these new machines and they ask us to blow into them. They have someone standing there with a camera. I don't want my licence taken away, sir, that's the only thing I have. I will have to pick up my taxi and return to the stand but if there is some place you wish to go to, please tell me, we can go there. You will drive me back? Why, sir, why take so much trouble? Where have I been since last night? Sir, I dropped you off and then returned to the taxi stand and found a customer who had to be dropped off at the international airport and then I just stayed there, picked up a passenger who had to go to Faridabad, and I have been on the road ever since. News? What news, sir? No, I haven't heard anything. Do I remember her face? No, sir, it was so dark I couldn't see anything. No, I have not seen them, neither mother nor child.

~

Sir, no, why are you doing this to me? Let me go, please, let me go, I don't need anything, I don't need the money, I don't know what I have done wrong. Tell me, sir, you don't tell me anything. You bring me here, you ask me to take a bath, you feed me, I will leave just now, on my own, no one will know that I came to your room. No, I don't remember anything from last night, I don't know why you keep asking me that, sir, no, I don't recall who they were, you told me they were your maids and they had missed the last Metro train and you were picking them up. That's all I know.

~

And Taxi Driver, smelling of shower gel and warm towels, single malt and shampoo, clean and fresh from head to toe, his hair soft to the touch, his face shaved smooth, is no more.

Minimum spray, minimum spatter.

He will leave the body in the hallway, slumped against the elevator, let them figure out where it came from. The last witness is gone, he has no reason to worry any more, he will now return home to Apartment Complex.

Thank you, Balloon Girl, for everything, he says, and looks up at the ceiling but she isn't there.

CHILD

CINEMA SCHOOL

MS Violets Rose carries Orphan, walks with him, speaking as if she's reading from a book.

~

'A cinema theatre isn't like any house at all. It's a very strange, very unusual place for a child to have his home. There's no bedroom, no living room, no dining room. There is no kitchen, no bathroom, too. Not to speak of a child's room. No bunk beds, no stickers on the window, no posters on the wall. Of either mice or funny men.

'There are only chairs and chairs, there is a stage and there is a screen. And at the back, high up, looking as if it's suspended in air in the dark, is the projection room, the inside of which no one can see except us. Many machines are kept here:

the projector which makes the film move and shines light through it, sometimes it gets so hot that you have to wear gloves to take the film off it. Then there are machines to regulate the sound and the lights in the theatre. There is a bench fixed to the floor where the projectionist changes the reels, every nineteen minutes for most films these days, by staining the top right-hand corner of the film with a white line that no one in the audience can make out. That line marks the place where the reel changes.

'The projection room has a long, narrow window, very similar to the one you have in a train. This window is made of special glass through which the image, riding on a beam of light, travels from moving film to the screen.'

~

More than the machines, though, the first thing that Orphan has to learn, to live in Europa, is how to cope with the constant dark, just the opposite of what a child his age is conditioned to learn. How much of Little House Orphan remembers is hard to tell: does he remember the light streaming in through the big windows in his bedroom? Or the colours of the sky, their brightness, their shade, to which Kalyani points when she tells him the story of the little cloud that brought a child? Because, from Europa, it's hard, almost impossible, to see the sky. It's sealed, soundproof, its four doors are all closed most of the time, marked by 'Exit' signs glowing in small red rectangles. There are several sources of light in Europa but they all work to heighten rather than banish darkness: the lights on the ceiling, in exactly a dozen rows, twenty in each row, like stars in the night sky. Switched on when people begin to walk into the theatre to take their seats before the movie. Dimmed to darkness when the curtains part. The brightest lights are those right above the screen. These are the stage lights, sixteen in all, but these are switched off, too, when the movie is on. They light up only during the interval, if there is one.

The only lights that are always kept switched on are the tiny ones, each one green in colour, fixed on the side of the last chairs in each row, to the left and to the right. These lamps show where each row is so that you can reach your seat in the dark. Ms Rose has spent such a long time in Europa that she can walk to any seat eyes closed. All it takes for her to adjust to light and dark is a blink of her eye. But she knows that Orphan, little more than a baby, is still learning how to walk, even the muscles of his eyes are still forming, he still sees blurred shapes.

~

So Ms Rose is his teacher.

First, she makes him walk between two rows of seats, getting him to use his hands for support and balance. Once Orphan gets tired after a couple of such trips, she lifts him up, carries him around, shows him the other corners in the theatre: the room in the wings behind the curtains where they keep all the cleaning equipment. Or the giant speakers behind the screen, spiders' cobwebs behind each. She gets him to walk up and down the steps. Once, holding the armrests of the chairs. Then, holding the railing that runs along the wall. Most surfaces in the theatre, because they have to absorb light and sound, are made of soft material: the steps are covered with carpeting, rich and red; the walls are padded, cushioned with black. All this helps Orphan because when he stumbles and falls – and he does stumble and fall a lot as he navigates his way between the seats – he doesn't hurt himself.

Let him trip, Ms Rose tells herself, he will have no major injuries, that's the only way he will learn.

So right through the morning, before the first show begins, she sits in her corner while Orphan goes up and down, right and left.

From one seat to the other, moving closer to the screen until he stops right at the edge of the stage.

~

Along with walking, Orphan begins learning the alphabet and numbers, too.

As his steps get more steady, Ms Rose begins to walk with him, pointing out the letter at the end of each row of seats, each one glowing in the dark. And when the overhead lights are switched on, she shows him the numbers on the seats, each a piece of shining plastic embossed in the upholstery. She holds Orphan's hand and runs his little fingers over each number so that he gets its shape as well.

Orphan will learn fast, she is sure of that. It's just a matter of time, she thinks, before she tells him the seat number and he finds the way to it on his own.

~

One morning, shortly before the beginning of the first show, after the seats have been cleaned, the floor and the aisles swept – the two janitors who vacuum the carpet every alternate day don't even notice Ms Rose or Orphan in the dark – Ms Rose climbs up onto the stage with Orphan, takes him right to the screen that's bathed in light from the four overheads.

She makes him touch the screen's white vinyl. She shows him how each square inch of the screen is dotted with tiny holes for the air to pass through from the speakers placed behind the screen. She shows him the red curtains, the black frames that move up or down, left or right, depending on the size of the film, its aspect ratio.

She leans into Orphan, lowers her lips to his ears, and whispers, 'There is something else I will show you. It will be our secret and it will be magic.'

And Ms Violets Rose smiles as she kisses Orphan on the tip of his nose. It tickles, it makes him laugh – his face bathed in light on the stage against the screen.

WOMAN

PHOTO ALBUM

AFTER that incident in the taxi, he becomes my secret.

So we meet when you are in school, this is when the city is not as generous as it is today, when it opens very few spaces for couples like us, closes very few eyes. Forcing us to meet in places, hurried and furtive, where we know no one will recognise us, between my classes in school, at a bus stop midway from his college to our home, sometimes a platform at the railway station, once even the waiting area of a hospital, on a bench, between waiting patients. We steal twenty minutes, half an hour to exchange words, to look at each other, sometimes let our hands brush so that we can return to our respective homes, assured that each of us is there for the other, that neither of us has slipped off the face of this earth.

~

'How is she doing?' he calls and asks me.

'She's sleeping,' I say.

'So long?'

'Yes. Or maybe she's awake, I don't know, I can't tell.'

'Hasn't it been almost ten hours since she arrived?'

'More than twelve, in fact.'

'Did she eat something?'

'No, nothing, she's locked herself in.'

'Just like her.'

'Yes. She hasn't changed . . . except.'

'Except?'

'She looks very tired. Her face is just as beautiful as I remember, except that someone has added many lines to it. There are marks, too. She's been hurt, maybe even beaten up. I see marks and smudges. I think she has been crying a lot. Or maybe it's dust from the journey.'

'On the way home, did she say anything?'

'Nothing, she kept her eyes closed all the way in the taxi.'

'Let her be. Let's wait for her to wake up.'

'That's what I have been doing all these years. Waiting, and now that she's here, I guess I don't wish to wait any more.'

'Be patient, she is with you now, she is in the same house.'

'Of course, but it doesn't feel like it. She is really holding me to that condition which she made me accept. No questions, Ma, she said, don't ask me anything. Otherwise, I am not coming.'

'So, don't. Don't ask her anything. It's as simple as that.'

'Easier for you to say because you are not here right now.'

'She will come round. Let her stay in the room as long as she wishes. She will have to get up, she will need to speak.'

'I don't like this, sitting here, waiting for her.'

'I know.'

'You know what worries me most? I don't even know if she's ill or something.'

'What makes you say that?'

'I don't know. Just looking at her, she is like a shadow, so thin, when I touched her hands, they were cold as if she had washed them in water with ice.'

'You want me to come over?'

'No, not now, don't. She isn't ready yet.'

~

So busy am I in keeping my secret that I let you keep yours as well, let you drift away from me until you are too far out into the sky that opens between us, in which, once in a while, we pass each other like clouds.

Like the day I discover your first bloodstains on the bed.

Or the morning your teacher tells me you are way behind the rest in class, that you are always distracted, that you haven't even been coming to school.

When I ask you where you have been, all I hear is silence. When I insist on an answer, you say, why don't you tell me where you have been and with whom.

~

He calls again: 'Have you had anything to eat?'

'I don't feel like eating when she hasn't,' I tell him.

'You have been sitting alone all this while?'

'What else will I do?'

'You should eat something, catch some sleep.'

'What if she wakes up in the middle of the night?'

'It is the middle of the night.'

'She doesn't even know her way around the house.'

'So?'

'I don't want her worrying when she wakes up.'

'Not to worry, just relax. She's a grown-up woman, she will find her way around the house. You are a light sleeper, if she opens her door I am sure that will wake you up.'

'It's just a few hours before morning. Let me stay awake.'

~

There is one evening when it's almost perfect. When I am the mother, you are the child. A few weeks after you turn nineteen. We are at home, right through the day there are reports of violence in the city, of homes having been set ablaze. There is curfew outside, draping the entire neighbourhood in a silence unfamiliar for so early in the day. It's December, freezing inside the house, and I have to switch on the electric heater. What comes back to me, of that night, at the remove of all these years, is that I am sitting in the living room with my school work. It's exam time so I am either working on a question paper or marking answer sheets. You walk in carrying a photo album which, you say, you found in your room, fallen in the gap between the books and the back of the cupboard. Most of the pictures in it have come unstuck, you say, we need to fix them back. You carry a glue stick I got from school.

I am not sure why but I put all my school work aside and I say, yes.

You are right, the album is in a mess.

The next three hours, four hours we sit together, we glue the pictures back.

Black and white.

Pictures of your father and me in the city, standing outside his college, outside my school.

Of you on your first birthday, in your school uniform waiting at the bus stop.

You and me with a suitcase at the railway station, you at the school sports day, you and your father on the Ferris wheel. There is a picture of your father giving a speech at what looks like a college function.

Ma, why are there so few pictures after Papa died, why did

we stop taking pictures, you ask. And I don't have a proper answer. Papa is the one who took the pictures, is all I can say, and he's gone. Where is the camera, you ask.

I tell you we have to look for it, maybe it's not working.

We will look for it first thing in the morning, you say, I want to take some pictures of you, of us, of the street outside under curfew. But, Ma, tell me about these pictures, you say.

So as we glue each picture back, you listen, sometime during the night, you rest your head in my lap, as if you are five years six years old, your eyes wide open as I tell you a fairy tale for the very first time.

You laugh when I tell you how difficult it is to buy a candle on your first birthday because it's a Sunday and all shops are closed and we finally get one but it's not a birthday candle, it's a tall one that's used to light the room. That's why the candle is the oddest, biggest thing in your birthday picture.

And you slip into sleep, I do not wish to wake you up. I keep looking at your face, your eyes closed, your hair tangled, in need of a comb or brush, a wash. The glue has dried on your fingers, your sweater is streaked with dust from the album and I stay perfectly still, I don't want to move.

It's been such a long time since I have held you, I want to feel your weight against me for as long as I can.

~

'It's raining,' he says when he calls back.

'I didn't even know.' I have been inside the house the whole time.

'It's very light rain but it will cool us down. We needed it.'

'What have you been doing?'

'I haven't been able to sleep since I knew she was here. I want to meet her but you are right, there's no hurry, I will wait.'

'I have told her about us, I don't know if she heard.'

'Don't make it about us. This is about her. Let's find out why she is here.'

'You are right.'

'I am up the whole night so let me know if you need anything.'

'Sure.'

'I love you,' he says.

MAN

LOVE LETTER

TAXI Driver is gone.

And he is back from The Leela, in Apartment Complex, in his house, in The Room.

This time, Balloon Girl doesn't follow him, she must be tired after all she's done for him through the day, and although he knows she will return if he wishes her to, he needs to be alone. His body aches as if he's been beaten all over which, in a way, he has, when Taxi Driver thrashed around while he held him down – like a fish out of water, just before it's sawed in two.

He lies down, imagines himself in the mortuary at AIIMS, on the cement counter, next to the beautiful dead woman still warm. His breath slows down, he opens his eyes and looks along the floor at the coloured umbrella in the corner, at the butterfly mobile that hovers above, catching a faint wind from the air conditioner below.

Earlier this morning, he aired The Room.

Gone is its stale smell; the oak wardrobe is open and, through its doors, he can see Kahini's winter clothes, coats and sweaters, shoes. He gets up, walks to the wardrobe, takes out a letter from its top drawer, lies down to read it. This is the first letter Kahini wrote to him, each word written in her hand and spoken in her voice, coming to his ears from another life.

~

Dear:

You tell me to write you a love letter and when I ask why, you say no one has written me one, that's why. A love letter on demand? I think about it, yes, I am in love with you so why shouldn't I write you one. About the first time we met. So if we do have a life and a future together, this letter will also serve as a record.

I meet you at a friend's house. By accident. Whose house I do not recall, there are many people in the room, there's some sort of a farewell for someone. Usually, I never do such things, going to places where I know no one, but this evening, I have a fight with my mother and I need to get away, I need to be alone, with strangers. It's raining because the entrance to the apartment is wet and muddy where everyone has wiped their shoes on the mat. Inside, the atmosphere isn't that of a party, that's quite clear. In fact, it's quite dull, like the room itself. Cement floor, bare walls, a mattress on the floor pushed against the wall. Some people sit on it, many sit on the floor, some stand. Someone offers me a glass of beer.

I stand in a corner, watch my friend move from one circle to another. Each minute seems to crawl like an hour, I need to use the washroom, someone points it out to me and on my way there, something happens, I am not quite sure what, I have a glass of beer in one hand and a paper napkin in the other. And the napkin, crumpled into a ball, falls to the floor. I bend to pick it up and I discover that I am a few feet away from four or five people who are standing

in a circle and chatting. And you are one of them, you are the one
I hear. You are the one speaking, the others are listening.

I hear you before I see you. Maybe it's the weak light in the room
or the fact that you are in half-shadow. I remember the words, all
of them. Because that's the sentence that scares me before it makes
my heart beat so hard I think everyone in the room can hear.

You say, there is a woman standing behind me who's just dropped
something on the floor and I can tell you right away that she doesn't
have a father, she doesn't have a father for a very long time and
that's why she's never happy. She always misses her father.

And you laugh before the sentences, the words, have even regis-
tered themselves on those standing around you. Their faces look
startled, their smiles awkward. They are all looking at me now,
they know I have heard but you act as if you think I am not there,
you slap the man next to you on his back and say, let's go for
another beer. They fidget, they turn, I hide myself in the washroom,
I lock myself in for at least ten minutes because I don't want to come
out, because I am frightened. I even cry, I think. What happens
next I am not going to write down, that's something you know.
What you may not know is that that is when I fall in love with
you.

Only yours
K.

~

His eyes closed, he can see Kahini sitting across from him
when they first meet for coffee.

She talks, she talks, she talks.

He listens.

And they laugh when she tells him her name means a story
and he says, so sit still so that I can read you. She tells him he
is right, her father is dead, she asks him how he knows about
her father and he says I have the sixth sense and they both

laugh over that. She tells him he frightens her. She tells him *The Exorcist* is released the year she is born and maybe that's why she loves things that frighten her. And they laugh over that, too. She tells him the small things first. Like how the window pane in her bedroom has a thin crack and although she has taped a cardboard strip to it, it gets so wet in the rain that the paper gives way, the wind keeps slipping in through the tear. Like however hard she tries, she is a terrible student in college, in her final year, and she has no idea how she got through the first three years. Like how difficult it is for her to fall asleep and how she is trying to find a way to get around that. And when she runs out of Alprax, which she gets by bribing the boy who works in the pharmacy, she does the train thing in her head. She imagines she is lying down on the roof of a train hurtling in the dark, very high speed, faster than sound, maybe, and all movements are such that she is perfectly balanced so that if she moves even a fraction of a millimetre, this balance will get disturbed and she will roll off the train's roof to certain death. She, therefore, lies still, hears the wind whistle and screech in her ears, the howl of the engine, sometimes she can smell the engine's exhaust, the odour of burnt diesel, and as night falls harder, the sounds begin to fade away, the movements get smoother and smoother, and all this stillness, all this concentration helps because soon the only sound she hears is the shuffle of the coaches, rhythmic, as they glide over the tracks, push her deeper and deeper into sleep.

The way you describe it, you make me want to go to sleep right here, right now, he says, and they laugh over that.

Kahini, you are such a story, he says.

And one morning, six months, seven months later, Kahini runs away from her house to come and live with him.

In Apartment Complex, New City.

CHILD

CYCLE RICKSHAW

THERE is a knock on her tarpaulin door.

'Kalyani?'

She knows the voice. It's Dr Chatterjee.

'Are you there, may I come in?'

She doesn't reply, she cannot reply, she is lying down on the floor, she tries to speak but each word tears at her insides in a fit of coughing so fierce it pulls her up, forces her to support herself by holding the wall next to her bed. Her head swims, she covers her mouth with a towel which only muffles the noise, brings tears to her eyes. He doesn't wait for her, he parts the sheet and steps inside. She raises her head to look at him but that hurts, so weak she is.

'You lie down,' he says, 'you don't need to get up.'

~

He sits on the floor next to her.

'I got your message,' says Dr Chatterjee. 'I tried calling you but no one was picking up. Remember I told you that you needed to see the doctor but you didn't listen. But you don't worry, I am here to help. Mrs Chopra said you called her and said it was TB. Can I take a look at the doctor's papers?'

Kalyani points to the plastic bag on the floor, propped up against the wall, which has all her reports, the prescription, the record of her medication.

Dr Chatterjee goes through her records. 'Seems all is on

course,' he says. 'You just have to keep taking your medicine and wait for it to work.'

Kalyani has gone back to sleep.

Her eyes closed, he can hear her breathe. Shrivelled, she almost disappears under her thin white sheet.

He looks around the house.

~

The last time he was here – and he's embarrassed remembering that – he was only interested in letting her know how he felt about her. He came with a proposition of sorts but his words got all mixed up, he never says them, and the moment passes. That's why he keeps avoiding her and it's only when she calls saying she is not well that he knows he has to see her again, help her in whichever way he can. That's the only way he can make up for the selfishness that brought him here last time, help him salve his guilt.

Next to a tiny gas stove and a kerosene lamp, squats a small pile of aluminium utensils, bowls, saucers, spoons, each one turned upside down to drain the water in which it was rinsed.

Where do the other four members of the family sleep?

The room is so small Dr Chatterjee cannot imagine the space he thinks they need. For, across from where Kalyani lies, barely four, five steps away, the floor ends in another corner of the room where there's a quilt wrapped around a pillow. Above it, on the wall, a row of nails is hammered into the cement, these serve as hooks from which clothes hang: two thin red towels, one yellow shirt, a girl's dress. From one nail hangs a calendar with a picture of a bunch of flowers, the only splash of colour in the room. An incense stick has burnt to its end, dropping a heap of ash on the floor, filling the room with the whiff of a sweetness that mixes with the odours of Kalyani's medicine.

'You must be Pinki,' he says to a girl who stands at the entrance, a look of shock and surprise on her face.

She is little more than a child.

'Yes,' she says. 'I am Kalyani's sister.'

'She told me about you, I worked with her in Little House,' he says, getting up, stepping out of the house.

'I will wait outside, you go in,' he says. 'I just came to check on her.'

'She stopped going to Little House long ago,' says the child.

'Yes, I know.'

'Are you Doctor Babu? She talks about you.'

'Yes,' he says. 'And where do you work, Pinki?'

'Across the Metro line.'

'And what do you do?

'I look after a child, a four-year-old boy.'

Dr Chatterjee watching, Pinki walks to Kalyani's bed, touches her forehead to check if she has fever, arranges her quilt and her sheet, pats them down, gets a glass of water, helps her sister to get up, helps her with the pills and then, with her thin, small arm behind Kalyani's neck, helps her lie down again.

'I am going for a walk in the neighbourhood, I will be back soon, I need to speak with your father,' he says.

'Yes,' she says. And Pinki gets back to work, her elder sister fast asleep, preparing her home for the night ahead.

~

The sun is setting, the first residents are returning home, maids and gardeners, nannies and cooks, most of them women and children. Most of the men will return later in the night, from their daily-wage factories off the highway or construction sites scattered across New City, driven home by trucks or hanging from footboards of buses crammed beyond capacity. Children play with mosquitoes in black-brown puddles of water that's leaked or dripped from no one knows where. Smoke rises from coal ovens being lit for the evening's cooking. Standing on the raised verandah, outside Kalyani's room, that runs all along the row of houses in this part of the slum, Dr Chatterjee is aware that he gets a second glance from almost everyone coming into the colony. Of course, he is not unwelcome. For there's not the slightest hint of hostility or menace in any eye, just the aware-ness, cold and clear, that he is only a transient who has strayed into their space. That he belongs to the world that exists across the street that skirts their slum, beyond the dumpster that's not been cleared in a month, beyond the Metro line, where restau-rants and apartments, villas and condominiums are. Where CCTVs record entry and exit to check for all suspicious move-ment, where laminated IDs screen suspects.

~

'Doctor Babu.' It's Baba, Kalyani's father. He has wheeled his rickshaw in, right up to the entrance to his house.

'Pinki told me you have been waiting. My shift is still on but I returned to check on Kalyani. She speaks a lot about you.'

'We all miss her at Little House,' says Dr Chatterjee. 'I heard she is not well.'

'Please come inside. Have some tea, Pinki says you have been here for a long time.'

'No need for any tea, I just wanted to find out how she's doing.'

'You have seen it for yourself, Doctor Babu, what can I say?'

'She will be all right. Her TB is the type that can be cured but it will take time and a lot of care.'

'That's what the doctor says.'

'Take my number,' says Dr Chatterjee. 'Call me any time if you have a problem.'

'There is only one problem, Doctor Babu,' says Baba. 'Money is always the problem. I have saved some but I don't know how long that will last. Kalyani's TB medicine I get for free but I have to buy fruits, fish every day. You have seen how she has become, as thin as a ghost. I don't know how long I can manage this. You know how it is, I drive a rickshaw, how much can I make? Pinki, you have seen her, she should be in school, but what can I do? We need her money too. Ma and Bhai bring in something but all of us are working very hard and I am frightened that one of us will fall ill.'

His words come in a rush, almost breathless, as if Dr Chatterjee, by his mere presence outside his house, has brought all the hope he needs.

'Here's some money for the fruit.' Dr Chatterjee hands him a 500-rupee note. 'This should take care of her share for a few weeks, buy fruit for everyone in the family. Let Pinki eat some, too, she is a child, she needs that.'

Baba doesn't know what to say, how to say it.

He reaches out to touch Dr Chatterjee's feet.

'No, no, no,' says Dr Chatterjee. 'You take care of Kalyani, I will keep sending you money for the fruit and the fish.'

'Please come in, please see Kalyani one time before you leave,' says Baba.

'I have seen her, she is sleeping.'

'No, please come in and take a look.'

~

The room is dark.

Pinki has lit an incense stick, its glowing tip the only light in the room. Kalyani lies in the shadows.

Dr Chatterjee sits down on the floor again, takes Kalyani's hand in his. It's cool, damp to the touch. There is no fever, he can smell sweat and sleep on her skin and in her clothes. Her wrist is so thin he's afraid the bones inside may break under pressure from his fingers. He gently lowers it, lets it rest on the bed. He feels a slight movement of her fingers.

Kalyani is awake, her eyes are open, she is looking at him. He smiles at her, unsure if she can see him in the dark. He covers her hand with his and she lets him, too weak to draw her hand back.

~

'Doctor Babu, let me drop you off at the Metro station in my rickshaw,' says Baba.

'No need, you go ahead, I will walk.'

'No, Doctor Babu, I won't let you,' says Baba. 'Please get in, I am going that way.'

Pinki is at the door, she smiles at him, he smiles back as the rickshaw begins to move.

It wends its way through the narrow lanes in the slum, almost scraping the walls on either side, sending dogs and chickens scurrying away. They are out on the street now, Baba says something but Dr Chatterjee cannot hear above the sound of the traffic. This is the evening rush-hour, cars headed for Delhi are backed up almost a mile, crawling to enter the highway. As Baba pedals the cycle rickshaw, Dr Chatterjee can see his thin shoulders strain and stretch under his thin vest, the veins in his calves distended under the skin, sweat dripping down his back, his entire frame balanced on the seat, pushing his slight weight forward, as frail as his daughter who lies in the dark.

MEANWHILE

AT THE PROTEST NOT FAR FROM
THE AIIMS MORTUARY

HE is eighteen and he loves her.

She is eighteen, too, and, of course, like anybody else in love anywhere in the world, he loves everything he sees in her.

The way she looks she talks she walks she turns she eats she bends she sits she writes she reads she lifts she carries the world she does anything. And, again, like anybody else in love anywhere, he loves everything about her that he cannot see and because they are both first-year medical students at the All India Institute of Medical Sciences, New Delhi, the country's finest medical college, ranked No. 1 in all college surveys, 200,000 taking the test for fewer than forty seats each year, when he thinks of what he cannot see, the first thing he thinks of is what lies inside her.

He loves her capillaries, blood flowing, red blood cells, layers of tissue, blue, red, white, dermis, bones, heart, which is very obvious, ribs, the pineal gland that regulates her waking and her sleeping, her uterus where he hopes one day there will be someone, his or her little heart beating because of their love, even her large intestine holding her waste, honey brown, her kidneys that keep her clean. Every Anatomy class, he thinks of her, sees something entirely new inside her, learns its name, falls in love with it. Looks it up on YouTube or

Google Images and finds someone somewhere in the world has taken a close-up picture with a sophisticated microscope-equipped camera that has enlarged the surface of the organ to make it appear like flowers, candy loops, sometimes a sea, roiling, blue-black, sometimes like the dust of stars blown across space.

~

Sitting behind her in class this morning, he falls in love with the lines she has drawn in her yellow exercise book, the cord of her phone charger that peeps out of a corner of her soft leather bag, a pen drive which she carries around her neck, the power button of her MacBook, its silver matching the collar of her white shirt, one end turned more sharply than the other.

He loves the way she raises her hand in class to speak because he can then see the skin around her elbow, hear her voice. He knows that each word she speaks is born inside her skull, in the folds of her brain, it touches her tongue, scrapes the roof of her mouth, her teeth, then travels, through her lips, parted, a hint of red, to reach his ears and his brain and tracing this journey inside his head makes him hard and this is a class, what if he is called on to stand up, to answer a question, and to distract his brain, to make the blood rush back, he looks out of the window and sees there is a crowd on campus, near the main entrance.

About fifty to hundred people, he counts six OB vans, one blue police van, several policemen with riot shields.

This is a protest against the government's move to bring a law to reserve seats for other backward castes, he reads placards, 'No to Quota, Yes to Merit', he softens, his eyes return to the blackboard, to her back, the crease in her shirt below the shoulder moving as she writes.

~

That afternoon, on his way to his hostel room, he discovers that she has joined the protesters and because she is the youngest and, by far, the most beautiful and because of the way her upturned collar moves as she raises her beautiful hand and because it leaves exposed her beautiful neck and the beautiful hair that falls over it, because of her shirt and how it clings to her, all the TV cameras are recording her, ensuring that her breasts, small and firm, are in the centre of the frame, being broadcast across the country.

He doesn't wish to share her with so many people but he can do little, so he stops to look. To listen to her, but the crowd by now is much bigger and he is on its outer periphery, so far away that all he can see is her face, her lips moving, four TV microphones inches away from her chin.

She is like his sun, he thinks, and he the distant planet, no, not a planet, he doesn't have that high an opinion of himself, he is mere dust orbiting far away, he tells himself, he is debris from dead spaceships, unnoticed, unfelt.

She looks up once, their eyes meet and he thinks she smiles at him but he isn't so sure. He moves closer, makes his way through the crowd that's getting more loud, more aggressive, 'No Quota Boys, No Quota Girls,' the chant is growing, 'No Quota Boys, No Quota Girls,' it's like a noise wave crashing into his ears, even she has joined the chant, 'No Quota Boys, No Quota Girls,' and he knows that this complicates matters a bit because he has decided to tell her how much he loves her but this is neither the time nor the place to say that because how can he tell her that he is Quota Boy, he is the son of a backward-caste father, who works as a lower-division clerk in the Health Ministry, and a backward-caste mother, and so he walks away. He takes the longer, quieter route to his hostel via the mortuary, where people wait to claim bodies of their kin, where he sees a man run inside, his wrist so slim his watch slides halfway to his elbow when he raises his arm to press a handkerchief to his mouth.

WOMAN

RUNNING AWAY

LIKE warmth that escapes in winter when you leave the door open leaving no trace except a chill, you run away from home one January morning many years ago.

~

The door to your room is ajar, that's unusual because you sleep late, because every morning I am the one who knocks on this door to wake you up, get you started. When I walk in, the windows in your room are closed, the air is stale. Your bed is made, the quilt folded, both cold to the touch. Outside, there is fog. Your room looks as if you were not here last night, or even the night before, as if it's been abandoned long ago.

I call out to you but all I hear is my voice.

I look in the closet, your clothes are there, in neat rows, your table is cleared, your chair pushed under it.

The lamp is disconnected, its cord neatly looped down the leg of the table, the plug on the floor like an open mouth.

Nothing seems to be missing – except you.

~

I run from room to room, I ask questions of the emptiness hoping you will answer:

Have you fallen down, have you tripped somewhere? Are

you hurt? Unable to respond, call for help? Are you in the bathroom, have you slipped on the wet floor, twisted your ankle? Are you in the kitchen searching for something? On the balcony, looking out, once again, waving at the ghost you think is your father? But all I see is the remains of the night. Cold and dark, only shadows.

Still calling out to you, I walk down the stairs. Everyone else in the building is asleep. I touch the banister that runs down the staircase, I feel no warmth of fingers recently brushed. Or dust, just disturbed.

I am on the street now, looking left and right, in front, but there is nothing there except the fog through which I see the lights, oncoming, receding, of a passing truck, a morning bus. I call out to you again, this time louder, running into the fog for a minute or two, I brush against something, someone I cannot see but it's not you.

~

I return to the house to look under the bed, under the table, under the chair, between the shoes, inside the cupboard, between the books on shelves, just in case you have transformed into a little girl playing hide and seek, the little girl who asks me about the woman, 12 feet tall.

Or the one who sleeps, with her head in my lap, glue drying on her fingers, photos in the album.

Maybe you have gone out for a walk in the fog, to see how cold it is, maybe you have gone out to speak to the birds, get them to wake up, make the morning show the day.

I keep the door open and I wait.

The sun is out, the fog begins to clear.

~

'She is not here,' I say.

'What do you mean?' he asks.

'She is not here, she is not in the house, she left. She has gone.'

'When?'

'I don't know. Seems like sometime in the night. Her room is cold, everything is in place, which means she has planned it.'

'Have you called the police?'

'Not yet.'

'I am coming over.'

~

We track you down, using an address you scribbled in a note-book you leave behind. It's of a shelter in the city.

When we ask about you, the woman in charge says, 'Sorry, ma'am, we cannot let you meet your daughter. She's run away from her house on her own and she is here seeking shelter. She says she is not safe in the house, she says she wants to be alone.'

'But she is alone,' I say, 'I need to see her.'

'No, she isn't, there is a man she is in love with, he will come and take her from here. Your daughter does not wish to speak with you.'

He holds my elbow. Just like he does on the day they bring your father dead.

'I know how this sounds to you, ma'am,' she says. 'I see it every day with parents who come here looking for their daughters and it's a very, very difficult thing for them to understand. She is an adult, she is fully within her rights to leave the house, she has the right to live where she wants to, with whom she wants to. My duty is to protect her interests.'

'Can I see her for a minute?' I ask. 'Her father is dead, I am the only one she has.'

The woman at the shelter looks at me and says, 'Yes, she told us that, ma'am, she told us about her father.'

'Please let me speak to her once, just once? I am her mother.'

~

When they bring you, I see that you are crying, you have been crying, I see that in your eyes.

I don't want to speak with you, Ma, please leave me alone, you say. I have found someone I love, I want to live with him, Ma. I know you love someone, I know that, why can't I do the same?

You are right, I should say. Of course, you are right, but I don't.

All I remember is that winter afternoon when you are eight years nine years old when you say, Ma, may I ask you something, may I ask you something, and I say, of course, baby, you may ask me anything and you say, Ma, when I am tired, when my legs hurt, when my eyes begin to close, I only need to call out to you, I only need to say, Ma, and you appear instantly, like magic, from wherever you are, from whatever you're doing, you come to me, you lift me up, you carry me.

But this time, I don't, I can't, so I walk away.

'She will be all right,' says the woman at the shelter, her hand on my back as she walks with me to the door – and out of your life.

MAN

NEW BABY

THEY love each other, he and Kahini, so they tell each other stories.

She tells him about her father, how the only thing she remembers about his death is ice and sawdust on the floor. He tells her about his father, an old man in glasses, like the man in the Gieve Patel painting, with bread and bananas in the rain.

She tells him about the home she has fled. A little house that can fit in your living room, she says. She tells him about the smoke from the coal oven on the balcony waking her up in the morning. The first night she sees her mother with a man in bed, a man who was her father's student. That frightens her, the sight of this person next to her mother, like a giant bird from some alien planet has entered the house, perched on the headboard of the bed.

~

They love each other.

So he watches her sleep.

It is as if she has closed her eyes but is, in fact, wide awake. Or is fighting sleep, so restless is she. He counts her move fifteen times in less than half an hour, more than twice every minute, her mind trapped in constant indecision. He watches her fingers twitch and tremble, her lips part and close, as if she is gasping for air. She changes sides, turns this way and then that, her legs cross and uncross. Eyes closed, she adjusts the pillow, sometimes folds it in half, sometimes pulls one end over her eyes only to remove it the next moment. She covers, uncovers her eyes with her arm; pulls a sheet over her, pushes it away, curls up, like a child in the cold, then lies on her stomach. Softly, he speaks her name, once, twice, thrice, he touches her shoulder, lets his hand rest there, but she doesn't move, she begins to settle, he can hear the rush and the intake of each breath, and just when he thinks she is now finally asleep, the movements begin again. He walks out of the room on tiptoe.

She watches him all the time.

She watches him when she stands on his doorstep, when she comes in from the cold and the fog and he waits for her with his house and his heart open. When she steps inside the house, she watches how he has made it their home, she feels the warmth he says he has bought for her, neatly folded, and then arranged it in a house like the one she has only seen in photographs. She watches him speak to her, each word measured, not one out of place. She watches his resolve to protect her from everything, including herself. She watches him with pride when he says each one of them has a past they are running away from and he will fill her days only with the present – and the promise of a future.

~

They love each other.

So they decide to get married.

They go to the Delhi government website and download the forms they need, they read and reread the instructions so many times that each one has it by heart. One, they need to give notice to the marriage officer who is the Sub-Divisional Magistrate, a notice that they intend to solemnise their marriage under the Special Marriage Act 1954. Two, they need separate affidavits from bride and groom giving date of birth, their present marital status; a declaration that they are not related to each other within the degree of prohibited relationships defined in the Special Marriage Act, those related by mother's blood and father's blood. Three, they need to get two copies of their passport-size photographs duly attested by a gazetted officer.

Both are required to be present when they submit these papers. A copy of the 'notice of intended marriage' will be pasted on the Magistrate's Office noticeboard with the announcement that any person may, within thirty days of issue of notice, file an objection to the intended marriage. If no objection is received, the Magistrate will register the marriage in the presence of three witnesses.

Who will be the three witnesses, he asks her, and she says, I don't know, you bring them, you are my only witness.

~

They love each other.

And when she finds out she is pregnant, she is not sure what to tell him.

CHILD

MOVIE SCENE

IT is her secret: Ms Violets Rose knows how to slip in and out of a movie.

~

She knows how to climb into the screen from either edge of the stage where the red curtains end and the black emptiness of the wings begins. She knows how to squeeze herself into the holes on the screen through which voice and music flow so that she becomes part of the movie, enters a scene of her choosing.

Of course, she is very, very careful. For she cannot afford to be noticed by those inside the film. Or those outside. Just in case the director or any member of the crew is watching, what

Ms Rose doesn't want is anyone saying, 'Look, that old woman wasn't there when we were filming the scene, where has she come from?'

What this means is that Ms Rose has to ensure that her entry to and exit from a scene is as inconspicuous as possible. That she only walks by. Or stands in a corner to look. Unseen and unheard by everyone else in the frame.

That's why she avoids scenes either dramatic or action-packed because she is worried she will be noticed. For example, if it's a chase sequence in an action movie, she cannot stand by the side of the road as cars screech by, planes crash or trains collide. She may not find her private corner when a ship on the high seas is caught in a raging gale. Or when a spaceship hurtles across galaxies.

She avoids scenes that are spare, where there are only one or two actors, these are tricky because it's harder to step into them and not be noticed. As an added precaution, Ms Rose doesn't allow her on-screen adventure, as she calls these trips, to last for more than a minute or, at the most, two. Anything longer and there is the risk of being trapped as a trespasser.

Or being found out – even by an alert member of the audience.

~

The first time Ms Rose takes Orphan with her into the screen, she is very cautious. She has never slipped into a movie with someone else. She is not sure how the little child will be affected, what kind of a disturbance he will set off. There is also the fear of separation. What if something goes wrong? What if she loses Orphan in the film, never to return? The memory of Bhow handing over the child to her floats in front of her eyes. She recalls how she feeds him in the dark, how she stands with him watching the sun rise. So she tells herself, aloud, so that Orphan, too, can hear, 'We will make it very short, twenty-five to thirty seconds. And let me choose a scene that you will like.'

The first movie she chooses for Orphan to enter is a Hindi movie in which, halfway through, there is a birthday party for a child in a park and there are so many children there, young and old, including babies in strollers, that no one notices when Ms Rose, carrying Orphan, steps into the scene. If someone in the theatre audience were looking, they would see the curtain tremble when Ms Rose climbed in but, of course, it's too dark and no one watching a movie in a theatre ever looks at what's happening off the screen, in the wings.

Once in the movie, Ms Rose lets Orphan walk all over a manicured patch of grass where other children his age are playing. She stands in one corner watching Orphan play with a pebble he has picked up from the ground. In the scene, all attention is focused on a seven-year-old girl whose birthday this is. Her parents, the two main stars of the film, are standing behind her, helping her blow the candles out and cut the cake. No one notices either when Ms Rose walks up to the table and, showing not the slightest hesitation, picks up a slice of cake and brings it to Orphan to taste before they climb out of the screen into the little dark room behind the curtains where they wait for the show to end and the credits to roll.

By then, Orphan is tired, he falls asleep.

So uneventful is this first time that Ms Rose is emboldened and chooses, for her next trip with Orphan, a movie set in Los Angeles in which a taxi driver, a young woman, barely eighteen or nineteen years old, picks up a casting agent at the airport and is driving her home.

They start talking and the agent says, I am looking for an actor with attitude and I think you are perfect for the part and the taxi driver says, I am sorry, I have no interest in the movie business, all I want is to be a mechanic just like my two brothers and I like driving the taxi and I want a family and, yes, I want children. I want to have a son, she says, and it's at this precise moment that Ms Rose enters the scene with Orphan, stands at the next traffic lights where the taxi stops for red. The taxi driver looks at Orphan, Ms Rose's heart skips a beat, the taxi driver smiles, the lights change. And Ms Rose knows that, for a second, Orphan may have found a mother and a home.

From Los Angeles, Ms Rose takes him into a scene in a village in West Bengal where Orphan looks at a steam-engine railway train for the first time in his life. It is a black-and-white movie and they stand behind a sister and her brother in a field, the wind blowing through bamboo grass. Orphan is frightened at the sight of the engine tearing down the tracks, its black smoke, he begins to cry but no one can hear this above the piercing whistle of the train. From the train in the village, one day they move to the boat in the sea. This movie is part of a special screening in Europa, a very short movie about a boy, ten or eleven years old, who builds a ship near New City and then drags it to the sea near Kolkata from where he sets sail, down the coastline to Antarctica, to get some ice for his father who is dying. Ms Rose knows that Orphan will never see the sea if he lives in The Mall and so one night, during the last show, she and Orphan enter the scene in which the boy is sailing in the Bay of Bengal. They climb into the boat, sit on its floor behind the boy, who is whistling a tune as he rows tirelessly across the calm sea. Ms Rose points out to Orphan fish that fly in the dark, seagulls, with wings brightly coloured, riding the white crest of waves that bounce back light from the moon.

WOMAN

GIANTS WAITING

TONIGHT is ending and she is back, the tall woman. There
she is, standing still, all 12 feet of her, drenched with streetlight. She knows where I am, I am sure of that, she doesn't
need me to open any doors or windows, she can walk in anytime, anywhere. Like she did last night.

Why is she here? Does she think I am tired? That my body
hurts? That I want her to carry me, help me fall asleep? Maybe
I should walk up to her and tell her that, unlike last night, I
am not sleeping, I am wide awake. That you, my child, are at
home with me and I am waiting for you to wake up. I will tell
her, thank you for last night, for the little walk we took, I like
being carried around but not today because I do not wish to
leave the house with my daughter sleeping.

So I wave to her, knock on the window pane to get her
attention, I switch on all the lights in the house so that she can
see I am in. But she stands still.

~

An hour goes by, she is still here.

I open the windows again.

This time, she looks up, I see her face clearly, like those of
goddesses in idols: perfectly shaped, bedecked with jewels,
earrings and necklaces that shine in the dark. Jasmine flowers,
bloodless white in black hair.

She gestures she's thirsty, that she wants something to drink.

304

I get a jug of chilled water, I put ice into that as well, it must be very hot outside and she's been standing there for quite a while. But when I step out of the house into the street, she is not there. I leave the water on the pavement, I look around but there is no one. No lingering fragrance of the flowers in her hair, nothing she has dropped.

A light drizzle has begun, I feel its first drops on my face.

All this while, I have been wide awake, waiting for you, but this brief interlude in the open, this slight wind, the night sky above me, the drops of rain, have all conspired, it seems, to tell my mind to start shutting down my body, to let go, force me to sleep. Suddenly, I sense myself in the dark, I am sleepwalking, every muscle in my body aches, each step requires an effort so strong that by the time I enter the house, an overwhelming exhaustion has come over me. Maybe the arrival of the tall woman has something to do with this. Maybe she is helping me fall asleep so that she can, like last night, walk into the house, lift me up, carry me.

But I will not fall asleep, I cannot. I need to be here for you when you wake up, so I wash my eyes and my face, I wet my hair, I let water drip down my neck and I wait.

~

She returns but not alone. This time, with many many more.

Giants in dozens, scores, hundreds, visible as far as my eyes can see. A massive gathering, a festive crowd of men, women and children, tall and taller, some so tall they tower above trees and streetlights, their heads shrouded by the dark. Some as tall as 50 feet or more, some part of the city's distant skyline, standing shoulder to shoulder with the buildings, their neons lighting their face. They are all out-side the house, crowding, any second some of them will be inside. They can break down walls, doors and windows, they cannot be stopped.

There's a knock on the door.

It's the tall woman, now dwarfed by others who stand behind her.

She opens her arms, bends down, invites me to climb into her lap.

No, I do not wish to go with you tonight, I tell her.

To which she smiles before she brings her face level with mine and she whispers in my ear that she knows you are here tonight and so she is not going to take me away. She says that she and her family and her friends have all come to see you, to thank you for that winter afternoon when you were eight years nine years old, when you thought them to life.

Can we see your little girl, she says, and I say you are sleeping in your room, that I would not wish you to be disturbed. But then I remember that winter afternoon, my promise to you that I will let you know, the gleam in your eyes when you say, Ma, let me know when you meet her, Ma, promise me that you will let me know, I want to see her, I want to see her carry you.

So I tell her, please wait outside. That, in a short while, just when day breaks, you will wake up and then you can meet each other.

Maybe you can carry me, I tell her, for a while so that my daughter can look.

And she says, of course, I will.

MAN

RED TOWEL

KAHINI tells him about the baby inside her.

In reply, he speaks as if he's reading from a script, standing on stage, stiff and awkward, his face white under the lights, his body unsure what to do with his hands and feet. As if he's standing in front of an audience he cannot see.

'Look around,' he tells her, 'look at all that I' – he corrects himself –'that we did together, built together. I haven't even told you how much money I have spent on this but money's not the issue, it never has been with you, it never will be. We need to do this all over again.'

She turns to look out of the window, finds it comforting that the night begins just beyond the glass, that from where she stands, she can reach out and touch the dark.

'We are not ready,' he says. 'I am not, you are not either.'

She wants to say to him, 'How do you know? What's there to be ready about?'

'I am ready,' she wants to say, without looking at him, because this is the first time they have had an argument. 'I am ready for whatever it is that sits inside me, that's fast asleep or wide awake, upside down, growing breathing feeding on my blood. That you are also responsible for.'

But she doesn't say any of this.

'I love you,' he says, 'we love each other, we are both running away from something. The last thing we need, before we have built our future, is this thing between us.'

'That is not a thing,' she wants to tell him, 'that is not between us,' she wants to tell him, 'it's inside me.' And why can't we keep running away, she thinks, the three of us, now, instead of just the two?

A bright yellow truck is speeding down the highway. So small, she can block it with a finger in front of her eye. She is trying not to listen, she is building a soundproof wall between them which his words keep climbing over.

'We need to get rid of it,' he says, and he leaves the room. 'You think about it.'

She thinks.

And for the first time since that winter morning when she leaves home, she thinks of going back to visit her mother. To tell her what she sees on the screen in the doctor's room, the smudge of grey moving against black. The gel on her stomach so cold she worries it may make the new heart inside tremble, she is relieved when the doctor wipes it away with warm tissue. She thinks of returning home so that she can stand on the balcony and wait for her father to appear so that she can tell him, in the silence that fills the space between them, what she hears when the doctor switches the speakers on: the sound of that smudge. That insistent beat, that drumming, getting loud and louder, like that of an approaching train in the night.

From where she stands, at the window in his house in Apartment Complex, if she tilts her head, she can see the Metro glide by. She hears him, in the next room, talking to someone on the phone.

'That will be perfect,' she hears him say, 'the earlier the better.'

~

'Have you decided?' he asks. 'I have made all arrangements, they say it won't take more than a couple of hours.'

~

Kahini knows she should say no, she should stand up, but when she looks around, she can only see the countless things she stands to lose.

Yes, he is right, they cannot go back to where they have come from: the small house where her mother clocks her last days or the village where his father lives alone, all their years spent with little to show except the ravages of time on body and mind and the vague comforts of a clean conscience.

No, he won't go back to that, he's made that clear. She, too, will not.

Not only because she loves him but also because – and she is proud of the fact that she has the courage to admit this, even if it's only to herself – she is an average woman with less than average skills and much, much more than average dreams but with neither the drive nor the means nor the luck to chase them on her own. That's why she likes his constant hunger for more, she craves it because it feeds her as well, it gives her all that she has started to like: the million-and-one things that she is losing count of that, together, make up the present and the promise of a future. From the 800-square-foot bathroom with white onyx tiles on the floor in Apartment Complex to the wardrobe that he got designed for her, its oak veneer, the double-glazed Fenestra glass through which New City reaches out to her, inviting her to build her home and live her life.

Will she let all this fall apart?

She will not.

~

So she goes with him the next day, just after daybreak – I chose a slot when there is no crowd in the clinic, he says – and signs the consent form, they talk to a nurse and a doctor, both

very welcoming, warm and smiling. She has never had sur-
gery.

They sign in and wait.

The TV in the lobby is playing a rerun of an old cricket
match. A nurse escorts them to a room where a doctor explains
the procedure in detail. He tells them about anaesthesia, dila-
tion, suction, mild cramps, a little blood, very quick.
Absolutely nothing to worry about, the nurse says, you won't
feel anything. He watches as they insert a cannula into the
vein just above her wrist, for the drips that she will need. They
ask her to change into a gown, drop her clothes into a clear
plastic bag that's so cold it must have been taken from a fridge.
She hands the bag to him, they tell him to wait outside.

Sir, please make yourself comfortable, says the nurse.

~

The bag in his lap, he looks straight ahead, at a framed print
on the wall. Of a baby, white, blue eyes.

He closes his eyes.

Naked, he enters Kahini, swims inside her womb in butterfly strokes upstream through the amniotic fluid, moves
towards the baby and as he gets closer and closer, he can hear
her heart above his head, he can hear the baby, too, their baby
is screaming now, air rising in bubbles from its mouth, only
partly formed. Before they scrape and suck the baby away, he
wants to touch it, to wrap himself around it.

Excuse me, sir, can I get you a glass of water, asks the nurse.

He opens his eyes with a start. The cold plastic bag with
Kahini's clothes covers his hardness. No, he says, I don't need
any water, thank you.

Just about half an hour, says the nurse.

~

Dressed in a gown that opens at the back, Kahini is told to lie on a bed, soft inverted V-shaped supports under her knees. Something enters her, probing, cold and sharp, the doctor asks her about her college, which subjects did she take, I have a daughter, too, he says, almost your age, he asks her about her father, which city did you grow up in, how old are you, you are so young, you will have a baby again, take your time, she feels the grey smudge move, she hears the sound of a train hurtling in the dark, then sliding off the tracks, she hears people screaming, the sound of metal twisting and snapping as the train's coaches crash into each other, move against the black sky like the little heart once did on the screen.

When she wakes up, they give her two wheat crackers and a cup of chilled orange juice. She gulps it down and when she rushes to the bathroom to throw up, she finds she is bleeding.

She washes herself, waits for two hours and returns home, emptied.

'Thank you,' he says, when they enter the house. 'We will do this right the next time.'

She cannot understand what he says because he speaks a language she has never heard.

~

That night, when they lie in bed, the 2 feet of distance between them, stretched tight across the bedsheet, folds over, tears, throwing open a chasm so deep that she falls into it, along with the entire night, and finds herself on the street in the city, carrying a newborn boy, perfectly formed, in a blood-red towel.

They are in an autorickshaw that comes to a stop outside a decrepit building, in front of a giant garbage heap. She can barely read the scrawl on a tin board at the entrance: 'Little House'.

A dog, black-and-white, looks at her as she walks up, leaves the baby at the doorstep, gets into the rickshaw that drives away. A wind, slight but searing, slaps her in the face, fills her eyes with water.

CHILD

EXIT BHOW

THREE weeks after David Headley, the Chicago-born alleged terrorist who was picked up by the FBI, reveals plans to target schools in New Delhi and intelligence agencies confirm that the threat does, indeed, have some basis, Mr Rajat Sharma, director of Little House, sends a letter to the Secretary of the Child Welfare Department that after 'much deliberation and assessment', he is 'constrained' to put on record that Little House is extremely vulnerable to a terrorist attack. And that all arrangements should be made to plug what he calls 'glaring holes' in the security of this building.

Times are always tense, it is always the season to play safe. Mr Sharma has gained some attention after the TV episode with Ms Priscilla Thomas – the wall collapse is now history, no one even remembers the name of the boy who has gone missing – so his letter promptly secures him an invitation to a two-day meeting of all security agencies with principals and parent–teacher representatives of the ten largest schools in the city.

Anyone wishing to speak is allowed to do so, the result being that the meeting, initially planned as a two-hour, one-day event, becomes a marathon talkfest that drags on and on into the hours well after midnight, in which speaker after speaker stands up, outlining the threats, wild and fanciful, limited only by the scope of their imagination.

One principal, for example, cites the siege of the school in Beslan, Georgia, by suspected Chechen terrorists and says, perhaps, the time has come for such a storming to happen here, at Shri Ram School, Delhi Public School or Modern School. That's the way you get eyeballs on TV.

Representatives from the American Embassy School and the British School say their campuses are the most threatened given the international demographics of the student community: sons and daughters of diplomats and expatriates, most of them from countries fighting in Iraq or Afghanistan.

One principal says that all Urdu-medium schools, because they have Muslim students, are the most secure since terrorists would never target children of their own religion.

To which another principal gets up to say, 'What kind of communal nonsense is that, sir? I have a better idea, why not take all these Muslim students, there are about 25,000 of them, and distribute them all over the city in all the other schools? Because it will serve two objectives. One, these students will get a decent education since Urdu medium schools, we all know, have abysmal facilities and terrible pass percentages. And, two, going by your logic, having a Muslim student in each class in each school in the city will be our insurance against a terror attack.'

Someone laughs nervously, someone applauds.

'In the heat of all these arguments, we are forgetting the cold light of reason,' says Mr Sharma, when his turn comes. The brief exposure to national TV has made him watch TED talks for hours to polish his public-speaking skills.

'Most of you, ladies and gentlemen, are from schools where

there's already very tight security because VVIPs send their sons and daughters there. They will be the first to complain the day they notice something amiss. And so you are safe. In some schools, as we all know, ministers' guards, special commandos, come to drop off the child and they wait outside during school hours which, by itself, is very reassuring. But that's not the case with Little House. I know this isn't a school but we do teach little children. Every child there is an orphan, every child an abandoned child. There will be no angry parents outside your office when terrorists hit Little House. Ladies and gentlemen, listen to me, please, this is the age of TV, this is the age of drama, of tears. The more the drama, the bigger the impact. Why did Mumbai work so well? Because they stormed five-star hotels. Now, imagine storming an orphanage, a home for the destitute and the homeless. Imagine killing one orphan every six hours, a small body being thrown out and no parents to grieve. The orphan has no one in the world except our dedicated staff, of course, but think of the power of that killing. It will strike fear in the hardest of hearts.'

Silence.

Whether it's the reason underpinning Mr Sharma's argument or the emotion that he invokes from the number of times he uses the word 'orphan' it isn't clear, but one thing is: no less a person than the Chief Minister herself is persuaded.

'Your point is noted, Mr Sharma, thank you very much,' she says. 'I don't do such a thing, I'm not authorised to do this but, at this moment itself, I am making an exception and clearing a metal detector and a security guard right away for Little House. The metal detector may take time but the guard should be there any day. Please work out the estimate and I am granting prior sanction. I am asking the ministers concerned to expedite the process.'

'Thank you, Madam Chief Minister. Tonight, the orphans

will sleep safe because in you they have found a parent,' says Mr Sharma. 'Just one more point, Madam CM. In front of Little House is a garbage heap that hasn't been cleared for days, months, years. It is a security threat to the building since it chokes our entrance, it may be used as a hiding place for explosives, I will be extremely grateful if something is done about it.'

'That's strange,' says the Chief Minister. 'What are our friends in the municipal corporation doing? Are they not clearing your garbage hoping that the stench will scare the terrorists away?'

Everyone laughs extra hard, to break the thick sombre mood created by Mr Sharma's scare speech.

~

Three days later, as a first step in the security upgrade, two bulldozers and a dump-truck, along with a dog-catcher squad, raze an illegal wall near Little House, clear the garbage dump, pick up Bhow to take her to a place from where she cannot return.

Their job done late in the evening, as the convoy of these vehicles stops near a traffic light, Bhow twists and turns, the lasso around her neck loosens, she wriggles out, squeezes herself through a chink in the door of the cage in which they have trapped her, grows flesh-coloured wings and flies away into the sky, towards the moon. The roads are crowded with angry and impatient drivers, so except for a few who have the time to look up at the evening sky, no one notices Bhow flying away into the night.

No one notices Bhow looking down one last time to see the lights of The Mall below, as she wags her tail, safe and happy in the realisation that she has found Orphan his home in New City.

MEANWHILE

HULKING BLACK MITSUBISHI
PAJERO AT THE LEELA

HER name is Nidhi, she is twenty years old, she is hiding, she hears them at the door.

~

Whore, Lover Girl, motherfucker, dry cunt, tear you right through, open your mouth, you, you want to love, you? They gulp their words before they throw them up, covered in the slime of a thousand years.

Number One says, we will slice your breasts, cut cut cut. We will make eight out of two. We will set them in two rows of four each, staple them to your skin on the chest, running from base of neck to waist. Just like a dog has. Row of teats.

Number Two says, bitch is hungry, bitch wants bone. You wait, we will show you. We have a bone for you, says Number Three.

There are six of them.

~

Number One is clearly the leader of the group, the way he walks he talks he laughs he frowns, the way each one of the others looks at him, looks up to him. He is the one whose brother she dares to fall in love with, dares to brainwash him into believing that he loves her too. They have to be stopped.

First, this girl.

Then, he will take care of his brother, teach him how not to put himself into such dirty, lower-caste cunt.

There are seven if you count the driver who got them here, eight if you count the driver's attendant who sat on the floor of the Mitsubishi Pajero, in front, at their feet. Driver is also the man whose job is to clean up afterwards.

Number One tells Driver, you will not touch her, all right? Use water, use soap, use hot water, cold water. You listen to me, he says, you can't even watch us, you stay out, this isn't a cinema show for free, you clean up when I tell you. You won't get to fuck, you know that, you know why?

Driver doesn't reply.

Because you are old, laughs Number One.

OK, says Driver.

~

They break down the door, walk in, Nidhi doesn't stand a chance.

How can she? How can she when there are eight men, youngest fifteen (Driver's Attendant), oldest forty-six (father of three)? How can she when six of them walk in, four already hard. How can she when Number Five and Number Seven hold her down, Number Three pees on her face, Number Two kicks her in the stomach, once, twice, thrice, four times, five, six? Driver's Attendant, the kid, the youngest of them all, counts this in his head.

Number Four and Number Five tear her clothes off, shirt, skirt, underwear one, underwear two? She wears a skirt, they say, she is The English Whore. Number Six is the first to rape her. Going right in, he says, right in, all the way in, cunt is dry but cunt is clear, like the highway.

Number Five splashes water between her legs, I can't go in just now, he says, I need to clean her first.

Go in, stay in, says Number One, go in, stay in, that will teach her a lesson, each one enters her except Driver and Driver's Attendant.

They gag her, make her throw up what she has had for dinner that evening. This mixes with the blood.

Driver, Driver? Where are you? Number One shouts.

Here, sir.

Stay right there, there is lots of work to do, hope you are ready, hope you got everything with you.

If she gets pregnant, Number Four asks, whose child will it be? They laugh. Not my brother's any more, says Number One.

Then they get together to hammer her face in, make her eyes meet her ears, her lips slide down her neck, her nose fall into a hole.

Driver, it's your job now, says Number One.

Driver has large plastic bags from Big Bazaar, Shoppers Stop, The Home Store. He layers them, one inside the other, so that they can take the weight of all that's strewn on the floor, her clothes, blood, theirs and hers. He scrubs, washes, scrubs, washes, dries up with towels, red and white and white that turns red.

'Is the whore dead?' Number One asks him, standing outside, impatient, ready to go.

Driver looks at her, she looks at him.

Her eyes are open, she is awake. He can see her breathe. She is trying to tell him something. 'Stay here until the police come,' Driver whispers to Nidhi. And then walks out to tell them, 'Her eyes are closed, she is dead.'

~

She will pull through, Driver hopes, as he drives them down the highway past The Mall, into The Leela, where guards in black suits check their car, open its doors for them to step out.

They get out, walk up the stairs into the hotel lobby, pass a man standing there waiting for his car, a man who smells as if he's freshly bathed, his wrist so slim his watch keeps sliding to his elbow every time he raises his arm.

They shout out to Driver and his attendant to wait for them until they finish dinner in the new Chinese restaurant at The Leela.

WOMAN

GABRIELA MISTRAL

HOW distracted I have been, I am near the end and I forget to tell you about the third author I am reading: Chilean poet Gabriela Mistral. She got the Nobel Prize in 1945, the year I am born; you read her acceptance speech and you will never know that, as one critic says, 'pain and anguish suffused her entire being.'

I will read you some lines from one of her poems and tell you a little about her.

~

When I walk all the things
of the earth awaken,
and they rise up and whisper
and it's their stories that they tell.

Gabriela is barely three years old when her father, a teacher in an elementary school, leaves the house to chase his dreams. Of writing poetry. His absence deeply affects both mother and daughter although Gabriela never blames him for her suffering. In a way, critics say, the legacy the father leaves behind for his daughter – a 'vagabond' soul – is what helps her succeed as a poet and as a teacher.

~

And the peoples who wander
leave them for me on the road
and I gather them where they've fallen
in cocoons made of footprints.

When she is nine years old, her teacher, who is blind, falsely accuses her of stealing sheets of paper belonging to the school. She orders Gabriela to leave the classroom, gets the children to even throw stones at her. When the teacher dies forty years later, Mistral happens to be in the same town, and she attends her funeral, places violets on her coffin. Asked if she remembered her teacher, she says, 'I can never forget memory.'

~

Stories run through my body
or purr in my lap.
They buzz, boil, and bee-drone.
They come to me uncalled
and don't leave me once told.

In 1906, when she is seventeen, Gabriela meets a man called Romelio Ureta who works as a railroad conductor and baggage clerk. Later that year, they meet again in a small town where she is teaching. The only detail available about their relationship is that Gabriela usually saved a seat for Ureta at the table. Three years later, Ureta shoots himself in the head. And, on his body, is found a postcard bearing her name. There are many versions of his death. According to one, a friend to whom he had loaned money from the railroad company refused to repay and he chose suicide to uphold his honour. One version says he is supposed to marry somebody else and to prevent that, he kills himself. His suicide is a defining moment in Mistral's life and a powerful influence on her poetry.

~

> *Those that come down from the trees*
> *braid and unbraid themselves,*
> *and weave me and wrap me*
> *until the sea drives them away.*
> *but the sea speaks endlessly*
> *and the more I tire, the more it tells me…*

In 1929, when she is forty, Gabriela loses her mother. Some of her finest poetry commemorates her mother's death. According to one critic, 'Mother and daughter commune in these poems, in a spiritual bond of penance and perseverance.'

~

> *People who are chewing the forest*
> *and those who break stone*
> *want stories at bedtime.*

The least documented tragedy in her life is the death of her nephew, Juan Miguel Godoy Mendoza, nicknamed Yin-Yin. Gabriela cares for him like a mother from his infancy to his death at eighteen. He is her father's grandson by an extramarital liaison. The baby's father surrenders the baby to Gabriela because the mother dies of tuberculosis. She takes him in and she transforms into a mother for him, only to watch him kill himself.

~

A father who leaves his daughter when she is a child; a lover who commits suicide; a child who, too, leaves her before he is an adult – so much of this seems real that perhaps that's why I, an old woman, sitting in a little house in a little town, three continents and two oceans away, read the poems of Gabriela Mistral and wish to share them with you.

> *Women looking for lost children who don't return*
> *and women who think they're alive*
> *and don't know that they're dead,*
> *ask for stories every night*
> *and I spend myself telling and telling.*

MAN

BALLERINA GIRL

IT'S Balloon Girl's voice, calling out his name, that wakes him up.

In The Room, the oak wardrobe's doors are open, Kahini's letter lies next to him. For a moment, he isn't sure where he is or where he was, and then his left foot begins to wake up from its sleep, stabbing his sole and his heel – he still has his shoes on – with countless needles, tying invisible weights to his ankle so heavy he cannot move. The throbbing pain in his arm, which he recollects from earlier in the evening, from his encounter with Taxi Driver at The Leela, begins to clear his head. She calls out his name again, her voice so near it seems she is inside the house and will walk into the room any time. That will be a big help, he thinks, given that he cannot move, because then he won't have to get up. She can do whatever she wishes in this room, it's hers now. Indeed, this entire house, which has been abandoned by Kahini, will now be Balloon Girl's.

And, justifiably so.

Because isn't she always there, whenever, wherever he summons her, for whatever?

Doesn't she always stand vigil, keep looking out for him, like she does at the mortuary?

Or, warn him of impending danger as she does in The Leela, when he has almost forgotten the fact that Taxi Driver is still around? Doesn't she always help him clear hurdles along his way? And then, most significantly, she is also helping him fight himself, make himself a better person.

At the Bird Park in Singapore, watching the lories perch on her, he wishes to hurt her, drink her blood, but now lying down in his house, listening to her call out to him, all that she fills him up with is love. All he wants to do now is to take her off this city's streets, grow her up, like a plant with flowers, nurture her soil and her water, share with her his own good fortune, his house, his home, his everything. Work hard and work long to give her all she deserves, all that she will never get otherwise. Free her from the swarm of flies, take her away from her mother, so selfish, who has reduced her to a withered body in a bundle of rags that smells, darts in and across the dark, runs to strangers in the hospital yard, offering red balloons in the night.

He wants to tell his friends Sukrit, Arsh and Aatish that no, he is now no longer alone, that Kahini may have left him but she wasn't his missing piece to begin with, the only person who loves him for who he is is Balloon Girl and now it will be her and him living happily ever after.

Even his father, his honest father with a conscience, would be proud if he took in a child from the street, cleaned her up, gave her his love, made her his own.

And that child is right now calling out to him.

~

'I am here,' says Balloon Girl.

Looking through the French windows of his living room, he falls in love again.

For, there she is, standing on the narrow ledge of his verandah, Red Balloon floating above her head, gleaming, taut, as if, in the night, it had gone back to Kailash Sahu and got itself filled with fresh helium.

Its string, this time fixed to a hook at the back of her white dress, is invisible in the dark – except when it catches one of the night lights in Apartment Complex – making it seem as if girl and balloon, unconnected, are floating in tandem.

And then, just before he can step out and respond to her call, she begins to dance. With an abandon that's both measured and unrestrained, child and adult. Like a ballerina he has only seen on TV or trapped in snow globes, she pirouettes on her bare feet, balancing herself on one toe and then the next, her jumps in between so daring and so graceful that he can feel his heart stop with awe and fear. One moment she soars into the sky, her arms outstretched, her head thrown back, a glittering brooch in her hair glinting in the dark, and the next she is still, as in marble, upright on the ledge, the entire weight of her tantalisingly balanced between beauty and death. The very next moment, she is all movement, a blur, the red of the balloon and the white of her dress against the black of the sky in patterns, delicate and tender, flirtatious and flamboyant. Child on the ledge, she transforms into a woman in mid-flight, making the night so fragile and fraught with danger that he remains rooted inside, unmoving, not knowing what to do next.

She calls out to him again.

'Come, join me,' she says.

CHILD

ORPHAN'S HOME

IF those who know Orphan, the staff at Little House, including Kalyani, Dr Chatterjee, Mrs Chopra, Uncle and Aunty, the men and women who live under the highway at the traffic lights, Bhow and his dog family, if they ask Ms Violets Rose, where can we find Orphan, she will sit them down in the seats in the cinema theatre, wait for them to get comfortable, for the lights to dim, and before there's any music, any movie, once she is sure that she has their undivided attention, she will tell them.

~

Look for Orphan right here.

He will be the shadow beneath your seat. Certain evenings, when you are watching a movie, you may feel his head move underneath you, his small hands scrape your armrest. There will be days when I won't be able to provide for him so please leave something on the tray or drop something on the floor – shreds of popcorn at the bottom of the box, flakes of chips, a beverage undrunk. Not exactly food a child should have but, at least, it will satiate his hunger, quench his thirst.

Once in a while, if you look carefully, you may see a shape quickly dart across the stage, turn the corner around the screen. You will see the red curtains move, that's Orphan stepping into the wings, maybe into the little storage room to lie down or wait. On-screen, you will see him, too, if you are lucky, in the scene into which I choose to place him.

Mainly those where a mother stands at a window looking out, the thought of a child in her eyes.

Or a scene where children play, in a park on a clear winter morning, the grass dappled by sunlight. A schoolyard, where there are slides, see-saws, monkeybars.

When the movie is over and you walk down the stairs, when the credits roll, turn around one last time to look underneath your chair and you may see Orphan peering out, his beautiful face lit by the floor lights, his baby eyes sparkling at you in the dark.

~

And if he's not there?

~

Step out of the theatre, walk down the corridors of The Mall, into any of the 208 stores and you may find Orphan.

In kids'-wear stores, he will be dressed in all you want him to wear, sitting between the mannequins in the display window. In toy stores, you are likely to find him in a quiet corner, playing with a train, if he is three years four years old, or just walking, crawling down an aisle looking at the boxes, if he is younger.

A few years later, if his language classes with me are any success, you may find him reading a book at Landmark Store, concealed by the large plastic bin that keeps discounted footballs and soft toys.

In the large anchor stores where they have many sections, he will surely be harder to trace, given the sheer number of places he has to hide. In the home furnishing section, look under beds, between quilts and behind mattresses. Between the boxes of silverware, behind the thicket of wires where they display lamps and lights, you may see him in a mirror, appear and disappear.

In the men's apparel or women's-wear section, you are likely to find him in the trial room, underneath the sofa or chair, covered by clothes left behind by a shopper.

Let him be there as you change, he won't look, don't frighten him away.

~

When you leave The Mall, when you are out in the parking lot, you may find Orphan under, or in between, the cars.

In the shadows that curve around the pillars. In the little cubicle in which the parking attendant sits to give you your ticket. That's why when you start your car, wait for a minute, look in all your mirrors, let him slip away just in case he is hiding underneath.

Drive down the highway and you will see him, maybe, holding on to another car in front or hiding in its trunk.

Sometimes, when he's daring, he will be perched on the highway signs, looking at the planes coming in to land. At other times, you may find him at the toll gates playing with mynah birds, or climbing the rafters in the roof, his face lit by the rising sun.

In the Metro, during rush-hour, he will be in the first coach meant for women and children, squeezed into a corner so that he doesn't get in anyone's way. At night, though, he will spread out, flit from one coach to the other, slip underneath the seats. Or stand in a corner and watch the passengers, a thin man whose watch keeps sliding to his elbow, a young woman and an older man, holding hands, listening to the voices inside each other's heads.

~

That's so many places for Orphan to live, they will say.

And if one them asks, Ms Rose, Ms Rose, which is the safest, most secure home of them all, Ms Rose will pause, take a deep breath, think hard before she answers.

WOMAN

WAKING UP

THIS is a summer night, hot, gathering dark, when I will go up the stairs, on tiptoe, walk into your room hoping to find you, curled up, a blue-jeans comma on the white sheet, the room so cold I will shiver before I switch off both fan and air conditioner, banish their noise into a sudden silence in which I will hear you breathe.

The water, condensed, drips down the wall outside.

Soon, it will be morning, I shall open the windows, let the sun in to wake you up – bright and soft before it begins to climb into the hard sky, char and scorch whatever it can see.

You will wake up, on this first day here, you will walk downstairs, sit at the kitchen table, across from me. Of course, you will be awkward, your toes will curl up so that they do not touch the floor because it's covered with dust of the day and the night gone by. You will despair when you find that you have retraced your steps to the past which you, so boldly, escaped.

You will feel the crushing weight of this despair – the walls will close in on you, squeeze both air and light out so that you will find it harder to see, harder to breathe. And when you watch me in the morning light, you will see your mother but you will also see a woman, very old and very weak, counting the hours, with nothing left to do.

Looking at me, therefore, you will be unsure where to begin, how to begin. But if you do decide to speak, I will help you by looking the other way so that we are not eye to eye. Because, after all, what we need are not eyes to judge but ears to lend. Maybe you will then tell me about the man you love and you will tell me about the baby you have lost. You will tell me about the hurt, cold and knotted, blue and grey and black, that you carry inside and outside. In the severe lines on your face and under your eyes. In all your bruises, in the burn marks across your back and on your arms, in the welts on your wrists and above your knees. So many of them, the hard prints of your pain.

You will tell me, Ma, I am tired, my eyes close, my legs hurt. But I am afraid, my child, I can no longer lift you up, I can no longer carry you or walk with you until you fall asleep but we are lucky the giants are here. Not one, not just the woman, 12 feet tall, but her friends and family, too, and they are going to be here as long as you are. They are very eager to help. They tell me they want to meet you. They are waiting outside.

As for your future, I am not sure if I can help. What I am sure of, however, is that I am your past. And although most of me is over and finished, I am hard and I am solid. I am all that has happened, not what may happen or what should happen. I exist and I am real, I am the ground you can stand on knowing that it is reliable, that I am time-tested. It is in this house where you come home when you are born, where you first find love. And now that you are back, it's in this house where we will find love again.

As I will tell you and as I will show you, there is enough for both of us and there's a lot left over for the lost child, we will give him a name and we will bring him home from wherever he is.

Can you hear me? You will wake up, won't you?

MAN

FALLING MAN

AS if drawn by invisible strings, he steps out of the living room onto the verandah, begins to walk towards Balloon Girl, step by heavy step. His left foot has woken up but, in his shoes, he can feel the remnants of the heaviness and pain from his sleep. His arm still hurts, he wants to rest it; he wants to take his shoes off to let his feet breathe. For, barring a few hours at The Leela – where he gave the shoes to Housekeeping to be polished – his feet have been trapped in them, through the heat of the day in the car and outside, the streets of New City and Paris and then Singapore and now, in his own house. But with Balloon Girl now barely a few feet away, dazzling in the dark, light rain falling on her face, his face, the discomfort he feels in his feet soon disappears and a music begins to fill his ears.

It's a symphony of sounds: the noise her bare feet make when they land on the ledge, the soft swish of her white dress, the wind sliding against the skin of Red Balloon, her breathing, sharp, fast, and, of course, the sounds of his own making, his shoes against the floor, the doors closing behind him – all working in perfect harmony like a piece of music that writes itself and then plays itself as well.

She calls out his name.

He is inches away from her. She sits on the ledge, offers him her hand to hold and once her fingers, soft and cold, curl tight around his, she stands up and begins to rise.

First, imperceptibly, off the ledge, and then the clearing between her feet and the ledge increases, a millimetre each second, so that in five minutes, she is a foot above, in the air, and slowly rising, and it's when her feet clear his head, it's then that he begins to rise.

~

They are both off the ledge now, in the air, the night sky waiting to receive them, Red Balloon lifting him and his love higher and higher.

He can see The Leela below, is that his room, the windows fogged, have they discovered Taxi Driver's body, he can see the highway unspool beneath them like a black ribbon, the mynah birds sleeping in the rafters, to his left is the glass dome of the New City Station in which, reflected, are the headlights of the day's first Metro getting ready to roll out and they float across the city, hand in hand, until she says, let's go home now.

And, he says, yes, let's.

And he marvels at how this little child has taken charge of him and how she will lead him now, from their fleeting present to their enduring future, where they will live happily ever after, and he feels a sudden calm descend over him. They are moving fast now as they come in, faster and faster, pulled down by the earth, the wind whistling across his face, back to where they took off from, he can see the verandah of his apartment and its ledge, a thin strip of red cement on which Balloon Girl danced, in perfect balance. Will she now land feet first?

Will she guide him down? Will she walk into his house with him? He asks of himself these questions and then stops worrying about the answers because he knows that Balloon Girl will take care of everything, just as she has done in the past, and that's why he doesn't even realise that she has let go.

That she and Red Balloon are flying higher and higher into the dark that drapes New City, and from up above she is watching him, the starlight in both her eyes, and when he looks up, he can see her crying, one tear drops, its wetness brushes his face and it's only when he brings his hand to his face to wipe it that he realises he is on his own and he is falling.

CHILD

LOVE STORIES

MS Rose, thank you for telling us where Orphan can be but which is the safest, most secure home of them all? Ms Rose will take a deep breath and say:

~

Beyond The Mall, there's another place, more secure than any of the ones I have just mentioned. It's a place where Orphan will always have a home, where he will be sheltered, fed, washed and clothed, where he will be told stories, where he will be taught letters and numbers, how to speak and how to listen, where someone will watch over him as he sleeps, where he will find love whenever he goes looking for it.

Such a place can only be another heart.

And one such heart in New City belongs to a woman named Kalyani Das. For Orphan to always have this place, she will, of course, have to be cured of her illness and united with her dreams.

Which is what I will do, says Ms Rose, give him a love story, which is what only I can do. Because take my name, she says, take all the letters in it, mix them up, throw them up in the air, look where they land, pick them up, one by one, and rearrange them to change my name.

~

Violets Rose.
　Love Stories.

MEANWHILE

A GIFT FOR APARTMENT
COMPLEX SECURITY GUARD

LIGHT rain drizzles the streets giving New City, baked by sun the entire day, the damp fragrance of dew. Thin sheets of water, blown across by a wind that's barely there, shimmer like curtains of glass that break, silently, around buildings, their hard angles where mortar and cement, bricks and paint together touch the sky through which he falls, head first.

Balloon Girl watching, her tears falling, he makes contact at the precise moment the front wheels of a giant truck slip into a pothole near the entrance to Apartment Complex. Tipping over its cargo of stone chips weighing almost a ton making a noise so loud that no one hears the thud of his body, the fall of kilograms, sixty, sixty-five, towards the centre of the earth.

No one hears his head open when it hits the concrete, no one watches it explode into streaks of black, red and brown. Hair and blood, tissue, skin, what lies between and beneath, splatter the wall behind the row of parked cars. Shards of his bones skitter away, as if each one were alive.

No one hears this except Security Guard because these sound like a shower of small stones thrown, in mischief, as a prank by boys in some upstairs apartment.

Who's there, asks Security Guard. Who is awake at this time doing this, he thinks?

He looks up, there is no one, just the faces of sleeping apartments, their window eyes closed.

~

Security Guard finds his body.

The neck has snapped, the face turned at so impossible an angle, it is draped in its own shadow. Security Guard sits down on his haunches, leans forward, crouches, then goes down on all fours, turns the body around to see who he is.

It's Sir.

Sir, who lives alone. Sir, who, last night, tells him to be more responsible at work, Sir who gives him 500 rupees for not letting the maid disturb him.

Sir, whose body is warm.

Sir, whose shoes are black, made of soft leather. Almost new.

Perfect fit for his son's feet.

~

His youngest son, who asks him – every time he calls home – for money to buy shoes. His youngest son, who, although Security Guard will never admit it to anybody, he loves the most. More than his other children because the boy works so hard, the boy never complains, the boy never makes his mother angry, the boy has done so well in school that his teacher says, let him study further, he deserves to be the first college graduate in the family.

That boy wants shoes and there's no use for Sir's shoes anymore.

Because the police will take Sir's body to the mortuary where the post-mortem man will throw these shoes away, maybe sell them for scrap.

But, no, he cannot, he will not defile Sir's body, he will not steal, but this is not stealing. Sir will not mind, Sir is a good man, because even that night when Sir warns of punishment, Sir never tells the estate manager anything.

So Security Guard looks left, Security Guard looks right, he looks over his shoulder, behind and in front, and when he is sure no one in New City is looking except the night and the rain, he sits down and pulls each shoe out, very slowly, just in case there is life still inside Sir, although he can feel the soles of his feet, through the socks, rapidly turning cold. Security Guard puts the shoes in the plastic bag in which he brings his dinner from home, then calls Main Gate of Apartment Complex to report a suicide.

WOMAN

SUMMER NIGHT

HE is dead, you do not need to worry any more, you have nothing and nobody to fear.

~

Balloon Girl, too, is safe, as she will fly away, across the night sky, into the star dust where children go once they die, her path lit by the fireflies I told you about, into the dark where Bhow has gone, too, jumping out of the moving van, bounding down the street like a plane taxiing for take-off before she lifts off the ground and enters the clouds.

Red Balloon, its gas slowly draining, weighed down by tiny raindrops, will begin to fall.

A light wind will push it clear of Apartment Complex but it may not be strong enough to take it where it should go.

So let's wait and watch and, if more force is needed, I shall summon the giants, get them to quickly form a huddle, put their heads together, blow and blow, send out a gust so powerful that it will push Red Balloon across the highway, nudge it into The Mall, through the glass doors, make it float three flights up the escalator, right up to Europa where it will slip in through the metal detector, enter the theatre, seek Orphan out and float down, come to rest, the shy balloon next to the little boy fast asleep, maybe the start of a new friendship.

Watching over both will be Ms Violets Rose, you know how special she is, she has marked out all the places where Orphan can live, in The Mall and outside. But we cannot take any chances.

~

What if Ms Rose leaves him one day, taking all her love stories with her?

What if Kalyani never gets well? What if the police demolish the slum, scatter her family?

What if developers tear down The Mall to build another, convert Europa into a store, wrench all its seats out, leaving Orphan no place to hide? Bhow gone, what if they chase him out of whichever space he slips into, don't let him sleep even under the highway?

It will then fall on us, you and me, both mothers, past and present, as it has fallen on all mothers since the first light of the first day, to make sure that Orphan always has a home. And that is why, once you wake up, we will build him a city.

ACKNOWLEDGEMENTS

My first and foremost debt is to *The Indian Express*. For providing me, since 1996, such incomparable employment – in the most free of newsrooms with the most passionate of storytellers. And, along with it, that rare freedom to drift away when there's an extra tug in the wind.

Katharina Narbutovic, director, Berliner Kunstlerprogramm. For your precious gift: one year in Berlin for this book to grow and write. Cornelia Zetzsche, who showed me the way to Katharina, I cannot thank you enough.

Unni Rajen Shanker, Editor, *The Indian Express*. I get leave of absence because of the assurance of your presence.

Uschi Seifried, projectionist at Filmhaus, Berlin, for helping me seek the places in a cinema hall where Orphan could hide.

Bloomsbury editors Diya Kar Hazra (New Delhi), Helen Garnons-Williams, Elizabeth Woabank (London), and Lea Beresford (New York). For the warmth with which you welcomed Woman, Man and Child and helped me build them a better home than the one they were first in.

Gillon Aitken and Shruti Debi, the champions. For your faith.

A NOTE ON THE AUTHOR

Raj Kamal Jha is Chief Editor of *The Indian Express*, which has won the International Press Institute's India Award for Excellence in Journalism three times. His novels include *The Blue Bedspread*, winner of the 2000 Commonwealth Writers' Prize for Best First Book (Eurasia) and a *New York Times* Notable Book of the Year; *If You Are Afraid of Heights*, a finalist for the Hutch–Crossword Book Award in 2003; and *Fireproof*, rated first in CNN–IBN's list of best books published in India in 2006. His novels have been translated into more than a dozen languages. Raj works in New Delhi and lives in Gurgaon.

A NOTE ON THE TYPE

Linotype Garamond Three – based on seventeenth-century copies of Claude Garamond's types, cut by Jean Jannon. This version was designed for American Type Founders in 1917, by Morris Fuller Benton and Thomas Maitland Cleland, and adapted for mechanical composition by Linotype in 1936.